'An absolute corker... A:
noir and
S

'Devil
Sunday Post

'Another delightfully mischievous whodunnit from
the author of *Helle and Death*'
i Paper

'One to be enjoyed'
Belfast Telegraph

'Will find favour with Conan Doyle fans thanks to Jensen's
bravura plotting and satisfying conclusion'
Crack

'Downbeat and funny at the same time. Oskar Jensen's writing is a
delightful mix of classic crime fiction and Robert Galbraith'
Ian Moore, author of *Death and Croissants*

'Witty, compelling, and what an intriguing, fiendish murder'
J.M. Hall, author of *A Spoonful of Murder*

'Rogues, rascals and an oversized dog – *Helle's Hound* has it all.
The most delicious murder I've read all year'
Marion Todd, author of *Old Bones Lie*

'A triumphant return for Torben! Charming and fun'
Sam Holland, author of *The Puppet Master*

HELLE'S HOUND

Also by Oskar Jensen and available from Viper

Helle and Death

HELLE'S HOUND

OSKAR JENSEN

VIPER

This paperback edition first published in 2025
First published in Great Britain in 2025 by
VIPER
an imprint of Profile Books Ltd
29 Cloth Fair
London
EC1A 7JQ
www.viperbooks.co.uk

Copyright © Oskar Jensen, 2025

Text design by Crow Books

1 3 5 7 9 10 8 6 4 2

Printed and bound in Great Britain by
CPI Group (UK) Ltd, Croydon, CR0 4YY

The moral right of the author has been asserted.

All rights reserved. Without limiting the rights under copyright reserved above, no part of this publication may be reproduced, stored or introduced into a retrieval system, or transmitted, in any form or by any means (electronic, mechanical, photocopying, recording or otherwise), without the prior written permission of both the copyright owner and the publisher of this book.

A CIP catalogue record for this book is available from the British Library.

Our product safety representative in the EU is Authorised Rep Compliance Ltd., Ground Floor, 71 Lower Baggot Street, Dublin, D02 P593, Ireland.
www.arccompliance.com

Paperback ISBN 978 1 80081 1782
eISBN 978 1 80081 1799

For Mark, Roger, and John

DANISH GLOSSARY

Absolut	Absolutely
Det svin	The swine, i.e. the bastard
Er du sindsygg?	Are you serious?
For fanden!	For the devil! (expletive)
For helvede!	For hell! (expletive)
For Satan!	For the devil! (again. Very Lutheran, the Danes, aren't they?)
Fuck dig	Fuck you
Gudskelov	Thank God
Gymnasium	Grammar school
Hej	Hi
Hold kæft!	Shut up! (Also as in 'No way!')
Hold op	Hang on
Hvad?	What?
Hyggelig	Cosy (but let's not get into all this again)
Ja	Yes
Klap lige hesten	Hold your horses (literally 'pat the horse')
Lort	Shit, damn, uh-oh
Mange tak	Many thanks
Narre	Fool
Pølse(r)	Hotdog(s)
Præcist	Exactly, precisely
Prosit	Cheers

Rigtig	Correct
Som du vil	As you wish, if you like
Strålende	Brilliant
Tak	Thanks
Tak for det	Thank you (for this)
Tilgiv mig	Forgive me
Vi ses	Be seeing you, ciao for now, laters! (Speaking of which, let's begin …)

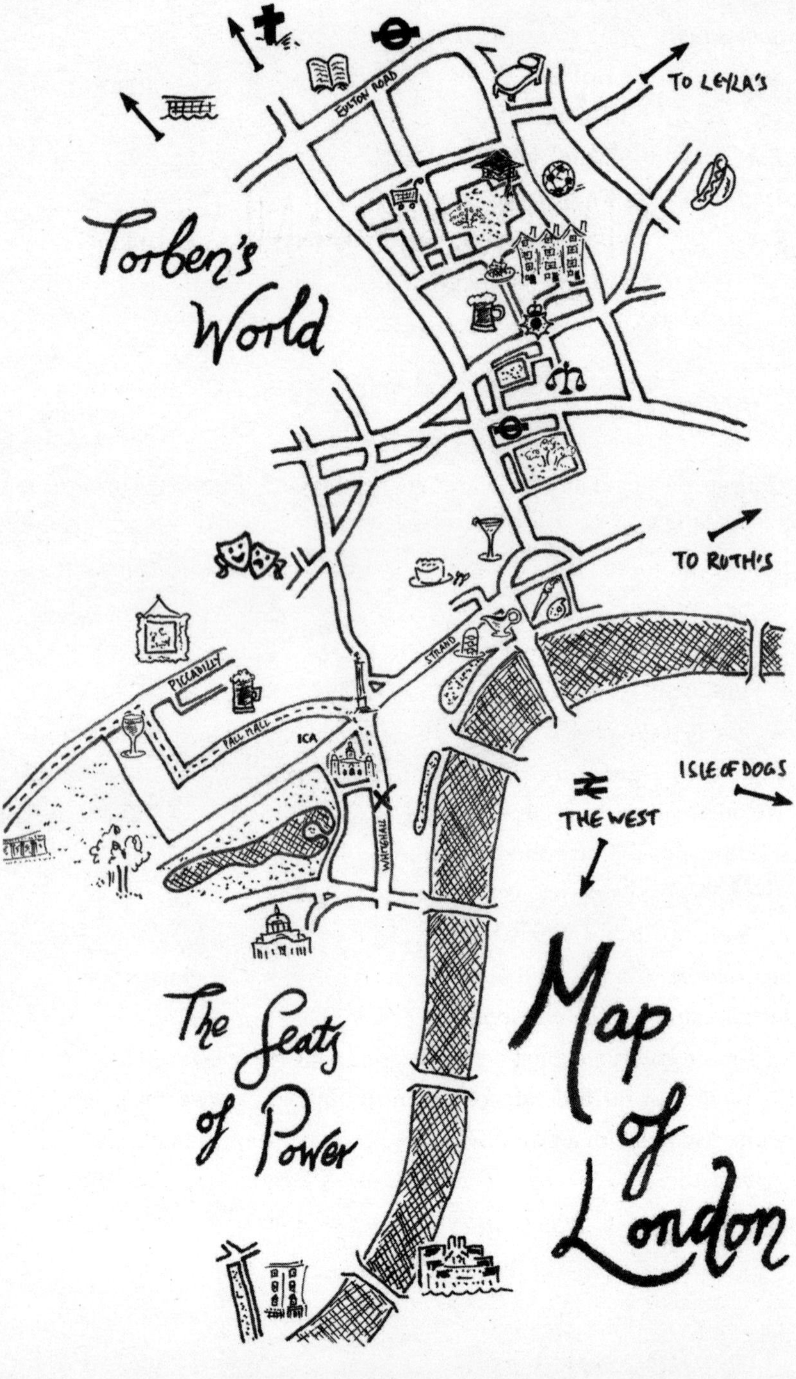

Torben's World
EUSTON ROAD
TO LEYLA'S
TO RUTH'S
STRAND
PICCADILLY
PALL MALL
ICA
WHITEHALL
ISLE OF DOGS
THE WEST
The Seats of Power
Map of London

I

THAMES EMBANKMENT

'Torben, darling, I am the bearer of grave tidings – Boris is no more.'

'What? Dead?!'

'Oh yes, quite dead. It was very sudden, apparently, too quick to feel any pain …'

'When did this happen?'

'Last night. He was hit by a bus, I believe.'

'*For helvede*. That's a brutal bit of karma.' Torben Helle looked around at the crowd of other Londoners walking on the Embankment. 'No one seems very excited,' he added.

His companion frowned. 'Excited?'

'Or shocked, or whatever. I mean to say – Boris!'

'Well, no, dear. Frankly I'm surprised you've taken it this much to heart; he was *very* old, after all, and he'd had a good innings. It's just such a shame for the children …'

Torben had the feeling he was missing something. '*His* children?'

'What? No, no, little Marko and the others, you know – my neighbours. As far as I'm aware Boris himself was neutered as a puppy.'

Only then did Torben remember the venerable animal in question, who so far as he knew had never held public office, and whose mercifully swift passing was unlikely to occasion much distress among the general public. Poor old Boris. The question was, which was more at fault – his memory, or his companion's rather dark sense of humour?

Dame Professor (Emerita) Charlotte Lazerton, Fellow of the British Academy et cetera et cetera, was one of the world's most eminent art historians, besides being his ex-supervisor. With her shock of pure white hair, Hermès scarf and exquisite bone structure, she looked like a piece of finely wrought jewellery, with cut-glass voice to match. Yet despite all these markers of respectability, he couldn't shake off the creeping suspicion that she had been pulling his leg.

He said as much.

'Nonsense,' she replied, 'I was doing nothing of the kind. Really, Torben, to accuse me of levity at a time of grief – I mean, W. T. Fuck?'

He stopped walking. '"W. T. Fuck?"'

'Yes,' she said, sounding – for the first time – a little abashed. 'That's what the young people say, isn't it?'

'You're getting confused with W. G. Grace,' said Torben. 'Or H. G. Wells.'

'Meaning, my contemporaries? The cheek of it! That's the problem with you millennials; you're all so ageist. Now keep walking, Torben. Mortimer isn't going to exercise himself.'

The two of them – well, three, counting Mortimer, Charlotte's Irish wolfhound – were heading west from Somerset House, along the Embankment on the north side of the Thames. It was an unseasonably warm spring day, perfect sky, trees in blossom – even the dirty old river itself was putting on a show, glinting with reflected light. Before long, they would make it to St James's Park, where the enormous dog would finally be allowed off his lead, and Torben could stop restraining an animal that weighed as much as he did. Ever sceptical of Charlotte's reassurances, he had taken the precaution of checking the Royal Parks FAQs before agreeing to this jaunt ...

'So,' said Torben, as Mortimer tugged him right, into the minor detour of Victoria Embankment Gardens, 'what's new this week?'

They had been meeting like this for a couple of months now, ever since Torben's unexpected legacy of £50,000 from an old university friend had allowed him to move out of Charlotte's spare room in Bloomsbury and rent his own studio. Well, 'friend' wasn't exactly the word; Anthony Dodd had been more of a frenemy. Not that they had known terms like that back as undergraduates. But unravelling the mystery of his death, at a reunion held at Bastle House – Dodd's remote Northumbrian mansion – had taught all of those caught up in it rather more than they'd bargained for.

Still, the affair had liberated Torben from his status as Charlotte's lodger. At the age of thirty-one, she had declared, it was high time for him to have his own place. 'You can catch up on all that wild bachelor sex you've not been having,' was how she had actually put it. Now, they spent two hours together each week pacing the London streets.

'Don't think I want you for the company and conversation, or anything soppy like that,' Charlotte insisted. 'I'm just using you as a free dog-walking service. Either he's grown too big, or I've shrunk too small, but he needs his daily workout, and even I, entitled boomer that I undoubtedly am, cannot afford to hire dear Ximena every day of the week.'

Ximena Podenco was Charlotte's regular dog walker, Torben had gathered: a young Mexican employed by a firm that charged exceedingly reasonable rates, so long as these were paid in cash. 'I said to her, "Visa?" and she looked terrified, but then again, I suspect we might not have been talking about quite the same thing, poor girl. So now of course I give her these great big tips, and it's practically as expensive as hiring someone legitimate …'

That all sounded about as blunt as Torben had come to expect from his old supervisor. Still, aside from Leyla Moradi, there wasn't anyone he could think of with whom he'd rather spend his time than Charlotte. And given that Leyla was a human rights barrister of his own age, certifiably gorgeous, and his one true unrequited love, whereas Charlotte was a retired professor who knew a lot about oil painting in Tsarist Russia, this was saying something. And, unlike Leyla, Charlotte always seemed to be in a good mood. Although right now …

'"What's new?"' she said, finally returning to his earlier question. 'Well, I'm afraid it's rather more a case of "what's ongoing".' Nimbly sidestepping a Deliveroo driver, she led them across Northumberland Avenue. 'You know, Torben dear, I'd much sooner not trouble you with this, but I feel I really should tell *somebody*, and since that little contretemps of yours at Bastle House has acquainted you with the serious side of life …'

'I'm all ears,' said Torben.

'Then you should probably see an otolaryngologist,' said Charlotte, in an admirable impression of her usual manner. 'In the meantime, however, you can listen to my problem. Torben, I think someone's tapping my 'phone calls.'

There was something about the way she pronounced 'phone' that made the contraction audible, and Torben almost smiled.

'Oh, I'm quite serious,' she said, as Mortimer broke aside to relieve himself against the statue of William Tyndale. And for once, she looked it. 'It sounds just like it did in the eighties, that same little click-pop noise. Really you'd think their methods would be more sophisticated by now, but then, I haven't changed my landline in forty years, so why would they bother—'

'Why were you wiretapped in the eighties?'

'Now, Torben, don't distract me, I'll lose my thread. The point is that they're doing it *now* – not that I can be entirely sure whether *they* means Millbank or Fleet Street – and it's a teensy bit concerning.'

He considered. Not for the first time, it occurred to him that Charlotte's chief vice was indulging herself by pretending to an old age that she had not, in reality, attained: some of her expressions, her mannerisms, must be those of her parents' generation. Whenever she answered her phone – sorry, her *'phone* – her first words were invariably 'London seven-four-two-six-triple-four-oh', delivered in a sort of trill that sounded like something out of a Noël Coward comedy. All charmingly eccentric, of course, but he worried that this pose of venerability might be self-fulfilling. 'You could finally get a mobile?' he suggested.

'Hmm,' said Charlotte. 'I think not, that smacks of defeatism. No, there's nothing to be *done* about it, I just wanted someone else to know in case … in case there are any more unpleasant developments. Not to put too fine a point on it, but I'm actually just a little bit scared.'

He hesitated. If Charlotte was prepared to admit to genuine emotion, this might actually be serious. '"Unpleasant developments"?' he prompted.

'Well, that's a euphemism, of course. Really I mean something positively nasty, but I didn't want to worry you, you're much too young to be cultivating morbid thoughts.' Charlotte sighed. 'You know, Torben, for more than seventy years on this earth, I was doing pretty well, *je ne regrette rien* and so on – in fact, there is only one action I sincerely regret in all those years, and that happened awfully long ago. But lately, this past year or so, I believe I have begun to act really rather foolishly.' She sniffed. 'Hence, you know – unpleasant developments.'

For an instant, as they crossed Whitehall just past the Cenotaph, Torben had a sense of dislocation. The expression on her face was entirely alien to him, no longer that of a cosy old don, but of a woman whose long and hard-fought life held secrets of unfathomable depth and importance.

'Oh, and I *also* think someone's stolen one of my bedroom slippers,' she added, rather spoiling the effect.

Walks with Charlotte – and, perforce, Mortimer – were one of a handful of regular commitments in Torben's London life. His slot for this was Monday (he suspected her of two-timing him with other susceptible colleagues; the city was full of art historians, critics, painters, whom she had mentored or fought with at some point in her career, and curiously, it was the rivals and antagonists who seemed most devoted to her, and might be good for the occasional dog walk). On Tuesday evenings he generally took the Central Line out to Stratford, where he trained with the Great Dane Handball Club for his weekly ration of ex-pat atmosphere and minor injuries. On Wednesday afternoons there was usually a research seminar he was expected to attend at the Courtauld, and this year he had wangled it so that the one master's degree module he was teaching happened right beforehand. He chilled on Thursday. Friday nights were dedicated to five-a-side football at his old international hall of residence, Oarwright College, where he had spent his first year as a postdoctoral fellow. This left the weekends free for inventing new reasons to see Leyla.

The rest of the working week he spent not writing his second book. Unaccountably, Taschen had given him an advance contract for a swanky coffee-table survey of Scandinavian domestic paintings of the nineteenth century, which they hoped would do very well on Instagram. They wanted to call it *Art of the Interior*. He was still fighting for it just to be called *Room*. Both titles were, of course, already taken, but originality did not seem to feature very high up the desiderata of commercial publishers. Either way, the real trick was smuggling in enough actual research to satisfy his employer and his grant funder without alienating his editor. Impressively, this was not even the most first-world of his struggles. He had also decided to give up meat, and sausages were proving to be a real problem.

There was the ScandiKitchen on Great Titchfield Street, for one thing. True, he still allowed himself the odd pickled herring, but to forgo their *pølser* was tantamount to blasphemy. Worse still, he did his weekly food shop at the Brunswick Centre branch of Waitrose – the only supermarket within walking distance, which told you all you needed to know about this part of Bloomsbury – and on a Saturday, there was this Polish guy outside whose hotdogs could be smelt from the other side of the square. Until recently, his *kiełbasa* had been the crowning glory of Torben's weekends. Now he couldn't even look the man in the eye. Instead he hurried past, hat pulled low over his face, whilst conducting an impassioned mental debate with Charlotte, who in recent years had expanded from art history to environmental activism. In part, this meant borderline illegal activity and orchestrating major campaigns. In part, it meant telling Torben off for eating sausages.

Charlotte always won these arguments in Torben's head, with her verifiable statistics about carbon emissions, her reasonable points about animal welfare, and her inspiring suggestions for the redistribution of land usage. Torben's counter arguments, which tended to be drawn from the *but it's delicious* school of philosophy, faltered in the face of imaginary Charlotte's flawless logic. *What about*

Mortimer? Torben had reasoned, assuming a hound that size came with a hefty carbon footprint. *Plant-based dog food; it's been around for decades*, came the answer. *Plus I know this enterprising chappie in Camden who sells London pigeon from his rickshaw*. Only in London. *Righteous smug eco git*, Torben said. Imaginary Charlotte looked disappointed in him, and gestured to a river contaminated with slurry from an under-regulated pig farm. Torben said sorry. By this point, unless he had been distracted by the spectacle of an eight-a-side game of football at Coram's Fields, or had contrived to trip over the leads of one of the army of professional dog walkers that had sprung up around Mecklenburgh Square, he had usually made it safely back to his studio flat.

Life, in short, was good to Torben Helle. Take today, for instance: a Sunday, six days after his stroll on the Embankment. Tomorrow, it would be his next dog-walking slot. He also planned to spend a few hours in the British Library consulting a PhD thesis from 2003 on Vilhelm Hammershøi and the concept of interiority, before walking off the stultifying after-effects with Charlotte and Mortimer. Tonight, he was going to a party at Cameron Plott's rooms in Oarwright College.

Cameron, whom he knew through football, was a student, and Torben would usually steer clear of student parties, so as to avoid meeting anyone he might teach. But this one would be safe enough: Cameron was studying for a PhD in mechanical engineering, and tended to socialise with the other footballers. This crowd – mostly male scientists, hailing from everywhere from Rio to Riyadh, Lagos to Lahore – was about as far as you could get from the art history crowd without actually leaving academia. Cameron himself was from somewhere in New Jersey. Torben's main task for the day was to prep for this party, which meant buying some beer, and catching up on last night's *Match of the Day*. Probably not in that order.

He groaned, stretching luxuriantly in the sunlight stealing in from a crack in the shutters. This involved his feet poking over the end of the bed with which the studio had come ready-equipped. But no matter: they could rest on the imitation leather of the one-and-a-half-seater sofa that, together with the bed and glass-topped table, comprised the entirety of the room's furnishings. Still, he had got lucky: a first-floor studio in this no man's land between Bloomsbury and Clerkenwell, carved out of a terraced house built, so *British History Online* had told him, in 1826. The kitchen was a whole other room; the extractor fan in the windowless en suite occasionally even worked. To have all this *and* be able to walk everywhere still seemed ridiculous, and he raised another mental toast to the memory of Anthony Dodd, whose atypical act of posthumous generosity was subsidising this lifestyle – at least until the autumn, when both the studio's lease and Torben's fellowship would come to an end. Even then, the cash would smooth the transition to whatever came next. *Prosit, Anthony!*

Torben allowed himself another catlike yawn. What was the time? Nine-thirty? No hurry yet. Gary Lineker and Ian Wright could wait a little longer. After all, he couldn't have *Match of the Day* without a cup of black coffee, and that meant going through to the kitchen, which meant getting out of bed … Might as well check his phone first. Sorry, his *'phone*. God, but he loved Sundays.

One missed call from late last night. Unknown number – so not Wilson, badgering him about his new podcast again, or Frances wanting a drunken gossip about Sara's weird home counties relatives. And a voicemail. Seriously? Who did he know who would leave a *voicemail*?

'Hello, is that … let me check … yes, this is a call for Torben Hell. Really, hell? Um, sorry, sir, yes, Torben Hell. This is Police Constable Meera Rampur. I'm looking at the appointments diary of Professor Charlotte Lazerton and I believe you're scheduled to meet on Monday lunchtime. As this appears to be one of Professor Lazerton's regular engagements I'm calling to inform you ... wait ... I mean, I'm afraid I have some bad news and you may wish to sit down at this stage. I regret to inform you that Professor Lazerton passed away on ...' – at this point, the line went silent for several seconds – 'actually, we're not quite sure when. Look, sir, perhaps you'd better call me back as soon as possible. Basically, she's dead. And, well, it's not a pretty sight.'

2
ISLINGTON & ST PANCRAS CEMETERY

'We therefore commit her body to the deep ...'

Leyla Moradi started in surprise. Admittedly, she hadn't attended many Anglican funeral services, but something about the wording seemed a bit off.

'... to be turned into corruption, looking for the resurrection of the body, when the sea shall give up her dead ...'

She risked a glance around. No, it wasn't just her: most people were looking a little disconcerted. And that was definitely grass beneath her feet, the only waves the motion of the trees, rippling in a light spring breeze. At her side, Torben gave a discreet cough, and she refocused.

'... and the life of the world to come, through our Lord Jesus Christ who at his coming shall change our vile body, that it may be like his glorious body, according to the mighty working whereby he is able to subdue all things to himself ...'

'I was talking to the chaplain beforehand,' Torben whispered to her in the next pause. 'Turns out that Charlotte found a loophole in the order of service. Apparently she's always quite liked the trappings of being buried at sea' – Leyla glanced down at the body in the grave, stitched inside a sailcloth cocoon – 'and she even had the cannonballs, a gift from some marine archaeologist she once met in New Orleans. See, they're weighing down either end. So, when she found out she couldn't have her *ideal* option—'

'Ssh!' said someone.

'Sorry,' they both said, automatically.

Leyla was quietly impressed. She'd never met Dame Charlotte – until a few months ago, Leyla hadn't even seen Torben in a decade – and was only here because he had asked her. It took quite a lot to drag her as far north as East Finchley, but these woodlands and their ancient gravestones were really rather magnificent, and she'd rarely seen such a crowd. OK, seventy-three wasn't old, but Torben said Charlotte had no family to speak of, only second cousins or removed cousins, Leyla never knew which was which, which meant that most people must be here because they *cared*. And there were hundreds of mourners of all ages, almost all of them adhering to the dress code on the invitation – 'any colour, so long as it isn't black' – many of whom looked surprisingly, well, chic.

Maybe it was because the deceased had become something of a minor celebrity in environmentalist circles, in recent years. Even Leyla's work as a barrister representing campaigning charities had brought up the name of Dame Charlotte Lazerton more than once. Or just maybe, she thought, looking up at the tears streaking Torben's face, it was because she had been a genuinely good person, whom people loved. Such things were possible, after all.

'Ach, *for helvede*, but at least that's over,' said Torben, as the service concluded and the throng began to break up. His face was still glistening, but he didn't seem to care. Leyla had a handkerchief, a silk Liberty one in a nod to the dress code; part of her wanted to take it out and—

'Well, come on, Leyla, cheer me up,' he said. 'I haven't dragged you ten kilometres out of town so you can be all deferential and respectful of my grief. If I wanted sympathy, I'd've asked Ruth.'

Harsh, thought Leyla. But also undeniably fair. She glanced around for inspiration. 'See that woman over there? I hear she's buried nine husbands,' she said, in a music-hall sort of voice.

'A gold digger?' said Torben.

'No, a grave digger: she's a sexton.'

Torben groaned.

'I had to improvise, OK?' said Leyla. They were allowing themselves to drift with the tide, back towards the cemetery gates. There was some sort of reception planned, organised by the Academy of Western Art in lieu of a family gathering, back in the centre of town.

'So,' said Leyla. 'You said she couldn't have her *ideal* choice of burial ...?'

'Ugh,' said Torben. 'Well, no. You see, what she *really* wanted was to be ... to be fed to the tigers at London Zoo. They're Sumatran tigers, critically endangered; she said she wanted to do her bit.'

'Ah,' said Leyla. 'I suppose the keepers aren't keen on giving their charges a taste for human flesh.'

'I think it was more a health and safety issue,' said Torben. 'The average human body nowadays contains so many dangerous chemicals that ...' His voice trailed off.

'Sorry,' said Leyla. 'Too soon? Too much?'

He shook his head. 'Unfortunate coincidence. They kept this bit out of the eulogy, obviously, but, when they found her ... you see, she'd been lying there for some time, several days maybe ...'

'A fall, wasn't it?' she said softly. He had told her before that the body had been found at the foot of the stairs.

Torben grimaced. 'So it seems. The point is, it was just her and Mortimer, her Irish wolfhound, in the house. Dogs that size, they take a lot of feeding, and of course, he couldn't get out, so ... well, the way the policewoman put it was that he'd "had a little nibble".' Torben looked like he was going to be sick.

'I'm so sorry,' she said. Side by side, her hand was very close to his. A simple matter to reach out; to squeeze it. Should she—?

'Torben!' came a voice from behind them; they both turned. A formidable-looking woman of middle years was advancing on them. 'A tragedy,' the woman said.

'Perhaps,' said Torben, reassembling his features. Now what on *earth* did he mean by that? 'Oh – Carmen Sabueso, Leyla Moradi,' he managed. 'Carmen edits the art history list for OUP,' he went on. 'She oversaw my book on Friedrich.'

Ah. This was shop; Leyla sensed power. Better play along for Torben's sake. 'I loved it,' she said, 'which always confused me – now I know who to actually credit.'

Sabueso smiled – the sort of tight-lipped smile people allowed themselves at funerals. 'Well, Charlotte had already done such a good job licking him into shape,' she said. 'Speaking of which, Torben, I have a new series, *Art Historiography in the 2020s* – shortish, accessible editions, around sixty thousand words, profiling seminal figures of our times – naturally the world needs a volume on dear Charlotte, and you were my first thought.'

Leyla started. Was this how publishing worked? The body barely in the ground five minutes, and already getting down to business ...

Sabueso was clearly taking Torben's silence as leave to continue. 'It needs, I think, the personal touch, not just a sober set of essays. As a close friend, new blood she's brought through, you'd be perfect for the introduction, and then I'd want you to interview a lot of her contemporaries – scholars, but public figures too, names people know – and document their impressions, anecdotes, reminiscences – you know, the sort of stuff they go for in the *London Review of Books*. A rounded picture of the real woman. I think, with her media profile, there's crossover potential … I mean, the wider public needs to read a fitting tribute to her impact.'

Still Torben said nothing.

'Well, think it over,' Sabueso said. 'But I'm looking to turn this one round quickly, before anyone else gets into gear. Trust me, it'll help open doors; I don't think you have your next position lined up, do you? Lovely to meet you, Leyla.' And with a final smile, she was gone.

'I thought the funeral service was meant to be the blood-chilling part,' said Leyla. 'Will you do it?'

'What? Oh, maybe.' Torben seemed not to be listening. Come to think of it, he'd barely spoken since the editor had shown up. Even now he wasn't looking at her, but instead—

'Leyla,' he said. His voice had changed; it was more awake, alert. 'Do you see that crowd over there?'

Her eyes followed the direction of his nod. Five mourners, conspicuous by their sombre black clothes, very formal, oddly out of place among the vivid colour all around. Doubly conspicuous by the shadowy presence of one or two bulky men a few paces back, also in black, wearing sunglasses.

She squinted. 'Isn't one of them that MP? Minister for whatever it is?' A Tory, she remembered that much; not the sort you'd expect to see in this sort of company. The politician – large, slow-moving – was being introduced to an austere but glamorous-looking woman by another dark-suited man, this one lean and bald. The body language of all three was stiff, awkward.

Torben nodded. 'And that's Professor Shani Rajapalayam, the art critic for the *Observer*. They seem to both know my old boss, Henrik Drever, the one making the introductions – he's in senior management now, hardly an academic at all anymore. I don't recognise the other two, but ...'

'But?' she prompted.

'No,' he shook his head. 'Nothing. I'm imagining things.'

But, thought Torben, was he though?

On the one hand, he'd mugged up on a lot of Agatha Christie since that reunion weekend in Northumberland. He'd read 'The Stymphalean Birds' and knew how misleading first impressions, premonitions, gut instincts could be. Sometimes a prickling sensation at the sight of some ill-omened figures in dark clothes was nothing but an overactive imagination at best, rank bigotry at worst. And yet. And yet ...

He had first clocked the five black-clad mourners at the graveside, all keeping well back. A patch of shadow amid the sunshine. They had not, he thought, come together, and though some seemed to know each other, they were clearly not a set. Perhaps there had been a natural gravitation, caused by embarrassment, a sense of being out of place in their crow-like garb. Even then, there was something about them, an attitude, an energy, that seemed a little out of kilter. It was not as if anyone was actually happy to be here, it *was* a funeral, but this was something more, a shared sense of – of discomfort? Maybe they were just hot in their suits. Three men and two women, all of them almost *too* funereal, all at least a generation older than him, all conspicuously rich, and worldly, and yet somehow not at ease. The light just – just slipped off them somehow. And then, those goons in the background – the MP's security detail? – was it only that, that had raised the hackles on the back of his neck?

He had glanced at them once or twice since, expecting the group to have dissolved; they must know so many other people here. Shani Rajapalayam had briefly embraced Carmen Sabueso; he had seen Drever gladhanding some other academics. Yet the sombre knot of them remained – a nagging doubt, a question.

As the crowd, its chatter now general, funnelled itself down Viaduct Road, Torben contrived to steer himself and Leyla alongside the one of them he knew to talk to – Henrik Drever, former head of his department. The shiny-headed Swede gave a tight-lipped smile. It suited his general demeanour, the little trimmed beard, the crispness of his white shirt. 'Awful, isn't it?' he said. 'Such a loss to scholarship.'

It was not quite how Torben would have put it, but he forced himself to nod. People were milling about now, suddenly uncertain, some starting the trek for the tube, others looking for taxis or consulting their Uber apps. 'Henrik, this is Leyla Moradi,' he said. 'She's with a set of chambers on Bedford Row.' He would like that, Torben thought; Drever's nostrils flared like a warhorse whenever he got a whiff of power. But it wasn't why he'd introduced her that way.

'Delighted,' murmured Drever, shaking Leyla's hand. 'Ah – I'm sure you both know Shani here, no?' He indicated the elegant, fine-boned woman at his side. 'Shani Rajapalayam, Torben Helle – you should talk actually; it would be good for you, Torben. And Leyla – Moradi, did you say? A ... barrister?' Smiles all round; Drever's sweeping gesture took in the others behind him, none of whom seemed overly keen to pursue their further acquaintance. But Torben was trying his best bright-eyed, ingenuous face, and was grateful to see Leyla beside him smouldering away, raising a characteristic eyebrow.

'Simon Grey, of course, a junior environment minister, though junior hardly seems ...' Drever had lowered his voice, trying to square the circle of fulfilling his social obligations without inconveniencing his reluctant companions. Grey, a rubicund, weary-looking man who would clearly never see either sixty or parts of himself below the waistline again, was already turning away and muttering at one of the security officers.

Drever resumed his *sotto voce* introductions, the light trace of his Swedish accent softening his words still further. 'The rest of us have only just met. This is Katherine Trigg, one of Charlotte's oldest friends, from her school days I believe' – he inclined his head infinitesimally towards a very short, white-haired woman, leaning on a stick with an air of great impatience – 'and Jonathan Azawakh, CMG, who, according to Simon here, practically runs some part of the civil service that we are not supposed to talk about. It's been a pleasure to make their acquaintance.' This fifth member of the group was a tall, bald black man dressed in a suit of such impeccable correctness that he would probably blend into the furniture at any official function of less *outré* appearance than this one.

As if on cue, two large people-carriers with tinted windows pulled up behind them. Grey and Azawakh, the government minister and the senior civil servant, made automatically for the opening doors of their vehicles. 'Look,' said Drever, 'Shani and I have been offered a lift in Simon's car; if you like, I'm sure I could ask—?' He spoke in the tones of a man who would rather gnaw off his own toes than finish that sentence, and Torben, mission accomplished, decided to spare him.

'It's no problem; we're taking the tube,' he said. 'Come on, Leyla.'

As the unsettling figures melted away inside the oversized cars, he and Leyla joined the now-dwindling trail of mourners heading south on Finchley High Road.

'What the hell was all that about?' said Leyla.

'I don't know,' said Torben. The mood was still on him, but its pull was ebbing. In the absence of those black-suited omens, he found that the late afternoon sunshine, the mundane surroundings of suburban London, were weakening the spell. All he had left was the fundamental, stomach-hollowing sense that something about each of those five mourners had not been right. And there could, of course, be a million explanations for each of those five cases. He tried to shrug the thought away.

The problem was, he could think of only one reason why something could not be right at Charlotte Lazerton's funeral. The same reason that had starved him of sleep ever since the news; ever since PC Rampur's pained description over too-sweet tea, in a private room of Holborn Police Station. The thing that had adulterated his grief, robbing him of what he really needed: the head and heart space to simply *mourn* the loss of his mentor, his inspiration, his friend.

For helvede, he thought. He knew exactly how Leyla would react if he told her the truth: that he was increasingly certain, in spite of all evidence to the contrary, that Charlotte Lazerton had been murdered.

3

THE RED LION

'Seriously, Torben, what the actual— no. No no no,' and Leyla reached for Torben's beer, and pulled it across the table. 'You're not having this back until you promise me you're joking. Either that, or your *completely understandable grief* has finally unseated what passes in your head for reason. We're not doing this again. Not after the last time.'

They had left the reception ('wake' seemed wrong) early – soulless, schmoozy, strangely divorced from the person it was meant to commemorate and who, despite looming over the gathering, courtesy of a wall projection, was entirely absent from the discussions around them. The function room was on Piccadilly, and a quick slip through Princes Arcade had got them to the relative normality of the Red Lion. Still, all the lacquer and Victorian glass and varnished panelling were exerting their influence; you could practically choke on the ghost of pipe-smoke past, smell the gas in the flower-head lamps. One glance at the insipid ales on tap and the crush of tourists had nearly sent Torben back out through the black and gold japanned portals, but Leyla had found the bottled Weissbier, parlayed them a corner table, and was now holding his drink hostage as she berated him. Still, it had gone much better than he could have hoped for. She had said 'we're'.

'I know, I know,' he said. 'Anthony Dodd wasn't murdered in the way I thought. But his death *was* staged to look like it. We weren't making things up back at Bastle House, we were correctly registering that the whole thing was fishy. And yes' – he held up his hands – 'you were right and I was wrong, but we *both* knew, right away, that it wasn't a natural death. Well, this is the same.'

'Tor, an old lady fell down her stairs. It's tragic, but—'

'*No!*' he said. '*Not* an old lady. Leyla, she was seventy-three, that's practically the prime of life these days.' Albeit, he thought to himself, a prime in which she had no longer been capable of walking her own dog. Admittedly, Mortimer wasn't just any dog, but he couldn't deny that ageing was real; it could not be dismissed on ideological grounds. And Charlotte had been a *much* older seventy-three than many others of her generation. Still. 'Just hear me out, because so long as you withhold that beer, I have nothing to do but talk.' He paused. 'Only – would you mind not gripping it so tight? Your hands will warm it up.'

Leyla did not slacken her grip, clearly taking this for a ruse.

'Well, anyway,' he said. 'Meera – that's PC Rampur – told me that, best guess, Charlotte died the, the day after I ... oh, *for Satan*.' It had not been like this with Anthony Dodd. How was he meant to state his case dispassionately when his throat clotted up and his eyes kept watering? It was different when you loved them.

Leyla passed him a quite staggeringly vivid handkerchief. '*Tak*,' he said, wiping his eyes. 'As I was saying, Charlotte died the day after I last saw her. It took four days for the lodger in her basement to get worried enough by the random barks and scrabbling, and the general lack of other activity, to get in a locksmith and find – well, find one desperate dog, and a body, lying at the foot of the stairs.'

'Mm,' said Leyla. 'All this presumably being confirmed by the post-mortem, which found no grounds for suspicion, plus no sign of a forced entry, nor a struggle …'

'And that's another thing,' said Torben. 'If there was nothing odd about it, why even *order* a post-mortem? I checked with NHS Online: it has to be ordered by a coroner or a hospital doctor, and there have to be grounds. The police officer, Meera, she referred to it as a matter of course – but it isn't. Which got me thinking. The day before she died, Charlotte told me she was scared. Someone had been wiretapping her landline. Either the press or MI5, she thought, but it could have been anyone, and she was worried there were about to be – how did she put it? – "unpleasant developments". She said she'd been making foolish decisions, and that there might be consequences.'

She had also thought, he reminded himself, that someone had stolen one of her slippers. Was Leyla right, that Charlotte had simply grown old before her time? Was it all a case of a brilliant mind losing its grip; of a body grown fallible?

Well, no, obviously not, because how damn condescending was that?

'And,' he said, now raising his voice over the hubbub, 'if you were a *criminal* barrister, you'd be rather less quick to accept the old "fell down the stairs" line – it's the oldest one in the book. Oh, she fell down some stairs. Oh, I just walked into a door. It's *always* cover for—'

'For domestic abuse,' said Leyla. 'Which I accept. But unless you're about to suggest Dame Charlotte was being knocked about by her dog, then—'

'But the *timing*, Leyla,' he persevered. 'It's too much of a—'

'Coincidence.'

'Look, would you stop doing that? If I can't have my beer, I surely *can* have my—'

23

'Sentences.'

'Oh, *fuck dig*,' he said. 'I should never have said anything.'

'It was those mourners in black, wasn't it?' she said, in an altogether gentler voice that he liked even less than her sceptical one. 'They spooked you.'

'Yes, yes they did. Leyla, I could smell it, there was something going on. Now, I'm not saying that we've just met Charlotte's murderer or anything, but …' Oh, what the hell, she thought he was mad anyway. 'You know, we actually might have done. Look, if you'd just murdered someone you knew and tried to pass it off as an accident, you'd go to their funeral, wouldn't you? To be on the safe side. And you'd make *damn* sure you'd wear black. And of course, it *would* be someone she knew, because she had to let them in – no struggle, no forced entry—'

'Tor, that's beyond a logical syllogism, that's – that's just being silly. Think about it: even if we accepted your addlepated theorising, surely that would mean *all* of them had done it. Since they were *all* dressed in black and acting a bit weird. A five-way murder?'

'No, of course not, I only meant that we *could*—'

'If *you* were a criminal barrister, rather than someone paid to wrap paintings in a string of polysyllables, you'd know that almost all murders are committed by close relatives. I didn't see a single relative in black, did you? Just some acquaintances who probably forgot to read the invite properly.'

'I don't think Charlotte actually *had* any close rel—'

'And OK, maybe I was being a bit ageist just now, I'm sorry. But why would anyone want to wiretap an old— I mean, a retired professor?'

He was damned if she was going to cut him off this time. He'd been thinking about this question for weeks. 'One who's repeatedly courted controversy for her environmental activism? One who recently led the campaign to make the Academy of Art put "Western" in its name and, until her untimely death, was in the running to be elected its next president on a reformist agenda? One whose principles were likely to jeopardise a series of major arts sponsorship deals from oil companies? One who told me she'd previously been wiretapped in the eighties and whose specialism in Tsarist Russian art frequently took her behind the Iron Curtain?'

Leyla blinked. 'OK, those – those were actually some really good points. I can see why she might have been worried someone was spying on her. But to go from that to *murder* ... Tor, I concede there may be a mystery here, and I can totally see why you want to uncover it. But you're falling into the same trap as before, only this time, it's you who's setting it. You want a puzzle to solve because, on some level, you need the catharsis. But can't you just, I don't know, do a bit of research, write an obituary for some magazine? Do the book that ghoul of an editor suggested; it might as well be you rather than someone who didn't truly care about her. It can't always be murder just because there might be some foul play involved: the stakes just aren't that high most of the time.' She shook her head in an insufferably wise sort of way. 'I get it, I do; that's why I've specialised in a branch of law that actually matters to people's lives. By contrast, most wrongdoing is petty, and petty is – well, it's a drag. What's fraud or theft or illicit surveillance, next to the big one? It's why they call them murder mysteries. No one wants to be the "mystery of the silver salver" solver.'

Torben frowned. 'Say that last bit again?'

Leyla paused. 'Actually, I'm not sure I can.'

He sighed. 'Leyla. I just don't want her to be dead.'

She nodded. 'I know, Torben, I know.' And she slid his beer back across the table.

*

Lord spare me from the solipsism of sad boys, Leyla thought, as she finally closed the door of Torben's building, and began the slow walk home to benighted East London. Frederick Street was quiet now that the great rumbling engine of the Gray's Inn Road was dormant; quiet and a little forlorn. The overflowing rubbish sacks, the intermittent scaffolding. Everything that bit too narrow, too grimy, as if the spirit of the age that had erected it had given up halfway with a shrug, uncomfortably aware of the hypocrisy that lay behind that era's elegant façade.

For fuck's sake, Leyla Moradi, listen to yourself. Torben's mood must be catching.

She quickened her pace, trying to stride off the irritation. It was very touching, how hard he had taken his old mentor's death. Indeed, she was all too conscious of how the part of his sorrow that was entirely selfless had called to her, the sincerity and the vulnerability taking hold of something inside her ribcage – could be her heart, could be her spleen, she wasn't an anatomist – and squeezing it till her breath shortened.

But she had been here before, too many times, with blue-eyed boys whose anguish read as authenticity. Nice, well-spoken, sensitive boys, albeit rarely as tall or as blond as Torben, whose winning ability to display their feelings fooled her into thinking this might extend to empathy, when all they really wanted was for someone else to jump into their sadness with them and wallow around in it, like some great big onanistic hot tub. Preferably naked. After the fifth or sixth time, one started to lose patience.

She turned right at the police station, relishing the ability to walk out across the road without risking her life in the process.

Was that what this was, this maundering on of Torben's about murder? Hadn't he learned from the last time? Was he seriously proposing to make it all about him *again*? The private fears that Charlotte had confided in *him*, the hunch that only *he* had felt ... though, now she was alone, Leyla was prepared to admit that to her, too, there had been something decidedly *off* about those five sombre figures at the funeral. Couldn't this boy, just for once, have the humility to be sad, and move on?

Alternatively, said the part of her that was very good at analysing briefs, but an infuriating know-it-all when it came to these late-night self-examinations, could it be that you're cross with him, because he spent the evening talking to you about crime, when you hoped – thought? – *hoped* that he'd wanted you there to comfort him?

To hold his hand at the funeral. To make sparkling conversation at the glamorous art-world function. To take his mind away from a dog-bitten old lady by means of this respectable yet suitably exuberant contemporary floral number by Stine Goya, which she had selected for her outfit today at least half because the designer was from Copenhagen? Hoped that they might go on, not to an overcrowded Victorian pub, but to some discreet wine bar a little nearer his place? Hoped that the evening might end ... differently?

Really, inner voice? You want to do this *now*? God but it's going to be a long walk home.

Actually she loved this walk. The irony was that the street she was climbing right now, Wharton Street, was where she had wanted to end up, her dream location, ever since her first foray up the hill to see the ballet at Sadler's Wells in the first month of her pupillage. From that night on, she had coveted one of these preposterously square, almost mausoleum-like houses – which she knew really wasn't selling it – preferably on the left-hand side, so you got the sun. There were cherry trees, like there had been at home; sometimes the blossom still made her cry. And all the gardens nearby, and the silly swanky shops. But above all, it was the sky. On this slope, there was an awful lot of sky.

Even then, nearly a decade ago, she had known it was a fantasy. But an aspirational one, something to work towards, the sort of home that befitted a hot-shot barrister. And of course, this was back when she'd still thought she'd go into commercial law, and had not followed the siren call of crusading causes, the irrefutable rightness of representing refugee charities, asylum appeal cases, campaigns for climate justice. Mostly she lost, but the wins actually mattered, and the work was infinitely more sustaining than another zero on her income. Still, it was goodbye to Wharton Street, unless she sold out and switched specialisms. And goodbye to it tonight, as she pressed on home. Something that was either a very large cat, or a young urban fox, flitted across her path, to crouch beneath a parked car, eyes on her passing, its fur ghostly pale. Oh, it was pathetic, but at times like this, she really did love London.

For now, she had a one-bed, second-floor flat in a shared ownership scheme on Haberdasher Street. Leafy, airy, half an hour's walk to work. The wrong side of the A501. Completely and utterly, appallingly alone.

4

ON PAPER

Art historian of Tsarist Russian oil painting who, in her final years, made a major contribution to environmental activism.

Charlotte Lazerton, who has died aged 73, was a former Deputy Director of the Academy of Western Art (AWA) and professor emerita at the Courtauld Institute, a college of the University of London. Her pioneering work on the art of nineteenth-century Russia did much to help thaw UK–Soviet diplomatic relations and forge cultural ties both before and after the dissolution of the USSR. In the course of a fifty-year career, she produced a series of magisterial works on leading painters and schools, whilst acting as mentor and inspiration to two generations of emerging scholars, artists and critics.

A leading light during the heyday of London's art schools in the 1970s and 80s, Lazerton was as much a champion of the contemporary as the historical, a tireless promoter of grassroots and early ages arts education, and a key figure in encouraging curatorial and knowledge exchange programmes between the UK and the rest of Europe, particularly in the Baltic region. Though she always regarded her true calling as that of the art historian and scholar, Lazerton's career was increasingly characterised as it progressed by selfless stints as an administrator and reformer. Her most notable and perhaps controversial achievement in this regard came when, in 2017, she instituted the decolonisation programme at the (then) Academy of Art, a bastion of the British establishment, as part of which the institution added 'Western' to its title in recognition of its geographically and ideologically limited preoccupations.

Charlotte Lazerton was born and raised in the parish of Stourpaine, near Blandford Forum, Dorset, the only child of Hugo and Henrietta Lazerton (née Henrietta Cabell-Fowell). Educated as a day pupil at nearby Brook Hall School, she was remembered by contemporaries as a rebellious teenager, repeatedly threatened with expulsion, permitted to remain solely on the strength of her academic record in the arts and her utility on the sports field. In due course this won her a scholarship to University College London, her ticket out of what she described in later years variously as 'a sleepy provincial Eden' and 'hell on earth'. Fellow students at UCL recall her aptitude for balancing rigorous academic study with an enthusiasm for the swinging sixties, and rumours of her voracious appetite for both scholarly and other forms of stimulation are legion.

Whatever her indulgences, Lazerton excelled as an art historian. As a postgraduate, she studied at Yale, Vienna, Rome and Paris, serving as an overseas representative on the Sorbonne Occupation Committee during the summer protests of 1968. Her first book, *The Brothers Briullov: Russian Artists in Rome*, was a seminal work of micro-historicism, often compared favourably with the best of the Annales school of history. This was followed by a biographical study of the painter Anton Ivanov, a freed serf, and his patrons the Chernetsovs.

It was this foray into social history that led Lazerton to focus on the field with which she is most closely associated: the Peredvizhniki or Itinerant Movement. Exemplified by genre painters such as Pavel Fedotov, Vasily Perov and Ilya Repin, this was less a coherent school in the western sense than a wider rejection of Tsarist and bourgeois society by a succession of artists of humble origins who adopted itinerant lifestyles. Mixing taboo-breaking satire with an attention to the conditions of Russia's serfs, the Peredvizhniki were political rather than artistic innovators. Across a series of books and exhibitions, Lazerton came to see her own work as inextricably linked to that of the itinerants. Not content merely to research their idealism, she sought to put it into practice, making the step from a research career to more public-facing and leadership roles in the 1980s and 90s.

It was during this period that Lazerton embarked upon a series of cultural missions to Moscow and St Petersburg (then Leningrad). She is also believed to have undertaken work of a more private nature for the British government. Lazerton received an OBE (1991), CBE (1999) and DBE (2012) in recognition of her contribution to Anglo-Russian relations, and of her work as a public ambassador for arts education within the UK. She has also been honoured by a number of other governments.

Holder of a personal chair at the Courtauld since 1981, Lazerton was an influential organiser at the British Academy and Royal Academy, as well as the AWA, of which she was the Deputy Director between 2000 and 2007. At the time of her death, she was considered by many to be the leading candidate in its inaugural presidential election, following a major restructuring: a post that, she stated, would allow her to implement much-needed reforms of the academy's hierarchy, as well as the founding of a cross-organisation committee to review the ethics of exhibition sponsorship by private companies.

An outspoken public figure during the Brexit referendum of 2016, her final years saw Lazerton turn her attention to environmental activism. A recognisable presence on the picket lines due to her lifelong love of Irish wolfhounds (on one memorable occasion when she led a demonstration on a bicycle, accompanied by two of her dogs, she was likened by journalists to Boudicca), her most successful contribution was a social media campaign called The Contrast. This was a crowd-sourced curatorial project in which iconic landscape paintings were paired with new photography of the same or similar locations, demonstrating the impact of deforestation, soil erosion, melting icecaps, and other forms of urban sprawl and habitat loss. The viral global popularity of this initiative is all the more remarkable given Lazerton herself never owned a mobile phone or used any computer besides that in her university office – and even then, only under extreme sufferance.

Unmarried and with no immediate surviving relatives, Dame Charlotte Lazerton's greatest legacy will endure in her works, her idealism, and the many friends, colleagues and sparring partners she made and inspired during the course of her career.

Well, thought Torben, looking up from a screen which had, for some unfathomable reason, gone all wet and blurry. You could do worse.

He had been looking out for obituaries every day since the funeral, growing increasingly aggrieved at the thought that she might not receive one. This was now the third broadsheet in five days to produce an account, and, from the sheer body of work it had to cover, he was beginning to understand the delay. How much had he himself been aware of? Half of this? Less?

So keen had he been to read this account – it was by Shani Rajapalayam, the critic he had been introduced to at the cemetery, one of those ill-omened, black-clad five – that he had wholly neglected the letter he had found waiting on the doormat. It must have arrived yesterday, Saturday, only he had come home late, rather worse for wear after an alumni event with Cameron Plott, Iqbal, Pedro and some of the other footballers. They had been stood drinks by one of Oarwright College's most precocious former residents, an absolute banker of a man by the name of Zak Cremello, and the evening had marked the definitive end of a period of (relative) ascetism, begun in the wake of the Bastle House affair. The college dinner had been safe enough – just a glass of free prosecco on arrival. But honestly, if they *would* coax him along to the Mikkeller brewpub on Exmouth Market, how was he supposed to answer for the consequences? The place was more or less his own personal Mecca, and it had undeniably been his patriotic duty as a Dane to make the most of it. Besides, it took his mind off – well, this.

Unwonted, he had a flashback of Zak Cremello, bottle-blond hair in a footballer's cut, his semi-wasted face leering into Torben's own. The sense that rose from him more strongly even than the early summer sweat, was that because he had bought the most expensive drinks in the place – because, if he had wanted to, he could have bought the place itself – he could treat it as a private fiefdom, ordering the staff about. How entitled, yet how fundamentally bored you must have to be, to get a kick out of that kind of boorishness – and the other young men there, more impressionable (or more drunk) looking up to Cremello as to a prophet. And Torben, too ashamed to stay but too implicated to call him out for what he was, slipping out with a whispered apology to the barman and a tip that probably exceeded the price of the drinks he had been bought … Oh the wearying, turgid, head-aching shame of it all. He just hoped he'd be allowed back in. He liked that bar.

Anyway, the letter. Bills aside, he didn't get many of these, certainly not with a handwritten address. And bearing a Dorset postmark. Dorset – where had he just … oh.

And Torben tore the letter open.

> *Hod Hill Manor*
> *Stourpaine*
> *Blandford Forum*
> *Dorset*
> *DT11 8TQ*

Dear Dr Helle,
Following the recent death of my cousin Charlotte Lazerton, I am writing in my capacity as executor for her estate to advise you that, under the terms of her will, you are listed as a beneficiary. ~~*Furtherm*~~

No, I really can't bear writing in this silly snooty way. My solicitor did offer to do the work himself and has supplied me with a template but, as I suspect Charlie named me executor because I was the only one of the family she could actually stand the sight of, I feel it incumbent upon me (the solicitor would like that phrase) to add the human touch to what is, whichever way you shake it, a horribly sorry and sad affair.

Firstly, I can tell from the will, and the fact she asks to write to you before practically anyone else, that you must have been close to Charlie: I offer my condolences. She was really something.

I'm afraid I do have rather a few of these to write, as my cousin has taken her belief in redistribution to some extreme – ~~split so many ways, I suspect, partly in order to spite the family, in fact there's barely a penny for any of them but why am I~~ so I will be brief. There are two items of the will that pertain to you. The first is a straightforward bequest and, given that you are presumably a very busy man, I'm not sure you're going to like it. You have been left the contents of Charlotte Lazerton's desk, viz., all papers, diaries, etc., on the condition that you attempt to put these in order and – I quote – 'see if there is anything redeemable amid the dross; if not, sell them as a job lot to an American museum or something'.

There is a recent codicil to this clause, in fact dated the day before Charlotte's death. It reads, 'I mean it, Torben, every damn scrap. In the event that I do not live to complete them, you may find the first draft of my memoirs particularly diverting.' She has then added, with a request not to paraphrase the words when informing you, that 'I am leaving you your duty in a <u>friendly spirit</u>'. She has underlined the last two words, so I'm doing the same.

Torben looked up from the page. He had been left her *desk*. Or rather, what was in it. *For helvede.* He remembered that desk, a mid-century colossus of a thing, itself half buried under a mound of loose papers. Suppressing a shudder, he returned to the letter.

The second item may prove more palatable. My cousin is using the larger part of her estate – savings, investments, proceeds from the sale of certain rather valuable paintings and the contents of the house in Bloomsbury, &c. – to set up a small arts foundation. This has several aims, ranging from the supply of artistic materials to inner-city primary schools, to the endowment of an undergraduate fellowship at the Ruskin; fear not, all this need not concern you, as you are disbarred (another nice legal term) from becoming a trustee. This is because you yourself benefit from being nominated as the first holder of the Peredvizhniki Fellowship, the aim of which is 'to facilitate the careers of international early-career art historians who do not hold a British passport'. Charlotte includes at this juncture some rather provocative rhetoric about a referendum of some years ago that, on balance, we trustees (I am one, you see) have seen fit to leave out of the rubric. The next section I am copying out of the official plans.

There is no financial consideration associated with this Fellowship. Rather, it stipulates that for a term of five years (60 months), the Fellow has the custodianship of 24 Little James Street, excepting the lower-ground-floor flat of 24A, the rent on which forms part of the Foundation's income. For the duration of this term, the Fellow will be regarded as the sole tenant of the house, free of charge. They will be permitted to entertain guests and cohabit with a partner (actually she writes 'or partners, so long as they all share the same bed'), but not to take lodgers. The Foundation will advertise for and administer the appointment of successive Fellows, but the outgoing recipient will be expected to serve on the appointing panel. The chief duty of the Fellow, besides the continuance of their regular professional activities in a 'manner likely to promote international concord', and the delivery of an annual lecture at Cockpit Studios, which stands across the road, is to renovate and furnish the house in accordance with their own aesthetic principles. Each new Fellow will receive the house unfurnished, and have the chance to reinvent its interior as far as their means allow. (I should note that all of this is of course subject to Listed Building Consent, which Charlotte seems to have forgotten. She notes that 'I have let the old place get a bit stale.')

All of this will, naturally, take some time to clear probate, though we have hopes of expediting matters here since my nephew knows a few people in that department. Yes, I know. Still, I wanted to write to you as soon as possible, not just because Charlotte requested it, but also to confirm your acceptance of the position, as doing so will naturally have an impact on your future plans. I enclose a receipt form which I am assured has some legal standing; please sign, date and return this asap.

Informally, I imagine you'll want a good look around the place. I gather you used to rent a room from Charlie, but these things look very different once they become your responsibility – take it from one who knows. To that end, I'll try and get someone in authority over to you with a set of keys. I am not sure if this would be better before or after they empty it of contents – from what I recall, it's a bit of a junk-shop in there – so am leaving this to fate; one never knows how quick these legal bods will be.

I think that's all. Ten more of these letters to go before lunch. You will make it nice, won't you, Dr Helle? And – you know – artistically coherent. Uncompromising. I think she'd like that.

Yours sincerely,
Beryl Cabell-Fowell

PS If you're ever passing this way, do pop in. I couldn't make the funeral – someone had to look after the animals, and I rarely travel nowadays in any case – and it would be nice to exchange stories about Charlie. She was a plucked 'un.

5

LITTLE JAMES STREET

The four of them looked up at it.

'A. Whole. House,' said Ruth Thompson.

'In WC1,' breathed Leyla.

'I dunno, isn't it a bit … skinny?' said Wilson Ho. 'That one's much bigger.'

It was one hour later. Immediately upon finishing Beryl Cabell-Fowell's letter, Torben had rung round his oldest friends, three of whom had been free to spend their Sunday lunchtime standing in a London street, gawping up at an assemblage of bricks, wood and slate.

'Hey, Leyla,' said Wilson. 'Isn't your office, like, just down there? I bet you'd kill for this.'

There was an awkward silence. Save it for later, Torben told himself.

'Built in the 1710s,' he said instead. 'And practically unique for London. See how the gable end faces the street?'

'It looks sort of – Dutch?' volunteered Ruth.

'Exactly: practically nothing in the capital was still being built this way round by the Georgian period; the roofs all began to face the other way. Even here, they only built these three houses' – he gestured to numbers 22 and 26 on either side – 'with a crosswise connecting bit of roof on the north side; you can't really see it from here, sort of a rudimentary escape route in case of fire. Anyway, that's why it's so narrow; each room occupies the whole width of the building, with the staircase running at right angles through the centre of the house. Two rooms per floor ...' He tailed off, feeling suddenly sick. Just saying the word 'staircase' had reminded him of the reason for his good fortune.

No one else seemed to notice this. 'That's impressively quick googling,' said Leyla. 'Or no, wait, this is where you used to lodge, isn't it?'

'That was his room,' said Ruth, pointing at the third-floor garret, a triangle of mellow brick framed by the steep rake of roof on either side. 'I only saw the inside once. Like a monk's cell, I thought, very austere. But I suppose there was nowhere to put anything ...'

Until their recent reunion, Torben had seen neither Leyla nor Wilson for the best part of a decade. Although 'best part' was very much *not* the phrase for it. Of his old undergraduate friends it was only Ruth, now a Metropolitan Police inspector, that he had stayed in close contact with, because of – well, reasons.

'And the basement's a separate flat,' said Leyla. 'That's still – what, eight rooms? You're going to have *eight rooms*?!'

'I've nothing to put in them though,' Torben offered up, aiming for exculpation. 'As in, *literally* nothing.'

'Oh boo bloody hoo,' she said. 'How many bathrooms?'

'Just the one, which made the whole lodging thing pretty, well, intimate,' said Torben. 'The top room that wasn't mine is a sort of attic store, I think, mostly full of paintings; bed and bathroom below; office and library on the first floor—'

'Oo, a *library*!' said the others, practically in unison.

'—with the kitchen and dining room at street level. Plus,' he said, allowing himself to get carried away, 'it's got just about all its historic features. Fireplaces, cornicing—'

'Oh, thank heaven for the cornicing! I was beginning to worry!'

'And I mean, obviously the kitchen and bathroom are retrofitted, plus there's this hideous landline setup at the top of the first set of stairs, all of it incredibly seventies—'

'You poor, *poor* boy!'

'Still,' he finished, having saved it up till last. 'It does have all the original panelling.'

They followed up the on-street ogle with a picnic in Brunswick Square Gardens.

'My treat,' said Torben. 'Given the circumstances.'

'Damn straight,' said Wilson.

It was like old times, except obviously not. They had never done this before in London. And in Oxford, their student loans had definitely not stretched to a few oozing Petit Saint Marcellins, sun-warmed, scooped from their ramekins with hunks of sourdough baguette and washed down by a bottle of Chiroubles.

Wilson held up his disposable coffee cup of wine. In his best Richard E. Grant manner, he declared it 'a perky little number. Floral notes of violet and peony ... summer berries ... the liquid evocation of that beach the tourists haven't found where you deflowered your French pen pal. What Mummy would have called a twink of a wine.'

Ruth snorted.

Torben found himself distracted by the sight of Leyla biting into a tomato. Her exquisite teeth, tearing the red flesh, flecks of juice on her throat. Sun-dappled, beneath the spread of the ancient plane tree, the undersides of its leaves impossibly green against the light.

'We should've got a saucisson.'

'And cut it how?'

'Or we could just … lie here …'

'We've still got this sexy little Langres to get through. I've saved some grapes.'

'The best cheese,' contributed Torben, 'is of course a well-aged Gamle Ole. But I'll allow that the French know their way around a cow's udder.'

'That,' said Wilson, 'is just the kind of batshit language I want from you, Tor—'

Ruth groaned.

Torben propped himself up on his elbows; eyed them warily. '—?'

'For my—'

'New podcast,' said Ruth. 'It was only a matter of time; practically everyone has one. Like most of them, Wilson's is a—'

'True crime pod, yeah,' said Wilson. 'As I've been trying to tell you for weeks. Ruth, why not eat some cheese for a minute?'

'Ouch,' said Leyla, from the sidelines.

'I've already got interviews with Frances and Sara in the can,' said Wilson, 'and I'm off to see Tom next week. The Bellinghams I'll do over Zoom; apparently Danny can get hold of a decent USB mic. I am *not* going back to Bastle House in a hurry.'

'Wait,' said Torben. 'Your true crime … is *us*?' He turned to Leyla. 'Did you know about this?'

Leyla suddenly became very interested in finishing off the leftovers.

'What … what are you calling it?' said Torben.

'I can't decide between "Crimeward Ho" and "Ho-rrible Histories",' said Wilson. 'I've got season one sorted though; I'm subtitling it "Hell Freezes Over".'

Torben couldn't decide if that was a compliment, or simply the stupidest thing he'd ever heard.

'You're my main man!' Wilson pressed on. 'The amateur detective of legend!'

'Ugh,' said Torben. 'I wouldn't be an amateur if you paid me to.'

'Hmm. That one needs work, I think,' said Wilson. 'Anyway, when can I book you in? All very casual, we can record at the theatre.' Wilson was an actor, and had finally made it to the West End, albeit in a supporting role. 'There's this old stationery cupboard that's practically soundproofed.'

Torben looked at the tall, handsome Hong Kong-er. While an unexamined part of himself would not be entirely averse to an hour in a cupboard with Wilson Ho, he wasn't sure he liked the sound of any of this.

'I've already told him not to,' said Ruth, wiping the last of the Langres from her fingers with a napkin. *Hold op* – the *last* of the Langres; had they really eaten the whole cheese?

'Besides asking for trouble from the Dodd estate,' Ruth went on, 'it's all, quite frankly, in very poor taste. A man *died*, Wilson.'

Wilson winced. 'Don't I know it. But that's what people want, Ruth. If you can't give them a mysterious death, they're just not interested.'

'No one wants to hear about the "mystery of the silver salver" solver,' said Torben.

'Love it,' said Wilson. 'We'll use that one.'

Leyla looked ready to throw an empty ramekin at Torben's head. He stuck his tongue out at her.

'So, if you're on board then,' said Wilson, 'that's everyone except Ruth. Sure I can't persuade you, Thompson? I'd've thought you'd be more, you know … demob happy.'

Leyla and Torben turned on Ruth. 'What's this?'

Ruth sighed. 'I ... I'm leaving the force. Tomorrow I hand in my notice: four more weeks and I'm done. On 18 June – hah, isn't that the anniversary of Waterloo? – I will no longer be a police officer.'

'*Er du sindssyg*?' said Torben. 'I thought this was your, your *calling* – and weren't you about to be fast-tracked to Chief Inspector or something?'

'This needs more wine,' said Leyla. 'But, Ruth, I'm confused, are we celebrating or—?'

Ruth made a gesture that looked a bit like an octopus trying to refuse second helpings. 'I really don't know,' she said. 'I'm just so – so very, very tired.'

Torben considered. 'I can think of literally a hundred reasons why you'd want to leave an institution like the Met,' he said. 'But haven't you always said—'

'Change comes from within, yeah,' said Ruth. 'But I've also always thought that, if something was hard and painful, then it was a reason to do it. For years I've seen so many colleagues risking their lives on the street; risking their sanity in the station. All of us convinced that it was worth it if we could make this institution *only* the force for good it's meant to be. But lately, I've begun thinking – actually, Wilson said it to me first – that if something's soul-destroying, maybe that's a reason ... *not* to do it?'

'Come here,' said Leyla, holding out her arms. Ruth went to her. Torben tried not to be jealous. Though actually, his chief feeling was one of – what even was that? Concern for his friend, obviously, who was already going through a messy divorce; surely this couldn't be unrelated. Plus the last thing the police force needed was a talent drain of its best young black officers. But jumbled up with that, could he, could he possibly be feeling – inconvenienced? He had been counting on Ruth as an influential police officer – but why? Hadn't he admitted that Leyla was right about Charlotte's death? He tried not to think about what Charlotte had said in the will. About what might be waiting for him when he got inside that house.

'I'll have to move back in with my parents for a bit,' Ruth was saying. 'Even with your specialist friend's advice, Leyla, the divorce settlement's stretched me pretty tight. And then I was thinking of entering local government …'

'Of *course* you are,' sighed Leyla. 'Seriously, what's wrong with taking a break from do-goodery?'

'You can hardly talk,' Wilson pointed out.

'At least I factor in holidays after a tough case,' said Leyla. 'I'm actually taking a lot of the next month off.'

Four weeks, Torben thought. Four weeks before Ruth was no longer a serving officer. Not a lot of time to work with.

Hypothetically speaking, of course.

Across the gardens, two figures were getting up from a bench, leaving in opposite directions. As one came nearer, Torben recognised Zak Cremello, the awful guy from the alumni event who'd stood them drinks: late thirties, dressed down with a classic rich-boy hoodie, excessively well groomed, his hair dyed peroxide blond. Zak raised a hand in greeting, and Torben steeled himself for the encounter. The man apparently hoovered up seven figures a week, thanks to some especially adventurous venture capitalism, and was about as high-maintenance as one might predict. Zak was eternally bored, restive and nearly impossible to keep on one topic for more than thirty seconds at a time without him bulldozing down the conversation in some unexpected and often unsavoury direction. Perhaps Torben could hand Cremello over to Wilson; they could bond over their playboy affectations.

Meanwhile, the other man was just leaving through the far gates. Funny thing. But Torben was almost certain it had been Henrik Drever.

6

SOMERSET HOUSE

The next day, Monday, Torben replaced his old afternoon dog walk with a trek out to Ruth's police station in East London, taking a bottle and a bouquet of flowers. They spent the evening discussing her decision, her future plans – and, in what he considered a laudable display of self-control, entirely ignoring the subject he really wanted her opinion on. Tuesday ended in a much-needed release of feeling on the handball pitch, a series of body-checks, passing triangles and jump shots serving to compensate for a day of total frustration: every time he attempted to get down to work, the vision of a narrow staircase rose before him. Despite himself, he read and re-read Beryl Cabell-Fowell's letter, always coming back to Charlotte's hasty codicil. *For helvede*, how long did he have to wait to see that desk, those memoirs? To see if he had been right to suspect – and if Charlotte had also suspected …

It was not until Wednesday that things began to happen.

Lunchtime, and Torben, stomach rumbling a little, turned from the sun-baked, crowded mess of Shaftesbury Avenue, down a grubby side street of the kind he thought they reserved exclusively for films about the seedier side of the 1960s. He found Wilson waiting at the stage door of the Hayford Theatre, chatting to two other actors who were taking drags of cigarettes. Torben wondered why Wilson, so conscious of his health, was standing so near, until he caught a whiff: Sobranies. How could something so disgusting smell so … delectable? *For fanden*, he should have fitted in a meal …

Wilson led him through an ill-lit labyrinth. 'That's my dressing-room,' he pointed out, the pride latent beneath the off-hand air.

'Want to show me?' said Torben.

Wilson looked horrified. 'Christ, no,' he said. 'You'd never take me for a human being again if you saw the state of it. Here we are. Thanks for doing this, by the way.'

They had halted outside a door labelled 'Stationary Cupboard'.

Torben resisted the impulse for fully two seconds. Then he pointed out the 'a'.

Wilson smiled. 'D'you see it moving?'

'Well …'

'Look,' said Wilson, 'if it hops, starts spinning round, even gives a very slight tremor, I'll get them to change the name.' He opened the door on a room that, though not large enough to swing a cat in, did just have space for a desk and two chairs, crammed between the shelves of printing paper, surplus drapery and empty egg cartons nailed to walls that made it into an ersatz recording studio.

Ten minutes later, they were in full swing. 'So, Dr Helle—'

'Why are you calling me Dr Helle?'

'Sounds more impressive. We'll edit out this bit. So, Dr Helle, when you finally hit upon the truth of Anthony Dodd's death—'

'*Hold op*, that wasn't me, that was Ley—'

'Work with me here, Tor, the audience wants a genius, not some bozo who gets the whole thing wrong ...'

'... OK, now, if I can take you back to the moment you first suspected there was something strange about Anthony Dodd's death? You instantly thought—'

'This is wrong, yes,' said Torben. And something prickled on the back of his neck. For a second, he was back there, in the icy bedroom. The harsh light of morning, the still figure.

'And, even knowing what we know now, faced with that situation again, you would still call it out? You'd say it was murder?'

Torben paused. Had Wilson been talking to Leyla?

'You know Aesop's fables?' he said, slowly. 'They're a global thing, not just—?'

Wilson nodded. Then he seemed to catch himself: gestures didn't work on audio. 'Yeah, I know them,' he said. 'Those mean fucking ants and the poor grasshopper, that fox stuck in a bottle, the hare that can't manage interval training?'

'*Præcist*,' Torben agreed. 'Well, do you remember the boy who cried wolf? Yes? What was the moral?'

Wilson took a second. 'Um, not to go shooting your mouth off, because people won't believe you? Not to make stuff up?'

'No,' said Torben. 'People have always got this wrong. Starting with Aesop. Because the boy died, didn't he?'

'Yeah ...' said Wilson, sounding a little uncertain.

'So,' and Torben leaned in towards the mic. 'That's the moral. Maybe there wasn't a wolf yesterday. Or the day before. But, one day, there *will* be a wolf. In the end, there is always a wolf. So don't get complacent. Don't stop listening. And if you see a glint of yellow eyes, a darkness stepping from between the trees, well then … you'd better be ready to shout.'

Three o'clock. More shaken than he cared to admit by his strange little speech, Torben had wrapped things up pretty quickly. Wilson seemed delighted with the results. 'I love the bit where you go mad and start ranting about wolves,' he had said. 'You come across as properly eccentric.'

Making his excuses, Torben had headed for the Strand, grabbing a salmon roll (he was not yet ready for the 'no fish' stage of his dietary journey) and black coffee from the Ole & Steen next to the Lyceum. Now, nerves still jangling and fingers only a little greasy, he turned to his seminar group: eleven MA students still showing up at the end of the year, long after the undergraduates had finished classes, for this final session on materiality. The seminar room was on the Thames side of Somerset House; high-ceilinged, high-windowed. From up here, London was mostly clouds and sky. Empty as air. He *had* planned this, hadn't he? Back before he got distracted? Their young faces raised expectantly. All of them so shiny.

Torben fished in his pocket, and brought out a box of Tordenskjold matches. The twelve of them were gathered around a large square table, and he chucked the box into the middle of it. 'So,' he said. 'What can you tell me about this?'

The students took turns to handle the matchbox, passing it round. As usual, it was Elodie Griffon who broke the silence. 'Matchbox, twenty-first century. Approximately forty by sixty by twenty millimetres' – she pronounced the final word in the French style – 'which is already interesting,' she said, reflecting, 'because I automatically give three measurements. Normally if we caption an artwork, we say two

– but all art is, I think, really in three dimensions …'

A boy whose name Torben knew was either John or James – or Jack? – leapt in, saying something about the digital and questioning the relevance, even the tyranny, of fixed dimensions in an interactive, screen-centred world, and they were off. Torben was proud of Elodie; she could always be relied upon to open up an angle.

'Torden … Tordenskjold,' someone was saying. 'Sorry, Torben, that's probably not how you pronounce it! But that's him, right, the guy whose portrait is on the matchbox? Who was he?'

'You tell me,' said Torben. 'You're looking at his portrait.'

'Well,' said another student, 'Danish, knowing you … and I'd say early eighteenth century, judging by the style, plus that looks like a wig …'

'Plus,' said Elodie, 'he looks like he has gout, which is *very* eighteenth century.'

'*Hej!*' Torben said. 'That's a national hero you're maligning.'

'Ah!' said Elodie. 'We have extorted a clue. So: a war hero – that's a uniform, and a medal …'

'Not actually Danish, by the way,' Torben admitted. 'Norwegian.'

'But,' said a boy, 'they were both part of the same kingdom at the time, so …'

'But is it *art*,' mused another, 'if it's a painting that's been mass-reproduced to sell matches? I'm reminded, obviously, of Andy Warhol …'

'Ironic,' said a young woman. 'If he's an admiral who's been posthumously press-ganged into the service of capitalism.'

'You're all losing sight of the material aspect,' Torben warned them. 'I mean, this is all excellent' – he was trying to remember you were meant to compliment them in between the important feedback – 'but … let me ask a more specific question. What can you tell me about *this* matchbox? This one *in particular*?'

For a minute, it stumped them. Elodie picked up the box again. 'It's faded,' she said. 'Like it's been lying in the sun. Which is unnatural for a matchbox, I suppose … There is a dent in the side, here, like it has been hit or – or thrown? – and a scratch mark on the back, or the indent of a fingernail. It is across some words. They are saying' – she peered more closely still – '*Alors!* They are saying "Made in Sweden".'

'I thought you said he was a Danish war hero?' said the boy. 'Which means he probably fought *against* the Swedes, no?'

'*Ouf!*' said Elodie. 'So, Torben is all happy with his heroic Danish matchbox, but then he reads the small print, feels betrayed, and – *voilà!* – throws it across the room, where it lies, ignored, by the window, until one day he realises he has a seminar to teach and no lesson plan prepared.'

Torben applauded. 'I googled it,' he said. 'Apparently matchmaking – making matches, I mean – was a big Swedish industry, and so a Danish patriot decided to start up this brand in response. They did very well. So well, in fact, that a Swedish company bought them out in the seventies. Elodie, you'll make a great detective – I mean, of art, art history …'

He tailed off. Once, at a dinner, he had disavowed the suggestion that art history was like detection. But if the two were indeed distinct, he might as well set aside work on his new book for the next four weeks. Because there was only one thing his mind wanted to focus on right now.

Five-fifteen. Heading home, Torben crossed Theobalds Road, shedding the clamour of Holborn for the better-heeled buzz of Lamb's Conduit Street. The south end still depressed him; a modern office block to the left, with Holborn Police Station opposite. But the sun was doing that thing where it danced in the leaves of the plane trees, slanted through buildings and struck sideways off glass, making him dizzy, lightening his tread. It was nearly summer, at last – his teaching term was over – each step rang out with the promise of holiday, which meant, to his mind, the freedom to concentrate on the things that really mattered. And despite the seriousness of the task he was contemplating, that licence, the gift of bending himself entirely towards something worthwhile, had him beaming like a madman.

Just ahead of him were two figures. One forging ahead with intent, the other scrabbling along in its wake. He blinked. Surely the first of those figures was—

'Mortimer!' he cried.

The gigantic hound stopped and turned. Seconds later, two enormous paws were on his shoulders and the beast's tongue was intent on exfoliating the entirety of Torben's face.

'So – so sorry!' said the police officer, trying to tug the dog back. 'I'm trying to train— oh! It's you!'

Torben recognised PC Rampur, the constable who had broken the news of Charlotte's death.

'Yes,' he said. 'Torben Helle. Don't worry, Mortimer and I are acquainted.' He scratched the wolfhound behind its ear, making a mental note to dry clean his jacket.

Meera Rampur looked awkward, young, friendly. He considered. '*Hej*,' he said. 'Could I maybe – maybe buy you a drink? I mean, a … platonic one?'

The officer goggled at him. 'No, obviously not, that's absolutely not allowed!' But she sounded more regretful than offended – whether at his caveat, or having to decline, he couldn't tell. But either worked for him.

'OK,' he said. 'In that case – *you* can buy *me* one. I'll take Mortimer, I'm – I'm sort of used to it.'

'Um, OK then,' she said. 'Actually I'm new to this post; where should we—?'

'The Perseverance is just up here,' Torben said, taking over the leash. *I'm new*. Really, he'd never have guessed.

'The pizza's good too,' he suggested, accepting the pint of unfiltered lager. The Perseverance was a great little pub – crowded and cosy, but festooned with enough dried seedheads, replete with enough old and deep-scored wood, to feel almost like they were out in the countryside. And he should have a wolfhound with him more often, he thought; this was the first time he'd been in here without other punters squeezing in close on either side. With an eighty-kilo monster lapping from a bowl at their feet, people seemed to be giving their nook a respectfully wide berth.

'Look,' said Meera, shuffling round next to him. 'I'm really sorry for that answerphone message, I – did you say pizza? Let me just check something ...' and she pulled a dog-eared copy of *Blackstone's Handbook for Policing Students* from her rucksack. A second later she was beaming at him. 'Turns out that, if we're off-duty, we *are* allowed to accept pizza.' Torben grinned back.

Two pints, a *Carciofi* and a *Napoletana* later, it was clear that what PC Rampur wanted was a friend. One who would make a better listener than Mortimer, the station's new mascot.

'He was left to someone in the will, of course,' she said. 'But actually, if a dog over a certain size has got up to – well, what this poor boy got up to after, you know – it's meant to be ... put down.' She was whispering. Torben was almost certain it was so that Mortimer wouldn't hear what she was saying.

'*For Satan!*' he said, as if horrified at what seemed a pretty reasonable, if heartless, policy.

'Only thing to do was to, you know, lose him from the books,' she said. 'Not that I should be telling members of the public, really. In fact, if you could forget that I—'

'My lips are stitched,' he said.

'Stitched?'

'Isn't that the saying? Like they did to Loki?'

'Sorry, I'm not really into Marvel.'

'Marvell wrote a version? I didn't know he was even aware of the Eddas.'

Meera laughed. It was clear that neither of them had a clue what the other one was talking about.

'So, how's he getting on?' said Torben, indicating Mortimer.

'Oh, he's the best!' said Meera. 'His first day on the beat, up by all those seedy little two-star hotels right before you get to King's Cross? He led us straight to this abandoned basement, turned out to be some sort of unlicensed sex dungeon!'

'*Hold kæft!*'

She nodded, wiping the beer foam from her upper lip. 'Deserted, but you could see kinky stuff had been going on – there was all this bondage gear – collars, gags, leads, even chains – crash mats for beds, probably so they could be wiped down' – Meera wrinkled her nose – 'and cocaine residue on the surfaces. I reckon he might do as a sniffer dog if he can make a beeline for a place like that from across the street!' She paused. 'Of course, if we followed up all his hunches, we'd have to arrest half the squirrels in central London, so his strike rate could do with a little improvement.'

Torben smiled. Then, like the lowest sort of worm imaginable, he let the smile falter and his gaze drop. From some hitherto unknown cesspit of his character, he summoned up a sort of choking sigh.

Meera frowned. 'Everything OK?'

He shrugged. 'Ach, my therapist says I'll be fine, that it's natural. The grief, you know?'

'Oh,' she said. 'Sorry, I shouldn't have joked about—'

'No, no, it's good to be taken outside of myself. And, you know, to talk about things connected with her ...' He allowed a light to come, ever so tentatively, into his eyes. 'Actually, that's something you might be able to help me with.'

'Really? I mean, sure, I want to help—'

'The therapist says,' and Torben added a touch of resolution into his voice, 'that the best thing, if it were possible, would be to hear it in detail from someone who was there. Someone who could paint the full picture of how my friend died. It would be – cathartic, you know? Give me closure?'

Meera was nodding, 'Of course, of course.'

Seriously? This was going to be easier than he'd thought.

'I was actually the first officer on the scene,' Meera began. 'I think I told you before, it was the lodger that called us in? Japanese guy, bit older than you, quite fit— I mean, athletic. Um, anyway, he'd called in a locksmith, so the door was open. And ... well, it was dark, you couldn't see much at first, just this short little hallway with a door to the right, and at the end ... the stairs go sideways, see, they're not facing you, so even though I'd heard, I didn't recognise – this, this little bundle.'

Meera paused, took a swig; seemed astonished to find her glass empty. 'They'd got Mortimer out, couldn't stop him apparently, he barrelled past them ... The officer with me was busy getting him under control so I just, just walked forwards. There was a light switch; I pressed it without thinking and ... you know, what surprised me was how *small* she was. Not especially short, they told me later, not for her age, five foot four or something, but she just looked like some ragdoll, all – are you *sure* you want to be hearing this? You've gone a bit ... green.'

Torben nodded. He needed to know.

'Well, there was this buzzing sort of drone and I thought, not even flies could ... and then I peered up the stairs to the right, saw the phone dangling off its hook up by the landing. Must've been like that for days. You don't see many phones like that anymore, still on cords. I took a step nearer and I could see – down her side, where he'd – poor thing, I mean, what was he supposed to do? It'd clearly been a last resort, he'd made a right mess of the kitchen, but he couldn't get in the fridge, could he?'

'No. No, I suppose not. Um, what sort of a mess?'

'Oh, a chair turned over, cupboard doors a bit bashed, things off the work surfaces – I think he'd got up there to nose about – and the front and back doors were both, well, gouged. Plus, of course, he'd been shut in for days so there were piles of – I mean, I won't forget that smell in a hurry ... sorry, I'm not exactly sure how this helps your therapy ...?'

'Er, she said I wouldn't know what details would give me, you know, release, until I heard them. It's like grief is a ... a locked cage around your heart, constricting it, and you need to find the right key.' Too much, Torben – surely that was too much? But no; Meera was laying a hand on his arm.

'Of course. You know, Dr Hell—'

'Call me Torben.'

'—Torben, sorry. You know, you're very in touch with your feelings. So ... well, I think that was it. I took the lodger and the locksmith downstairs to the guy's flat, made them cups of tea, took statements – they were pretty shaken up too – while my colleague watched the door.'

'No signs of a struggle, a forced entry, anything like that?'

'Oh God, bless you no, nothing like that, quite the opposite. Except for where our friend here had been panicking about, it was all very, what's the word, genteel. I had a peek in the front room – obviously I didn't look upstairs because, you know, at the foot ... but anyway, I just thought I'd have a check on my way out and it was this perfect parlour, tea for two on the table, the lot. Only other thing I noticed were these strange brown and orange patches on the hall rug, but it turned out that was—'

'Just the pattern, yes,' said Torben. 'She took a rather perverse delight in the worst excesses of the 1970s. So there really was nothing in the post-mortem?'

'Nothing, at least not so far as I heard. Don't think they even bothered to send through a copy, which saved a lot of time on the paperwork, I can tell you. No, sorry, Torben, your friend just had a nasty trip on the stairs. Probably running to answer the phone or something.'

'I'd told her to get a mobile,' Torben said. 'She always loved that spot on the landing, though. With the doors open, you got the light from both front and back windows, plus the staircase up and down – she said it was the airiest space you could get in WC1 without investing in a rooftop terrace ...'

'She sounds like a lovely woman, your friend.'

'Yes. Yes, she was.'

*

Later. Tipsy, garlic-breathed, and prickling with self-loathing for the slimy way in which he had played a kind young woman, Torben threw himself down on his bed. Idly, he opened his laptop, typed 'Charlotte Lazerton' into YouTube, clicked the first video. An interview clip from some arts programme, about a decade ago. Charlotte was looking resplendent, sporting a tweed trouser suit in a houndstooth check of the sort Torben knew, because Wilson had told him, that you were absolutely *never* meant to wear on television; apparently it went all Bridget Riley on the screen.

The clip began with the art critic Brian Sewell at the end of another of his self-consciously 'controversial' statements. As the clip started, he was saying: 'whereas in the olden days—'

'Why *do* we say "in olden days"?' Charlotte cut in. 'The world was younger then.'

The camera panned across to centre on her. The checks on her suit did indeed go a bit funny. 'You know, Brian dear, the trouble with you is you will always keep up this dreadful guff about how things used to be so much more sophisticated – people so much more learned – when you must know perfectly well how silly you're being. Now, I know my school wasn't quite so up itself as yours, but it *was* private and I *did* go to a "proper university", and frankly it was all *so* much more rudimentary than it is nowadays. The sophistication of young scholars in the twenty-first century, the sheer amount of critical *thought* – in our day, Brian, we were left to wander down these jolly little rabbit holes and ferret out arcana and we thought we were being *clever*, when we were really just being single-minded … no, don't interrupt, you've had your turn' – the camera cut briefly to a close-up on Sewell's face, which was taking on an interesting hue

– 'and what you've done is compounded this *catastrophic* slippage by equating "old" and "older". We didn't know *more* in the past, we knew less, *because there was less to know* – modernity isn't youthful, and the past isn't mature, it's quite the reverse. Why oh why does no one realise that the world is getting *older*, not younger. The coming generation aren't naïve, their idealism isn't "childish" – they know so much more than we ever did! So don't you *dare* sit there and wiffle on about "in my day" as if that was an age of wise old grownups, because it damn well wasn't, and next to this *magnificent* young performance artist we're *supposed* to be discussing, or that handsome young rapper they just had on, or any teenager who's worried about the planet and wants that multinational company we're not meant to name on here to stop sponsoring exhibitions like the one we're coming on to next – there you go, darling,' and she turned to the presenter, 'I've done your link for you – compared to them in their maturity and wisdom, *you*, Sewell, are an *infant* and should bloody well do some *growing up*. That's probably my bit done, isn't it?'

The clip ended as the shot returned to the presenter, still hastily reassembling their expression.

Torben lay back, not sure whether to laugh or cry. All he knew for certain is that he was desperately glad he'd never had to try and chair a discussion with Charlotte on live television. Then, because he was still a little drunk, he sent the URL to Leyla with the message, '*This is the person I think was murdered. Want to help me avenge them?*'

The next day, Thursday, a solicitor came to see Torben. He had with him the keys to 24 Little James Street.

7

AROUND A DESK

Leyla clocked off at 18:22 – early, by her chambers' standards. Just two WhatsApps, both Torben again – not another video, just the message 'Have house, come fydr sorj', followed by the addendum 'fydr sorj = after work'. From which, she deduced, he was rather excited by it.

Well, for *this* she was happy to indulge him. The video had been very satisfying, but he would have to do rather more than that to convince her there was anything worth investigating. Like, find some actual evidence of wrongdoing. And *not* just the sort of aesthetic inconsistencies that had started all the trouble last time.

Still – last time. She had liked him like that. Driven. Dynamic. Sort of ... potent.

At work, they'd recently concluded a major case on which she'd been a junior, opposing a new coalmine on behalf of a group of adorably committed schoolchildren whose right to a future standard of living, they had argued, was materially impaired by such developments. They had lost, obviously, but with reasonable grounds for an appeal – the date of which had been set far enough off that, right now, she had been allowed to mix some long-overdue annual leave with some more humdrum casework. Meaning she might actually have some free time this summer, and no particular plans.

If – and it was a colossal if – Torben was actually right this time ... then maybe it could be fun?

She stood on the broad pavement of Bedford Row, blinking in the early evening sun. A light breeze was stirring the *very* green leaves of what she thought might be young plane trees. Torben's new house – *God*, what an expression, she wasn't sure whether it made her want to murder him or marry him – was literally a minute or two's walk away, and she set off, narrowly avoiding another of those damn professional dog walkers coaxing along about half a dozen poodles, and skipping across the main road in the hair's breadth between a bus and a bike.

Walking up Great James Street, she felt rather than took in the narrowing of space, the loss of the trees ... was dimly aware of an official-looking Brazilian flag, a very bijou little address for such a large country ... noted the blue plaque opposite and laughed aloud at the description: it had to be a sign, an omen!

> *Dorothy L.*
> *Sayers*
> *1893–1957*
> *Writer of*
> *Detective Stories*
> *lived here*
> *1921–1929*

And then, at the turn of the street, there it was: the little trio of Dutch-looking houses, numbers 22–26. There were black iron railings, a little bridge, steps down to the basement flat alongside. A simple door, nothing flash – except seriously, was that a boot-jack, sunk into the pavement? Knowing full well her patent leather shoes were spotless, Leyla gave them a scrape anyway; in future, she thought, she would always do this; maybe she'd find somewhere muddy to walk first on purpose. And Torben would have to clean it, of course.

Her hand rose to the bell beside the deep blue door – then withdrew. At the centre of the door was a lion's head knocker, ancient and black. Well of course there was. Start as you mean to go on, Leyla Moradi. And she raised her hand, and knocked.

Well, that was anti-climactic. After a full minute of nothing, then another bout of knocking and waiting, Leyla was about to give up, when a thought struck her, and she reached for the door handle. The door opened.

A close, dim hall, somehow expectant. Her heels clacked on tiles, aged to softness, worn down in the centre. A bare lightbulb dangled above. On either side, simple panelling rose to the ceiling. The room to her right was empty, just a supremely hideous wall-to-wall carpet pulled up at one side.

He must be here *somewhere*. Beyond the stairs, an open doorway disclosed a bare kitchen, still scarred by the scrabbling of that poor, poor dog. Here, the window looked over a tiny walled garden – more of a yard – paved, but with old stone, and a strip of border at the back from which a pear tree rose, espaliered against the rosy brick wall. Also, there were dustbins, and a line of washing: evidently the yard was shared with the downstairs lodger. Ah well.

Not, of course, that it was any concern of hers.

This door – also lacerated with claw marks – was locked. Almost reluctantly, she returned to the foot of the stairs. Leyla realised she had been ignoring them, and even now forced herself to stand squarely at their feet, trying not to think about the fact that this spot was almost certainly where …

Swiftly, she began to climb.

Something about a panelled staircase, especially one this enclosed: it felt like she was on a ship. Obviously, the best way to live was somewhere warm and dry, on a plateau or hillside, in a white and airy space open to the winds, with room to run, an open atrium, a little pool, sky and water brought inside. But, if you were stupid enough to live somewhere cold and wet, then this was what she wanted: the squared circle of elegant snugness, a sense of history that wrapped round you like a mantle. Her feet made no sound on the grubby stair carpet.

At the top of the stairs above her she could see a Bakelite phone, coiled plastic wire dangling in a loop. It seemed by far the most antiquated thing she had seen in this three-hundred-year-old house. Another window on the landing looked onto the brick wall of the adjacent house, and she realised why this style hadn't caught on; the light it lent the staircase was somehow second-hand, desultory. But now she had reached the landing, and was hit by a sudden swimming of brightness from either side. To the right, a glimpse of barren bookcases, warped with age, a couple of dead flies on the nearest shelf. To the left a bright, square room, uncarpeted. A fireplace, its black grate ancient and filthy, its surround of plain stone, the edges worn. Another large and lovely window, the trees beyond masking London. And in the centre of the floor, his back to her, kneeling amid stack upon stack of papers, was Torben.

She chuckled, and he turned to look up at her, his expression one of total incomprehension, a baby's face – despite the blond beard – or that of someone slowly returning from very far away. Those blue, blue eyes, finally filling with recognition. A little punch, somewhere in the region of her heart. They had both been caught, unguarded.

'I've emptied it,' he said, thumping the desk behind him, and it was only now she took it in: a beast of a thing, squat and ugly, sharp-cornered.

'Three motives, so far,' he said, gesturing to different parts of the floor. 'Obviously, ninety-nine per cent of this stuff is just work – catalogues, *endless* notes, draft manuscripts and articles; there's even the start of an abandoned card-index somewhere. And she was *very* good at doodling, I'm talking Leonardo level; there are some excellent geometric designs, and then some of her drawings are just *filthy*, I mean look at this' – he rummaged about, and held up a pen-and-ink sketch, a few very free lines, but clearly a rather debauched rendering of a threesome. Leyla squinted, trying to place the various naked limbs: two women and a man, she thought, but couldn't quite be sure, because one of the heads was shoved right up—

'Puts me in mind of Henry Fuseli,' Torben said.

'Right,' said Leyla. Whoever *he* was. There was a scribbled caption on the sketch: 'Self, SR, nice boy called Matteo, Rome '88.' Feeling suddenly prurient, Leyla hastily set the picture aside.

'One day, I'll have to sort it all,' Torben went on. 'But for now, I think *these* are the really important documents: her diaries' – indicating a pile of Leuchtturms – 'this first draft of her memoirs' – a perilously teetering stack of exercise books – 'and this little folder' – a thick card binder labelled 'AWA Presidency Run – campaign notes'. She noticed a fourth item set aside with the three, it looked more coherent – several hundred A4 pages bound in a hard cover. His eyes followed hers. 'Yes, and that – I'll come to that later.' Was that a blush, or was the mania just flushing his features?

He sat back. 'Of course, I've not had time to make a real start on any of it; there's bound to be loads more, but I was *right*, Leyla, I was categorically *right* to suspect foul play, Charlotte did too, and you'll never believe who—'

'Torben,' she said. Blessedly, he stopped. She looked down at him, interested in this rare chance to survey him from above, reality finally aligning with her sense of their natural stations. Took in his rumpled clothes, the especially distrait look of his shock of blond hair. In all essentials, an over-excited child. 'Torben, have you even had *lunch* today?'

'Well ...'

'Look, if you want me to listen to any of this, you're going to have to give me dinner.'

He paused, glanced back at the papers. 'Could we make it a take-away?' he said.

She sent him to collect it, taking the chance to poke about the rest of the house. That library, overlooking the street – the total *desolation* of a room built for books, stripped naked, skeletal. Evidently they had let him in as soon as the place had been emptied; even with friends in the right places, you couldn't clear probate half this quickly, but it seemed sensible to have someone occupying the place – did this mean they were technically trespassing? – it *definitely* meant Torben wasn't meant to be messing about with her papers yet, but that ship had not only sailed, it had practically circumnavigated the globe ... either way, it felt distinctly uncanny to wander such a bare-boned house.

Up the next flight, her sense of being on the *Mary Celeste* continued, except she wasn't sure that ship had an avocado three-piece of loo, sink and bathtub. Strangely, the top floor felt far less eerie, the sloping eaves lending its deserted state a certain rightness. This room at the front must have been Torben's – a peak artist-in-the-garret existence, romantic as anything, which probably didn't quite offset the inconvenience of living in a space three metres by four, where a step to either side required a duck of the head, and the only vertical space was a strip either side of the window or the door. The rear room – the box room, had he said it had been? – was still less workable, with a great hatch built into one side that must be the fire escape passage to the next-door house that Torben had told them about. Idly, she tried the handle, and the hatch swung open, sending spiders scurrying. A draught of cold air from the queer little wooden tunnel. Hastily, she closed it again. If she wasn't entirely certain she should even be in number 24, then she certainly had no desire to commit an accidental trespass in the adjacent house.

Far below, the rattle of the door. She had, after all, only sent him as far as Salaam Namaste. Leyla glanced at her watch. Nearly eight! She hoped she hadn't under-ordered.

They ate standing in the kitchen, the little foil cartons spilling over every available surface. 'Papadums, chutneys, one rice, one roti,' Torben checked off. 'Bhel puri – why do you *always* go for the bhel puri, Leyla, it just fills you up on nothing – one soft-shell crab, provenance unknown – but I checked, and the Keralan fish curry *is* tilapia, so I'm having some of that; apparently it's as eco-friendly as fish can get – two dals, one makhani, one tadka; one okra … Leyla, are you *really* proposing we eat all of this, or were you just trying to bankrupt me?'

She gave him one of her go-to looks. 'Torben, when have you and I ever failed to finish a meal?'

'Fair point,' he said.

'Um,' she said, 'you *did* remember to ask for some cutlery, didn't you?'

'Oh *for helvede*!'

Luckily she had a knife and fork in her lunchbox; they took turns, passing dishes back and forth.

'I told you one roti is never enough,' she said a little later, looking mournfully at the caramelised sauces, in every hue of ochre, still adhering to the inside of the trays.

Torben grinned, and lifted a carton to his mouth. His tongue was shockingly large and pink, almost leonine. It was grotesque, and yet—

Leyla grabbed at another of the empties. 'I call this one,' she said. 'Oo good, it's the makhani ...'

It wasn't flirting, not exactly. But it was rich, and creamy, and tasted very, very good.

'OK,' she conceded at last. 'You've earned it. I'll give you half an hour.'

Disconcertingly, his enthusiasm did not seem to have dipped. She'd hoped he'd find the prospect of negotiating the stairs after that meal rather off-putting, but he bounded up them like an especially annoying subspecies of ibex. Feeling more like a hippo, and resigned to an extra hour in the gym on Saturday to atone, Leyla dragged herself after him.

'Here,' he said, balling up his jacket and placing it before her as if he were Sir Walter Raleigh with his sodding cloak. But it *was* good to sit down.

'I suppose it's too much to ask,' she said, 'that you might be systematic about this?'

He opened his mouth – then shut it. A good sign. She could practically see him rummaging through the mental chaos, trying to tidy.

'First, before any of this – the codicil to Charlotte's will,' he said.

'I don't think I actually showed you the letter that quotes it directly, did I?'

She took the folded sheaves of paper. 'Hod Hill Manor ...?'

'Family home, I think. Next page – no, the other side ...'

She found the passage.

'I mean it, Torben, every damn scrap. In the event that I do not live to complete them, you may find the first draft of my memoirs particularly diverting.' She has then added, with a request not to paraphrase the words when informing you, that 'I am leaving you your duty in a <u>friendly spirit</u>'. She has underlined the last two words, so I'm doing the same.

Leyla's legal mind noted the insistence upon specificity. Those last words were clearly significant. Noted too the implication that might be put upon 'In the event that I do not live to complete them', coupled with the timing of the codicil – the day before she died. Circumstantial, but certainly suggestive.

She looked up. Torben was a picture of impatience. And she *had* promised him half an hour. '"Friendly spirit" – it's a code?'

'Exactly!'

'Interesting. So her suspicions extended beyond physical danger, to the possibility of surveillance, or of someone going through her things ...'

'Leyla, she literally told me she was being wire-tapped.'

'Fair point. So presumably the message has some special meaning to you alone ... I mean, the only friendly spirit I can think of is Casper the Friendly Ghost. Well, a good single malt would fit the bill too, I admit—'

'You were right the first time,' he said. The next second, he deposited in her lap that bound volume she had clocked earlier. It weighed more than she had reckoned with, especially on top of the curry, and she glared up at him.

'It's my doctoral thesis,' he said, sounding slightly sheepish. 'Her marked-up supervisor's copy. She kept it in her desk.'

It would have been more touching, she thought, if that desk hadn't also contained about half the papers in the greater London area. She opened it. 'Of course – your thesis was on *Caspar* David Friedrich …'

'It's at the end of the acknowledgements,' he said.

Leyla flicked to the page. His final words had been to state the eternal debt he owed to Charlotte. Below this, a hasty hand had scribbled just two sentences.

In that case – should anything untoward happen – MM, KT, HD, SG – perhaps SR too. It'll be one of them, and though I probably deserve it, I think you should find out which.

'Charlotte's writing?' Leyla asked.

He nodded.

'You know, Torben, if I were a melodramatic sort of person … I'd have to say it sounds like she thought someone might try and kill her.' She paused. 'Which probably only means that her paranoia has rubbed off on you, and is now starting to work on me. But I'm still listening. These initials – surely they're not—?'

'The ones we met at the funeral! At least, most of them are.' Released from silence, he practically leapt down her throat. 'I made a note of their names after Henrik Drever – HD, of course – introduced us. He's the senior-academic-turned-management-stooge, remember, the Swede with the bald head and the power handshake? And we both recognised the MP Simon Grey – SG – he's a junior environment minister, recently reappointed, having been on the backbenches since John Major's government. SR is Shani Rajapalayam, also an art historian, journalist, public figure – she wrote Charlotte's best obituary. The most stylishly dressed, if you recall. And then KT – Katherine Trigg – apparently an old schoolfriend who went into finance, I don't know much about her yet.'

'Not the civil servant, then?' said Leyla.

'Jonathan Azawakh ... so not MM, but I can't find a connection to any other MM online, and on a quick flick through these' – he indicated the piles of papers around him – 'MM, who comes up a lot, especially in the eighties, definitely sounds like someone from a hush-hush branch of the establishment, which chimes with what Drever said ... Either way, my reasoning was sound: Charlotte's own suspicions of the people who could do her harm tally with those who seemed most out of place at her funeral. Which all fits: if there was bad blood between her and each of them, no wonder they stood out. Only in one case – I'm presuming one case – it was more than just ill-feeling. We just have to work out which.'

Leyla glanced over the rest of Beryl Cabell-Fowell's letter. 'It sounds like her family knew in advance they weren't in for much in the will,' she mused. 'So bang goes the most obvious motive for murder.' She caught herself. 'Speaking hypothetically, of course. OK, so you've got some semi-reasonable grounds for suspicion concerning either four or five people – depending on who this MM is ...'

For a moment, she thought about pointing out the various branches of logic. If Charlotte *had* been murdered, for example, it might have been by someone entirely unsuspected, not one of these sets of initials. But it seemed madness to mention this. Because the only reason she could see for thinking there had been a murder was that Charlotte had suspected these people. Which meant that the only reasonable thing to do, if they were going to do this at all, was to trust Charlotte's reasoning and build a case around what she had left Torben in the desk. The circularity made her head hurt. 'So,' she said instead, 'have you found anything in all of this that backs up the cryptic little message from beyond the grave?'

'Well, I've made a start,' he said. 'I had to trust that, having been left the contents of the desk first, then given this clue, Charlotte made sure anything I might find useful was somewhere among it all. The first thing I checked was her appointments diary, this calendar one here.' He held up a hardback from Persephone Books and Leyla was struck, rather uncomfortably, by the realisation that she used the exact same one. 'Meera mentioned it when she first called me.'

'Meera?'

'PC Rampur. We went for a drink yesterday. Several, actually.'

'Is that even legal?'

'Oh, it's OK if she pays. But it's why she notified me in the first place, because I was a regular feature in the diary, so I thought I'd check. Probably lots worth following up, but I obviously began with the day they think she was killed.'

'The day they think she *died*,' Leyla amended.

'*Som du vil*. The point is, she was meant to be having tea that afternoon with Simon Grey. SG – the government minister on the list? Here, at home. So we need to find out if that happened: if so, it places him at the scene of the crime; if not, then why not? Or did he arrive too late, get no reply, and go away?'

'If so, presumably he'd have tried to contact her by other means,' said Leyla. 'That landline on the stairs – it was her only phone?'

He nodded. 'And off the hook, according to Meera, so even if he rang ... *But*, also according to Meera, there was tea for two laid out downstairs. Only, she didn't say if it had been *used* – oh, *for helvede*!

She said she just glanced in, so she almost certainly didn't see, even if she could remember – you know they have honestly left not a damn thing, not one single thing, in this house, except that useless old phone and this desk?' And he thumped it again, more exercised than she had seen him in a long time. 'Stripped and cleaned, the whole place, not a fingerprint, not a bloodstain; they had to leave *this*, because it was in the will ...' He looked at her, a little manic. 'The rest of the will – can we apply to see it? All of it?'

'Not yet,' Leyla said. 'The lawyer who gave you the keys – did he say the will had cleared probate?'

'I don't think so.'

'Thought not,' she said. 'They've just handed you the keys early so someone's looking after the house. It'll be months until the will's available to read.'

'*Lort*,' he said. 'I was sort of setting myself a deadline of Ruth's notice period.'

'You are *not* dragging Ruth into this again.'

'Obviously I'll try not to ... Anyway, we can't cross-reference our suspicions with who benefits from the will, but from the sound of Beryl's letter, that's probably a dead end anyway ... so ... where was I before we got sidetracked?'

He looked as tired as she felt. 'SG,' she prompted. 'Simon Grey.'

'Yes! Yes yes yes ... it's all in here' – and he slapped the diaries, causing them to slide to the floor – 'I've only had a glance, and it's *fucking* odd reading someone's private diaries, I can tell you, but I am *literally* obliged to do it by the terms of that will ... She and Simon Grey used to be friends, but *real* friends, I think, in the nineties – he was one of those Ken Clarke types, extremely pro-Europe, I think it's how they knew each other – but then I opened this recent volume and it sprang apart at a two-page rant about a "betrayal" of some kind;

I haven't read it all, her handwriting really goes to hell when she's angry ... but there's a motive there, I'm sure of it!'

'Torben—'

'And Henrik Drever too!' he said, actually getting up and pacing like a detective in a film, and looking every bit as ludicrous. 'HD – my old boss – definite contender for the AWA presidency, and now probably a shoe-in. His election manifesto's in this folder, annotated; his whole programme runs directly counter to Charlotte's. But he was a distant *second* favourite before she was murdered. That gives him an obvious reason to have wanted her out of the way: it cleared the path to his shot at the big prize.'

Ludicrous, yes, and spouting clichés, but she couldn't fault his logic.

'I admit I have nothing on Trigg or Rajapalayam as yet, but I'm sure it's all in here. If only she had written down Jonathan Azawakh's initials!' He sank to his haunches, hand hovering over the unfinished memoir, a mishmash of loose sheets and stacked notebooks. 'What did Drever tell us? That he runs some part of the civil service that we're not allowed to know about? A spy, in other words! Which would explain the wire-tapping, and why she hid that final message in a cryptic clue about my thesis, because a spy would go through her papers after he killed her.'

Leyla couldn't help it; she laughed out loud.

'Fair enough,' said Torben. 'Except that even the *Observer* states that she was deep inside Anglo-Russian affairs in the 1980s; it's where her damehood came from. Exactly the period, in fact, that she was about to cover in her memoir, the memoir that she labelled as "particularly diverting" in a codicil she wrote the day before she died. Exactly the period, moreover, when Anthony Blunt, another great art historian, was dying in disgrace for being exposed as a Soviet agent.

And in the memoir, the account stops just as she's about to go for a meeting with someone she describes as a "sober-suited chappie from the Foreign Office". Well, I say "stops"' – and he brandished the pages of a lined A4 notebook before her – 'but what I actually mean is, the page ends. *And the rest of the pages in the book have been carefully cut out.*'

Leyla stared, incredulous. She had expected him to have a theory. She was ready to concede that it stacked up with Charlotte's own concerns. That being the case, circumstantial corroboration was bound to come up. But solid, material evidence that the papers – the same papers Charlotte had specifically directed his attention towards – had been tampered with? No wonder he looked wired.

'I have to hand it to you,' she said, checking her wristwatch. 'Seven minutes still left on the clock, and you've actually convinced me. Torben – I'm in.'

8

24A

'We need a plan,' said Torben.

'We need,' said Leyla, 'to go to bed.' She paused. 'But yes, a plan sounds good. Can we make it a bit more rigorous than the last time?'

Torben suspected that 'the last time' was going to be weaponised by Leyla for the rest of their lives.

'There are two clear lines of enquiry,' he said. 'Interviews, and reading. I'll look after the latter, since I'm contracted to sort all this out anyway, but I'll put my notes in a shared Google Doc or something, so you have access to everything.'

'I'm glad to hear you don't think this conspiracy of Charlotte's extends to Silicon Valley,' said Leyla. 'But really – interviews? We're not shut in a house with these people this time, Torben, and we've zero authority – how do you propose to make people talk? You can't take them all for flirty drinks.'

'I was *not* flirting with Meera,' he said, which he sort of believed. 'Anyway, we start with the neighbours. Top priority is the tenant of 24A, downstairs. Meera said he's Japanese, late thirties, I think she fancied him—'

'Bags I get to talk to him.'

'*No*, he's *my* new neighbour. Must have moved in after I left, because it used to be some home counties lobbyist called Dave. So it's completely natural that I introduce myself, accidentally discover he found my close personal friend's body, and want to hear all about it.'

'I concede the point,' said Leyla. 'What about either side?'

'The Posavacs have number 22; their family runs an antiques shop on Gray's Inn Road, I think they've been here since the forties. Might make sense to do that one together, I can introduce you – the grandmother always said I should bring round— oh, never mind.' Flushing, he avoided looking at Leyla's face, not sure which expression he feared seeing more: outrage, or amusement.

'And at 26?' said Leyla.

'Actually, I don't think I know. A fashion designer or something, they're very private. Could be tricky. Still, it gives me an excuse to introduce myself.'

'You could bake them something,' said Leyla, eyebrow arched. 'Maybe I want to do the fashion designer! I could pretend to be the lucky bastard living here, couldn't I?'

'Not for long you couldn't,' said Torben. 'What if they clocked you leaving in the evenings, or heading home from work? And you'd have to explain me being here all the time.'

He kept his real reason to himself. There was a strong chance the neighbour was a woman, and, as he couldn't help having noticed lately, Leyla was not always the greatest of hits with her own sex.

'The person we could really do with seeing,' he said, only partly to change the subject, 'is Ximena Podenco.'

'Who?'

'She used to walk Mortimer a few times a week. And the appointments diary indicates she was down for that Tuesday afternoon – probably overlapping with Simon Grey, even. Clearly, since Mortimer was locked in, she either got him back in time or arrived too late to take him out. Either way, it makes her the likeliest to have seen something.'

'Well, can't we get hold of her easily enough?' said Leyla. 'There must be a number.'

For answer, Torben tapped a very small pile of business cards and leaflets.

Leyla picked one up. 'Pest control?' she said, waving a tiny photograph of what looked like a cross between a Ghostbuster and an astronaut, embossed with the legend 'Bloomsbury Fumigators'.

'Not that one.'

'Ah.' Leyla found the right card, and held it up to the light. '"London's first choice for pet perambulation. Five-star service at one-star prices. Large breeds a speciality, call now." Well, and have you called?'

He nodded. 'Twice, before you got here. I remember her getting them on a recommendation from a colleague, or maybe a neighbour – she didn't say who – a few months back; she'd finally caved in and stopped walking him on her own, but the rates charged by other companies had been ... well, I think her phrase was "cunting ridiculous". Anyway, the people from this card are very friendly when you get through to them. Right up until the point when you ask to speak to a named dog walker. Then they hang up.'

'Hmm. Maybe they don't give out details in case their people go freelance, start undercutting them?'

'Could be.' What had Charlotte said, in their last – their *final* conversation? She had mentioned Ximena; something about visa issues. 'Or else they think we're from the Home Office. There's no website for the business – I googled – mind you, there wasn't one for the pest control people either; I thought I'd test it as a sort of controlled experiment, so probably it's just an overhead they think they can do without. Still, I get the sense that their right-to-work checks might be less than stringent.'

'Ah,' said Leyla. 'Well, we'd just better hope we bump into her. She's presumably still working the same area. Any idea what she looks like?'

Torben shrugged. 'I'd guess young, Latina, and hidden behind another gargantuan canine. Keep your eyes peeled. Ugh. *Eyes peeled*, what a revolting expression.'

'Positively Dalí-esque,' said Leyla. 'Um, Torben, you haven't said anything about interviewing ... well, not to put too fine a point on it: the sodding suspects.'

'I was afraid you might mention that,' he said. 'The thing is, Leyla ... Charlotte's past, her work, her connections – that's literally an open book. The neighbours are fine, it's the most natural thing in the world that we'd want to talk about that day, even if it is going to be pretty ghoulish gossiping about something so raw—'

'Whereas conducting an investigation into it is psychologically unimpeachable, I suppose.'

'*Hold kæft*! My point is: I had a hunch about those five people, and you felt it too, you *know* you did. It turns out that was more than instinct; it was a symptom of whatever it was that meant Charlotte thought them each capable of doing her in. A couple of hours up here has provided a plausible and timely motive for three of them, and I'm sure the others will come too with a little more work. But, Leyla – Henrik Drever is a senior professor and Dean of my faculty. Shani Rajapalayam is one of the country's leading art critics. Katherine Trigg appears to be an ex-City slicker. Jonathan Azawakh – if he somehow is MM – is also a high-up civil servant and God knows what besides. Simon Grey is actually part of the government. Forget being able to compel them to tell us anything. Forget having a convincing reason to ask them questions. How do we even go about getting fifteen minutes of their time in the first place?'

Only after he had booked Leyla a taxi and hauled himself back to his rental flat, vowing never again to let Leyla order the food, did it occur to Torben that he was not just investigating a murder. He was moving house. He had been *given* the house of his dreams – this was not a figure of speech: a disconcerting number of his dreams involved the eighteenth-century domestic vernacular – for a five-year lease, and his immediate response had been to feel so utterly overwhelmed with gratitude and unworthiness that he had sublimated the whole lot into a single-minded desire to be worthy of Charlotte's bequest. In this, he was doing the 'duty' she had referred to in the codicil: she had begun to fear foul play, she suspected it was because of something in her past, she was directing him to *get* the bastards. But in fact, when you read the whole of the will that related to him, he was *also* meant to manage her legacy. Which meant editing her papers – but also restoring and looking after her house. Which meant living in it. Which meant giving notice; moving his few belongings; setting up things like insurance and utilities and internet and council tax. Which meant working out the exact aesthetic. Was he meant to go more Dennis Severs, or – and this was his first impulse and a lot cheaper, though infinitely more painstaking – more Lars Sjöberg?

No, Torben. What it meant was, before any of that, was *buying a bed*.

Start as you mean to go on, Torben. He opened his laptop, went to eBay. Antiques … antique furniture … Beds … Filters: pre-1800.

It was what Charlotte would have wanted.

*

Ruth and Wilson helped him move in that weekend, each lending a wheelie suitcase to the cause of migrating Torben's possessions through a few hundred metres of extremely central London. It did not, he thought, take an amateur detective to observe how frequently the two of them seemed to be doing things together recently. It had started with badminton, which he'd never really classed as a gateway drug before, but then he was re-evaluating a lot of things these days.

Leyla managed to materialise at his side just as the three of them had lugged the last case up to the second floor – to the room that was, hypothetically at any rate, a bedroom. For the first time it occurred to Torben that it might have made more sense to wait for his new bed to be couriered over before moving all his things, vacating the comfortable studio flat. Well, he could make a nest out of the bedding … *or* see if one of these three would put him up?

'Better sleep on my sofa,' said Leyla. 'I've been here ten seconds, and already I feel competent in advising you *not* to try and crash whatever it is – frankly I don't think even *they* know at this point – that these two have going on.' She considered. Their two tall, beautiful, exceptionally athletic friends, glowing with effort and their limbs sort of shimmering with a light gloss of sweat, were just returning from a 'moment's rest' on the floor below. 'Unless you *do* want to crash it?'

'Crashing?' said Ruth. 'Yes, I think we're all crashing a bit in this heat; who'd have thought it, we're going to have a genuinely hot English summer … shame you missed the actual move, Leyla.'

'I am immune to passive aggression, Inspector Thompson,' said Leyla. 'I lack the residual guilt that comes of growing up in a Christian culture.'

'Only inspector for three more weeks!' said Ruth.

'So,' added Wilson, 'if you guys want any inside assistance, I'm guessing you'd better step on it.'

Torben blushed.

'We've just seen your incident room, haven't we?' said Ruth. 'All your wild theories laid out like wall-to-wall carpeting. I know you were left her papers, Tor. But I don't imagine they came sorted into personal files with Post-its reading "Suspect One: Azawakh" and so on.'

'And Leyla's clearly changed her mind,' contributed Wilson, 'or she wouldn't be wasting her Saturday alongside us poor saps. I'm fully booked, myself, but if you could record a few voice notes, sort of "in the moment"? It'd make recording series two a lot easier.' He paused. 'I'm kinda hoping it's not the civil servant or the MP though. I don't think there's enough ad revenue in the world to hire the kind of legal team I'd need to make *that* version of the podcast.'

'Ruth,' said Torben, doing the easy thing and ignoring Wilson, 'is that a serious offer? You'd be willing to – actually I don't even know what that might mean …'

'Strictly advisory is what it means,' Ruth said. 'And nothing with a trail, sorry. No way can I go pulling out the case file for you. But I *do* think I can probably hook you up with the officer responsible.'

'I've spoken quite a lot to Meera Rampur, the constable on the scene,' Torben said. 'She's very … new.'

'Someone will have been in charge,' said Ruth. 'The SIO. They'll have signed everything off, read the reports, liaised with forensics – well, not that they'd have got forensics in for this, but with the medical officer, anyway.'

'Ruth – *mange tak!*'

Ruth smiled. 'You know, I could get used to this feeling. A maverick. A whistle-blower. A loose cannon!'

'Wait a sec,' said Wilson, scrabbling in his pocket. 'Let me get this down on tape.'

'I wasn't being strategically late, as it happens,' murmured Leyla, once the others had left. Torben realised that she had been looking more than usually smug. 'Like a fool I came here first, rather than going to the studio with your stuff in. And then I was held up a good half an hour, on account of my very productive interview with a certain Kai Kishu.'

'Leyla, who is Kai Ki— oh, *no*, Leyla, you didn't! You got the downstairs neighbour after all?!'

'Uh-huh. Your tame constable wasn't wrong, he's a little bit dreamy. A chef, it turns out; he runs the kitchen of a pretty decent sushi place just off Regent Street, I've eaten there myself. He showed me his Santoku knives, they are beauties. Plus, Torben, you should see his forearms. Muscles like cords of rope …'

He found her teasing rather comforting. Surely she wouldn't bother, unless—

'How, I hear you ask, did I get to see his knives? Because we bumped into each other outside the front step, both turning in, and he invited me in for a cup of tea.'

'Don't tell me, you got the full ceremony.'

'No, as it happens, a big mug of builder's, which will teach *you* to make stereotypical cultural assumptions, even in jest.'

'And what was your excuse? Your cover story?'

'Oh, Torben,' she laughed. 'You silly boy. If a single man asks *me* inside his home and I say yes, do you *really* think he's going to bother asking himself why? Trust me, he had far more interesting things on his mind!'

*

The lower-level flat had been surprisingly airy. Old stone floors and a vaulted ceiling; light flooding through from the area above. Shame about all the black faux-leather upholstery; a definite red flag for a bachelor residence, at least in her recent experience. And within five minutes, Leyla had the sense that, were she willing to prolong her stay, she would have plenty of leisure to examine the bedroom and bathroom too. It took all her tact to keep the conversation from becoming intimate without imposing a fatal degree of detachment.

'So, Kai,' she had managed at last, leaning in over her teacup (he had, in truth, made a *very* great show of serving her a fancy pot of jasmine). 'My friend who's moving in upstairs tells me you were the one who actually *found* her …'

Kai nodded. 'Yeah. I was growing worried, because I had not seen the old lady for three, four days, but there were these noises – scratches and howls. Coming back off a shift and hearing them again I think, no, there is something wrong here, so I call the locksmith – always easier not to trouble the police, if you know what I mean; they are very busy people and best left alone – and get the door unlocked. He's scared to open it, but I step forward, and as soon as I'm in, *wham*, this huge thing, like a wolf, it leaps at me, but I know how to handle wild beasts, so I go into this roll, taking the force of the blow on my arm like this …'

'From this point on,' Leyla said to Torben, 'it got the teeniest bit subjective. But he *did* confirm that the phone was off the hook, mentioned a pile-up of post on the mat, and best of all, he stepped into the front room for air, once he'd seen the, you know. I suppose he was trying not to be sick. But he clocked the formal tea service; probably only remembered it because we had one in front of us too—'

'I thought you said builder's?'

'I lied. Now, listen: *the tea had been drunk*. Not cleared away, you notice. But the cups were empty, with those little dregs and bits you get from loose-leaf. You know what this means?'

'Yes! This places Simon Grey *inside the house* around the time it happened! Leyla, I could kiss you.'

She looked at him. There was something hard in her eyes that had not been there before.

'Go on then,' was all she said.

The problem was, she said it only in her head. In reality, Torben's words fell into a silence only intermittently broken during the half hour's walk they shared back to her flat on Haberdasher Street.

Probably for the best, she thought. Either it would have been bad, in which case— no, don't even go there. Or it would have been good, in which case it would have led to more, and she didn't fancy those bare boards. The desk was obviously out, and while the thought of the kitchen worktop had a certain seedy appeal that she could, at a pinch, have leant into, the lingering smell of Thursday's curry was not exactly an aphrodisiac. So they'd have had to do this walk anyway, which would have given them both time to think, and second guess, and then Torben would have seen the state of her bedroom, and probably ended things there and then on sanitary grounds …

Had she, thought Torben, been about to say something? And if so … No, the chances of being right with two hunches in a row were vanishingly small. This was *Leyla* he was talking about – he should count himself lucky she was willing to play along at all, let alone think she might actually be into him. Now get a grip, and focus on things where you might have a hope in hell of succeeding: you need to fix a date for the Posavacs, tackle the other neighbour, get that police contact from Ruth, make a proper start on Charlotte's papers …

They had reached the crest of Wharton Street. It was dusk; London was still, and quiet, a residual heat now rising from the pavement. Torben sighed. 'You know, Leyla, once I get kicked out of Little James Street … I think if I could live anywhere in London, this would be it.'

9

TWO BEDROOMS

What Torben, acutely conscious of Ruth's last month of service ticking down, was already thinking of as 'week two of four', was upon them almost before they realised. Torben spent the Sunday further rationalising Charlotte's papers – Leyla might as well have an *actual* day off for once – and he also managed to run into one of the Posavacs and get the two of them invited for Sunday lunch in a week's time. So far, a postcard (carefully selected from a stack Torben always had in reserve, the spoils of far too many exhibitions) and a knock had produced no results from the other neighbour, so that side of the operation would just have to await developments. Meanwhile, Leyla had promised to use any free evenings she could spare on profiling the suspects Charlotte had indicated. They'd set a date – a working date, alas – for Wednesday night.

Bemoaning once more his old mentor's insistence on using paper and pen, rather than text-searchable word documents, Torben set about what was clearly going to be a Herculean task. But the more he read, especially in the old diaries, the more lucid it became. Charlotte had a fondness for using sets of initials, and based on context, he was pretty confident that her final clue had not been a one-off; this was how she'd always referred to those people. So throughout her papers, SG was *always* Simon Grey, HD Henrik Drever, SR Shani Rajapalayam ... Disconcertingly, unless she had known a number of senior civil servants of Nigerian extraction (or at any rate, civil servants who cooked her jollof and moi moi in their Pimlico townhouse) and who were concerned with diplomatic affairs, then Jonathan Azawakh really did seem to be MM. This aberration continued to puzzle Torben until he found himself looking at a long-hand allusion to a 'Man from the Ministry' for three long minutes, before realising why he had stopped reading on. Man from the Ministry. MM. It was perfect – a most Lazerton-like piece of flippancy that served the purpose of disguising his identity should MM himself, or rather JA, ever cast his eye over these papers in a semi-official capacity. That sealed it: the five names from the funeral *were* the five in Charlotte's mind. Elated, he messaged Leyla at once.

Rather more troubling was the fact that, unless he had missed something, there was no KT for Katherine Trigg in any of the diaries, and these went back more than thirty years. But at least there was nothing, from what he'd scanned so far, to implicate anybody else not on that hurried list of initials; five suspects were more than enough to be getting on with.

He needed to be systematic. Maybe the unfinished memoir, in which the most eloquent evidence seemed to be that surgical excision in the 1980s, held more secrets in its earlier chapters – though not, he was pretty sure, in the section about her schooldays, which promised to be fascinating but seemed unlikely to yield motives for murder, and for which reason he was reserving that substantial chunk of memoir for more pleasurable reading once this affair was over. But perhaps something from her days as a student protester in Paris? The whole thing was certainly cosmopolitan – while mentions of 'SG' tended to show up in London only, 'HD' was encountered as a precocious tyro at conferences in Stockholm, New York, Berlin, Prague; 'SR' in Amsterdam, Rome, Edinburgh, Rio, Tokyo; MM – or rather, Jonathan Azawakh – in St Petersburg, Istanbul, Washington … While converting the frail, grey-bobbed Katherine Trigg into a long-ago schoolgirl was an imaginative stretch too far, he could easily see a young Henrik Drever networking his socks off at foreign conferences, and the suave Shani Rajapalayam sashaying about all the glamorous art-world functions of the 1990s.

He realised he was in that early, scattergun phase of research he knew so well, when a topic was still fresh, a revelation at every turn. This was when you made the most electrifying discoveries, those flashes of insight, the memory of which sustained you in the long hours – months – years that followed. But it was also when you ran around yapping at your material like a puppy in a park of pigeons. The moment had come for folders and sub-folders … a scanner … summary documents he could walk Leyla through in those brief windows of time, normally no more than thirty minutes per evening, when she was actually prepared to tolerate his earnestness.

His mind went back to the night before. Her flat had been … poignant, was that the word? Nice sofa, squishy but still elegant, in a vivid emerald green. A lot of jewel colours in general, compensating for the standard white walls. Cactuses rather than full-on plants. And the place smelt *divine*, a blend of her personal fragrance (still Le Labo Oud 27), a St Eval scent diffuser – the sort that actually worked – and a muskier undertone that was just, well, her.

But fundamentally, it all remained just a little bit sad. A space so ready and willing to be a home, yet called upon, thus far, simply to be a domicile.

He imagined his own studio, the one he had just vacated, to be the same; probably most of the people he knew in London lived in similar holding patterns. For some reason, he had hoped Leyla's might be different.

The next day, Monday, brought with it two arrivals that were each, in their way, of seismic significance. The first was his new – or rather, extremely old – bed. Torben helped the courier carry each section upstairs, fussing at the landings and corners like a mother hen, for all that it was swaddled in layers of cloth and bubble wrap. A five-minute dash down the road later he had procured two screwdrivers, both cross- and flat-headed. Left alone, he took time over the bed's assembly, relishing the fit of every piece. The slats were modern, of course – he wasn't a total idiot – but the rest had to be 1770s, maybe even older? Scraped down to the original off-white paint, with six legs to spread the weight, delicate tracery along the edges – beading, simple flowers – and high, solid head- and footboards, tricked out to resemble ionic architecture, with a swag done in relief at the foot and a sort of raised bow figure, in very intricate carving work, at the head.

Stepping back, he surveyed the finished bed. Its lines were perfect: the only thing standing in a room that seemed made for it. It was far and away the most magnificent thing he'd ever owned, and the silliest thing he'd ever bought. The best thing was, it would take a double mattress, which he had also remembered to procure, and the whole structure showed no signs of collapsing beneath him. It might even do for two, though where *that* idea had come from …

The second arrival was a WhatsApp from Ruth. *His names Gary Bassett and hes your Meeras boss. Have fixed meeting for tmorow eve but impt I brief you first. CALL ME LATER!*

Ruth picked up on the second ring, at one minute past six that evening. 'Look,' she said, before Torben could speak, 'my phone has a problem with apostrophes, OK? The auto-correct seems to be stuck ...'

'*Hvad?*' Apparently, this was what his friends worried about: that he'd judge their grammar. It was a sobering and, on balance, a displeasing thought, but it was the last thing on his mind right now. 'Ruth, you've *really* got hold of him? This is wonderful!'

'Yes, it's amazing what you can do when you're not worried about how it might affect your future career prospects. Trust me, over the last few years of being a black woman police officer in the Met, I have stored up a *lot* of debts to call in. Mostly from people I might've made complaints about ... plus I knew the station, it wasn't hard. So: Gary Bassett, early forties, incipient paunch, going grey. West Ham fan, favours a dark beer, has two daughters and, surprisingly, a Pekinese. Just back from a one-week break in Marbella, and lives – inconveniently – in Barking. Enjoys golf, classic rock—'

'Ruth, Ruth! *Klap lige hesten*! I need a pen ...'

She said it all again, more slowly. 'I actually got a lot of this from Meera. First letting you take her to the pub, now this – frankly, I'm a little concerned for *her* career prospects if she keeps being this open about work stuff. Point is, *he* doesn't know you'll know this. I thought it might help if you could drop in a touch of Holmesian deduction. But the thing you really need to know is—'

'Why on *earth* a serving senior officer would agree to talk to some random civilian about a presumably confidential case?'

'Yeah,' said Ruth. 'That. We didn't speak for long, and I was careful to tread delicately, but I got the impression he wasn't entirely satisfied with the final verdict either. And if there's one way of guaranteeing a man will talk for as long as you could want, it's making sure he has a theory to share. If he thinks he's spotted something no one else has noticed—'

'*Tak*, Ruth, I am familiar with the scenario you describe,' said Torben. Why did chats with Ruth always end up with him feeling bad about himself on some level?

'*But*,' she said, 'that's only half of it. The other half's you.'

'Me?'

'Yup. It transpires that our Bassett is obsessed with Nordic Noir.'

'*For fanden!*'

'That's the stuff, Tor. He can't get enough of *The Bridge*, *The Killing*, *Wallander*, all those other ones I haven't heard of on BBC4 and Walter Presents … I popped by his office for this chat and there was a stack of Jo Nesbøs, Ragnar Jónassons, the lot. Even a poster of Sofie Gråbøl. When I told him you were a Danish detective – which may have been stretching the truth, but is technically accurate right now – with suspicions about a case he was involved in, he jumped at the chance of meeting up. Just throw in a lot of *for helvedes* and wear that jumper you had on back in Bastlehaugh, he'll lap it up.'

'But it's boiling outside!'

'Trust me, it will help. The man expects knitwear, you give him knitwear.'

'Speaking of "where" …?'

'That Mikkeller brewpub place you're always on about. Seven-thirty.'

And really, thought Torben, how could it be anywhere else? 'Ruth, I can't even begin to thank you …'

'It's nothing,' she said. 'Hey, it might even end up solving a murder. Which would make a nice change. And those were lovely flowers last week; they're still going strong now.'

Ruth really was the best.

Wait – tomorrow evening was Tuesday. That meant missing handball training!

The screen was swimming before Leyla's eyes. This was like pulling an all-nighter as an undergrad again – less familiar and mind-numbing than an ongoing brief that she had to take home with her, but just as arduous. Still, she was determined to have something good to show Torben on Wednesday. Not that she was competitive or anything. Already, now that the civil servant was confirmed as MM, she'd thrown together the beginnings of a dossier on each of Azawakh, Drever, Grey, Rajapalayam and Trigg: dates of birth, photos, video clips, websites, social media profiles, likeliest means of contact, key biographical details. The downside of dealing with five powerful Londoners was that they had no obvious way of tackling them at this stage of their investigation. The upside was that four of them had Wikipedia pages.

She'd begun with the suspect Torben actually knew a bit, as he seemed the one they were most likely to get to speak to. Henrik Drever's path to power seemed pre-ordained. Educated at Lundsbergs, Uppsala and Oxford. Professor by forty, a head of department role leading to a full-scale sidestep into senior management; he was now a pro-vice-chancellor, whatever that was, presumably nothing good. His internet presence was currently dominated by this quest to become head of the Academy of Western Art – which would, thereafter, return to its original name of the Academy of Art if he had his way – as articulated in a series of slick, professionally directed videos and a manifesto formatted in a very serious-looking font. The result, she noted, was scheduled for 16 June, two weeks on Saturday, and – now that Charlotte Lazerton was definitively off the ballot list

– Drever looked like a dead cert. He was handsome, she supposed, in a bland kind of way. Close-trimmed beard, compensating for a bald head. Straight nose, strong jaw. A touch short for her liking, at least for a Swede. But the nearest he seemed to come to expressing actual humanity was in a blog post written for the Ritz, nominally focusing on the history of its porcelain. It looked like Drever had started the article with an eye to countering post-colonial narratives of imperial atrocities in the tea trade. But within a paragraph or two, any trace of ideology had been abandoned, in favour of a paean in praise of the English tea service. Drever, it seemed, was that strangest sort of European, albeit a sort that apparently existed in surprising numbers in the more exalted professions: a fully paid-up Anglophile.

Leyla glanced at the cup on the bedside table. The tea within was jasmine silver needle from Fortnum's. The only problem was, it had gone stone cold.

She sighed, and re-plumped the pillow at her back; she couldn't afford to slip down, and off to sleep. Drever was, at least, an open book compared with Jonathan Azawakh, CMG. His name cropped up on various lists – including, of course, the New Year's Honours, for his various gongs; it turned out 'CMG' was an especially fancy order of chivalry – but the only extensive profiles were of the 'senior civil servant is an inspiration to London's Nigerian community' variety: well-intentioned, even moving, but so far as insights into his professional activities were concerned, entirely useless. Just one portrait photo that got used everywhere, professionally shot: tall, well-built, good-looking but starting to weather. From the difficulty of establishing exactly which departments he'd worked in, Leyla assumed Azawakh was Intelligence – MI6 seemed a safe bet – and it all lent further circumstantial credence to the general theory and the missing memoir pages, but in looking for a direct connection to Lazerton, her old diaries would be a much better bet than the internet. That was the problem with being able to find anything online. The people who had the power to remove it could find it too.

For now, she was setting aside Simon Grey and Shani Rajapalayam. The sheer volume of content available on an MP who'd been in parliament since 1990, and one of the UK's leading cultural journalists, was more than even she was prepared to assimilate in a spare evening or two. Hopefully one or both of them could be ruled out before she had to get to grips with their digital footprint.

Which just left Katherine Trigg, the old schoolfriend. No Wikipedia to help her out here. In fact, no public profile at all, so far as Leyla could divine. She'd been a director of some firm in the City, one of those asset-net-wealth-management-hedge-fund-foundation corporations that made Leyla want to set fire to the whole square mile, and damn the carbon emissions. But she hadn't been listed or indexed anywhere since the early 2000s – seemingly she'd had the good sense, or luck, to take early retirement before the 2008 crash. She had been to school with Lazerton; a black-and-white photograph on Friends Reunited, which Leyla had dug up via archive.org, had confirmed that much of Drever's brief introduction. If it hadn't been for the caption, it would have been hard to connect the short, brittle woman at the funeral with the athletic teenager beaming back at her from the screen. Leyla saved the photo to show Torben later; it was sure to amuse him. But in the last decade or more, Trigg's only appearance online had been in the form of a blogspot site with one single entry.

Hello world! My name's Katherine – or Kitty if we get to know one another! And I hope that's exactly what we're going to do, as I document my new mission: to write the first proper bioscopy of renowned barista, screenwriter and novelist, John Mortimer QC. Stay with me on my journey as I document the life of this wonderful man, from the Dragon School and Braised nose College Oxford, to the Inner Temple, to the BBC, to Rumpole of the Baileys. I'll be posting weekly updates, so stay tuned – and expect to read all about it in a bookshop near you, very, very soon!

The post was dated more than seven years ago. Leyla had checked on Amazon, and even on the British Library online catalogue, but had been unsurprised to discover that Trigg's long-awaited 'bioscopy' was going to remain awaited for the foreseeable future.

It seemed a harmless enough way to spend one's retirement. Still, Trigg had shown herself fully prepared to murder the English language. Why not an old schoolfriend as well?

Three kilometres away, Torben too was busy researching from the rather tentative comfort of his new bed. He had got the number of candidates down to four: a good evening's work, he flattered himself. But which was most likely to fit the bill? The one with the new webbing and re-upholstered cushions? Or the one with free delivery within the M25?

10

EXMOUTH MARKET

Leaving 24 Little James Street early the next evening, Torben nearly collided with someone walking very quickly, in *very* high heels. Reeling, perilously close to self-impalement upon the iron area railings, Torben fought against the overpowering scent of a fragrance he was very glad not to be able to identify. He had the fleeting impression of a tall woman, all angles, mounting the steps of number 26. Before he had time to muster more than a strangled 'Excuse me—' she had slipped inside and shut the door.

So: that was the other neighbour. Not the friendliest soul in the world. Or perhaps, not unreasonably, she was suspicious of strange men who wore thick woollen sailor's jumpers from Andersen-Andersen when it was at least 25 degrees Celsius.

Luckily, the Mikkeller brewpub had let him reserve an outside table. Even more luckily, no one seemed to be working who had also been on shift during millionaire playboy Zak Cremello's godawful binge the other week. By the time a man answering to Bassett's description – grizzled, four-square, no-nonsense – turned up, Torben was settled under the merciful shade of an awning, feet itching inside his most epic pair of Trippen leather boots, thighs a little chafed by walking here in skinny jeans, his jaw enflamed where his beard line met the thick upper edge of the indigo jumper neck. On the plus side: he was sipping an exquisite Viennese-style lager; his guest would hopefully not check the alcohol percentage of the pint of Baltic porter awaiting him; and an androgynous server with an entirely predictable and really rather good portfolio of tattoos was already shimmying over with the food.

'Gary!' said Torben, risking the familiarity, leaning into the roll of the 'r'.

The policeman swung round, his elbow millimetres from laying waste to the neighbouring table's drinks. His eyes lit up. '*Hej hej!*' he said. 'Torben Helle, I presume?' He gave the surname the full treatment; you could practically hear his tongue click against the inside of his lower incisors.

'*Hej*,' said Torben, gesturing to the seat opposite; to the plates between. He fought back his instinctual smile: Ruth had made it clear that Bassett expected terse monosyllables with a hint of underlying pathological disorder, and he'd hate to disappoint the man. 'I got you a *pølse*. Thought you'd be hungry. That OK?'

'Thanks,' said Bassett, his gaze already devouring the hotdog. They clinked their glasses. If Bassett was taken aback by the strength of his beer, he did a good job of disguising it. Perfect. He'd probably be good for a couple more.

'How's your dog?' said Torben, after five minutes on Saga Norén's car and suicide rates in the Arctic Circle.

'Delicious, thanks,' said Bassett. 'Fancy another?'

Torben glanced down at the remnants of his own portion rather wistfully. True to his new principles, he had ordered the vegan version – mushroom, red peppers, some sort of protein – and it was clear that his search for a convincing sausage substitute was not yet at an end. Maybe, for the sake of the investigation, he could allow himself just the one …

'Actually,' he said, 'I meant your pet, not the *pølse*. Happy to have you back from your minibreak in the Med?'

Bassett goggled at him. 'Who—? How—?'

Torben waved away the question. 'You've got quite the tan for a senior officer who has to endure more deskwork than they'd like. From the way the skin's peeling on your neck and forearms, I'm guessing a short break somewhere pretty hot – but not too far away, or the flight time wouldn't be worth it, and not so extreme that you'd take care with the suntan lotion. You really should, by the way. At a guess, either the south of Portugal or the Costa del Sol – Marbella perhaps? – because of the golf courses; your walk and musculature indicates a golfer's swing, and the sunburn is consistent with wearing a polo shirt in overhead sun. As for the dog, there is a series of minute hairs on your shoe and ankle – by the length, and the height they reach, I'd surmise a toy breed, probably either a Yorkshire Terrier or a Peki—'

'Fuck me!'

'It's nothing,' Torben said. 'And I'd love another one, *tak*, but this really *is* on me; it's the least I can do when you made time to see me, especially on a night when the Irons are playing their last post-season friendly.'

Bassett's mouth opened again, and then his gaze flicked down to his cufflinks, which bore the West Ham emblem of two crossed hammers, and he grinned.

I should probably have spotted those myself, Torben thought.

*

'You wanted to talk about the Lazerton case, right?' said Bassett at last. 'I mean, I *say* case ...'

Torben nodded. 'She was a close friend.'

'So I gathered,' said Bassett, 'since you were the last person seen with her before she died.'

Torben had been practising Leyla's single eyebrow lift, but didn't quite feel confident enough to try it out. 'Is that so?' he said.

Bassett nodded. 'Tall blond bloke with a beard, dressed in "classic Lamb's Conduit Street with a Scandi twist", is how I think she put it.'

'The neighbour?' Torben hazarded. 'At number 26?'

'That's right. Lucia Segugio, interior designer, tray cheek.'

This last statement confused Torben until he realised it was meant to be French.

'Sadly,' Bassett went on, 'no one seems to have seen anything on the day we think she ... died' – Torben noted the hesitation – 'so I haven't been able to corroborate the—'

'Tea for two,' Torben finished.

'You *have* done your homework,' Bassett said. Torben was glad the policeman didn't seem to have done his: if Torben were the last person witnessed in Charlotte's company, he'd rather the police weren't also aware of how well he'd done out of the will. He was through with people suspecting him of murder.

'You clearly think the death was suspicious,' Torben stated. 'Your recall of details; the fact that you ordered a PM—'

'It's not just the post-mortem neither,' said Bassett. 'It came back clean – but with the major caveat that where the wolfhound had been at her— sorry, mate, but you know what I mean ... anyway, they couldn't swear that wasn't obscuring a blow or wound that might indicate a struggle, a push. Now, there's nothing suspicious in a senior citizen, living alone, falling down dead and getting munched on by their pooch. In fact, dogs are hazards; they trip people up, or knock them over, and after that they're just obeying nature. Happens all the time: old gent in a townhouse in Knightsbridge conked out a few months back, got nibbled by his Leonberger. Saw a report of this biddy with a St Bernard, had a flat in Mayfair – well, let's just say the old mountain rescue dog was having an off day. Just the other week we had another one here, a pensioner on Doughty Street took a tumble over their Newfoundland. People get lonely, they think a big dog's going to protect them. Truth is, you need to be in good shape with something that size and weight around the house. Now, take Selden, my little Peke, no harm to ... sorry, seem to have lost my thread. Yeah, point is, they couldn't rule out an attack beneath the posthumous damage. *And* it was just a superficial survey, they didn't even do bloods – cost-cutting, see: if I couldn't produce sufficient grounds to investigate further, they weren't going to blow time or budget on the full medical works.'

'And you couldn't overrule that decision?' said Torben.

'Directive from upstairs, wasn't it? And more to the point, all this was communicated verbally.'

'And that's important?'

Bassett laughed. 'Hell yes! Basically, when it comes to a crime scene, if it isn't written up, logged, on file – then it didn't happen. As far as the record goes, there *were* no results from the PM, not even negative ones. I'm the only one who was told. They weren't keen on ordering forensics either, but I know some people, so I nipped over to their office and convinced them to do a basic sweep of the staircase, the hall, the front room ...'

'Which day did this take place?'

'Monday 30th April. Two days after we found her: probably six since it happened.'

'Isn't that pretty late to find uncorrupted DNA evidence?'

Bassett nodded. 'Yeah, but I'd hoped for something from the teacups at least, if not the stair-rail, the handles ... but guess what came back?'

'Nothing?'

'But *absolutely* nothing. Sweet FA. Like there'd been a malfunction or something. Dr Helle, that house had had a rampaging great dog all over it until the Saturday. Your friend's corpse had been lying there nearly a week. And two of my officers, plus the downstairs lodger, had been on the scene not forty-eight hours before I got those guys in there. But so far as the forensic record shows, that house was a literal vacuum. Empty. Diddly squat.'

'*For helvede*,' said Torben. He wasn't even putting it on.

'Which is why,' said Bassett, doing a pretty good job of fixing Torben with his gaze for a man who had had three pints of 8.3% stout, 'I'm talking to you. Because this case is officially closed: accidental death, we all move on. But I reckon there's been a cover-up.'

'At the Metropolitan Police?' said Torben, hoping he sounded incredulous rather than sarcastic. From Bassett's solemn nod, he seemed to have got away with it.

'Well,' said Bassett, 'thanks for the dinner. And the chat. Here's my card, with my private number – I can't take any action myself, you get me, but if you find anything ...' He winked. They both stood.

'In the meantime,' the policeman said, '*vi ses*.'

'Well?' said Torben.

It was Wednesday evening in Leyla's kitchen. Before them were the remnants – in truth, no more than crumbs – of two Jon Bon Chovy pizzas from Sodo's on the corner; they had even sourced another bottle of Chiroubles, which Torben had decided was now his go-to summer wine.

Leyla ran a napkin round her mouth, catching the smear of tomato that had been giving him secret amusement for the past ten minutes. 'It's a hell of a story,' she conceded. 'This may just be the wine talking. But I'm starting to think that she really was pushed.'

'Or,' said Torben, 'that there was something slipped into her tea? Just enough to make her dizzy, so that when she took a call, at the top of the stairs … That's why they wouldn't let Bassett order blood tests, because someone in authority knew what would show up.'

'That points to the MP,' said Leyla. 'Grey. He was the invitee, wasn't he? I can just see it – your rookie police officer phones round everyone in that appointments calendar, cross-referencing the names with the numbers in Charlotte's private phone book, contacting everyone from a certain Doctor Hell to an unknown bloke called Simon Grey, thus alerting his ministerial team to the fact the police have made the connection. If he did it, then he'd have his people get someone in there like a shot! But – but we *thought* the pages removed from that last volume of the memoir pointed to Azawakh, didn't we? Because it sounded like they were about to reveal important state secrets about his work in the Cold War? Which tallies with the secret clean-up too: he'd either leave no traces, or make sure that any evidence was conveniently wiped …'

'It comes down,' said Torben, 'to who we think is likelier to have suppressed a routine police investigation. The government, or the secret service. I'm inclined to call it a draw.'

'So we're nixing the other three suspects?' said Leyla. 'Just when I've put together these beautiful Google Docs?' She gestured to her laptop, open beside them at a photo of Shani Rajapalayam – roguish smile, razor-sharp cheekbones, glossy dark hair piled high. An aesthetic not so far removed from Leyla's own.

'Pfff …' Torben was beginning to regret the half-bottle, on top of the previous night's beer. True, it seemed to be what all the other detectives did, but maybe – just maybe – the consumption of alcohol was not necessarily beneficial to the deductive process. 'Not yet,' he decided. 'There's always a chance Bassett got the wrong end of the stick. Maybe there really *was* an error with the forensics, or the whole thing looked so innocuous no one could be bothered to do the paperwork. Negligence, laziness, human error, lack of time – these are surely much likelier explanations than corruption?'

'When it comes to the establishment,' Leyla said, 'such qualities need not be mutually exclusive.'

'Well, that's just it,' said Torben. 'The establishment. Do we know for sure that Drever or Rajapalayam – or even Trigg, who must be loaded – don't have friends in the right places to just, just make this all go away?' He gestured to Leyla's MacBook. 'Drever went to Lundsbergs. That's where half the Swedish royal family was educated, not to mention who knows how many politicians. Rajapalayam has been at the top of Fleet Street for decades, Trigg worked in the City … *for helvede*, they all know *each other* now, don't they, at least to say hello to? We met them *together*! Drever seemed to know Grey and Rajapalayam; Grey obviously knew Azawakh. If Azawakh or Grey could have ordered the cover-up on their own behalf, why not for each other, or a friend – or a friend of a friend?'

And which, he thought, was the more naïve proposition? That the two of them had somehow stumbled into a cover-up operation straight out of the conspiracy theorist's handbook? Or that a senior figure in British public life had been on the verge of being caught out

... and *hadn't* pulled whatever strings it took to hush it up?

Generally speaking, he thought cynics were more naïve than optimists – the assumption that others are up to no good and not to be trusted seemed, on balance, more foolish and indeed dangerous than seeing the best in everyone. In this case, however, he was prepared to make an exception.

'But,' Leyla was saying, 'that would mean that we are literally no further forward. At all. We get the inside scoop from the senior investigating officer, and all it tells us is that any of them could still have done it?'

'Worse,' said Torben. 'It means we can't read anything into the *absence* of evidence. A lack of witnesses, DNA, whatever, doesn't let them off the hook. It'll take a proper, verifiable alibi to rule any of them out. We need to find out what they were doing on that day.'

'If only,' said Leyla for perhaps the tenth time that week, 'we had a reason to interview them. To get a grip, not just on their movements, but on their psychology – for all we know, one has an obvious tell, or the cold dead eyes of a killer, or a guilty conscience just begging to be let out ... but without direct access, we're stumped.'

'Leyla,' said Torben. 'Pass me your laptop?'

She did so, frowning.

'When I need a morale boost,' he explained, 'I watch one of Charlotte's old interviews on YouTube. You'll love this one,' he said, navigating to the site, 'it's only short—'

Torben stopped. Below the search bar, three thumbnails featured the top 'recommended for you' videos for Leyla. One was a trailer for an arthouse film that he, too, would quite like to see. The other two were ...

'"Best of Mikkel Hansen",' he read aloud. '"Mikkel Hansen – Top 10 Goals of all time".'

He looked at Leyla. Leyla looked down at their plates.

Mikkel Hansen was the star player of the Danish men's handball team.

For maybe seven seconds, neither of them spoke.

'One of the ways,' Leyla managed at last, 'in which fiction holds the advantage over life, is in its ability to close a scene at the right moment. Two characters get into a contretemps, or come to the peak of a conversation, and the writer simply can't think how they're going to carry on. So instead, fiction simply draws the veil, and no one ever need worry about what to say next, or how to get out of the embarrassment. The author simply … ends the chapter.'

II
NUMBER 22

'Nice try,' said Torben. 'But you're not getting out of it that easily. Mikkel Hansen videos?!'

'I thought,' said Leyla, who seemed to have recovered herself, 'that you were meant to be a detective? It's simple enough – I find out that you play this wilfully literalist sport – really, football, handball, basketball, netball, won't someone exercise their nominative imagination as well as their limbs? – you even drag me along to watch a session; I am left none the wiser. In attempting to comprehend my friend's eccentric pastime, I turn to the internet and in so doing, I stumble upon this genuinely god-like hunk. You could learn a lot from him. And I don't just mean the bit where you jump up high and hand the ball very very hard.'

'Oh,' said Torben.

She had, she thought, just about got away with that one.

Eventually, they watched the video of Dame Charlotte, this time giving a vox pop live on some online news channel whilst at a climate emergency rally. The young man holding the mic made the mistake of saying that there were two sides to every story – what about the rights of the motorists they were inconveniencing by blocking the road?

The shaky camera just about stabilised on Charlotte's gaunt features. She looked as outraged as an owl whose feathers had been brushed the wrong way. 'Oh yes, that's the lesson of history, isn't it – that we should beware extreme positions? The right-thinking person always lands somewhere in the middle, don't they?'

In the edge of the shot, the young man nodded encouragement.

'Consensus, that's the grown-up solution!' Charlotte went on, now looking straight down the camera lens. 'A judicious sense of proportion. And history bears us out, doesn't it? Take the Middle Ages, the Reformation – some people want to worship a different god – do we burn them to death, or leave them be? Ah no, moderation is our watchword; let's just burn them halfway dead. Can two consenting adults have sex irrespective of their gender or class or colour? It's a polarising question – we should probably equivocate. Slavery. Apartheid. Should we have them or shouldn't we? These things are never black or white, so the answer must be somewhere in the middle. Suffrage, education, welfare – should they be universal, or the preserve of a rich male elite? Well, it's complicated. So of course this principle applies to climate change too: continuing to heat the planet by a tiny degree or two in the interests of the 0.1 per cent – well, they have families and pets too, it can't all be about those bloody polar bears or the entire population of Pakistan—'

Too late, the interviewer tried to call a halt, but she would not be stopped.

'And as for this "whataboutery", as you young people say – there's nothing the English love more than an ad hominem attack, a chance to call hypocrisy, down tools and go home. David Cameron – "the pig-shagger" – voted Remain, and Nick Clegg – "the tuition-fee Judas" – supported proportional representation, so those causes were beyond the pale. Gandhi took young women to his bed as a test of his chastity – so much for non-violent protest and a free India. Florence Nightingale and Mother Theresa are both a bit problematic – better not have any more nurses. Hitler was a vegetarian, so anyone avoiding meat must be a bit suspicious—'

Finally the reporter got in a 'Dame Charlotte Lazerton, thank you very much.' As the camera panned away to capture a wide shot of the crowd, you could just make out the hip-flask in her still-gesticulating hand.

'I can see,' said Leyla, 'why someone killed her. But at least it clears the path for making her a saint.'

Another random collision in the street – he really needed to watch where he was going more carefully; it was all this early summer sunshine. Apology already forming on his lips, Torben hastily converted the words into a gulp of astonishment, as a vast and rubbery tongue wriggled its way around his face.

'Mortimer!' he said at last. 'And Meera!'

'Hi,' she said. Same rucksack, same route as before. Curious. Did she always end up being the one who had to take the dog home?

It was, he now noticed, an Arsenal-branded rucksack. He looked her over. Decent trainers, clearly swapped at the end of the day for her police-regulation footwear. An athletic bearing.

'Meera,' he said, on an impulse. 'Friday nights, seven o'clock – there's a regular five-a-side football session that we play on the Calthorpe Project pitch, very casual, and we're allowed the odd guest. On AstroTurf. You should come!'

She started, then smiled. 'Thanks! That's – that's just over there, isn't it? I'd love to. But how did you know I played?'

'Oh – someone must've mentioned it,' he said.

Leyla had considered her outfit carefully for Sunday lunch at the Posavacs'. Nothing too showy, but enough to signal she was making an effort and appreciated the neighbourly attention. In the end, she had plumped for a light, short-sleeved top in a strong block colour, beneath an unstructured linen trouser suit, with her newest pair of sandals, all very summery, with just enough decorum to pass muster.

Arriving at Little James Street, she found that Torben had dressed exactly the same.

'My t-shirt's cotton,' he pointed out. 'You're in silk. It's different.'

'I still say you should change.'

'They'll reckon it's sweet.'

'Torben,' she said, 'do the Posavac family think that we're an item?'

'I left it ambiguous,' he admitted. 'Thought it might make me seem more respectable – providing you behave, of course – and, more to the point, explain why you're there. So don't grumble!'

'Fine.'

'I'm actually matchmaking all over the place,' he went on. It sounded like he wanted to change the subject. 'On Friday night I managed to set up Meera – the police officer, you remember? – with Cameron Plott, the most American member of my football crowd. They both love dogs, and he told Meera this story of Zak's …'

Torben proceeded to regale Leyla with a lengthy anecdote, which was third-hand at best, and had probably grown in the telling.

Apparently this Zak Cremello, who sounded ghastly, had done some dog-sitting for family friends as an undergraduate, the dog in question being a snow-white poodle. Being rich, young and entitled, he had decided to host a secret party in the friends' home. Everyone had drunk far too much WKD Blue – Leyla shuddered involuntarily at the name, it brought back memories she too would rather forget – and someone had been sick all over the poodle. Cremello had had to take it for an all-over haircut before the friends returned, to find their dog newly shorn, looking half its usual size, and still a very pale blue.

'By the way,' he finished up, 'that is just the sort of off-colour story *not* to tell my new neighbours.'

'Mm,' said Leyla, who was not generally in the habit of spreading the boasts of immature frat-boys. 'So the key things to establish are: did any of the family see Simon Grey on the Tuesday afternoon – or anyone else, for that matter – and whether they noticed someone snooping about for the rest of that week. And, if so, why they didn't tell DS Bassett: we'll have to watch out for signs that someone's got to them, a threat, a bribe … reticence, awkward silences, sudden forgetfulness – anyone keeping anything quiet.'

'… such a *lovely* colour on you—'

'… and I said to him, if *that's* what they're spending my business rates on—'

'More *kava*, Leyla, Torben?'

'Mila, dear, will you find out where I left that fish knife – my grandmother's, you know—'

'… and so *sweet* for you to be matching—'

'… I mean, really, the *state* of those *bins*—'

'Oh! The *soparnik*, I almost forgot!'

113

'It reminds me of when Domagoj, my eldest – that's him over there – was in love with this *awful* girl from Peckham—'

'*Mati*, you know we're still engaged?!'

'Just let them rest for five minutes first; the chard retains water, it can scald the tongue …'

All right, Leyla conceded; unwonted taciturnity on the part of their hosts did not seem likely to be a problem.

It was dizzying, this house that, at the level of brick and plaster, was more or less the twin of Number 24. At some stage of its life – presumably before listed building consent became a thing, though she was fast learning not to put anything past this family – an extension had been added to the ground floor and the rear wall knocked through, to form a long, staggered kitchen space that, like the rest of the house Leyla had seen so far, seemed simply too full to be allowed. The Posavac residence was less a family home than an Ali Baba's cave, fecund with the overspill from their antiques shop a few streets away. She was, at that moment, parked on a faded ikat cushion that padded a long, scarred pew, her knees bumping against the underside of an immense refectory table. It groaned beneath a merry jumble of majolica and pewter, stoneware and silver. Above, innumerable copper pans (actually, she *had* counted – there were seventeen) hung from a series of lines drawn taut across the ceiling. The air was thick with the smells of cooking and old tobacco, of too many people on a hot summer Sunday. The *kava* bubbled continually on an immense range cooker of untold antiquity, the aroma of coffee cutting through the fug of the rest like a promise, like a song. On her right, Torben was jammed close up beside her, seeming overlarge, overlong, in the crowded space. On her left, a small boy was wedged between her and the bench-end: he wore a shirt, a tie and a smitten expression. She had already had to remove his hand from her leg. Now, he was trying to give her one of his salted sardines. Well, if it would appease the little pest ... Hastily, she leant forward over the table, just saving her silk top from the light shower of fish-steeped oil. Hoping no one would mind, Leyla licked the oil off her fingers. The child beamed at her.

'More *soparnik*?' offered young Mrs Posavac – distinguished, at her own firm insistence, from *old* Mrs Posavac, her mother-in-law, who was rocking away in a corner and had apparently been a very successful call-girl in her day, though Torben was beginning to think he might have misheard.

'Mm,' said Leyla beside him. 'It's just like spana—'

He trod on her foot, just in time. To compare a Dalmatian delicacy to its Greek cousin seemed unlikely to endear them to their hosts. And speaking of Dalmatians.

'I'm sorry for your loss,' he said *sotto voce* to young Mrs Posavac. 'Charlotte told me what happened to Boris.'

Mrs Posavac's smile had a hint of a wobble in it. 'Thank you,' she said. 'We do miss him. Still, compared to what happened next ...'

Torben sat up a little straighter. Was this the way in they had been looking for?

'...But I *am* glad it's you who is taking over the house from dear Professor Lazerton,' she went on. 'She had many young lodgers over the thirty years or more we've been neighbours – Alex, Clara, Shani, Rodri – but you were much the nicest. And one of the handsomest, which is saying something; she always went for pretty ones.'

Beside him, Leyla made a sudden choking sound. Well, she would just have to learn how to handle her chard.

'It's all happened so suddenly,' he said, raising his voice a little to take in all of the table. 'It seems no time at all since I moved out; even less since I saw her last. I still remember the look on her face as we said goodbye. It was the day before she died – in fact, I think I must have been the last person to see her ... that Monday afternoon,' he finished, stressing the words slightly. Was no one going to pick up on his cue?

'They found her on a Saturday, didn't they, Torben? The 28th of April?' That was Leyla, falsely bright.

'Yes,' he said, hoping he didn't sound too much like a children's pantomime, 'but the police officer who rang me up said she probably *died* on the Tuesday beforehand – the 24th.'

Was it his imagination, or was there a slight stir, a wince, at the words 'police officer'?

One of the younger family members – Ema? – leaned across the table. 'We all feel a bit guilty about that,' she said. 'Tuesday is when we reopen the shop after two days off; it's all hands on deck with changing over the stock, processing online orders that have come in, packing and posting ... there's no one at home here during the day. So if she fell and called out – maybe she was lying there for hours, crying for help – well, any other day, someone might have heard her and been able to do something.'

That hurt; Torben hadn't really entertained that possibility. With his mind wholly focused on murder, the thought of a potential intervention, a rescue, hadn't crossed his mind. But whether Charlotte had been drugged and left to chance, or pushed and left for dead, it still admitted this horrible hypothetical: if a neighbour had been home, there was just a chance they could have saved her.

And the other, less human part of his brain filed away a corresponding thought. Did whoever was responsible for Charlotte's murder know the Posavacs' routine, and choose the day accordingly? He caught Leyla's eye. It looked like the point had not escaped her either.

'Well,' he said aloud, 'she was meant to have a visitor that day anyway – she left me her appointments diary – it's not like she was a lonely old woman. Just bad luck, you shouldn't blame yourselves. I suppose, since no one was here, you don't know if anyone came ...?'

Obviously not, you fool – and now he had pushed the whole thing that bit too far; the almost festive mood was stretched. A touch too brightly to be convincing, young Mrs Posavac switched the plates. '*Brodet!*' she proclaimed, as a pan of polenta did the rounds, and she lowered a great tureen of stew on to the table. It smelt of the sea, in the best conceivable way.

'I saw him!' piped up the small boy next to Leyla, apparently only just catching up with the conversation. 'We was let home early, coz Miss Barker got took poorly. A big fat man in a suit was coming out of next door when I come down the road. His face was all red, sort of like a balloon. He didn't see me though.'

That sounded like a pretty good description of the MP on their list of suspects. Leyla turned to the boy. 'You're sure it was Number 24? Not two doors down? What time was this?'

The child sat a little taller, pleased with the attention. 'Dunno. After two. An' I *think* it was ... yeah, it was denifitely next door.' He sounded less certain than his statement.

Torben rummaged for his phone; pulled up a picture of Simon Grey. 'Was this the man?'

The boy shrugged. 'Man inna suit. About that fat, anyway.' He paused, evidently keen to do better. '*But* I saw the others, too!'

'Others?'

'The cover-ups. They went in the Sunday after.'

'The *Monday*, Marko dear,' corrected young Mrs Posavac. 'He means the policemen,' she explained. 'In those special overalls. *Covered up*, not *cover-ups*. We all saw them, didn't we, Marko, it made you late for school. Can you remember what they called it?'

'Frenziks,' said Marko, his face mutinous. 'But it *was* Sunday, only you all weren't awake yet. An' I saw the frenzik cover-ups from my window. It was a big black man who went in first.'

Torben felt a shock, almost electric, pass between himself and Leyla. He did some quick googling. 'This man?' he asked, showing Marko the only photo of Jonathan Azawakh he had been able to find – the studio portrait, well-lit and debonair, taken for an outreach charity.

'Nah,' said the boy. 'Not him.'

'Give me that,' Leyla whispered. A moment's fumbling, then she showed Marko another picture. 'Was it him?'

'Dunno,' said Marko. 'But I think so. It looks more like him than the last one anyway.'

Leyla sighed. 'Thank you, Marko,' she said.

'It *was* Monday, you know,' said Ema. 'That child is a fantasist.'

'Oh, it doesn't matter,' said Torben. 'We were just being nosy. What I *really* want to know is, what goes in the *brodet*? You make your own stock?'

Soon they were back on safer territory; the last thing they wanted was for his new neighbours to – he allowed himself the pun as he pried another one open – clam up.

As they moved on to pudding, Leyla took advantage of the change-over to return Torben his phone, with a pointed tap of the tab, still open, that she had shown little Marko; the photo he had tentatively identified as the man who had led the forensic team on – on whichever day it had been.

It was a still of Samuel L. Jackson from the 2007 film *Cleaner*.

Two cups of *kava* and about a dozen little pastries later, they finally got up. It took a lot of effort. On the point of making his farewells, a final question occurred to Torben.

'Oh,' he said. 'I meant to ask. Do you know anything about sourcing Gustavian furniture?'

'Well,' said Leyla, trying to lean back against Torben's kitchen worktop and finding it irritatingly situated at the level of her coccyx – she didn't think she could make the Herculean effort necessary to hop up on to the worktop itself – 'that's an hour of antiques chat I'll never get back.'

'But won't you be glad when I have some chairs you can sit on?' Torben countered. 'Even a sofa!'

'While I'm delighted that your Columbo-style "just one more thing" yielded great results,' she said, 'I can't help wishing they'd been more germane to the enquiry. Did we actually learn anything, except confirming what we already knew?'

'Depends on how you rate your admirer Marko as a witness,' Torben conceded. 'He seemed … less than reliable.'

'Agreed,' she said. 'I have the funny feeling he was prepared to agree to anything I said: a quality that males only ever exhibit when it's unhelpful. And unless we can suddenly crack your elusive Lucia Segugio on the other side of this wall, I think we've exhausted our potential for witness testimony. No one's been ruled out, more's the pity, and no one's been conclusively pinned down – though predictably, it's the men who are hogging the picture at the moment.'

'Azawakh and Grey, at any rate,' said Torben. 'Whom we can also bracket as the two best-placed to make things easy for themselves, and difficult for us.'

'Can we please go through MOM now?' said Leyla. 'I want to impose some order on this thing before we give it up as a bad job.'

'MOM?'

'Or OMM, if you prefer. Method, Opportunity, Motive. Some people put it the other way round, but there's a Lord Peter Wimsey line about method coming first that made sense at the time I read it.'

'I'll get some paper,' said Torben. 'And at least we've got all night – I must have had six cups of coffee.'

An hour later, they both regarded the table they had drawn up.

'I think this merits a *for helvede*?' said Leyla.

'Yup,' said Torben. 'In the conventional sense of, "well that was a bloody waste of time".'

	Method	Opportunity	Motive
Jonathan Azawakh (MM)	Push?	TBC	Cover-up (spy stuff)
Henrik Drever (HD)	Ditto?	TBC	Rivalry/gain (AWA presidency)
Simon Grey (SG)	Drugged tea	High – on scene (?)	Revenge? (betrayal – Europe? Eco?)
Shani Rajapalayam (SR)	?	TBC	???! FFS Torben why is she even here?! Charlotte just paranoid?
Katherine Trigg (KT)	?	TBC	Personal history? (see school photo)

'How,' said Leyla, feeling like a stuck record, 'are we meant to get to the bottom of this if we can't interrogate the suspects? It's so frustrating – not only are they the people we want to know about; they're the people likeliest to be useful even if they're *not* involved. All of them know different sides to Charlotte – her early years, her career before your time, her activism, her diplomatic stuff – even the innocent ones could tell us all sorts of things, controversies, stories, that would help give us a rounded picture … wait. Torben. Why are you staring at me like that?'

'"A rounded picture" – Carmen Sabueso!'

'Who?'

'The editor of that book series, the one who collared me at the funeral! She wanted me to interview friends of Charlotte's in the public eye, didn't she? It would be the perfect pretext.'

'Hah – I said at the time you should do it. Clearly, I was thinking ahead. You'd better email her pronto, then you'll have a legit cover story to produce if questioned. Even so, these are busy people, and diverting as a chat with you can intermittently be, it's not exactly going on *Oprah*. What makes you think they'll say yes?'

Maybe it was just the coffee, but Torben's heart was thumping like mad. 'They came to the funeral, didn't they? Despite all looking like they'd rather be miles away. If they've got anything to hide, even if it's just guilt over an unresolved quarrel, they'll want to be on record as a good sport.'

'A funeral,' Leyla pointed out, 'is a social obligation. An interview is voluntary.'

'Then I'll make it worth their while! Do it over dinner. Politicians, journalists, academics – they're hardly going to turn down a free meal if I pick the places carefully.' He paused. He would have to offer them *very* nice dinners. Admittedly, he was no longer paying rent, but he was out of a job soon, and already splurging on furniture.

'Leyla – when I say yes to Carmen, do you think she'll stump up for interview expenses?'

And Leyla's mocking laugh rang throughout the empty house.

12

LIMBO

Torben had Henrik Drever's email – if it came to that, he knew where his office was. For Jonathan Azawakh and Simon Grey, they'd have to go through secretaries: a triple-pronged assault of phone, email and letter (on Courtauld-headed notepaper) seemed their best bet. Their friend Frances Adair knew a junior critic on the *Observer* arts desk – in fact, it sounded like they might have dated. Frances was currently on some sort of retreat with her partner, Sara, which at last report seemed mostly to consist of sketching an endless series of Sara's frowns as she tried to write up the final version of her PhD thesis. Still, they could wangle a contact out of her by phone; it beat going through the official channels. That would get them to Shani Rajapalayam. Which just left Katherine Trigg. But—

'Luckily,' said Leyla, looking up, 'she's not ex-directory. I have a London address and a landline!'

'*Strålende!*' said Torben. 'That's my Monday morning taken care of then.'

'And what am *I* going to do,' asked Leyla, 'while you swan about setting up dinner dates? I suppose I'm not invited?'

He considered. 'It might be stretching the credulity of even the most entitled boomer to believe that an early-career scholar could have an amanuensis. Unless you want to pose as my co-editor of the volume?'

She shook her head. 'Too risky. You're forgetting, Drever introduced us all at the funeral. Normally I'd take a chance on their sort forgetting an unimportant face in an instant, but I happened to be wearing a rather sensational dress at the time. Besides, they could look me up. The beauty of this plan is that it's genuine. The bugger of it is that it's entirely your pigeon.'

'My what?'

'Look it up, apparently it's a thing.'

'I thought,' he said, declining this offer, 'that you'd probably be happy enough to get back to real work for a few days, but—'

'I've been bitten now, haven't I?' said Leyla. 'Much to my annoyance. So I'm taking a tiny bit of overdue leave here and there, on days where I don't have meetings already scheduled. How about this: you do front of house, I stay in the kitchen.'

Torben blinked. 'You're literally proposing to hide in restaurant kitchens?'

'It's a metaphor, *Dummkopf*. I can keep up the investigation online – whatever they tell you, I can try to corroborate it.' She paused. 'And already, now we've switched the focus to suspects, I suppose I can look for evidence of their movements around that day. Opportunity, Tor – the big unknown O in the middle of our table of shame!'

'Leyla – *tak*,' he said. Then, as it seemed almost like a logical thing to say at this point, he went on. 'Um, and I've been thinking. You work two minutes away. It makes sense – especially if you're going to be doing extra-curricular internet stalking – that I cut you a spare set of keys for the house. I know it's not exactly *hyggelig* just yet, but …'

But Leyla was smiling at him. It was one of her nicer smiles.

'Purely for convenient detective work?' she said.

'Oh, *absolut*,' he said. 'Though I was also wondering – if you happened to be free early on Tuesday evening ...'

'Yes?' Her smile got even better.

'You might be able to take receipt of a sofa for me? It's the only time they can deliver, and I've got handball practice.'

Men, thought Leyla, as she schlepped back up Wharton Street. It was not the first word that had come to mind, or the rudest, but it was possibly the most damning. And the worst of it was, she probably *would* end up staying in and signing for his bloody sofa, because, firstly, it was almost certainly *lovely* and she wanted a piece of it; secondly, she was damned if she was subjecting her bum to that kitchen worktop a day longer than necessary; and thirdly, Charlotte Lazerton had in all likelihood been murdered by another of these self-interested male fuckers, and both she and her killer deserved justice, not least in the name of feminism. If it took lowering herself – voluntarily, she had to admit – to the status of Torben's PA for a few days, then that was a bitter irony that would just have to be sweetened by nailing the bastard. God, she mixed her metaphors worse than she did her drinks ...

It was no consolation that Torben's plan seemed, in essence, such a good one. To seize upon this wholly legitimate reason for interviewing their suspects in a friendly, even convivial setting, with no suggestion of crime to raise the hackles – or the defences. The worst thing about police questioning, Leyla thought, was that it was antagonistic by its very nature. You were on one side, the police on the other, and even the most unassailably innocent citizen was hardly likely to answer the questions to their true best knowledge. It was hard to perform with the tape running, across a desk, the long arm of the law snaking into your recollections. Even if you had nothing to hide, a police interview put you on your guard. It was a shame for the officers, too; it meant they so rarely got people at their best. It probably gave them a warped view of human nature.

Now, turn that interview into a deferential invitation for reminiscences, in a comfortable chair, with a glass of wine – throw in a free meal – and who wouldn't unbend a little? She herself, she thought, would unspool her innermost secrets for three courses at Moro and a half-bottle of good Albariño.

And of course, she now remembered just such a meal, with Torben, the night they had celebrated the Dodd inheritance.

Sign for his sodding sofa, indeed. Git.

Torben winced. This house was more than three hundred years old; he wasn't sure its timbers could take many more door slams like that one. Not one of his finest moments.

Back at his *Gymnasium* school, he had briefly tried hurdling. He still remembered the sharp edge of that metal bar, the gash on his shin, when he flunked a jump off the wrong foot. The way the pain, so unanticipated, so sudden, had left him at once gasping and indignant.

Well, he had fluffed this too. But Leyla was hard, wasn't she? Cynical, quicksilver, out of his league. So when he had taken what seemed the extreme risk of offering her her own set of keys – a gesture with such a presumption of intimacy as to be bordering on the insolent – the safe play was surely to defuse the situation with an off-hand comment, something unambiguously practical. Wasn't it? To undercut the flagrant proposition with an unromantic aside, making the step towards each other safe for both of them to negotiate without losing face? Because if it looked like an outright come-on, as if suddenly having a house was meant to make him eligible in her lovely, lovely eyes, she would surely raise an eyebrow and walk away?

Only, Leyla had responded so well to the naked offer. And a little less well to the undercut.

It was just possible, he conceded, that he might have overthought things a little.

Leyla fished out her earbuds. The little *blub* noise of the Bluetooth connection, somehow steadying, as she stormed up the hill. As Dory Previn's fragile, faux-confident voice began to sing 'The Lady with the Braid', to her mind the most perfect expression of female vulnerability ever committed to record, Leyla's pace quickened, to fall in step with the music. Going home – or what passed for home these days. A long, lonely ride indeed.

Monday morning, week three of four, and Torben had agreed to edit the book, fired off three emails to suspects, received two auto-replies, and left four voicemails before the coffee had finished dripping through the filter. He was slowly getting the hang of this sparse house, of living on four floors. So many stairs between rooms. His childhood home had been a one-storey farmhouse, arranged around three sides of a courtyard; ever since, he had lived in flats. If nothing else, the aerobic exercise would do him good. And he liked the emptiness, the austerity of the antique bed, resplendent in the centre of bare boards – the carpets and underlay were all gathered in the spare room, awaiting house clearers.

That had been something, the slow process of slicing, ripping, hauling up strip by strip, layer by layer. Hell on his calves, as he was now discovering. But also rather like peeling off enormous scabs, allowing the raw wood to breathe. Then hours of hunting down rogue staples and tacks left in the boards – at first with the aid of a torch, until he realised by repeated example that the most effective way was simply to tread the floor in socks, allowing the nails to make their presence known to the underside of his feet … there was maybe a moral there, if only he could find it. But it had something to do with Leyla.

And he'd figured out the idiosyncrasies of the shower – *gudskelov*, the water pressure was good – got a temporary rail for his clothes, made full use of the bookcases. By Wednesday he'd have the makings of a living room. Well, a sofa and a couple of upturned cardboard boxes. Next on the list were chairs and a table – a shame that genuine Gustavian baroque chairs were *quite* so covetable, and therefore expensive – it was something about the curves of their backs, so much more delectable than their Queen Anne equivalents. What he really wanted was a Mora clock, and damn the anachronism – but it probably made more sense to prioritise the floorboards – he was reading up on limewash – and then to source some form of storage. And as of this month, he was starting to save a decent chunk of his salary; once the Taschen advance came through, in about a year at this rate, as long as one of the academic posts he was applying for came off and he didn't bankrupt himself by wining and dining potential murderers, then he'd be able to start thinking about the bathroom, the kitchen. Oh – and of course the landline, its baleful Bakelite still haunting the staircase.

The vision of the telephone recalled him to his purpose. First stop: his department, an odd place to visit in what was now technically his vacation period, but a reliable source of official-looking writing paper, all watermarks and corporate headings. And he knew just the cupboard to look in. It wasn't likely to have moved since he had last been there, being very much a stationary stationery cupboard.

It also happened to be on the same floor as Henrik Drever's office. And the man himself was in! Screwing his courage to the sticking place – OK, not the best literary reference when murder was involved – Torben knocked.

Standing, Drever was always that little bit shorter than you expected him to be, and, judging by the way he straightened his spine and stared Torben in the eye, this was something of which he was all too conscious. As usual, he was dressed in chinos and a crisp white shirt, sleeves rolled up. His neat grey beard was trim as ever, practically painted on to his jaw beneath a gleaming bald head. But Torben fancied he was ill – hay fever, maybe? – there was a redness at his septum, around his eyes, a wild and slightly bloodshot look that might equally be the result of too much screen-staring. There was always something about Drever that Torben couldn't quite place, this man both of his world and not, the scholar who had sold his soul to the machine …

'Torben! *Hej*. I got your email.' And Drever seized his hand in a classic corporate shake. As ever, he spoke as if addressing a room full of people, projecting to the back wall, flashing his teeth. 'And look: congratulations. That's a good book series, it'll do wonders for your H-index, and it'll be good for you to edit something like this. It's a key leadership indicator.'

Torben, who neither knew nor cared what an H-index might be, forced a smile. Only now was it dawning on him that this was not just a convenient cover story; he was actually committing to a significant project here. He'd need to find real contributors, do Charlotte justice ...

'So. I can't do dinner any time soon,' Drever was saying – luckily the man was used to monologuing without interruption; Torben had been miles away – 'but an afternoon slot's just opened up tomorrow, my— I've had a cancellation. Shall we do tea? At the Savoy?'

'At the – er, *ja*, why not?' Torben shrugged off his surprise. *For fanden*, tea at the Savoy sounded expensive. At least it was just around the corner.

'Not the whole – how do they say it here – the whole shebang,' Drever clarified, a little wistfully. 'No time. But a pot of tea, maybe a scone ... you can do three-thirty.'

If there was a question mark at the end of that sentence, Torben had missed it. But he thought he could stretch to a couple of scones. '*Tak*, Henrik. Tomorrow then.'

Drever had already turned back to his desk. Rather relieved that he had a day to steel himself before facing the man again, Torben left the office.

One down, he told himself. Four to go.

Barrelling down the too-narrow stairs, Torben found himself brought up short by a slender figure, pinning something to a noticeboard. He stopped. 'Elodie?' His best student. 'Term's over – shouldn't you be off at a rave or something?'

She smiled up at him and pressed a leaflet to his chest. 'Torben!' The space was too small, he took a step back. Disconcertingly, his nose informed him that she, like Leyla, favoured a Le Labo perfume. 'You *must* come. 16th June; that's the Saturday after next. We are meeting at Bomber Command, as usual. Midday exactly.'

Bomber Command? For a second, he thought he must have tripped on the stairs and concussed himself into a parallel universe.

'You are going to love the float,' Elodie was saying. 'It's a homage to Charlotte Lazerton's activism. We have taken your stuff about materiality very much to heart!' And she skipped off, leaving him still holding the flyer.

He found himself looking at an ad for a climate rally – only, one with unusually high production values. The colours really popped … Obviously, that was not the point, and there were some hair-raising, well-sourced facts on the reverse of the sort that momentarily gave him the swooping, fight-or-flight bodily response of someone who genuinely realised they, like everyone else, were in mortal danger from the catastrophic heating of the planet. Then it passed, as it always did. But he *did* like the look of the float – there was a photo – a scale model of the *Titanic*, apparently about the size of a milk van, impaled upon an iceberg made of white text, illegible at this resolution. The flyer encouraged any orchestral musicians reading it to bring their instruments; they were going to recreate the band playing on while the ship went down.

It also had an accessibility statement: 'For anyone wishing to march but deterred by mobility issues, this float comes equipped with deckchairs.'

Torben considered. He had to admit, it was what Charlotte would have wanted. OK, the Saturday after next: Ruth's last weekend as a police officer. Either they'd have solved the case by then, or their single best ally in bringing about an arrest would be given her carriage clock or whatever it was, and be getting the hell out of her job, taking their chances of success with her – since Gary Bassett had made very clear he could assist behind the scenes, but not stick his neck out.

Whichever it was, solution or failure, he couldn't think of a better way to set the seal on the investigation than by marching for the planet.

And maybe Leyla would think a bit better of him for it, too.

Leyla's phone flashed. Squinting in the noon sun of Red Lion Square – she was on her lunchbreak, indulging in an empanada from the ramshackle garden café – Leyla navigated to the link Torben had WhatsApped her. A protest march?

Frowning, and getting grease all over her phone in the process, she messaged back. *Since when did YOU go on marches?*

The reply was swift. *It's about time.*

Leyla scrubbed at the screen with a paper napkin. *I thought you claimed that you found the very act of subsuming yourself within a collective to be inherently alienating and, therefore, both counter-productive and making you feel a bit silly?* Not great grammar, but it would have to do at speed.

I say all kinds of shit, he replied. *Was probably drunk at the time.* Then – *You coming?*

She paused. It was true enough, and it *was* about time he got over his piddling inhibitions. The planet was burning, wasn't it? Still, she thought she could smell a rat.

Who invited you? she wrote.

A pause, this time, before his reply. *Elodie Griffon. One of my students. BTW am in queue at that shop on Coram Street to get keys cut. It's my turn – vi ses.*

Without really knowing why, Leyla began to google Elodie Griffon. It had become almost second nature since she had started profiling their five suspects.

A pigeon was making moves on her empanada, but Leyla wasn't interested.

Elodie Griffon, it transpired, was twenty-two years old. She was blonde. Petite. Slim as a boy. And very, very, very, very, very, *very* French.

The old Iranian – Torben was *pretty* sure he was Iranian – held the keys of 24 Little James Street up to the light. His brow furrowed.

'Will there be a problem?' said Torben. The front door key was ancient, quite distinctive.

'Alas, yes,' the shopkeeper said. 'Something specialist like this' – and he held up the main key – 'it's not easy. But it's not a problem for *me*, it will just cost you more. No, it's just that I recognise the set; I've handled them before, quite recently.'

Something, possibly a bomb or a howitzer, went off in the region of Torben's stomach. 'Can you – can you remember who you copied the key for? I've inherited the house, you see, it might be a security issue …'

'Yes, yes,' the man waved away the explanation. 'I remember. A very loud man, with a shiny head and prissy little beard. Fifties, maybe – the sort that looks after themselves, you know? He had a Nordic air about him, like you yourself. What else … Oh, yes. It was an unusually hot day; everyone was rumpled and sweaty. But this man, he was wearing an immaculate, crisp white shirt.'

13

THE SAVOY HOTEL

Someone was tinkling – the only possible verb for the situation – on a grand piano. The piano was imprisoned in some sort of Raj-style birdcage. The cage sat in the centre of a vast carpet, the design of which reminded Torben of an all-too-vivid fever dream he'd had after eating rather too much of an overripe Gamle Ole. Also afloat upon this fantastical rug were an assortment of chairs, sofas, tables, all of them overflowing with crockery, cakes, teapots and the sort of clientele that, however varied they might be in age, colour, creed, were fundamentally indistinguishable in one overriding particular: they fairly stank of money. Unconsciously, Torben's hand moved to straighten a tie that was not there. He was faintly surprised he'd been allowed past the doorman.

'Torben!' Henrik Drever was discreetly tucked away at a corner table, his own tie bearing the dark green background and subtle stripe that Torben – thanks to Leyla's research – recognised as that of Lundsbergs school. It fairly blared out against the crisp white shirt. Clearly the formal setting demanded something more than his usual open collar. And he had to hand it to the man: the tie was immaculate, the thin end a perfect centimetre shorter than the thick, just peeking out discreetly, the knot above in harmonious proportion to the whole. Yet for all his sleek appearance, there was a sheen on his forehead, and he was fidgeting slightly – presumably the combination of a closed neck and a hot early summer afternoon were taking their toll.

Drever beckoned Torben over. 'Will you join me in a cup of tea?'

Still a little disoriented, Torben glanced down at the table. 'I'm not sure there'll be room. It's quite a small cup.'

'Coffee then?' Jokes were clearly not part of Drever's portfolio.

'*Tak*,' said Torben, sitting down. 'Everyone else seems to have one of those cake stands, are you sure we can just—?'

Drever shrugged. 'They know me here.' And he gestured to a waiter.

'So,' he continued, 'you wanted a statement on Charlotte?'

'More a conversation,' Torben demurred, bringing out his phone. 'Carmen Sabueso – I think you know her, by the way? – wants me to capture people's personal memories, more than their professional opinions – oh, do you mind if I record this?'

'Not at all,' said Drever, who seemed unconcerned by the question – in fact, his attention seemed to be half elsewhere, eyes scanning the room for the returning waiter. The need, perhaps, to play the consummate host, on this, his home terrain?

'*Tak*,' said Torben again. 'So, if I might start with a general question – how would you sum up your friendship with Charlotte Lazerton?'

'Oh, Charlotte and I go back decades. We're old – how should I put it – sparring partners? But we never did let our intellectual – ah, contentions – get in the way of our good personal relations. Quite the opposite; no one liked a fight more than Charlotte. I think she appreciated having colleagues who put up a bit of resistance, gave her a challenge, you know?'

Torben nodded. 'Could you give me an example? I believe, for instance, you had different views on the future direction of the Academy of Western Art?'

As he put the question, he became aware of a low but rising rattle, rhythmic, largely masked by the general hum and the pianist's competent but unenthused take on 'Prelude to a Kiss'. What was it? But Drever was already answering.

'—Academy of Art, as it used to be, of course – and could be again, don't forget; it comes down to the next president to ratify the name change, and the election concludes at the end of next week. But yes, that's a good example. From the outside, this might look like a typical instance of the so-called "culture wars" that apparently infect our discourse. But really, it comes down to two considered interpretations – both, I should stress, perfectly valid – over the remit and mission of one of our most venerable and distinguished artistic institutions. Should we be, as dear Charlotte maintained, chasing this zeitgeist of decolonisation and endless apologism? Or, as I put it in my presidential manifesto, is this a chance to reassert the timeless values upon which the Academy was founded: high standards, the classical lineage, the universal truths of aesthetics and beauty? Actually, I have a copy here – you're a member, aren't you, Torben? There's still time to cast your vote!'

And he brought forth an extremely shiny leaflet. Torben just had time to notice the discreet logo of the multinational corporation that seemed to be bankrolling Drever's bid, when the waiter arrived with the coffee. He made quite a production of rearranging the table, of pouring, and amid it all Drever stood up.

'Bathroom,' he murmured to Torben, and dashed off. Torben thanked the waiter, then, for want of anything better to do, considered the election leaflet. If Charlotte had read this, he thought

– and of course she had, there was an annotated copy in her desk – well then, it must surely have resulted in more than a mere difference of opinion. A convoluted defence of corporate sponsorship by foreign regimes and fossil fuel companies, rooted in an idealised representation of the patronage system that had funded the great works of the Renaissance. A series of mooted partnerships with business and industry that Charlotte would probably have described as the prostitution of the Academy's cultural prestige to the highest bidder. Forget 'sparring partners' – he was faintly surprised that Charlotte had not been the one to kill Drever, rather than the reverse.

Not, he told himself, that there was any evidence Drever had killed Charlotte. Not yet, anyway.

'Sorry about that,' said Drever, oozing back into his seat. He seemed altogether calmer, more assured, and Torben was able to place that rattling noise by virtue of its absence – it must have been the other man's knee, jogging the table from underneath. Clearly the Swede had really needed the loo.

'No problem,' said Torben. 'OK, this is a question I've been told to ask every interviewee, to build up a sort of collage of quotations – can you share with me your last memory of Charlotte? You know, the final time you spoke, that sort of thing.' He tried to make the question as off-hand as possible without overegging it, but Drever seemed unconcerned.

'I'm afraid it's nothing very profound,' he said. 'Nothing to put in the history books, anyway. You know we were near neighbours?'

'No,' said Torben, his heart beating a little faster.

Drever nodded. 'I live on Doughty Mews,' he said, 'it's only a minute or so from her house – her old house, I should say. And thanks to some quirk of custom or bylaw or something, it entitles both of us to the use of the gardens in Mecklenburgh Square – perhaps you know them?'

'I do, actually,' said Torben, his surprise entirely unfeigned. 'I used to play tennis there when I was living in Oarwright College.'

'Then you'll know,' said Drever, 'that you need a key to access them – hence this long preamble: the last time we met was not at work, but when I managed, somehow, to lose my garden key. Rather than go through the shameful business of applying for a new one, I asked if I could borrow hers and make a copy. And I'm glad I did – it means my last memory of Charlotte was not of a steely debate, or a committee meeting, but a twinkle in her eye as she did her neighbour a favour. "Losing your key and sneaking a replacement?" she said. "Henrik, I never took you for a lowly sinner like the rest of us." I'm not sure entirely what she meant by that – but it was the last time I saw her laugh. I appreciated that. And the favour, of course.'

Another man, Torben thought, might have mustered up a tear, or at least a wistful expression. But Drever was po-faced as he delivered the anecdote. And his impersonation of Charlotte's cut-glass accent definitely came under the heading of 'too soon'.

'And you didn't see her when you returned the original key?'

Drever shook his head. 'I posted them back through the letterbox; she may have been in, she may not. Either way, I'm glad our last meeting was a friendly one.' He seemed keen to stress the point.

'And can you remember exactly when this was?' said Torben, certain his heartbeat must be at least as audible as Drever's knee had been. He hadn't missed the plural 'them' in that last answer. If Drever had in fact copied the *front* door key, was laying this false trail of the garden access in order to put him off the scent … He pressed on. 'She died – I'm not sure if you know this – on Tuesday 24th April. I can only imagine the poignancy if you posted back the—'

Drever shook his head. 'No. No, it can't have been any time as late as that. You see, the week she died, I was away at a conference. In Brussels.'

'I still think he did it, mind,' said Torben.

'Tor, he *can't* have done,' said Leyla, turning her laptop so he could see the screen. 'It all checks out. Three-day conference in Brussels. Keynote speech. There are pictures: here he is, droning on about the academy as a civic corporation; here he is schmoozing at the reception; here's a thread where he live-tweets another speaker …'

'Three days – which three?' Torben leapt upon the point.

She shrugged. 'Monday 23rd to Wednesday 25th. And we know she died on the Tuesday—'

'We *think* she died on the Tuesday—'

'The police seem pretty certain. And then there are the used tea things, and the diary entry and the Posavacs' testimony …'

'Have you got the conference programme? Which day was he speaking?'

'Monday. But the reception was—'

'Brussels is on the Eurostar,' Torben said. 'The house is fifteen minutes' walk from St Pancras.'

'And if it comes to it, I'm sure the police will be able to check whether he flitted to and fro like a thief in the night, to do in his old adversary in the middle of a busy social event,' said Leyla, actually rolling her eyes. 'But for now, what we have is a big fat alibi. MOM, remember? And as far as we're concerned, the O in the middle of that anagram has just shrunk to the size of a squirrel's sphincter. Time to move on to the next one, Torben!'

'But he's such a *bastard*.'

'Well, by all accounts so is Simon Grey. The others might be too, beneath the surface. What happened to objectivity?'

'What happened to intuition? And "objectively", his is the clear-cut case. Not just a big job on the line, a career-changing presidency, but by the sound of it, a series of juicy corporate cheques into the bargain. He lives on Doughty Mews, those houses cost literal millions, as in two, three million – not to mention his penchant for tea at the Savoy. He might be in urgent need of the extra income. And the keys, Leyla – he admits to having had a means of entry!'

'Or he told what he considered to be a moving anecdote – by his desiccated standards, anyway – unaware that the possession of a set of her keys could in any way be seen as compromising, because he has *no idea that she was murdered*. You've said yourself that she was a bit all over the place. He might have asked for the garden key and got given the whole lot by mistake, which is why your man in the shop recognised them. Would Drever even mention the keys, unsolicited, if there was anything underhand about having had access to them?'

'If he knows I'm living in the house, then yes, of course he would! He'd know I might find out they'd been copied, and want to get in first with an innocent-sounding cover story.'

'Torben, look me in the eyes and tell me one thing: is this all just because he's Swedish?'

'Arghhh! Don't make me say it.'

'Say what? That you're a bigoted Dane who doesn't trust his neighbours?'

'For helvede!'

'Oh, that.'

*

Ordered by Leyla to take a walk, so that he might 'cool off his great fat head', Torben found himself turning left at the striking, triangular slice of house at the end of Doughty Street – down Roger Street – and up Doughty Mews. Which, he wondered, was Drever's residence? Remembering the Swede's exquisite cup of Darjeeling, his money was on one of the more ostentatious addresses, half-hidden by climbing roses and wisteria, pink-painted bricks above colourful front doors.

Best not to linger. Emerging onto Guilford Street, he was only half-surprised to find that his feet were leading him towards the private gardens in the centre of Mecklenburgh Square, screened by a towering profusion of plane trees.

He was nearly at the gate when a jerk around knee level sent him flying, to land with an ignominious bump on sun-warmed tarmac. Glancing up, he saw a harassed young woman reeling in a trio of mastiffs, whose taut-stretched leads must have been the boobytrap of which he had fallen foul. She looked far too slight a person to be entrusted with beasts that size – and where the dogs were sleek, groomed and glossy, she was a shabby slip of a thing. Half shame-faced, half smiling, she hastened towards him, dogs milling everywhere, but he was already on his feet.

'Sorry!' she said, with a thick eastern European accent.

'My fault entirely,' he said, grinning back. Then a thought struck him. The young woman was evidently a professional. 'Can I ask a rather random question?' he said. 'You don't happen to have met a fellow dog walker by the name of Ximena Podenco, do you?'

Her rueful smile vanished. 'No,' she said. 'I know no one of that name. Sorry, I must keep these dogs exercised ...' and she was gone, leaving behind her only an ache in Torben's backside, an unsightly deposit by one of her charges – and the unmistakeable scent of fear.

14

THE WOLSELEY

'But this is fucking *gold*, Tor,' said Wilson. 'High-quality audio of the suspects discussing the victim? And you're saying I can't have it for the podcast?'

'*No*,' said Torben, for the third time. He had stopped by the Hayford Theatre to see how rehearsals were going and to update Wilson on the investigation, and he was already regretting it. 'If you won't take it from me, ask Leyla; you'd be in breach of who knows how many confidentiality—'

Wilson waved this away. 'I won't release it till you've caught whichever bastard it is, obviously. Then the rest will be relaxed, and the culprit won't be in any position to complain.'

Torben did not think this was how either the law or these sorts of people worked, and said so. But he kept his real concern to himself. Ever since yesterday's run-in with the dog walker in Mecklenburgh Square, he had been thinking more seriously about the risks they were running. Of the presumed cover-up that had so far only extended to minor corruption – but that might, plausibly, go rather further. Especially if politics, espionage, big business were involved. For the sake of their own safety as much as everything else, he realised, he ought to pin a lot of their hopes on his next interview; hope that the supposedly least well-connected of the suspects should be the one to let something slip, that the motive should be no more than bad blood, something personal. An anti-climax, maybe, but a reassuring one. He was off to dine with Katherine Trigg.

As he stretched his legs down Shaftesbury Avenue, he began to wonder if it was just missing handball last night that had put him so much on edge. It had been worth it – the eBayed sofa, when unwrapped, was magnificent in a rickety, decadent, austere sort of way, and a well-placed bolster would hide the slightly dubious-looking stain. And the sacrifice had gone some way towards mollifying Leyla, who had been sounding frankly mutinous after their disagreement over Drever's alibi. But that weekly unleashing of energy on the handball court was not just a luxury, it had become foundational to his equilibrium. Now, unspent, he knew himself to be fidgety, cramped, and all his chemicals and hormones that little bit askew. He felt ready to launch himself at someone, in violence or passion – if that someone were Leyla, it might be either – and the last thing he was in the mood for was a genteel sit-down with a septuagenarian. Nonetheless, she had responded with alacrity to his invitation, and this was her only free night for a week or more. It was already Wednesday of the third week of Ruth's notice period – and they were running out of time. So. Three courses it was. The worst thing was, Leyla had not interpreted this dinner as the act of a martyr. If anything, she seemed to think he was somehow lucky to be off for supper at the Wolseley. Sometimes she just didn't understand.

'Sometimes,' said Leyla, 'I just don't understand what he's playing at.'

For the first time in what felt like far too long, she was having dinner at the Thompsons' – Ruth's family home, a cheery semi-detached out in Leytonstone. And yes, she was playing up to the attention of Ruth's parents and sister, but it was what they wanted. An honest, warm-hearted, pious, community-minded family, they desperately needed the odd injection of gossip and rancour into their general bonhomie, and the risqué – but, crucially, chaste – travails of Ruth's glamorous barrister friend were as catnip to their open, concerned, almost ludicrously transparent interest. Ruth, clattering pans around in the background, said nothing.

'Young men these days,' said Mr Thompson – his name, she knew, was Joe, but to Leyla he would always be Mr Thompson – 'have no sense of duty. And they don't know a good woman when they see one! Now, in my day, we knew better than to look a gift horse in the mouth—'

'And who are you calling a horse, Joe Thompson, I'd like to know?' chipped in Ruth's mother. 'Me or Leyla?'

'Don't answer that, Dad,' said Mary, Ruth's younger sister. 'Not if you know what's good for you.'

'Dinner's up!' said Ruth, heaving an enormous pan of rice and peas into the middle of the table, and going back for the side dishes. A fragrant steam wafted over them, and Leyla, stomach rumbling, let the subject of Torben's 'shilly-shallying', as Mrs Thompson called it, slide away.

Entering through the art deco doors of the Wolseley, Torben felt that same self-consciousness as in the Savoy. Weren't years of an Oxford education meant to inure you to this sort of thing, to make you feel at home anywhere? Right now, he felt he stood out mostly for not looking like a chess piece; the place was a masterclass in monochrome, all chequerboard tiles and gargantuan, squared-off, black and white pillars that rose to a vaulted ceiling. Maybe this was how Alice had felt in Wonderland.

Five minutes later, he was altogether more comfortable, ensconced at a corner table, mentally reviewing the goods on his yet-to-arrive guest. In deference to the occasion, he was in a light linen suit, in the pocket of which was a printout of the old school photograph Leyla had unearthed. And up his sleeve – metaphorically speaking, obviously, he had no wish to spoil the line of his jacket more than absolutely necessary – were all the facts he had cribbed about Katherine Trigg's pet obsession; the writer and barrister John Mortimer, whose biography she claimed to be writing in that one single blogpost; along with everything Leyla had been able to tell him about *Rumpole of the Bailey* – a television, book and radio series, written by Mortimer. Apparently it featured a lot of legal insight, humour and compassion for the underdog that Torben should praise – and a lot of casual misogyny that he would do better not to mention.

A stir among the waiting staff; this was surely her – yes – frailer even than he had remembered her, walking with the aid of a rather natty cane – she must have come in a taxi – and leaning indulgently on the arm of a strapping young waiter. Hair in a white bob, dressed in a demure velvet skirt suit pitched somewhere between Theresa May and Mary Poppins, and with a definite glint in her eye as Torben was pointed out to her. Hastily he rose to greet her, and she flushed with something like pleasure at the attention. This would, perhaps, be easier than he had thought. To his own surprise and slight discomfort, he was usually a hit with older women.

*

'What's an acceptable age range, do you think, Ruth? Shall we say ... mid twenties to late thirties? For reference, this French girl is nine years younger than Torben and has somehow persuaded him to go on a climate march for the first time in his life.'

Ruth and Leyla had retired to Ruth's childhood bedroom; the décor and stuffed animals mingled awkwardly with the trappings of the professional police officer. They were both sitting, cross-legged, on the single bed, and for a moment, Leyla's indignant emphasis upon Elodie Griffon's age drew attention to their own incongruity. Really, it was shameful that Ruth should be reduced to this, however temporarily, just because she had found the courage to split from the man whose attitude to marriage had been far more infantilising than any number of fluffy rabbits and glow-in-the-dark stars stuck to the ceiling could ever be.

'I thought,' said Ruth, in the slow, calm voice that Leyla recognised at once as the one she used for de-escalation, 'that you were meant to be cyberstalking murder suspects? Not setting up yet another dating profile.'

'I deleted all the old ones,' said Leyla. 'Besides, the other stuff's run dry. Take Katherine Trigg – Torben's dinner date for tonight. You know how many photographs of her I found online? One! A school team portrait – lacrosse, if you'd believe it, of all the public-school clichés, not even jolly hockey sticks ...'

Ruth shifted a little awkwardly beside her on the bed, and Leyla remembered that Ruth had, rather incongruously, gone in for both hockey and badminton at her comprehensive.

'It's not even a *good* photo,' Leyla moved on swiftly. 'All grainy. They must be sixteen, seventeen – I found the picture for the year after, when they'd've been in, what do you call it, the upper sixth form, and it's much better quality, but Trigg isn't in that one for some reason, just Charlotte ... speaking of which, I need to choose *my* photo for this app. You can help me pick.'

'Well, log in to your Instagram then,' said Ruth, passing her a laptop. 'I'd rather see them full-size. Phone pictures are always so unsatisfactory.' Sometimes Ruth really did sound more like a maiden aunt than could be good for her. But then, if she was cultivating this thing with Wilson, there was no need for Ruth to reconcile herself to the realities of online dating.

It wasn't that Leyla felt threatened by the Griffon child, exactly. But the fact that she had registered even the tiniest trace of pique, coming on top of the take-receipt-of-this-sofa debacle, had forced her to confront the unpalatable truth that she did seem to be developing a liking for Torben after all. Still, if he was going to beat around the bush, she might as well check there was nothing better on offer. Who knew, maybe London had acquired some genuinely eligible men in the past few months. Stranger things had happened. The last thing she wanted was to settle too soon, and she had the feeling that Torben was the sort who would stick around ...

While Ruth scrolled through Instagram, making intermittent noises of admiration and shock at Leyla's images, Leyla swiped through the potential matches that had loaded based on her initial preferences. 'God,' she said, 'aren't there meant to be eight million or so people in London? And yet the first person I match with is a boy I did my Bar course with who I know for a fact is only into heiresses.'

Ruth looked over. 'He looks far too boring for you. Really, I don't know why you're putting yourself through this again, it seems so much effort when you're already juggling a job *and* a murder enquiry.'

'Fuck,' said Leyla. 'Sorry, Ruth. But look who's just come up.'

'Zak Cremello,' Ruth read. 'Should I have heard of him?'

'Some venture capitalist that Torben knows. A multimillionaire and, by all accounts, the absolute epitome of arsedom. Is this really the sort of man I'm meant to be compatible with?'

'Well, I know this lovely boy with a house in Bloomsbury, some sort of art historian,' said Ruth. 'I'll hook you up if you like. Oh, and if you *must* carry on with this pretence that you're still on the market, then use literally any picture of you in existence, Leyla, you honestly cannot go wrong …'

Ruth was openly giggling now as she explored further. 'Leyla, why have you favourited so many photos of – let me see – Danish handball captain Mikkel Hansen?'

Could the woman sitting across from him *really* be an ex-captain of a lacrosse team, even at school level? Admittedly, it would have been a long time ago, but her frame, stature, bearing, quite apart from the use of the stick, spoke of a habitually sedentary existence that must stretch back decades.

So far, the toughest part of their dinner had been the ordering. Trigg, who apparently knew this place well, had opted for the chicken soup with dumplings, a sort of Mittel-European Jewish classic, followed up by the Wiener Holstein. This, the menu informed him, was a normal veal schnitzel augmented with anchovies, capers and a fried egg. It sounded like very heaven and was going to cost him a small fortune. And while Torben had allowed himself the indulgence of some pickled herring to begin with, his choice of main had been mushroom gnocchi: solid and unspectacular at the best of times, but practically gruel when set next to that dreamboat of a schnitzel.

The reality had borne out his worst fears. Those golden breadcrumbs. The action of her knife easing through the soft flesh beneath. That umami hit, he could just imagine the pungency, setting off the rounded flavour beneath. *For fanden.* It was hard to warm to someone when they had so comprehensively out-ordered you.

It would have been difficult in any case. Stock-exchange wizard she might once have been, but Katherine Trigg was now something of a monomaniac – he had seen it in other retirees suddenly free to devote themselves to a true passion – and if the subject were not her ongoing, much maligned biography of 'the Great Author', it was hard to keep her attention. At one point, she had asked who the big funders in his line of work were, and when his reply had included the Marie Curie foundation, she had started talking, rather vaguely, about free makeup samples. It had taken him several minutes to realise she must have heard *Marie Claire* foundation. She did not even seem particularly keen to discuss Charlotte, the ostensible reason she was here in the first place.

'Oh, a *lot* of water under that bridge, you know,' she said.

'You were estranged, I believe – but more recently, you'd started seeing each other again?' He posed as question what he took to be fact; though her initials were absent from thirty years' worth of records, she had cropped up a couple of times in this year's appointments diary.

'Ye-es,' she drawled slowly, as if uncertain that was the word she meant. 'We both thought it was time for a … rapprochement.'

'Might I ask why you quarrelled in the first place?' he tried. She pursed her lips, considering another forkful of divine-smelling schnitzel. He tried again. 'Not to speak to each other for – how long can it have been? – and then to reconcile, only to have her taken from you almost at once, that seems extremely cruel!'

'Fifty-six years!' said Katherine. The thought of so much time seemed, somehow, to give her comfort.

'So … what prompted the change of heart?'

'You know, John Mortimer's divorce from his first wife was a very bitter affair, but by the time she died, they had become the best of friends again. He was a very big-hearted man.' She seemed to consider this a satisfactory answer. 'He was sent down, you know, from his Oxford college, for a homosexual relationship with another boy. Still, it didn't seem to hold him back, either in his career or his more – ah – more conventional *amours*.'

Either she was raving, or there was some incredibly juicy subtext swimming about just beneath the reach of Torben's hook. Time for his trump card, perhaps.

'Katherine, I wonder if I could share this with you – the book series editor is keen on personal images where possible, and it's one of the few photographs we have of Charlotte's schooldays. I'm hoping you can provide some context.' And he retrieved the printout from his pocket.

An unknown hand, presumably one of the other players, had annotated the team portrait at the bottom, giving surnames left to right. If the captioning could be believed, the wiry, terrier-like girl squeezed tight beside Charlotte, their arms round each other, was an earlier incarnation of the woman now putting the cutlery together on her empty plate. She was dwarfed, in the image, less by Charlotte's height, which was unexceptionable, than by a sense of personality. Well, that and the protective gear, something like a ninja turtle, that, as goalkeeper, only Charlotte was wearing.

'Mm, I see.' Was it only Torben's imagination, or had the room temperature just dropped several degrees? Maybe the staff had left the door open? 'Yes, that's the Brook Hall lacrosse team. We were in the lower sixth.'

He waited for more. But the pursed mouth was back in force, putting him uncomfortably in mind of – what had been Leyla's phrase? – a squirrel's sphincter?

'Well, thank you for an enjoyable evening,' said Katherine, in tones more appropriate to a funeral. 'No, I shan't stay for dessert, I really must be going.' And she mimed to a waiter to call her a cab.

Oh, God, what had been wrong with the picture? They had been getting on so well! In desperation, he held up his hand.

'Katherine, if I may, there's just one question I'm asking all my interviewees – if you wouldn't mind giving me one more minute – I'd love to hear … what can you remember of the final time you saw Charlotte? Your last memory of her?'

She paused, hesitated … then resumed her seat.

'Leyla,' said Ruth, 'has Torben been sending you random clips of his old professor?'

'Of course,' said Leyla. 'At first it seemed sort of obsessive. But I rather like them. She's in danger of becoming my role model.'

'Amal Clooney will be devastated,' said Ruth. 'Well, there's this clip, from a podcast I think, that I've listened to a couple of times recently, while I've been trying to process my divorce from Jon. Listen …' and she brought up an interview. There was no video, just a placeholder image with the legend *Artlover Podcast: Valentine's Day Special*. Charlotte was already in mid-flow when the clip began.

'You know, Shani, I do think people – especially young people – underestimate the danger of solipsism – selfishness – self-love – that inheres in "being in love with someone". It is so easy to assume that you are thinking only of the other, when in fact you are thinking, predominantly, of your Love – your ear hears the proper noun as synonymous with their name, but your mind dwells on the love itself. Thus your role, your yearning to please, your devotion, occupies far more of your energy than the stuff that makes up the other's life. By which I mean, less their mood, their person even, than what they like for breakfast, or how they worry for their little sister's eczema.'

'It sounds,' said the interviewer's voice, rather caustically for what was presumably quite a fluffy podcast, 'like you're speaking from experience.'

'Oh, but naturally!' said Charlotte. 'That's what wisdom is, isn't it? The accumulation of an awful lot of mistakes. Sometimes when I think about all my own past idiocies I see them before me in a glittering pyramid of folly, like the Ferrero Rocher in that old advertisement. They're what qualifies me to talk such sententious guff now. But the point stands. We place Love upon a pedestal – apologies, my metaphors all seem to be about classical architecture today – when we should be busy surveying the foundations. If you, listener, aren't certain whether your beloved is worth the candle, then next time they profess their undying devotion and offer to slay you a dragon, ask them to fetch you your favourite childhood story, or buy you some more of your favourite *comfortable* underwear, and see what they come up with. But only, of course, if you think yourself capable of reciprocating.'

'Dame Charlotte, it's Valentine's Day, and you're on a public podcast – are there any idiocies in particular for which you'd care to apologise on air? I'm sure the listeners would be fascinated.'

'Oh no, I don't think so. Best keep those sweeties wrapped up, much more seemly. Really, it's so terribly indulgent, isn't it, regret? So – what's the *mot juste*? – so "first world". After a certain age, we, who are free, torment ourselves with the paths not taken, the lives we could have lived; in a word, with regrets. Yet is this not simply the luxury of having agency, of having choice? Regret is something you can only afford to feel if you had alternatives available, the power to make choices. We forget that, for most people across the world and across history, a life is made up of very few choices and, if lived over again a dozen times, it would end up looking very much the same.'

'Well, speaking of "across the world", that brings me on to your next choice of painting—'

Ruth ended the audio.

'And exactly what,' said Leyla, aware she was sounding every bit as chippy as the interviewer, 'was that in aid of? All that stuff about love and chocolates?'

'Oh, I don't know,' said Ruth, off-hand. 'There just might be a moral there, if you care to fish for it, about what really matters between two people, and what is just distraction.'

'She must have been distracted by something,' said Katherine. 'Because she answered the phone in that merry way of hers – you know, "London seven-four-two-six-triple-four-oh", as if it was still the fifties – and I said, oh, something like, "Hello, dear, it's Katherine," and then there was this funny sort of noise and the line went silent. Landline on the blink, I daresay. Still, it's a nice detail for your memory section, isn't it? Right up to the end, she was still performing this charming version of the elderly eccentric.'

As opposed, thought Torben, to this charm*less* version of the elderly eccentric. 'And when did you say this final phone call was?'

Again, the pursed lips, but in thought this time. 'A Tuesday, I think. Yes, I'm sure of it, because they were cleaning the windows. Yes, the Tuesday of the week before that silly little girl from the police called round to tell me she'd ... passed.' And she stood up to leave.

Torben couldn't help it. 'But that – that was the day she died!' he said. 'Katherine, this might be very important: can you remember *exactly* when in the day this call took place?'

'You mean—?' She had gone very white. 'Oh my. That sound ... *that* was the sound of her ...' She looked on the point of fainting. 'No, I'm sorry, I can't recall the exact time. I believe that's my taxi now; I'm sorry but I really *must* be going. It was *so* nice having this little talk, thank you for the supper.'

And, at quite a creditable pace considering her mobility issues, Katherine Trigg swept out of the restaurant. Breathing hard in both elation and frustration, Torben checked his phone, ensuring the recording had saved. It was crucial that he and Leyla could listen back to every detail of this conversation.

'Assuming,' said Ruth, 'that nothing definitive comes out of Torben's conversation with the old schoolfriend this evening, who's your money on for your killer?'

'Well, Drever's alibi rules him out, even if Tor's too hung up on national prejudice to admit it,' said Leyla. 'Logically, it's the MP – he's the only one we can place on the scene, and after all, he is—'

'Actually, Leyla, you'd be surprised how principled most politicians can be.' It was the closest she'd heard Ruth come to an actual rebuke in what seemed like forever. 'You don't go into politics if you don't seriously want to do good in the world, it's just not worth the hassle. It's just that—'

'Different people's takes on morality vary?' said Leyla.

'Not often to the extent that murder becomes an available option.'

'*You*,' said Leyla, 'will be the best local politician of all time, and one day we will continue this conversation in your mayor's office at City Hall. But you really do have to stop seeing the best in everyone all the time. They'll only take advantage.'

'Let them,' said Ruth. 'I'd sooner that than choose to see the *worst* in people.' She paused. 'Except for those two guys on your dating app. Frankly, they looked like absolute dicks.'

Sometimes, Ruth didn't sound entirely like a maiden aunt after all.

Since, for now at least, Ruth still had work in the morning, Leyla soon called it a night. Heading downstairs, she found that Ruth's mother was still up. 'I wanted a word,' she whispered, pulling Leyla into the kitchen before she could leave. 'I had to say – don't pity her.'

Leyla's eyes and nostrils flared. 'I would never—'

And there must have been something in her manner that convinced the worried older woman, because her whole body relaxed, and she laid a palm soft against Leyla's cheek. 'She did the right thing, didn't she, our Ruth?' she said. 'That boy, that husband of hers – he never knew what a treasure he was holding.'

'He wasn't fit to lick her boots,' Leyla said.

'Well …' Mrs Thompson demurred. Clearly, there were limits. 'But we are so, so proud of her, Joe and I. The police, that boy – it's their loss. Whatever she does next—'

'Will be brilliant,' said Leyla. 'I don't doubt it.'

'You're a good girl now,' Mrs Thompson sniffed. 'Too skinny, mind.'

'Good night, Mrs Thompson.'

'Good night, Leyla. And God bless.'

'Um, yes … the same to you …'

15

ST GEORGE'S SQUARE

The sofa creaked a little ominously as Leyla sat back, the recording at an end. First, she said nothing at all. Then, she said, 'Bugger me.' Finally, she said, 'Torben, you're an idiot.'

'Why?'

'At the end there – you more or less gave the whole thing away! Listen back to, um, this bit …' and she found the spot. Perched either side of the phone, they both heard him say again, 'Katherine, this might be very important: can you remember *exactly* when in the day this call took place?'

'You sound,' Leyla said, pausing the recording, 'exactly like an amateur detective. It couldn't be clearer that you're treating the death as suspicious. No wonder she makes her excuses and skedaddles.'

'But I had to ask!' he protested. 'She was leaving anyway. And if we could fix the exact moment of Charlotte's murder – it might be enough to pin it on Simon Grey—'

'Or rule him out entirely,' she said. Ever since last night's conversation with Ruth, she'd been trying to be more fair-minded. 'What was it future sex-pest Marko Posavac said? The fat man in the suit left the house "after two". We can corroborate that, even narrow it down further – it was as Marko got home, and, especially if he goes to that school just round the corner, it'll be easy to determine exactly when his class were sent home early. *Early*, remember – so before three o'clock, I'd imagine, which leaves plenty of time for someone else to—'

'Wait,' said Torben. 'Say we call it quarter or half past two as a working hypothesis. That's when Simon Grey *leaves* Charlotte's house. There's something off about that, isn't there? When do people normally finish taking afternoon tea with a friend in civilised society? Four o'clock, maybe? If Grey left in a hurry by two-thirty, doesn't that suggest something out of the ordinary – a need to, as you so eloquently put it, skedaddle?'

He paused. 'If he *pushed* her, and if we could match the time of Trigg's phone call to his departure, then that would clinch it. But what about the alternative method – that he slipped something in her tea to make her dizzy, induce a fall? In that case, the phone call *would* have come after his departure – the only way it lets him off the hook entirely, which is a very dated and unfortunate pun I did *not* mean to make, is if Trigg called much *earlier* – but in that case, his visit, entry and departure make no sense whatsoever. Unless he found the door open, saw the body, lost his nerve and bolted? Wait, I'm confusing myself …'

'Not only yourself,' said Leyla. 'You've gone from total certainty to three contradictory scenarios, all equally implausible, and you didn't even *get* the time of the phone call. Which, by the way, does not surprise me. Look, forget Grey for a minute, it's Trigg who was pigging out on schnitzel. And I'm much more interested in what this new evidence says about her as a suspect than as a witness.'

'Leyla, you didn't *see* her. I doubt if she could push so much as a Slinky down the stairs.'

'A Slinky?'

'*Ja* – it's a sort of children's toy. Made of this coiled spring – you really don't …? Look, the Slinky is not germane; the point is, I'm not actually sure she could have climbed the stairs in the first place, and if she *did* put through a phone call from her home – which, by the way, is somewhere in Belgravia and quite a journey even by taxi – then that gives her a pretty solid alibi.'

'Which is probably why she mentioned it, just to be on the safe side,' said Leyla. 'That whole swooning act at the end – saying that Charlotte had "passed" – the whole thing sounds pretty contrived on the recording. Like she was engineering the chance to perform her surprise and distress. Having spent the previous hour or so sizing you up as just the sort of gallant milksop likely to fall for the helpless-old-lady routine.'

'But—'

'Hup, I'm not finished … No, how about this: she knows a log of the phone call will exist, so she draws attention to it in a way that shows her in an innocent light, and places her far from the scene of the crime. But what if – work with me here, Tor – what if that phone call, which by the sound of it was *the last significant action before Charlotte's death* – what if it wasn't a coincidence? Not something that happened at the same time as the murder … but the means by which the murder was carried out?!'

Torben took a moment. 'You think Katherine Trigg murdered Charlotte … down the phone line?'

'Maybe.'

'How?'

'Well,' said Leyla, 'that bit needs some work, I admit.'

*

'Look,' said Torben, knowing it was more than his life was worth to laugh. 'The logical thing to do before anything else is to see if we can trace that phone call. I'll get on to my tame policeman, Detective Sergeant Bassett, see if he can oblige – oh, and I may as well see if he can ask questions at Marko Posavac's school, to check exactly when his class was sent home early on the day of the murder – perhaps Meera could do that. If those two question marks become facts, we have the exact time of death, and locations for two of our five suspects. It's progress, Leyla!'

'*Three* of our suspects,' she said. 'Since we know Drever was in Brussels.'

He shot Leyla a look that bounced right off her. 'Now, where did I put Gary Bassett's card …?'

They found it, eventually, in a neat pile on Charlotte's desk, along with the old, dog-eared business cards for pest control and the dog walkers.

'Even your subconscious is a little bit anal,' Leyla observed.

'Why is it,' said Torben, ignoring this, 'that when you've lost something, you always find it in the last place you look?'

Leyla raised an eyebrow. How was she so *good* at that …

'No, but really,' he said. 'Why not keep looking after you've found it, until you've looked everywhere – who knows, might it not be somewhere else as well? Wouldn't that constitute – what's the phrase? – due diligence? A good historian doesn't stop searching the archive just because they found the first thing they were looking for. Isn't it negligent to stop looking, simply because you've got what you were after?'

'"These are deep waters, Watson,"' said Leyla. 'You sound like someone who never invested in a STONi locator. What's your point?'

'I don't know,' he said. 'Perhaps that, after I've given Gary a call, I should go back to Charlotte's memoirs ... I'd set aside the early chapters, the schooldays stuff. But something Katherine Trigg said – or, no, something she *didn't* say – was it about the photograph? It just makes me think there might be something there ...'

'Hah!' said Leyla. 'So you *do* think Trigg could have killed her. Down the ... down the phone line ...'

'Leyla,' said Torben, 'can I ask you something? When you check your wrist, what do you see – the time? Your watch? Or both?'

'The – the time?'

'Yes, I thought so.' And, pleased to have concluded the conversation on this rather brilliant if gnomic observation, he turned to his phone. Time to put the Bassett on the scent.

The memoirs, however, were disappointing. Based on Katherine's identification of the photo as being taken during their spell in the lower sixth form, Torben had skimmed the account of that time and the year following, trying not to get absorbed in the contours of the lyrical modernist prose. He had found what he was looking for – hah! – almost at once. The problem was, it was a note to self from Charlotte.

Query: all the brouhaha over self, KT & RS – to include, or still too sensitive? K v touchy, R poss. litigious – best check. Poss. rapprochement w/K? TBC.

Reluctantly, Torben photographed the note and sent it to Leyla. Hadn't he felt like Alice, last night? But it was Leyla who was likelier to go chasing down this particular rabbit hole ...

He turned again to the final exercise book in the series, those last pages before the neat excision. He'd counted – there was definitely a good quarter of the book's pages missing. It was not as if the account was abbreviated mid-sentence: Charlotte had already structured the memoir in chapters, which meant there was a natural break which, to the casual reader, might look like the end of the volume. As he had quoted to Leyla, the chapter ended, in classic cliff-hanger style, on the eve of a meeting with a 'sober-suited chappie from the Foreign Office'. This was in 1984, the year before Gorbachev came to power in the USSR and initiated the first in a series of summits with Reagan that – and Torben admitted to himself that his knowledge of Cold War history was very much the child's ABC version – would lead to military de-escalation and a thawing of relations. In 1984, Charlotte had been in her prime and in her pomp, an endowed professor at the Courtauld at an enviably young age, and already *the* recognised world authority on the Peredvizhniki Movement. She had just returned from her first cultural mission to Russia, visiting not just Leningrad and Moscow but, true to her principles and her subject, embarking on an extensive tour of the regions – that was to say, the westernmost regions. It was quite a big place, the USSR.

Though Torben had not read every word, the trip seemed to have been highly successful, and Charlotte had done much to advance Anglo-Russian relations on a personal – which was to say, sexual – level, as much as in the cultural and political spheres. Not that Torben was counting, but she had put in some extensive nights of networking with at least three museum curators, an ambassadorial attaché, a young woman of no stated occupation, and two of her own security detail – the latter pair concurrently. At the same time, a series of loans for a major exhibition had been agreed, a conference set up, and a commission established. To her credit, Charlotte not only gave these issues equal prominence with her romantic encounters, she made them sound almost as interesting. Then, on her return to grey old Blighty ... the literal tap on the shoulder. A polite murmur in the ear. And a formal invitation to—

Torben's phone buzzed beside him. One new message, number withheld.

Dear Dr Helle, I was delighted to learn of your request to interview me. I have such fond memories of Charlotte. You mention dinner – why not come to mine? 7pm tonight. 124 St George's Square SW1, Flat B. No need to bring a bottle, but your friend Ms Moradi is very welcome to join us. Best, Jonathan Azawakh.

Oh *lort*.

'I'm not sure which I find more disconcerting,' said Leyla. 'The subtle implication of omniscience – "your friend Ms Moradi" is a frankly terrifying touch – or the absolute certainty that we'd both come. No means of reply, just a few hours' notice. It's a summons. I don't like it.'

'It's honest, anyway,' said Torben. 'No false pretence that we have any choice in the matter. I wonder if this really *is* his place, or some sort of ... safe house?'

'The whole point about safe houses,' Leyla pointed out, 'is that you don't go divulging their location to all and sundry. Besides, I looked it up. St George's Square is peak palatial real estate. Pimlico, effectively on the river.'

Torben tried some quick mental geography. 'So – just across the bridge from MI6? That weird shiny building from the Bond films?'

'I don't think we're going to be subjected to rendition,' Leyla mused. 'It all seems rather more like the velvet-glove tactic.'

'Have you ever seen anyone put on a velvet glove? It sounds way more disturbing than an iron fist.'

'Look at it this way: at least you're not paying for this dinner. *I* get to come along for once. And it's a Thursday night. You don't even have to miss your five-a-side football session.'

'Yes, but, Leyla, in order to play five-a-side football, you need kneecaps.'

'Ableist.'

St George's Square was, if anything, even more imposing than either the Savoy or the Wolseley. Approaching from the north and already reeling from an onslaught of thrusting porticos – Torben was sure he'd contracted something debilitating on Lupus Street – they found themselves walking the entire length of what felt not unlike a gauntlet – 'an execution squad, more like,' said Leyla – of early Victorian townhouses. Plunged into shadow by the looming trees of the long garden at their right, menaced by six storeys of pedimented privilege at their left, Torben and Leyla finally reached number 124, the last house in the row.

It didn't help that they'd been walking more and more slowly, the nearer they came.

'I think, since this is patently all my fault, I should do the honours,' said Torben, stretching out his finger to the buzzer for Flat B. Behind, to either side, arrow-tipped iron railings hemmed them in; the plunge to the basement level felt like a moat. Torben steeled himself to push.

And the door swung open. 'You made it!' beamed Jonathan Azawakh, CMG. Torben blinked. The Man from the Ministry was wearing an oven mitt and matching apron. Both were covered in a pattern of cartoon chickens.

*

'Apologies if we've rather overdressed!' said Leyla, following Azawakh's crumpled cord trousers up the communal staircase to the first floor.

'Not at all!' he smiled over his shoulder. 'I could do with a bit of glamour around the place. I don't know what Bedford Row is like, but all day at work I've seen nothing but dull suits and duller ties. Here, this is me,' and he held open the door.

Leyla had guessed as much by the scents wafting out of the first-floor flat. All manner of alliums, something fiery, something sweet ... so, he really *had* meant it about dinner at his place. He had also just demonstrated that he knew where she worked. She glanced around as Azawakh took their jackets – it was a balmy night – and they removed their shoes.

Everything screamed 'bachelor pad'. Or rather, everything *murmured* 'bachelor pad' in a low, gravelly, venerable voice. The main living space – double aspect, heaps of windows, a distant glimpse of river – was painted a deep, Venetian red, the walls festooned with oil paintings suspended from the high picture rail. The faded leather sofas and swag-shaded standard lamps were doing an excellent impression of a gentleman's club circa 1900, and only a bowl of plantain crisps and some sort of putty-coloured hummus laid out on a coffee table struck a more contemporary note. At a level pitched low enough not to impinge, but high enough that it was discernible rather than annoying, she recognised the first of Bach's cello suites, emanating from an unseen speaker system.

'Drink?' Azawakh called over his shoulder, already busying himself at a cabinet. 'Cocktail? Sherry? Akvavit?'

Leyla caught Torben rolling his eyes at the last suggestion, which was rich – he was no stranger to cultural stereotypes. At least it looked like the interrogation was going to be of the genteel kind. And this was a world she knew well from her day job. 'Whatever goes best with the nibbles,' she smiled at him. 'Surprise us! Lovely curtains, by the way.' And she moved over to finger the entirely ordinary fabric. No way was she going to be fazed by this display.

Torben, following her lead, went to examine some of the oil paintings as their host fixed the drinks. 'You have a Carl Holsøe?' he said, relishing a pale, sun-drenched interior that would make a fine addition to the *other* book he was meant to be working on.

'Possibly just his brother Niels; it's disputed,' Azawakh admitted, handing each of them something gin-based with a cucumber garnish that tasted of citrus, grenadine and Angostura. He really was doing this properly. 'But I will admit to owning a genuine—'

'Ben Enwonwu!' breathed Torben, recognising the style. It was an unfinished pencil sketch, preparatory material for a composition of dancing figures that, in the final painting, would have been well beyond the budget of even the most senior civil servant. Torben stepped back. It was certainly an eclectic collection, united only by an exquisite taste and a preference for the representational over the abstract. He noted two or three things that were almost certainly Russian – one, to be fair, was an actual landscape of the Kremlin – and felt a slight shiver. But he couldn't help but warm to the sensibility that had gathered together these works.

'It's a family heirloom, actually,' said Azawakh, standing close beside him. 'Practically the only thing we brought with us from Lagos in '75.'

Torben's brain raced. Hadn't there been a coup, a military dictatorship …?

Azawakh went on, his voice almost wistful. 'First we went to Oxford, a tutor at my old college took us in for some months – I had only recently graduated – then London, of course, where I joined the … ah, the civil service. I began, of course, on the West African station, but like many others, I was soon reassigned to work on – how might your generation put it? – the "big bad".'

He wandered back to the open-plan kitchen, stirring pots and testing flavours. Torben and Leyla sipped their drinks, exchanging glances. Why was he—?

'I am telling you, of course, only what you have probably divined from context, and what is available online,' he said, still smiling, 'because it is always nice to be on the same page. After all, I've enjoyed your book on Friedrich, Dr Helle, and I know a couple of people at your chambers, Ms Moradi—'

'Please, call me Leyla,' she said, and Torben suppressed a frown. He had wanted to use that line.

'Leyla,' Azawakh, or, as Torben supposed he should now think of him, Jonathan, amended. 'Do help yourself to the dip, by the way. I can't claim to have made it myself, but it's fresh from Borough Market.'

Nothing loth, Torben sank into one of the sofas – it exhaled most satisfactorily – and began to scoop up hummus with the plantain. Leyla raised an eyebrow, and he met her gaze defiantly. He needed ballast to counteract the cocktail, didn't he?

'Anyway, you'll need the backstory for the book, won't you?' said Jonathan, now ladling soup into bowls. The aroma, even from halfway across the room, was to die for. Though Torben hoped it wouldn't actually come to that.

'Do you make your own stock?' he asked Jonathan, trying to match him in genial chit chat. 'I've always been too scared to do it properly in flats, in case the neighbours complain.'

'Oh, they're used to my cooking,' said Jonathan. 'I've been here thirty-five years – I could never have afforded it otherwise. My downstairs neighbour, now, she's just inherited the flat from an unmarried aunt who kept a pair of Tibetan Mastiffs. She's been trying to air out the smell of dog for six weeks, with no success. And upstairs gets through twenty Marlboros a day, so no one's exactly in a position to complain about a few simmering fishbones.'

He shot them both another smile. 'Oh, you should be recording this, you know, in case there's something you can use for your … book.' He paused. 'Who else is contributing, by the way? I imagine it's mostly scholars and campaigners, not just unqualified old friends with an amateur interest in collecting like me?'

For a moment, Torben felt an internal lurch that had nothing to do with the investigation. Jonathan had hit him where it hurt – there was, after all, a *real* book he would have to pull together once all this was done. Presumably the other man had checked this. Was he simply being mocked? 'Oh,' he said, 'the usual suspects, as you say, though not everyone's signed up yet. Please don't underestimate the value of your own contribution; the point is to avoid the whole thing being a product of the ivory tower.'

'Well, don't worry, I'm coming up to my first meeting with dear old Charlotte.' Jonathan chuckled. 'I say "old", and of course she was six years my senior – I confess I was a little overawed in the beginning. Her charisma, her intellect, her style … Pepper soup,' he pronounced, placing two bowls upon the coffee table. It looked as if the first course, at least, was to be eaten at the sofas, and Torben wondered whether the awkwardness of spooning soup from a recumbent position was the sort of interrogation tactic they taught you at MI6, or a devious invention of Jonathan's own.

'You will pardon me, I'm sure, if I confine myself to our personal relations,' said Jonathan, settling himself apparently at ease on the edge of the opposite sofa. 'After all, our professional collaborations are hardly likely to be of interest to your readers. But I have many fond memories of my time with Charlotte, even if it was duty that brought us together in the first place. Dinners, dances, a couple of unforgettable private viewings, which before you ask is *not* a euphemism; whatever you may have heard, Charlotte was capable of purely platonic friendships.' He chuckled. 'All the same, I have two or three anecdotes that might be valuable in shedding a light on her own artistic preferences – her curious obsession with seventies décor, for instance – and on her dealings with prominent intellectuals. They have the advantage of being printable, unlike the stories some other mutual acquaintances might share with you. How is the soup, by the way?'

Torben blinked, and took a hasty sip. Heat, nutmeg, smoke, stock ... 'I think,' he said, since Leyla evidently still had her mouth full, 'that it's the best I've ever tasted.'

By the time she had finished her jollof, a main course for which, blessedly, they had sat at a proper table, Leyla was having to fight to keep herself alert. What she really wanted to do was to curl up on one of those sofas and just sleep it all off. Perhaps it was the fear. Perhaps it was just the food. Either way, she knew herself to be at a strategic disadvantage. Torben seemed to be doing a little better. He was, at least, entirely upright in his chair.

The anecdotes had not helped. Their host had been right – they *were* printable, alas, and undeniably expanded her own image of Dame Charlotte. Until now, the things she had watched and heard online had been largely combative, confrontational. These stories put her in a much more mellow light. But that last one, about advising Jonathan on garden design for his family home down in Micheldever, Hants, had not exactly been the sort of scintillating tale that she needed if she were to stay entirely awake.

'And your final memory of Charlotte?' Torben said.

Leyla shifted. If he was trotting out this line, perhaps he too was crashing.

For the first time, Jonathan Azawakh looked troubled. 'Actually, it was a quarrel. Nearly a year ago – we didn't speak after that. She told me she was planning to write her memoirs. "Warts and all?" I asked.' He sighed. 'Once she had finished lecturing me on the unreliability of Horace Walpole as a source for that phrase, and that actually it was the Cooper miniature of Cromwell, not the famous portrait by Lely, that has the best warts, she confirmed that, yes, she was planning to be as candid as possible.'

Leyla thought back to the note Torben had uncovered, in which Charlotte had wondered whether to include whatever the Trigg story was. Clearly 'as candid as possible' had its limits, even to a woman as forthright as Charlotte Lazerton.

'And you, I imagine, suggested that such a policy might not be wholly ... diplomatic?' Torben ventured.

Jonathan nodded. Then said 'yes', presumably for the benefit of the tape. 'It was unfortunate. But I am still of that opinion. It cost me what I could not have known were the final months of Charlotte's friendship, but I stand by it. And I would advise anyone else who might be inclined towards her, shall we say, idealistic interpretation of transparency, to think twice before they placed such principles, commendable as they are, above the public interest.'

The sudden shift in his manner irritated Leyla. That such a splendid cook could turn out to be so po-faced in defence of the established order. 'Even in a case of murder?' she shot back, before she quite knew what she was saying.

There was a moment's silence.

'Murder?' said Azawakh (Jonathan be damned, thought Leyla). 'I honestly don't know what you might mean by that.'

In for a penny, she thought. 'By murder, I mean,' she went on, 'when a person of sound mind unlawfully kills another person and they have the intention to kill or to cause grievous bodily harm. That's the definition I'm used to at any rate, though I concede your place of work might employ a more elastic one.'

Torben seemed to be having some sort of choking fit. Even Azawakh resorted to clearing his throat. 'Really, Ms Moradi,' he said, also reverting to surnames, 'I'm surprised at you. I am aware that your friend here has a taste for such melodramatic hypothesising – I allude of course to the affair at Bastlehaugh – but that someone called to the Bar should indulge such ... wait, is this a millennial thing? My own children are very into true crime, I know ...'

'Bastlehaugh?' Torben had joined the fight. 'So you've been looking into police files?'

'On the contrary,' said Azawakh, who seemed to have regained his equilibrium. 'I have listened to the first two episodes of *Crimeward Ho*. Quite an entertaining podcast; I like the lo-fi production values. It sounds a bit like it was recorded in a stationery cupboard.'

Torben nodded. 'No squeaking wheels, no engine noise, no wind rushing past.'

Perhaps he was just tipsy, rather than belligerent, Leyla thought.

Azawakh looked nonplussed but carried on regardless. 'Really, you two, I work for a government-funded agency. Do you think we could possibly spare the resources to look into you officially?' He shook his head indulgently, a headmaster ticking off a pair of scamps for their first offence. 'But really, Leyla' – it was back to 'Leyla' again – 'you don't want to be bandying words like "murder" around. Even at mate's rates, a defamation case might be beyond your means. If, that is, whoever was concerned chose to go through the courts. In general, I find, the sort of individual who might take exception to what you've just said is likelier to prefer a more ... discreet ... form of settlement.' He smiled again. 'Now – can I interest either of you in dessert?'

Torben just couldn't help himself. He wanted to get out as soon as possible, but he really *did* need the loo. 'I'll show you the way,' said Azawakh, leading him down a corridor, floored with deep-stained boards. As they passed an open doorway, Torben instinctively glanced into the room beyond. And ground to a halt. Hanging from a peg on the wall opposite, illuminated by a wall-light above, was a full-body PPE suit, helmet and all. The sort you wore to prevent DNA contamination. The sort Samuel L. Jackson wore in *Cleaner*.

'Yes,' said Azawakh, in honeyed tones. 'You've discovered my guilty secret. You see, I've recently developed a passion for urban beekeeping. The bathroom's just at the end there.'

Torben had no choice but to walk on, in the full knowledge that Azawakh had orchestrated the whole thing. Beekeeping indeed. They had been meant to see that suit. *For helvede*. Now, just when he was in such desperate need of a piss, he couldn't make himself go after all.

16

LAMB'S CONDUIT STREET

They walked back to Little James Street. It was already late, and would take them more than an hour. But neither of them fancied standing on the edge of the platform at Pimlico, waiting for the tube.

'I know it sounds silly,' Leyla said, 'but I'm checking each way *twice* before crossing the road.'

'Me too.'

'Can I – can I stay with you tonight? Just … just, you know. I'll take the sofa.'

'*For fanden* will you take the sofa. I'm not having my eighteenth-century furniture ruined just because we've both been spooked by a – well, by a spook. We're sharing the bed. Top to toe if you like.'

'That's … that's very gentlemanly of you. But it's June, and we've walked a long way. I don't exactly fancy snuggling up to your feet.'

'That's the spirit! For a moment, I thought you were really worried.'

'I *am* worried.'

They walked on.

'But you heard him,' said Torben eventually. 'Having no resources to bother with us was one of the only things he said that had the ring of truth about it.'

'These things can be done on the cheap. A word in an ear.'

'Maybe showing me the hazmat suit was all he thought it needed. A clear signal—'

'That we'd be mad not to heed.'

They were walking along the Embankment now, past the gardens where Torben had been dragged along by Mortimer as Charlotte told him of tapped phones, of nameless fears. Strangers loomed in the summer dark. At their right, the river, shining.

'I still can't make up my mind,' Leyla went on after a minute, 'what he meant by showing us that. A sign that he did it, or that he was involved in the cover-up?'

'Unless,' said Torben, 'he's actually innocent, thinks we're sticking our noses in, causing trouble for respectable public figures with no justification, and just wanted to say, "watch out, we have ways of making you ... not talk".'

'Yes,' said Leyla, 'and if you believe that, you might as well believe he's actually just a friendly beekeeper.'

'I was just trying to state all the possibilities,' said Torben. 'No; clearly, he's up to his neck in this business. But his memories of Charlotte, the fondness – that seemed genuine. Compared to Drever's coldness, Trigg's downright animosity ...'

'You're talking,' said Leyla, 'as if our investigation is still ongoing.'

'Of course it bloody is!'

'Good. Just – just checking.'

'After all,' said Torben, 'it would almost be *more* suspicious if we stopped interviewing subjects for the book, wouldn't it? And I've got lunch with Shani Rajapalayam on Saturday, that took three people owing favours to each other to set up.'

'Plus,' Leyla observed, 'it's at Honey & Co.'

'There is that,' he conceded.

'Most people in this situation wonder if they're being brave or foolish. Very few of them add gluttony into the equation.'

'I am hungry,' said Torben, 'for justice.'

Altogether, they were feeling a little less shaken by the time they got back to Torben's house. Still, the shock, the lateness of the hour, the large and excellent meal, all combined to subdue any other emotions either of them might have been feeling. In the quiet dark, they slipped into bed. Without thought, he held her, felt her spine settle against him. Tried to decide if this moment was worth the risk of sudden assassination, and concluded that, on balance, it probably was. Prepared nonetheless for a night of lying awake, heart jolting at every creak of board or growl of traffic.

Within minutes, they were asleep.

Any awkwardness the next morning may have held was dispelled by the WhatsApp message on Torben's phone. It was from Gary Bassett. He had traced the phone call. Katherine Trigg had not been lying about calling Charlotte on the day of her death. And the call had been placed at 15:22.

'Late enough, in other words,' said Leyla, 'to clear Simon Grey of pushing her downstairs. But, on the other hand, probably about as long after his departure as it might take for a small dosage to work its stuff. It clears nobody.'

'Except Trigg herself,' said Torben. 'Unless you're still convinced an ex-City slicker with a mania for biography has also invented a means of murder by telecommunication.'

'I told you, I need time to think about that,' said Leyla. 'Besides, we've only her word that *she* made the call. She could have arranged for an accomplice to use her phone, or rigged some sort of auto-dial thing, in order to give herself an alibi.'

In the brilliant sunshine of another hot summer day, the fears of the night before seemed altogether less credible. 'The more I listen to us,' Torben said, 'the more I think Jonathan Azawakh went to a lot of trouble over that dinner for nothing. Treating us like people worth intimidating – we still don't have the first sodding idea what happened, do we?' He paused, his face a little redder than the heat warranted. 'Um, how did you sleep, by the way?'

'Surprisingly well, for someone who'd just been threatened by MI6,' said Leyla.

In fact, she *had* woken in the night. Lain there convinced she was in for five hours of insomniac worrying. And, warm, held, barely conscious of a scent that she found infinitely comforting, she had drifted off again almost immediately.

It was perhaps the most disconcerting part of the whole situation.

That evening, Torben played football as usual, finding himself on an impromptu team with both Cameron and Meera, who had an excellent and rather unexpected facility for turning a defender with her back to goal. The two of them, he couldn't help but notice, looked for every opportunity to pass to each other, and bickered like mad if one of them missed what the other considered to be an easy shot. It made him feel all avuncular.

He himself had never played better. The last twenty-four hours had acted as a tonic, dread giving way in turn to caution, shock, fear … and all of it swept away in one flood tide of certainty: cocooned against the world, Leyla in his arms, her scent, her softness – that this was right, and good, and what his life should be.

True, he had had to adjust his position very quickly on waking so as not to come across as too ... forward ...

But even then. Would she really have minded?

Still. They had been scared. It was no sort of time to take advantage. He had waited so long, it was all so *big*, the risk of disaster so great ... Safer, surely, to take it slowly. As with the investigation, he could not afford to act until he was certain his suspicions were justified.

Leyla went to work. And then she went home. Last night had been – well, it didn't matter what it had been. It had taken place under conditions that they were neither capable nor desirous of replicating. And Torben had not explicitly invited her to stay on the Friday night as well. And, despite the relative lull between court appearances, she had a steady trickle of casework mounting up from all the time off. This weekend, while he interviewed Shani, she would catch up on her job, then take herself away. Nowhere too quiet or remote though, where some spook might pounce on her; somewhere reassuringly populated. Something at Sadler's Wells, perhaps, and maybe she could have Ruth round on Sunday. Wilson too, if need be. Maybe even schedule a date via that app. Though having spent an evening listening to Azawakh's rambling stories and veiled hints, she wasn't sure she was up for more of the same from the Zak Cremellos of this world.

Dickens had Seven Dials. For Conrad and Ray Davies, it had been Soho. But Torben's heart of London was unashamedly Lamb's Conduit Street. The stretch between the Langham Gallery towards the south end, and The Lamb itself at the north, was more or less his spiritual home from home. There was the odd post-war block among the Georgian architecture, to stop it feeling too unreal. Any number of shops he felt too poor even to window-shop at. The People's Supermarket for blood oranges in season and good fresh bread; a reliable pub in The Perseverance. Excellent coffee at both ends of the street – Redemption Roasters got extra marks for its mission to rehabilitate prisoners – which must be at least partly responsible for the constant, light, well-heeled buzz of the place. There were old-school, exorbitant things like florists, half their stock out on the pavement, merry rivulets of water running down the street. Dark panelling, faded awnings, an undertaker's that, for as long as he could remember, had a window display consisting of an antique map and a model tall ship. Part of him wanted to find out why. Most of him liked the unresolved oddity. Today, however, he was here to have questions answered, not leave them open. Time to interview Shani Rajapalayam.

His first impressions of Honey & Co., the eatery he had judged most likely to appeal to her, were distinctly troubling. It was not only that today's bill might hit him where it hurt. Much worse than that: he was afraid he'd want to come back. Often. It was the scent of the candles, the Scandi-meets-North Africa simplicity of the pale wood, paler walls, vast windows and ticking-striped cushions … those plants, so very *very* green … the fact that the menu that had just been placed before him was secured with a large wooden peg – a peg! – all of which he listed, somewhat disingenuously, before admitting that all the waitresses were— But he could not finish that sentence, even to himself. Was there a loophole, he wondered, in employment legislation, that allowed discrimination on purely aesthetic grounds? He would have to ask Leyla. On top of which, they all seemed genuinely *happy*. Except, perhaps, when one of them was called over to the round table in the corner, where four City boys in shirt-sleeves were rah-ing happily, attending closely to their wine glasses, and leaving most of their food untouched. One of them had a shock of peroxide-blond hair.

He still had five minutes in hand. Time enough to conduct a mental review of everything they had assembled between them on Shani.

Some thirteen years younger than Charlotte, born to parents who had emigrated from Tamil Nadu back when it was still Madras State, she had started out as a regular academic. The Ruskin; the University of London; her path had perhaps first intersected with Charlotte's when she began her PhD back in 1982. He would have to wait for more on that relationship. The public record spoke instead of a meteoric rise, precocious radio appearances, the swift transition to television, increasing visibility on both Channel 4 and BBC Arts programmes, with a guaranteed slot every time the Turner Prize looked like generating some headlines. Professor at thirty-eight, back when such things still happened … an irregular column for the *Evening Standard* before, back in the early noughties, she had bagged the gig at the *Observer* that she held to this day. Choosing the most traditional of areas to specialise in – the Italian Renaissance – she had stirred up the field from the first, with a radical reappraisal of the influence of the Islamic and even Zoroastrian worlds upon Quattrocento painters, then a pioneering study of representations of race in early history painting, and of course she had been the driving force behind the first exhibition devoted to Artemisia Gentileschi's female contemporaries. All in all, she was something of a professional hero of Torben's. But he was well aware of that old advice, never to meet one's heroes. He had heard rumours – who in his sector had not? – about some less than savoury dealings with younger scholars, of hostile reviews and petty gatekeeping. Of a fondness for overseas conferences that gave her the full keynote treatment – taxis on tap, lavish honorariums. He hoped these rumours were exactly that, motivated by jealousy or prejudice. And she was here to be interviewed, after all. He had no objection to interviewing someone only artificially charming, if it helped fill in the very many gaps in their investigation without wrecking both his respect for a former idol and his lunch. Speaking of which ... he glanced down at the menu.

'Whatever we're having, it has to end with the cheesecake.' He looked up. Shani Rajapalayam had arrived.

'—absolutely *terrified* of peacocks!' Shani ended.

'Peacocks?! I never knew that,' laughed Torben.

'Yes, it was awfully unfortunate because we were putting on a "Rethinking the Raj" exhibition for the British Library – just one of those small public ones on the mezzanine level – but they'd sourced this *fabulous* original wallpaper, a bit faded but all the better for it, that was all iridescent tail feathers, and I had this taxidermied monster of a bird that we'd twice tried and failed to repatriate to Mysuru – none of their museums wanted it because it was *riddled* with beetles, but they didn't really show ... anyway, one day Charlotte popped round to finalise the display, and I thought I'd surprise her with this peacock – Torben, I swear to you, she jumped three feet off the floor, and then took a swing at it with her umbrella!'

'The umbrella bit I *can* believe.'

'Mm, I think she was taking the anti-orientalism a touch too far.'

Shani smiled at him over her glass. She had ordered a Greek red from a vineyard called something like Lyrarakis, and asked for it to be lightly chilled. Here, he thought, was someone unlikely to be impressed by his Chiroubles theory. He had also noticed her eye travel lower down the wine list the second he confirmed that the lunch was 'on expenses'. They were getting along famously. And everything they had ordered had been delicious. He just hoped that, before the meal's end, the conversation would reveal something a little more nourishing.

A shadow across the ransacked plates; a whiff of rather musky cologne. Looking up, he recognised one of the – what to call them these days? Yuppy was outdated; wanker perhaps overly judgemental – one of the men from the corner table, anyway. It was Zak Cremello of the shocking hair; the one he'd *thought* he'd seen meeting Henrik Drever in the park, when was it, weeks ago now …

'Shani! Torben! Thought I recognised you both. Well, that and I clocked the words *chiaroscuro* and *craquelure* being spouted by people who can afford to eat here and reckoned, even in Bloomsbury, what are the chances—'

'*Hej*, Zak,' said Torben, as enthusiastically as he could manage.

Shani didn't seem that pleased to see him either. 'Not your normal haunt, I'd have thought, Zak?' she ventured.

'Couple of mates are having their wedding reception back at Oarwright in a couple of hours,' he said. 'Noble Rot was fully booked – like, actually fully booked, not just the pretend sort where a place will bump someone's reservation and claim a mix-up if you promise to order three bottles of Bolly or slip them a fat wad, pardon my *entendres* – and these guys said this was the next-best place to load up nearby.' His gesture took in the other men, one of whom was still trying to coax a couple of drops out of the final bottle left on their table.

'By load up, I take it you don't mean on carbs,' Torben observed. Cremello actually *winked* at him. Then slapped his shoulder. *Det svin*.

'Look, great to catch up, guys – let's do this again, yeah?' And with that, Zak Cremello had left the building.

Torben and Shani eyed one another. 'How about,' she said, slowly, 'I don't enquire where you had the misfortune to make so unlikely an acquaintance, and you return the favour?'

'Agreed,' he smiled.

Zak popped his head back round the corner. 'Oh, Tor, I nearly forgot – if you've not been here before – you've *got* to try the cheesecake.'

Torben scanned the dessert menu. 'You know, I'm really not sure I can manage anything else. Maybe we should just share a pot of tea …?'

They had covered a lot of ground in the past ninety minutes. Torben was now much better versed in how one might almond-crust an aubergine. More to the point, he had on record not merely Shani's last meeting with Charlotte – a meandering stroll back from the Beeb two weeks before Charlotte's death, after both appearing on a rather tempestuous edition of Radio 4's *Front Row*, courtesy of some other guest bringing up the British Museum's sponsorship deals – but also their *first* meeting. 1978: an impressionable Shani, still in her teens, had dared to ask a question after a visiting lecture by Charlotte at the Exam Schools on Oxford's High Street. Charlotte had responded with a laugh, a considered answer, and an invitation to the afterparty – and it had been a proper afterparty too, not stilted glasses of sherry in some moth-stalked senior common room. The years between those two anecdotes had been filled with enough incident, both recounted and discreetly hinted at, to demonstrate to Torben that, despite having lived in her spare room and walked her dog, there were hinterlands to Charlotte Lazerton where he had never trod. With the aid of a carafe of zesty Retsina, he had even coaxed out an account of how Shani had spent the days around Charlotte's death – a whirl of publishers' parties, copy deadlines and editorial meetings that, dutifully followed up, seemed likely to produce nothing but ambiguity. Without access to her personal diary and a corroborating witness, she was no more in or out than any of the others – except, he had to admit, the Brussels-based Henrik Drever.

He had also clocked her gaze following the wriggling bottom, encased in skinny grey jeans, of their latest waitress, as she cleared detritus from the City boys' table. Interesting.

Another shadow over their dessert menus, somehow more angular than the last. 'Shani, *bella*, don't say I've caught you with your latest beau!'

'Lucia!' Somehow, Shani managed to inject something of the head girl into this reproof-cum-greeting.

Torben looked up. Blinked. Looked again.

Surely, this was his elusive next-door neighbour.

Two minutes later, Torben had secured two things of value. The first was a private invitation for a drink at his new neighbour's, later that same evening. The second was Shani's startled shutting down of the woman he now knew as Lucia Segugio, when she had begun to say, 'Shani, *carissima*, where have you been hiding yourself? I can't have seen you since you came round that—' at which point Lucia had been politely but ruthlessly talked over by his dining companion. Something to follow up at their drink later, anyway.

'Well, I must dash,' said Lucia, a little ruffled by Shani's abrupt treatment. 'Oh, Torben, if you are contemplating dessert, you must try' – he steeled himself – 'the plum pistachio cake. It is *heavenly*.'

Well. He had not expected that.

It turned out the cheesecake was worth talking about. Feta, honey, thyme, berries, at once light as cloud and rich as a kingdom, all atop an impossible bird's nest of kadaif pastry. He shared it with Shani, and tipped generously. OK, this would probably mean another month before he could afford such luxuries as kitchen chairs or a table. But – always assuming he could stagger the few metres back home without toppling into a gutter, send Leyla the recording, get through his interview with Lucia Segugio, and hopefully spend hours this evening debating all the implications with Leyla while she raised her eyebrows and swore at him in three languages – this had been an afternoon well spent. Well spent. A phrase that just about summed him up.

17

NUMBER 26

Leyla's office was on the top floor of 45 Bedford Row: the end of the street furthest from the traffic, and high enough that the view was mostly sky, and the pale green of a breeze-tossed treetop. The room itself was more or less a broom cupboard. But the brass plaque on the outside of the door had her name literally etched into it, presumably with lasers. It spoke of a permanence, a legitimacy, that she had encountered nowhere else in life. It was the main reason she preferred to do her weekend work here at her desk, rather than in her poky, lonely flat.

When Torben's email arrived, late on Saturday afternoon, that desk was slowly disappearing under a stack of reference works and papers, and Leyla was on her fourth cup of coffee. She skimmed his message, downloaded the WeTransfer audio, listened to a random thirty seconds from about an hour in. She glanced at the files beside her, spilling from their customary binding of pink ribbon. The effect was tethering. She had needed the reminder that she was Leyla Moradi, called to the Bar, a glamorous London lawyer, prepping for a high-profile yet reassuringly distant case. Not a second-year undergraduate, scribbling away mid-essay crisis, while her would-be love interest rutted away on a moonlit balcony a couple of staircases away.

Because, by the sound of the recording, Torben had been having the time of his life, sharing small plates with an infamous art critic. And he was now proposing to walk, like Daniel, into the den of some Italian cougar for yet more drinks, while she, Leyla, got to read up on precedents and draft hypothetical counterarguments. Not that she was worried – she would back herself over some random neighbour any day. No, it was the injustice of the thing. Being left out of the fun. Reduced, despite herself, to a supporting role. She glanced at the hand that was still fingering the ribbon. A very faint tremble in the tendons. But that was probably just the coffee.

She had done some more digging. Not on Shani Rajapalayam; her proclivities were an open book, an equal-opportunities sexual predator of renown. No; on Lucia Segugio. A quick check of the electoral roll and the listed buildings register had confirmed Gary Bassett's casual identification of Torben's neighbour. Then the profiles in the interior design magazines had led Leyla to the three divorces, the fashion shoots, the legendary parties.

To think that she had gone so far as to google poor little Elodie. Compared to Shani and Lucia, Elodie Griffon was a kitten.

One cold shower and two coffees later, Torben felt almost alive. He'd backed up the Rajapalayam interview, updated Leyla, written up what seemed the most salient points. Now – what to take as an offering for Lucia? And, more to the point, what to wear? She'd literally run away from him the first time they met, and he'd been wearing his best jumper. *For helvede.* Maybe he wasn't cut out for Bloomsbury after all.

Abandoning any thought of getting some actual work done, Leyla had plugged in, and taken herself off to pace brisk laps of Lincoln's Inn Fields as she listened to the full recording of the Rajapalayam conversation. Even for early June in London, it was a hot afternoon, too hot; the tennis courts were empty, and she seemed to be the only thing moving at any sort of pace. Woe betide the tourist who strayed across her path as she forced herself to digest every minute of Torben's lunchtime adventure. Really, the sounds the two of them made over that sodding cheesecake were practically orgasmic. If only that pigeon would come near enough to kick …

Back in her office, shoulder blades sticky with righteous sweat, the small of her back a positive puddle, she tried to cool off in every possible sense; to take stock, think over what she had just heard – and decide whether that light, self-assured voice could have belonged to a murderer. She tried to reach, nerves straining, for objectivity, as a mountaineer stretches for the next ledge. Most of it had sounded benign. A lot had even sounded natural. But she had heard – had heard *something* important. A fact, a phrase, a detail, that if brought into contact with something *else* she knew about the case, would come to life; a chemical reaction, a great big fizzing *gotcha*. Whether it implicated Rajapalayam, or one of the others, she couldn't yet say. But she knew that it was there, in Shani's conversation.

Leyla got up. Nothing for it; she would have to listen to the whole thing again.

It was not, thought Torben, how *he* would have decorated Number 26. Where the Posavacs' had been an Aladdin's cave of curios and warm, homely chaos, Lucia Segugio had gone for monochrome throughout, taking her lead from the chequerboard hallway, and chucking white emulsion, black leather and Carrara marble at everything that dared expose itself to view. A low hum of air conditioning kept the baking June evening at bay, as artificial as the rest of it.

'I *love* what you've done with the place,' he said. That was how you played this game, right?

'No you don't, but it is sweet of you to say so,' Lucia smiled, steering him towards the kitchen with a hand on his arm. She accepted the bottle of Chiroubles without comment – after Shani, his hopes of impressing had not been high – and found a space for it in a gleaming chrome wine rack that looked like it had come from the set of a high-budget sci-fi. Instead, she poured out two tiny glasses of something called Cynar. From the way she wielded the bottle, he guessed this was meant to be ironic, and he smiled in what he hoped was a knowing fashion. What was it about a rich woman in her – forties? – that made him feel like a gauche teenager?

'Didn't we bump into each other the other week?' said Lucia, appraising him. 'I am sorry for disappearing in such a hurry, I was late for a Zoom – but actually, was that you? You were wearing rather more, rather outlandish …?'

'It's a long story.'

Lucia flapped an exquisitely manicured hand. Clearly she had no time for long stories. At least, not if they were told by other people.

'I would not,' she said, 'be in London at all, of course, if I did not have to be on the spot – they are letting me guest edit an issue of *Elle Decoration*, the fools! But really, this summer, this heat … I have a little place in the hills above Lecco, a shack really, a shepherd's house – just a pool, a few terraces for vines, you know – normally I am there, you should visit in fact …' She pulled herself together. 'And I was for a long time in Milan, New York, this is why we have never met, I want to apologise for this – Charlotte told me you were her last lodger, her favourite.'

'She did?' Torben was not sure which surprised him more – the rabbit-punch of pride at hearing he had been her favourite, or the fact that Charlotte and Lucia had been on intimate terms.

Lucia nodded. 'Yes, I knew all about the idea of her Trust, that you would be the, how do they say, custodian of the house. We talked a lot in the spring, the weeks before her death, when she—'

Lucia broke off. Cradling her triangular face in her hands, elbows on the marble kitchen island – he feared she might lacerate her palms on those cheekbones – she contemplated him. 'I think I trust you,' she said at last. It was not a question.

'*Tak*,' he said, disarmed despite himself.

'You know she was worried, someone was—'

'Tapping her phone,' he said. It was a gesture of faith, a declaration. A gamble.

'Yes, yes!' She nodded vigorously. 'Like she knows something is afoot, but she won't say what. Personally, my first thoughts are of a diagnosis, something in the brain, maybe it causes paranoia as it grows … But now it is me who is paranoid. Torben, I have something to tell you. I do not tell the police, it is not' – she clicked her fingers, searching – 'not *serious*, not worth it maybe. But when I see you, this good little boy who Charlotte liked and trusted, having lunch with Shani – discussing Charlotte …?'

Torben explained the interview, the book.

'Ah.' Lucia sounded relieved. 'Then you and Shani are not …?'

'It was our first conversation,' said Torben, sparing her the task of ending her question.

'I, as you can imagine, have had a thousand conversations with Shani,' said Lucia. 'We have been sort-of-friends for twenty years, maybe more. Torben, can I tell you a story? Two stories?'

'Please,' he said.

'OK – one, the week before Charlotte died, Shani comes to see me. Practically invites herself for lunch, like she has something important to discuss. Now, I am only just landed back in the country after two months away, I am jet-lagged, it is not convenient. But obviously I say yes – you don't say no to Shani, you don't even want to. But the chat is all same old, same old, some gossip, some plans. I start to wonder why she is here. Then she excuses herself and goes upstairs, to the bathroom. She is gone some five, ten minutes? Then she comes down, we talk a little more, it is all very pleasant, she leaves, mwah mwah, darling, *carissima*, *ciao* …'

Lucia performed a very convincing impression of her own manners in Honey & Co., earlier that afternoon.

'Now, Torben, I am not Mr Sherlock Holmes, but I have an eye for details. One: Shani takes her handbag when she goes upstairs. And this is normal – even you, a boy, know this about women – but in a public place, you know, not so much here, in the house of her friend. And it is a *very* large handbag, I think perhaps Mulberry from the days when they were still … *Allora*! The point is, it is no mere clutch or purse. Two: when she returns, yes she is groomed, very neat, this too I expect. But not so much do I expect the cobweb in her hair.'

Cobweb? And then it hit him. The escape hatch on the top floor – the connecting passage – a route between the houses! But already, Lucia was carrying on with her tale.

'Three – and I hate to shock you, really I do, but there is no delicate way of putting this – I wander up to the bathroom myself, the minute she is gone – there is only one, the same as yours, on the second floor – and there is no smell, but none! And I let you into a little secret, Torben; even when it is we ladies who spend that much time in the bathroom, there is still a smell. So. It is all a little strange. But I think no more about it. And that is story number one.'

Torben nodded. Hesitated. Then asked, carefully, 'You say this took place the week before she died – you mean ...?'

'Oh, I can look it up!' Lucia fished for her phone, scrolled through her e-diary. 'Yes – the police called me with the news at the weekend, the last weekend in April, and this was the week before ... does this matter?'

'Maybe,' said Torben, trying to get a message to his heart to dial down the volume a little. 'I mean, I don't know the ending of these stories yet ...'

'Ah, it is not in here,' said Lucia, tossing her head. 'She rings me up and comes on the same day, this I remember. It cannot have been the Thursday, I see I was in meetings all afternoon ... no, I forget. Monday? Wednesday?'

'Tuesday?'

'*Si*, early in the week, one day, what does it matter – I thought it was the Swedish who are meant to be the anally retentive ones?'

That did it; Torben was *not* going to be compared to a Swede. He could circle back to this later. 'Sorry,' he said.

Lucia poured them each another shot. Apparently, he was forgiven. 'Now, where was I ... Ah! So the second story begins at a party back in February. Actually I had hoped to meet you there – she had told me such things! – but you were away at some reunion ... As you know, Charlotte used her walls as a permanently rotating gallery, always in flux – pictures would go up for a month, a year, two, then come down, to be sold, given as presents, or in most cases—'

'Hoarded in the box room,' said Torben. 'Remember, I used to sleep across the hallway from that shapeshifting den of art. It gave me nightmares once; I dreamt of all the portraits coming to life like paint-zombies.' That had been after another overripe Gamle Ole, but she didn't need to know that.

'*Si* – always, her preference was for portraiture, nudes, the human form; she said it resisted trends and united genres.'

Torben smiled. 'The way she put it to *me* was something like, "Tits, arse and cocks. Doesn't matter whose gaze it is or how noble the intention, we'll always paint them and we'll always want to look at them."'

Lucia laughed. 'Exactly that! And at this time of the party in February, she had on the wall a painting, a small nude, no bigger than – than your two hands, side by side.'

Torben dutifully held up his hands. She nodded rather approvingly.

'Hmm, OK, you have long fingers, so maybe a little smaller. It was a Lucian Freud; a nude, a young woman, but not his late style, you know, not so *harsh*, unsparing; I would put its date as maybe the late seventies ... anyway, for me, it was all about the light. The girl in the picture, her skin was dark, but it glowed like – like nothing else I have ever seen, not outside a gallery. I told Charlotte that I loved it, she shrugged it off as just another dirty picture she'd acquired, somewhere along the line ... and when I am next in the house, it is gone. Victim to that endless curation, I thought, and I thought too, what a shame, for her to remove it when it gave me such pleasure.

'And I say to myself, well, that is that. Until I get a letter, some weeks ago now, sometime in May, from the executor of Charlotte's will. Such a nice letter, very warm. And I find I have been left the little Freud painting as a gift. Is that not the most charming, the most thoughtful?'

Torben agreed. It did not exactly compare to his own great good fortune, but it was certainly a lovely gesture. And it spoke to the fact that Charlotte had been amending many parts of her will in the months before her death. She had sensed what was coming.

'*But*,' said Lucia, now raising a melodramatic hand, 'then the men come, they clear the house, time passes, and I receive a second letter, also from the executor. This one, it is all apologies. Charlotte has left clear instructions: the picture is in the little box room, apparently there is a system after all, they are numbered – but it cannot be found, it has vanished – but *completely* vanished! And then she writes of something called ademption, that the law does not allow for compensation in these cases; that if she had free rein she would give me first pick of another painting, but since the proceeds are to set up this charity, well – and *poof* goes my little memento—'

Little memento was a nice way of putting it, he thought. Not that he had any wish to be vulgar, but a Freud in oils, even that small … well, maybe the price it might fetch *was* a small sum to someone like Lucia, what did he know?

'And that is story number two,' Lucia finished up. 'Now, when I tell you that Shani was also at the party in February, and had some sort of intensely whispered – I think you say "spat"? – with Charlotte, I wonder if you can put the stories together for me?'

Torben rose. 'I think,' he said, 'that I would like to go … to the bathroom.'

She smiled, and got up too. 'Or perhaps … a little further?'

'Perhaps.'

She *almost* had it, Leyla thought. She had expanded her walk now, taking to the streets, past the restaurant where the conversation in her ears had taken place, in case that might, in whatever unlikely way, help. It did not. Trying to keep to the lengthening shadows, out of the still-too-hot sun, she refocused her attention on the voices in her head.

'So we used to have this awful parlour game,' Shani was saying. 'One of us would name some canonical cultural figure, and the other would have to improvise a joke. Like "Isadora Duncan? No, is a door" – that one's just silly – or, for Purcell, we came up with "Dido of Carthage, whatever happened to her?" Because of the—'

'—Aria, her lament. Yes, we played that one too,' said Torben's voice. 'I remember one for Burns – "O my love is like a red, red rose: you can buy it for a fiver at a petrol station."'

Shani audibly sniggered.

No, Leyla thought, that was definitely *not* the important bit. Tossers. But it had been *some* story of Shani's, one that connected up with – with what? And now she was doubling back, turning right into Little James Street … and yes, her pace might be slowing a bit as she approached the little trio of gable-ended houses.

Number 26, as befitted the last in a row, had exposed windows on the western side. Small windows, giving on to the staircase – that one higher up was what Torben had told her was called a Yorkshire, the sashes sliding horizontally. And there he was, and there was Lucia Segugio, heading upstairs. Lucia had a glass in one hand, the other playing lightly somewhere around Torben's shoulder. And there she was – she, Leyla – juggling two jobs on a Saturday evening, stuck outside.

Git. Maybe she should've arranged some dates after all, if only to teach him a lesson. Some dates … That was a thought. Torben was meant to be interviewing Simon Grey over lunch on Monday. Leyla had a sudden premonition that, when Torben got to the restaurant, he might discover – or, just maybe, *not* discover – that there had been an unannounced change of plans; that his guest was lunching elsewhere, with another companion.

Lucia's top floor was of a piece with the rest: a single open-plan space, as close to New York loft style as you could get with sloping ceilings. And at the rear, there was the same escape hatch, the mirror image of the one he supposed was now his own – except on this side of the connecting passage, it was painted in pristine gloss white.

Well, almost pristine. Because the door had clearly been painted shut. But now, there were little flakes of paint, speckling the boards beneath like settling snow. And a neat cut, such as might be made with a Stanley knife, freeing the hatch so that it might, again, be used. Torben pried his fingers into the tiny gap; eased it open. Stooping, illuminated by the torch from his phone, he could make out the corresponding door less than a metre away. He knelt, stuck an arm in, gave it an experimental shove. His own hatch swung open.

'Signora Segugio, it has been a pleasure. If you can remember the exact date this happened, then *please* – try and remember. We might be talking more than a simple act of theft. You can leave the rest with me. For now – thank you for a lovely evening, but I think I should be heading home.' And, fully conscious that his words were infinitely more dignified than his posture, he dropped to all fours, and wriggled his way through the hatch.

18

MAIDEN LANE / THE STRAND

The building opposite had a plaque to Voltaire. *Voltaire!* It was so strange, this storied street that felt half back-alley, half tourist trap. Right now, however, Leyla was the one laying a trap. She had seen Torben hurry through the door of Rules five minutes ago, hot and bothered, clearly keen to be in situ when Simon Grey arrived. Well, he was going to be disappointed. But it was a lesson he needed to learn.

Her plan of revenge relied on two factors, one of them being that a Danish pedant with all the time in the world on his hands and an ulterior motive would arrive for lunch early, while a member of the government doing a stranger a favour out of either gluttony or guilt, when parliament had just returned for its final session before summer recess, would be five minutes late at the very least.

She checked her watch, checked that Torben's table was not in the window, and sidled into position. Her final check was made with the aid of a pocket mirror. Taking out her Liberty silk handkerchief, she dabbed the beads of perspiration from her brow, steering well clear of the makeup she had applied for the first time in what felt like forever. Yes, she would do.

A black cab pulled up alongside her. As she had suspected, Grey had chosen not to use his official ministerial car and driver for this somewhat unorthodox appointment – a first hint of subterfuge suggestive, surely, of an uneasy conscience. A few seconds' fumbling around inside – he was paying in cash too, and not even asking for a receipt; the fact he was not expensing the cab was the second mark against him – and Grey emerged. For a second, she thought of their old university friend Tom Goring, writ large. Red of face, blue of tie, thin of hair, stuffed of shirt. It almost sounded like a rhyme from a fairy tale.

Leyla stepped forward. 'Mr Grey?'

'Yes?' he grunted, his eyes on the door of Rules. For a second she remembered the random fact that it was unwise to stand between a hippopotamus and the river. But in fairness, being accosted on the street was probably an occupational hazard that had long since ceased to hold any appeal for the politician. And they were standing directly in the glare of the midday sun. Leyla sidestepped under the restaurant awning.

'Mr Grey, I am *so* sorry, but there has been a change of plan. Dr Helle sends his apologies, but he is unable to honour his lunch engagement.'

'Eh? What kind of tomfool—'

'I am, however, pleased to inform you that I'm here to take his place. The shake-up has necessitated a change of venue, but it's just over th—'

'Change? To where?'

'Simpson's.'

'Ah. Yes, well, very good. Lead on!' The overloaded machinery that was Simon Grey's body stirred into forward motion, and Leyla was relieved that her substitute location really was just around the corner.

'By the way,' he said, almost as an afterthought. 'To whom do I ... or have we met before?'

'Leyla Moradi,' she smiled. 'I'm Dr Helle's co-editor of the volume.'

'Jolly good.'

Torben checked his watch. Twelve-fifteen. Already the head waiter had been giving him sidelong glances. He checked his phone. The secretary had confirmed the appointment: noon exactly on Monday 11th June. Surely they'd have the decency to notify him of any change in plans as well?

The glass window of The North Face made for an excellent mirror, and Leyla risked a glance. Grey, a half-step behind on the narrow pavement, was paying close attention to the seat of her too-tight skirt. So far, so good.

She had double-baited her hook, first with the restaurant, then with herself. That had been the second factor in her plan. Sometimes, she thought, it was nice when men played up to type. You knew where you were with this sort. The terms of engagement were clear. Not for nothing had she spent the last decade negotiating the London legal scene.

'You know, Ms ... Ms Moradi, I was under the impression you were some sort of lawyer,' Grey said, evidently happy to have placed his dim recollection of her face. Not that it was her face he was paying most attention to.

She was prepared for this. 'That's right. I advised Charlotte Lazerton on copyright during the "Contrast" campaign. We've liaised over environmental law ever since but I also have a sideline in academia – some articles on forgery cases, disputed ownership – which is why the press paired me up with Dr Helle, to ensure a spread of expertise.'

'Ah, yes. The absent Dr Helle.' They were waiting at the lights, ready to cross the Strand. Both of them now lightly sweating. 'Where did you say the devil had got to?'

'Food poisoning. I gather he rather overindulged himself,' Leyla said, without the slightest sense of compunction. 'Last minute onset, very explosive. He cancelled the reservation online, then messaged me, asking me to call your secretary and make his apologies – I rather think he's confined to the bathroom for the duration – but I happened to have a free afternoon, and hated the thought of inconveniencing you.' She toyed with the thought of adding, *And I wasn't going to pass up the chance to meet* the *Simon Grey*. But no; that would almost certainly be overdoing things. 'Sadly, I couldn't get another booking at Rules at such short notice, but when I mentioned your name to the receptionist at Simpson's, a table magically became free.'

'Really!' Grey harrumphed, clearly more indignant at the institution that had turned him down than flattered by his pull at the one that had obliged. 'Well, I've always said you can rely on Simpson's. These hallowed portals are the sort of thing that makes this city. I'll lay you any odds they're still here, filling the bellies of hardworking families, when you and I are long gone.'

'I'm sure you're right, Mr Grey,' said Leyla, as the hallowed portals were held open before them by a little man in a hat. For some people, this was the real world. It explained a lot, she thought.

At twenty past, Torben conceded that he would have to order more than the black coffee he had been eking out for the past ten minutes. No one had actually said anything yet; Rules had been here since 1798, and was a stranger to such modern evils as impatience and discourtesy. But there was a moral force bent upon him that he could not withstand. Grey was clearly not coming. Whether that made him into more or less of a suspect was unclear – on balance, probably less? But it was precious little to go on.

From dark, oak-panelled walls, Grey's predecessors in office glowered down. Churchill, slumped into a chair, his photograph rubbing shoulders with a stuffed and mounted gazelle's head that looked, if anything, the livelier of the two. A rather startling mural of Thatcher, armour-clad as a sort of stylised Britannia. This was Grey's home turf. So why hadn't he come?

Frustrated, Torben turned to the menu. Maybe he should just have lunch for one? His eyes roved over the rich array, from cocktails, oysters and spatchcocked game birds, to words like 'rump' and 'haunch', 'sticky' and 'curd'. Something funny happened in his stomach. He blinked. A month ago, ethics and finances notwithstanding, he would have wanted to order the lot. But after the couple of weeks he'd been having … Before his eyes, there rose a vision of a light, shop-bought salad and a glass of water. It seemed like very heaven.

'Before anything else, Ms Moradi, I'd like to make one thing clear,' said Grey, snuggling himself into a reassuringly sturdy seat and mopping his forehead with the table napkin.

She raised her eyebrows in enquiry.

'I don't care what we do about starters, I can take 'em or leave 'em. But I am having the beef from the trolley, followed by the treacle sponge. And if you've any sense, so will you.'

*

While he waited for the purse-lipped waiter to fetch the card machine for the sake of a single pot of coffee, Torben began to jot things down in a pocket notebook – this was hardly the place to use a screen at the table. On the walk over, he had listened to the episode of *Front Row*, conveniently archived on BBC Sounds, that had allegedly constituted Shani's last evening with Charlotte. What had Shani called it? Tempestuous? Possibly so, but the row over sponsorship sounded, to his newly primed ear, more like a sideshow to distract from the real tension in that recording studio. Charlotte and Shani barely addressed a word directly to each other, and when they did, they were chillingly polite. Charlotte didn't insult her colleague so much as once – a sure sign of something wrong. Had there *really* been a walk home afterwards? If there had, he didn't think it could have resembled the merry stroll of Shani's memory.

His first action on Saturday night – after finding a way to secure the top-floor hatch against another unsolicited entry – had been to go back through Charlotte's appointments diary. There was only one scheduled appearance by Shani that post-dated the night of the February party. And that had been heavily crossed out.

A coherent narrative, starkly at odds with the rosy recollections he had been served up on Lamb's Conduit Street, was starting to emerge. At its centre was undoubtedly a felony. The only question was – how grave?

As a spectacle, it fell somewhere between the Russian ballet and the Roman colosseum, Leyla thought. To the accompaniment of mid-tempo lounge piano, a man in a white apron – a tattoo-less man, to boot! – was slicing butter-soft rounds of roast rib of beef from a whole side of cow; the meat was bloody, oleaginous. He was doing this at a stainless-steel trolley parked at the side of their exquisitely white-clothed table, every so often flopping another slice of hot pink beef on to one or other of their plates, where they lay seductively beside a golden Yorkshire pudding. Also on the trolley, albeit very much cast in supporting roles, were a steaming gravy-boat – of gravy, naturally – and a mound of creamed horseradish – also, for some reason, in a gravy-boat.

Simon Grey sank back with a long sigh of satisfaction. Between his plateful of cow and the cut of Leyla's top, he was certainly getting his pound of flesh. She judged the time right to steer the conversation a little.

'Simon' – she had been strongly encouraged to call him Simon – 'I've just realised something. You understand, as both an editor and a lawyer, I'm keen to be as accurate as possible.'

'Of course, my dear, of course,' he agreed, through a happy mouthful of meat. On the plain white plate, the vivid red of blood was mingling with the deep brown of the gravy, making little patterns.

'Well, it's just that I'm not sure your last memory of Charlotte *can* have been that reception you described at the AWA, because in my briefing notes from Dr Helle, he mentions a meeting for tea at her house, considerably *after* that event—'

'No, I don't think so.'

'Well, you see, he got it from Charlotte's appointments diary. And when we spoke to her neighbours – for colour, you know, the great woman at home sort of thing – one of them *did* mention seeing you—'

'Ah, yes. Apologies. I misspoke.'

'Please, don't worry; I'm terribly forgetful myself. It's just, it would be incredibly valuable to be able to include a record of what might, by the sound of things, be Charlotte Lazerton's last words.'

His eyes widened. Then they narrowed. 'Surely not … her last words?'

'I'm afraid so. You see, we haven't been able to find anyone who saw her alive after that afternoon.'

'Really? Well, in that case … let's see … You know, I think this calls for a second helping of beef?'

Leyla beckoned the waiter over. Simon Grey spread his hands. Crinkled his piggy little eyes. And began to talk.

What if, Torben thought, this was another *Murder on the Orient Express*? Grey drugs the tea, Trigg calls to distract her, Rajapalayam administers the push from behind, Azawakh cleans up the evidence, and Drever … Drever profits?

Well, it was a hot afternoon, and he'd had a whole pot of coffee. He could forgive himself the odd idiotic thought.

19

UP IN THE AIR

Flushed, pensive, unusually nervous, Leyla let herself in to 24 Little James Street. Torben was in; all the windows were open in the summer heat, and she could hear music playing somewhere upstairs. Beautiful music. Extremely loud.

It was coming from the library. Easing open the door, Leyla was blasted with a swell of strings, a limpid female voice, the sudden thrill of woodwind. Torben was on the floor in nothing but shorts, knee protectors and a face mask, apparently scouring the floorboards clean by hand. For a moment he persisted, oblivious. She watched a bead of sweat begin the long journey down his spine. There was something childlike to his absorption in the task, the precision of his movements … the infinitesimally small proportion of floor that he had covered.

Then the track – the movement? – ended, and he became aware of her presence. Looked up, face red, the mask distorting his cheeks into a chipmunk's, pushing out his ears. He whipped it off, leaving redder marks where the elastic had bit in. Reached out to stop the music that had just restarted.

'Berlioz,' he said, as if that explained anything. '*Les nuits d'été*; Anne Sofie von Otter.'

'Right,' she said.

'Just songs, really,' he went on. 'But in many ways, they're like a mirror to the different things a heart does. The first one has this giddy, palpating rush to it; the second one does this sort of swoon, it's exactly like the feeling I get when ... Anyway, I've been trying to think things out,' he interrupted himself, getting to his feet rather gingerly, stretching his legs. 'Simon Grey was a no-show, so—'

'About that,' she said.

Luckily, Torben seemed too tired to be more than tokenistically angry. And also, somehow, very mellow. She remembered she was still wearing her seduction outfit, perhaps it was helping.

'I need a shower,' he said, after a mere two minutes or so of shouting. 'And maybe it worked out for the best – I concede you may have been a more sympathetic interrogator than I in this case. Look, come along up; you can look chastely the other way and debrief me.'

For a second, she was tempted to make a joke about debriefing him. But a glance at his face told her it was still too soon.

'... and first he claimed to have misspoken – *yes*, like a genuine politician! – but when I pressed him, he came out with this whole story of a reconciliation. How they had been very close as recently as 2016, during the referendum campaign – finally on the same side, you know, appearing at the same events, rekindling the old friendship they'd enjoyed during his years in opposition, when they'd last had a common enemy in Tony Blair ... *But* that in the reshuffle, after all the fallout that summer, he had finally got back into government as a junior minister in DEFRA—'

'Remind me?' came Torben's disembodied voice, from the other side of the over-bath shower curtains.

'Department for the Environment, Food and Rural Affairs,' Leyla glossed, 'which as you can readily appreciate is an intrinsically dangerous cocktail of cross-purposes, but anyway. Soon after that, they were both at a fundraiser at a cultural institution that he declined to name, and he claims that there was a miscommunication between them concerning his links to British Oil—'

'British Oil!' Torben practically shouted. There was a rattle of curtains. Leyla started back. She just had time to glimpse a streak of bare and surprisingly hairy Danish male, before he and his towel were out of the bathroom. She tracked the wet footprints across the corridor and found him, towel now hitched rather perilously around his middle, riffling through a recent volume of Charlotte's personal diary.

'Here it is!' he said. 'The Great Betrayal, she calls it. And it sounds like much more than a miscommunication – apparently he got so drunk that he accidentally let slip something about taking a six-figure backhander from British Oil, in exchange for approving a new drilling site in what had been earmarked to be protected waters. You should read the entry, Leyla, she's – well, her language gets rather creative. And then, that same night and still presumably sloshed, Grey compounded the indiscretion by sending *her* a panicked email, admitting that he'd let this slip, that was actually meant for his contact at BO—'

'BO? Really?'

'Yes; it must've led to some highly predictable protest slogans over the years. But the misdirected email – one of those message-your-spouse-instead-of-your-lover things – sounds like it was definitely incriminating. A written admission of corruption; at least, that's how Charlotte read it.'

'Wait,' said Leyla. 'Charlotte didn't have a computer, did she?'

'She was still an academic,' Torben pointed out. 'She had a work office, a desktop, an email address. She just didn't check it more than about once a month. That must be what Grey hoped for in this case, that she never read the email – it sounds like he knew her ways pretty well – but no such luck' – he flipped through a few more pages – 'because Charlotte claims to have printed off the email and kept it for a rainy day.'

He stood up. The towel just about stayed in place, which was probably for the best, thought Leyla. She rather liked what it did to his waist. Maybe she should always cancel his fancy lunches, it was clearly good for him …

'How did Grey finish his explanation?' Torben asked.

'He claimed she had invited him over to bury the hatchet,' Leyla said. 'Claimed that Charlotte had admitted she had read more into the situation than had been fair, and that they had agreed that, in this age of petty culture wars and an unhelpfully polarised public discourse, they should both put friendship and sentiment above petty differences. The way he painted it, it was all very touching.'

'Whereas I bet, in reality,' said Torben, 'she was testing the waters for her memoirs. There's a self-censored bit about Trigg, from her teens, where she makes a note wondering whether or not to include a certain compromising story. Calls Trigg "touchy" and says someone labelled RS is "litigious". The Simon Grey exposé is the sort of explosive allegation she'd have loved to get out in the public realm – imagine the mayhem, the embarrassment for the government – but would even Charlotte have dared? It could only have ended in Grey's disgrace, or a ruinous legal case for her and her publishers …'

'Either way,' Leyla mused, 'the whole thing remains purely conjectural. Unless, of course, that email is somewhere among all these papers?'

They hunted for ten minutes without success.

'Maybe she left it with her solicitor, or her bank, or something?' Leyla said at last.

Torben shook his head. 'Remember the codicil in her will? She more or less told me that everything of relevance was in these papers – she would surely have had the email sent to me separately if she'd stashed it somewhere else. No, I bet it *was* here ... until it went the same way as those excised pages.'

And at the same time, Leyla wondered? Or separately? It sounded increasingly like everyone had made off with something from Charlotte Lazerton's treasure trove. Azawakh's appearance in the memoirs, Lucia Segugio's promised painting ... and Grey's misdirected email? Had the same hand been responsible for the disappearance of all three?

She was about to put this impossible question to Torben, when his towel finally decided to change the subject. Fatally loosened by the search of the desk, it gave up its long struggle, and slid, very gracefully, to the floor.

An hour later, Torben felt it was almost safe to look Leyla in the eye. They had both been very grown up about the whole thing. That was what he didn't like. There was something in Leyla's studied professionalism, the way she had refrained from comment, or indeed speech of any kind, that made him fear there was a pent-up volcano of laughter, just waiting to explode. He couldn't begin to imagine how things would have gone had their places been reversed. Probably he'd have dropped dead on the spot. But at least he would have died happy.

For now, they had gone back to their table of suspects, newly armed with the fruits of five interviews, and had another go.

'Azawakh—' he had begun.

'Has all but formally announced to us that he was in charge of the cover-up. At least an accessory, for sure.'

'Though I *was* wondering – could his surprise, at the mention of murder, have been genuine?'

'You sweet summer child.'

'No, but hear me out – Azawakh's clean-up team went in on *Sunday*, the day *after* the body had been discovered and the police officially involved. Don't you think, if he'd been in on the whole thing, they'd have gone in immediately, say, on the Wednesday?'

'And risk being seen by someone like Marko Posavac? Surely that would be just *too* suspicious, Torben – a team of forensics with zero explanation. And then what, they'd have spirited away the body? No, the way I see it, they had no choice but to wait for it to be reported officially as an accident, and then make sure there was nothing incriminating if anyone chose to go into it more thoroughly …'

'OK, you have a point. But if he *had* been directly involved in the murder – would he really have gone back in himself? Allowed himself to be linked to the crime scene by potential witnesses?'

'Better that, surely, than entrust the whole job to someone else. Who better to know what needed covering up?'

'But they went too far, didn't they? Sterilised the whole damn place, not even a dog hair! That's not exactly the act of someone with inside knowledge …'

There had been a lot of this sort of conversation. It was frustrating, and it made his head hurt.

But it beat talking about the towel incident.

*

Eventually, they had a new MOM table on which they were agreed. It looked substantially better than the first version. Torben, digging out one of those four-colour pens he had last used, he suspected, for exam revision a full decade earlier, had even used different inks to indicate the relative significance of each element. At last, everyone had a motive – of greater or lesser clarity. There was a wide spectrum of opportunity, though they had resorted to using the fourth colour for Trigg and Drever as a 'neutral', to accommodate their differences of opinion in these two cases. And the method seemed as straightforward as before – though one cell of the table still remained tantalisingly empty.

Torben stood back a little from the page. And these people were meant to have been Charlotte's friends? He had a momentary image of a wounded lion surrounded by circling hyenas. And every pack of hyenas had to have its alpha. That being said, weren't hyenas matriarchal? Perhaps the parallel would only reinforce Leyla's pet theory. 'When you boil it down to this level,' he said instead, 'you lose a lot of the nuance. But it's pretty clear who stands out as our main suspect.'

And they each placed a finger upon a name.

The only problem was, it wasn't the same name.

Leyla laughed. 'Well, it was a good try. So what now; go back to your DS Gary Bassett, put him on the scent? He was the Senior Investigating Officer; there are things he can do that we can't.'

'N-no,' said Torben, the negative apparently drawn out despite himself. 'In all conscience, I don't think we can, not with Azawakh peering over our shoulders. We've been left alone so far, but I suspect that's because we've done nothing especially provocative just yet. The things we'd want from Bassett' – and he indicated a different name with each item – 'passport control data, CCTV footage, a search warrant, requisitioned emails, time logs … they all leave a trail, of request and authorisation. Even if Bassett managed to get any of them, which is far from guaranteed since he's not actually conducting an official investigation anymore, we'd be exposing him to repercussions. Risking his career.'

'So it's down to us after all? I rather thought we were at the limit of our powers – and the licence that Azawakh's allowing us. We've completed the interviews, for which we had a legitimate excuse. I don't see what more the two of us can achieve … We need … we need—'

'A cat!' said Torben.

'What? Is this some other esoteric Danish expression?'

'Leyla, what was that thing you said before we started these interviews – something about a pigeon?'

'I thought you were on about cats?' And Leyla thought of pigeons she had known recently. The ones unkicked in Lincoln's Inn Fields. The one that had snaffled the last of her empanada in Red Lion Square. All of them mute witnesses to her various frustrations with the entirely confusing Dane at her side.

'Something about this "being my pigeon". And it's another English saying, isn't it – in fact I think it's a Poirot novel – a cat among the pigeons? And here we have five fat pigeons, all refusing to budge, all of them complacently pecking the seed of security—'

'You may be at risk of overstretching this metaphor, Torben—'

'When what they need is a cat set among them. Something to shake them all up! And then we see who takes flight, or gets eaten, or—'

'A cat …' An image was forming in Leyla's mind, of unsighted birds, intent on one direction, while behind them, creeping up from afar, armed with secret knowledge … 'Torben, are you thinking what I'm thinking?'

'The climate march!' Torben shouted, his every feature alight with enthusiasm. 'We flush them out! Send an email that compels the guilty party, or maybe parties, to gather for the protest rally. Say that it concerns the truth about the murder of Charlotte – that it's their only chance – fill their thoughts with paranoia, and force them to march while we observe them. They'll be miles from their comfort zones ...'

He was pacing now, actually pacing, as he elaborated on the idea. 'Whoever's implicated will come, so it'll narrow the field. If they're guilty, they'll be desperate to find out what someone knows, to hush it up. If they're complicit, they'll think someone's blabbed ... try to control the narrative ... so seeing who shows up will already do half the job for us. The rally – the float, my students' float! – will be a constant reminder of Charlotte and her activism. Elodie said it was a homage to her. If only one person comes, we're sorted. If there are more ... well, say we insist they have to stick it out as far as Parliament Square, that would give them, what, two hours together? On edge? Something's *bound* to come out. And when it does, we'll be on the spot, ready to record.'

Leyla looked at him. 'Um, no, Torben,' she said at last. 'No, that wasn't what I was thinking at all.'

He felt a moment's disappointment. Part of him, he was coming to realise, more or less lived for those moments when he and Leyla vibrated to the same idea. But what did it matter if they weren't perfectly attuned this time: he had his cat! Thank God for the pigeon metaphor; it had got him there – the London street, the crowd ...

'Torben,' Leyla said, speaking in a sympathetic, patient tone he immediately distrusted. 'What's Jonathan Azawakh going to think

– what are *any* of them going to think – when he gets an email from you of all people, with some cock-and-bull setup—'

'It won't *be* from me, *narre*, it'll be anonymous!'

'And you think a senior MI6 official isn't going to be able to trace who registered definitelynotatrap@gmail.com, do you? Remember, Tor, he doesn't have to bump you off – you've only got settled status, you're not a UK citizen; he could arrange to have you deported in a shot on that kind of evidence.'

That gave him pause. But only for a moment. 'Zak Cremello!' he said.

'What?!'

'Friend of a friend. The venture capital genius, or whatever he is, remember? He's got this flagship company that sounds legitimate, but he's always dropping self-aggrandising hints that he's no stranger to the black market or the dark web. I'm not sure if his less-publicised ventures are just the sort of hobbies a bored rich boy runs to keep the thrill alive, or where he actually makes his real money, but either way he'll know how to send an untraceable email.'

'And on the day itself? You'll be in disguise I suppose?'

'Why not? I could wear one of those Guy Fawkes masks from *V for Vendetta* – in fact, it's perfect: all sorts of people will be dressed up, or hiding their faces. And I bet that'll include Simon Grey at least.'

He loved the idea of turning the tables on Azawakh, of playing the spy himself. The only way, he thought, that it didn't work, was if they *were* all in on it together, as a consortium. Which was, as he had told himself three times already, a ridiculous proposition. Why it should keep popping back into his mind ... But otherwise, even if a couple of them had been in partnership – say, Grey and Azawakh, to pick the most obvious pairing – there'd still be doubt in everyone's mind. The suspicion that someone they had thought of as a friend had smelt a rat …

'OK,' she said at last. 'You have a brilliant, foolproof plan that will definitely lead to busy members of the establishment showing up at a climate rally, and to at least one of them, against their own best interests, saying something incriminating. I wish you joy of it, I really do. But, Torben – I think this has to be just your pigeon, too. Sorry.'

'You mean … you mean you won't come?' It was, in every way possible, a desolating thought.

'For one thing, I'm not supposed to. There are expectations of impartiality that govern what someone in my position, representing the kind of clients I do, can get up to in my private life. If I were recognised …'

'You could be masked too! A nice Zorro or something?'

She shook her head. 'The march is on Saturday, isn't it? Ruth's last weekend on duty?'

'Yes …'

'I know you were thinking of that as some kind of deadline, for whatever reason, and fair enough, since Ruth seems perfectly happy to play along. But in that case, our time is running out, and no offence, but your undeniably ingenious plan comes with a rather high margin for error. Now, I've got to be in the office for a couple of days, and this will take time to arrange anyway. But while you've been working out how to choreograph pigeons, I think I've hit on another avenue of enquiry. One we should frankly have pursued much, much earlier. No, I'm *not* going to tell you what it is – let's just say that, while you seem bent on walking very slowly through central London, I intend to take a train to the country.'

'That's really all you're going to tell me?' he said. 'When I've spelt out every last detail of my Machiavellian scheme?'

'Yup.'

'So this is, what, a bet? Whose method gets us to the truth?'

'If you like.'

'What are we playing for?'

Leyla gave him a very, very long look. He couldn't tell if it was more calculating, dangerous, dirty or amused. But it was probably the highlight of his year so far.

'It's going to be a long train journey,' she said. 'I'll mull it over.'

20

FOURTEEN INBOXES, ONE DOORMAT

Danish Torben

Gary, I need to report a missing person. She's not in the online database. Ximena Podenco, female, age range 18–25, as far as I know she's from Mexico. No specific description but I think slim, average height, dark hair. And probably not 'on the books'. She'd need witness protection or whatever – basically if you find her, can she please not be deported? I'm only naming her in extremis. Tak for det. **23:53**

11th June
Haberdasher Street
London

Dear Beryl (if I may),
We have never met, but I am working with Torben Helle, to whom you once extended a very kind invitation to call on you if ever he found himself in Dorset. In taking the liberty of writing to you, I'm building up to asking an even greater one – that I might call on you in his stead, as soon as humanly possible.

Wow, writing an actual letter by hand really does make

you change tone, doesn't it? Sorry. I'm a barrister, my name's Leyla Moradi, you can look me up – give me a piece of headed notepaper and I slip too easily into formality! The point is: we've been looking into the death of your cousin Charlotte Lazerton, in concert with two of the police officers involved at the time, and I'm very sorry to inform you that we have strong grounds for believing Dame Charlotte's death was not entirely natural.

I can tell you much more in person. Please believe me when I write that time is very much of the essence, and I would deeply appreciate a few hours of your company, if that might be possible, later this week. I am more than happy to travel to you and will answer all your questions, if you will do me the enormous favour of reciprocating. I believe you may be in possession of the information we need to make sense of this appalling case.

As this is really rather urgent for reasons I'll explain in person, I'd appreciate it if you could reply asap by telephone or email; I enclose my number and address. Message or call any time, and please do believe me when I say I am very much looking forward to meeting you.

Yours in haste, and in hope,
Leyla Moradi

Subject: Request for email data
From: Torben Helle
Sent: Tue, 12 June, 09:00
To: IT-Support-Desk

Hello!

Sorry to trouble you this late in the academic year but I wonder if you can help me.

I'm working on two concurrent projects about our late colleague Professor Charlotte Lazerton that have hit the same technical hitch:

1. I am charged by the terms of her will to edit her correspondence and writings.
2. I am also editing an academic volume in tribute to her life for this book series.

On both counts, in order to follow up key sources, I find myself requiring access to official email correspondence. Do you know if there is any possible means of granting access to Professor Lazerton's Office 365 account, or more likely retrieving/downloading the data from it? I can provide authorisation from Head of Faculty if it would help.

Many thanks for your time and any assistance you can provide!

Torben

Torben Helle
Postdoctoral Fellow in Nordic Art
MA, MSt, DPhil (Oxon), FSA, FRHistS, FHEA

Leyla

Frances I have a MASSIVE favour to ask 23:49

Today

    Frances
    ... ? 07:31

Leyla

You know your friend/ex on the Observer? 07:32

    Frances
    Are you and Tor still doing this? FFS it's been weeks! 07:44

Leyla

Srsly just one tiny thing please please please 07:45

    Frances
    Aye? 07:48

Leyla

Thank you thank you OK, we just need an overview of Shah Rajasthan's movements or meetings on 23–25 April this year. Nothing dodgy, just a schedule, whatever. And for anything on pm of Tue 24, confirmation she was actually there. 07:50

FFS Shani RajapalayM 07:50

Rajapalayam 07:51

    Frances
    🙄 07:56

Leyla

Offer them whatever it takes. Money, sexual favours, a nice portrait. Legal advice for free, for life. Just – please? 07:58

And the same for you, obvs. 08:00

Except the sex. 08:01

Unless that would help? 08:01

OK sorry sorry. I will owe you FOREVER 08:09

Frances
Fine 08:16

Leyla
🖤 08:16

Subject: Re. Charlotte Lazerton's Murder
From: Unknown Address
Sent: Tue, 12 June, 18:11
To: Undisclosed Recipients

I am in possession of sensitive information concerning the murder of Dame Charlotte Lazerton and the subsequent suppression of this fact. If you wish to hear more, and to avoid this information being passed on to both the press and the police, then I advise you to attend the Climate Crisis Rally taking place this Saturday 16 June. Be at the Bomber Command Memorial at 12:00 precisely. There is a float designed to honour Professor Lazerton's recent work, modelled on the Titanic. Form part of the march beside this float. Do not leave the procession until it reaches Parliament Square. Compliance is in your best interests. Tell no one. Come alone. Message ends //

Subject: Re: Re. Charlotte Lazerton's Murder
From: Simon Grey
Sent: Tue, 12 June, 20:53
To: Unknown Address

Who the fuck is this and how do you have my private email address? I don't know what you're playing at but I do NOT condone such irresponsible rumourmongering and will be taking the strongest possible measures in this matter to ensure you do not get away with attempting to intimidate a member of Her Majesty's Government.

Subject: Mail Delivery Failed: Re: Re. Charlotte Lazerton's Murder
From: Mail Delivery System
Sent: Tue, 12 June, 20:54
To: Simon Grey

The following address(es) failed: Unknown Address <ohno@you_dont.com>

Subject: FWD: Request for email data
From: Amy Schiller
Sent: Wed, 13 June, 09:19
To: Pierre Basenji
Cc: Torben Helle

See below – can you advise? Thx Amy

Subject: Autoreply: Re: FWD: Request for email data
From: Pierre Basenji
Sent: Wed, 13 June, 09:20
To: Amy Schiller

Thank you for your message. I am out of the office until Monday 18 June. If your query is urgent, please contact Amy Schiller at amy.schiller@courtauld.ac.uk
Best wishes
Pierre Basenji

Subject: Quick auditing enquiry
From: Leyla Moradi
Sent: Wed, 13 June, 10:00
To: Maria Artois

Dear Professor Artois,
I am writing to you in your capacity as host organiser of the recent international conference Art, Heritage and Society in a Global Future, held at your Brussels campus on 23–25 April.

I represent a law firm currently undertaking consultancy work in the UK Higher Education Sector. One of the services we provide our partner institutions is a randomised audit of expense claims to ensure compliance with HMRC. In this instance, I am auditing the subsistence claims entered by <Insert name hereProfessor Henrik Drever> relating to a keynote speech given at your conference.

We find that the easiest way to approve these claims is by light-touch informal enquiry. To that end, could you please confirm that <Professor Henrik Drever> was physically present on your campus during some of each of the following times?

Monday 23 April 11:00–13:00 CET
Monday 23 April 13:00–17:00 CET
Tuesday 24 April 09:00–13:00 CET
Tuesday 24 April 13:00–17:00 CET
Wednesday 25 April 09:00–13:00 CET
Wednesday 25 April 13:00–15:00 CET

Many thanks for your cooperation in this matter.
Yours sincerely,
Leyla Moradi
Barrister, 45 Bedford Row

Subject: Re: Re: FWD: Request for email data
From: Oliver Dachs
Sent: Wed, 13 June, 16:42
To: Torben Helle
Cc: Amy Schiller

Unfortunately, data protection laws mean we are not able to assist you in this matter.
Kind regards
Oliver Dachs

Beryl
Can be free Friday. Waterloo to Poole, X8 to Blandford Forum.
Message ETA and will meet you off bus. Pack an overnight bag.
Just come. Beryl. **17:05**

Subject: Re: Item #0194
From: Torben Helle
Sent: Wed, 13 June, 20:22
To: Giles Hamilton

Hello

I am interested in purchasing this rather fabulous chest of drawers.
Could you please quote for delivery to London WC1N 2NW? Also, you say
it is Swedish, c.1770 – do you have more details of the provenance?
Best wishes
Torben Helle

21

EN ROUTE

Obviously, thought Leyla, it would have been better to have Torben along for the ride. But he might not have played up satisfactorily to his allotted part of Dr Watson. Certainly, as the train pulled out of Waterloo station, she was feeling thoroughly Holmesian, even if, she suspected, Holmes had not had to pay the equivalent of a week's grocery shopping for a weekend return fare. Still, inflation notwithstanding, what could be more in keeping with the Conan Doyle aesthetic than jumping on a train headed out of the old metropolis, bound for the west country? She even had sandwiches and an enormous newspaper. No deerstalker, but then she had a feeling that wasn't actually canon, and obviously no pipe – she wondered once again why individual train companies made a point of insisting it was their policy not to allow smoking, as if they were exercising some kind of unique sovereignty within the bounds of this metal tube, rather than it simply being the law, and their private policy wholly irrelevant … Well, she'd sort of answered her own question there, hadn't she? Five minutes into the journey and she'd already solved one mystery. It all came down to the illusion of power. An illusion that, if successful, became self-realising, and thereby no longer illusory …

God, listen to yourself, Leyla Moradi. This was clearly what spending too much time with Torben did to you.

Probably for the best, thought Torben, not to have Leyla along for the ride tomorrow. His own role was that of hidden observer, and that was going to be hard enough. He couldn't imagine the two of them in that situation for any length of time without one or other flaring up, flouncing off, generally blowing the gaff. *To blow the gaff.* And people said *his* idioms were eccentric.

Wordplay was on his mind right now. He was making a collection of conundrums and paradoxes, just on the off-chance that Leyla might find any of them diverting. Much as she would hate to admit it, there was something about her legalistic mind that enjoyed geeking out over contradictions; it was one of the things he had noticed about her recently. Part of her soft and ticklish underbelly; his way in. Since words were all he had to take her heart away, and all that jazz. Perhaps she'd like this one: if vampires can't see their reflections, why are they always in black tie? Surely the bow ties would be a nightmare?

He caught himself. Was this what his brain did when you turned everything else off? He was in an unlooked-for limbo, everything resting on tomorrow. No Leyla. No news from Gary Bassett. Maybe it had been a mistake to have Zak disable replies to the email address he had given him; it would have been good to see if any of his five fishes were writhing on the hook. As it was, he was just – waiting. He had his theories, but until someone's nerve broke, that was all they were.

So here he was, unable to concentrate, quite incapable of working, and it was still hours to go until football. He glanced out of the window. If Azawakh had detailed anyone to watch him, they would be having a boring time of it. But the street was practically deserted. Someone – an owner, alas, to judge by the expensive outfit, not a professional he could rush out and question – was walking an Alsatian. It had stopped by the lamp-post opposite, and was ... well, yes. He was glad to see the owner had a heavy-duty disposal bag. What was it about the defecation of large dogs that he found so disconcerting? The way they cocked their legs to urinate was almost charming, but this – all hunched on their hind legs, the squat – it positively revolted him. Maybe it was that, in shifting towards a bipedal state, they became that much more anthropomorphic, and therefore obscene ... maybe he just had a complex.

God, he really missed having Leyla here.

How was it possible, she mused, that the good people of Poole had allowed the three-letter abbreviation of their station used by National Rail to be POO? According to her app, they were currently about halfway between WOK and WIN, both towns rather more favoured by that shortening process, and would soon be pulling in to BSK – not BAS – for Basingstoke, so some latitude was clearly possible ... Leyla suppressed a shudder of unlooked-for fear as she remembered Jonathan Azawakh telling them about his family's house down in Micheldever, and it dawned on her that this was almost certainly his Friday commuter route home, hopefully some hours later than this; he would have to change at BSK for Micheldever – or rather, MIC – except, if Torben's plan had worked, he might just be giving that train a miss this evening, remaining in London for the climate march ...

A message flashed up on her phone, and she clicked on it immediately, but it was only her service provider informing her the next month's bill was due. No word as yet from either Frances or the Belgian conference organiser. Which meant all five suspects were still in play. Which was far from ideal. Whatever she was hoping to get from Beryl Cabell-Fowell – preferably straightforward answers rather than further questions – it was unlikely to be more than circumstantial. A stacking of the odds, rather than a definitive verdict.

Now, if she really *were* Sherlock Holmes, the person waiting at the other end of this train ... and, she remembered, additional rural bus service ... that person would supply her with *the* crucial piece of the puzzle. They would explain how Katherine Trigg had been able to murder Dame Charlotte down a phone line, for instance, which was still Leyla's preferred theory, if only because Torben had found it so preposterous.

The tannoy came on, crackly as ever, just about intelligible. Something about signalling issues further down the line, around Southampton. Oh joy.

Sherlock Holmes never had to contend with Network Rail in the age of austerity. Say what you like about fin de siècle serialised detective fiction: at least they made the trains run on time.

Some hours later, wedged into a top-deck window seat next to a teen with a *very* involved personal life, living every sway of the X8 and nursing an incipient sense of travel sickness, Leyla found herself almost nostalgic for the train. On the other hand, Dorset in June was positively idyllic, which was to say fluffy, all hedges and copses and fields of gently rippling wheat. And the road signs said things like Lytchett Matravers, Kingston Lacy or Charlton Marshall, all of which made her think it was time to ditch Holmes: she was in Miss Marple territory now.

She looked up Kingston Lacy. The National Trust property seemed a thoroughly Torbenish sort of place. Ugh, now she felt sick again. From looking at the screen, obviously, not the association of ideas … oh thank fuck, this was Blandford Forum they were coming into … and this, a couple more queasy lurches sideways up the hill, must be her stop. Salvation! All very quaint and olde worlde. Someone had even seen fit to park one of those funny old three-wheeled cars, what were they called, something to do with a bird? Yes, a Ferrari-red Reliant Robin, from the wound-down window of which a woman in a headscarf was now leaning out and waving … waving to her.

Oh no. Please no.

'How could you tell it was me?' said Leyla, strapping herself into the passenger seat with the same sense of 'fuck it, here goes' as Julius Caesar allegedly felt when crossing the Rubicon.

Beryl Cabell-Fowell laughed. It was a rich, rather deep sound; it put Leyla in mind of plum cake. 'Look at yourself, dear. This is Blandford. You're the most interesting thing to show up here since they opened the M&S Foodhall.' And she did something with the gearstick that made Leyla wonder if it was, by some anatomical sleight of hand, secretly wired up to her own intestines.

'How – how far is it to Hod Hill Manor?' she asked.

'Oh, ten minutes, at the outside. Unless you want me to really step on it?' There was something in Beryl's voice that suggested she would be delighted to do just that.

'Um, no, if it's all right with you, I'd … there's really no need.'

Beryl twinkled at her. 'Yes, the bus does that to some people. Don't worry yourself. I'll take it nice and easy, we can have a cup of tea, and then we can talk all about which bastard murdered my cousin.'

22

HOD HILL

More fields, trees, hedges … Leyla, alive to every jolt and thunk of this three-wheeled rattlebox of torture, was finding it difficult to process either the scenery or Beryl's last statement. Something about tea … and also murder?

They were juddering up through one of those green tunnels, all cocooned between banks, trees almost meeting overhead. Emerging onto the open crest of the valley felt like some sort of release.

'That's Hod Hill itself to the left,' Beryl nodded, as if their conversation had been entirely humdrum. 'You can't really tell for the hedges, but it's an Iron Age hillfort. Now, this is Stourpaine' – a thatched cottage; an ancient coaching inn called the pale, no, the *White* Horse; a church spire – 'and we're just out the other side. I was wondering whether, reading between the lines of your letter, your Torben Helle himself was the wrong 'un, but we can get to all that once you're feeling a bit more alive yourself.'

Leyla's attempt to answer manifested only as an 'oof' of air, as she was taken aback by a sudden lurch left, off the main road, up a winding dirt track. Steadying herself, she caught sight of a low-slung manor house up ahead, nestled into the slope of the hill, a rise of tall green trees behind. Despite the fact they were in the south, and it was summer, she was getting flashbacks to another country house. These did little for the state of her insides. Yet she couldn't help but feel a little underwhelmed when they pulled up well short of the house – 'pulled up' being the tranquil euphemism for the almighty jerk the death-trap gave as it abruptly ceased all forward motion – coming to quivering rest beside another one of those thatched cottages she had clocked back in the village.

'Here we are,' announced Beryl, in tones altogether more placid than Leyla thought fit for the situation. And then, 'Oh no you don't, my lad! *Down*, Rodger! I said *down*.' And she interposed herself between Leyla and some calf-sized dervish of an animal, a dog to judge from its deep, happy barking, just before it was able to knock Leyla over or lick her face off or whatever else was on its tiny mind.

'Oh, but he's beautiful!' she said, tactically. Then realised that she meant it. The creature had a lovely long, straggly coat, very thick, a gorgeous sort of grey fading to blond, and one of those big moppety heads, all silly floppy ears, big button nose, hair over its eyes, lolling tongue. It looked like the sort of puppet of a dog they made for old children's television programmes. Leyla put out her hand to the beast, let him nuzzle it. 'Good boy. Roger, was it?'

'Yes, Rodger; he's an otterhound,' said Beryl. 'But don't worry, he's never hunted a thing in his life. At least, he's never *caught* anything. Between you and me, if it came to it I'd put my money on the otter, but don't tell Rodger. The breed name's a sort of relic, really.'

For the first time, Leyla had a moment to take in her companion. She seemed a good candidate for the name of relic herself – wax jacket despite the summer heat, a pair of wellies, the faded, rather moth-eaten headscarf ... could that possibly be straw sticking out?

'We're not going up to the manor then?' she asked.

'Good lord no,' said Beryl. 'That's where my people live, and trust me, you do *not* want to waste your time making small talk with them. I bung the manor on the address when I want to sound grand, but I'm only the mad aunt; unless it's Christmas or a big birthday, I make shift in this hovel.' She gestured to the picture-perfect cottage behind her. Yes, it looked ready to fall down at the slightest breath of wind, but there was honeysuckle all the way up the wall, and a climbing rose trained over the doorway. Between the fragrance of flowers and the country air, Leyla was already feeling three parts human.

'Tea?' said Beryl.

And that would do the rest of the job.

In ten minutes, Leyla was unpacked in the spare bedroom – one of just two upstairs rooms – all undulating floorboards and sloping beams, with those roses peeking in at the window and a deeply touching crock of flowers on her bedside table. She followed the sound of the whistling kettle, and relieved Beryl of a tray heaving with tea things. There was a little veranda to the back of the cottage, facing southwest down the slope, with vines growing up the trellis and over their heads. That slope descended through a wildflower meadow to a dainty little stream with tall trees along its banks. Bees were humming somewhere nearby. Swallows dipped in perfect arabesques. As they sat in two wicker rocking chairs, Leyla had the sudden premonition that they would be ensconced here for hours, till the midsummer sun finally went down. She could think of nothing she would like better.

Oh, and also, it turned out there was cake.

*

Torben had decided, reluctantly, to give Friday football a miss. The odds of injury were vanishingly long, but after his ankle sprain back in February, he knew better than to risk any chance of immobilising himself before a big day. Trying to ignore the intense hormonal comedown that always accompanied a cancelled session, he busied himself with his mask and costume for the march.

Anonymity would be key. He had already taken Elodie into his confidence by email – he couldn't risk being outed by his students, who had spent so much more time with him than whichever of the five suspects might be drawn out to play, and would almost certainly recognise him whatever he wore. Not that he had told her the truth, of course. Just that, for reasons he could only explain after the event, her group would be joined tomorrow by a masked and cloaked figure they were to refer to, if at all, as Ben Catesby.

Even in disguise, he had a deplorable weakness for allusion.

'So why exactly,' said Leyla at last, 'did you say you thought someone had murdered your cousin?'

'Well, haven't they?' said Beryl.

They had finished the pot of tea, and the seedcake. Leyla had clocked a bottle of sherry waiting in the wings, and wanted to cut to the chase before proceedings reached that stage.

'Yes,' she admitted. 'We're pretty definite about that: there's been an official cover-up. Someone sent in a clean-up operation in advance of the official forensics team, and even that report was probably doctored. Plus we found evidence that key, compromising pages had been surgically removed from Charlotte's memoirs. Either someone physically pushed her down that staircase, or she was induced to fall—'

'Induced?'

'Yes, we think drugs, or maybe, I don't know ...' Leyla stopped herself before she said the word 'hypnotism', which had somehow edged itself to the tip of her tongue, and would surely have scotched all credibility she may have had with this woman.

Beryl nodded. 'No one who knew Charlotte well could ever have bought the idea of her simply falling down her staircase. She was spry as a – as a spring chicken, and she could have navigated that house blindfolded, on her head. In fact I think she once did exactly that for a bet. She wasn't some, some doddery old biddy!'

Leyla glanced at the small figure beside her, almost Charlotte's age herself, and brimming with vitality.

'Quite,' she agreed. 'That was Torben's immediate reaction too. Oh, and rest assured he is *not* under suspicion; in fact, it's his investigation, we're just pursuing different leads right now.'

'Hmm,' said Beryl. 'Well, if you're sure. I mean, he did stand to gain an awful lot by her will. And I'm on episode three of *Crimeward Ho*, young lady: while I don't want any spoilers, from what I've heard so far I would warn you to be on your guard with that young man. There are certain indications ...'

Leyla's laugh, unbidden, uncontrollable, at least had the effect of quashing that particular line of enquiry. 'So,' she said at last, 'that's why your reply was so urgent, so insistent?'

'Exactly,' said Beryl. 'Knew you must be on to something. And if there's justice to be done, I want to play my part. Best person I ever met, cousin Charlie. You know she left me her dog Mortimer in the will? Impossible, of course, but still ...'

Was it Leyla's imagination, or was there a sudden glisten to those acute grey eyes? 'I've got good news on that front,' she said. 'He's not been put down; he's been adopted by the local police station.'

This news appeared to act as a tonic on her hostess. For several minutes, Leyla battled a flood of canine reminiscences, centred on wolfhounds Dame Charlotte had owned over the years. Reading between the lines, Leyla was starting to wonder if there was something like hero-worship at the back of the two women's relationship. Gently, she set about steering the conversation back to the case.

'... we have five suspects,' she eventually managed. 'That's really why I'm here. I wondered whether you might know something that would help us pin down one of them.'

'Oh good, I love a list!' Beryl actually rubbed her hands. 'Let's take them in order from least to most promising, shall we?'

'Um – right,' said Leyla. It was a little like having a mirror held too close to her face. This veering between a righteous sense of retribution and a gleeful enjoyment of the sport of detection – of all the people she knew with any experience of it, only Ruth seemed to be above this sort of double standard. She recognised it well from her day job, the ability to care deeply about a case to the point of total self-sacrifice, yet both relish the game she was playing, and remain on good, even jocular terms with the lawyers on the other side. It was, she suspected, a particularly English form of hypocrisy, one that had not featured on her own citizenship test. But, she had to admit, one she was now capable of passing with flying colours.

'Number one then,' she said, mentally reshuffling their suspects into her own preferred order. 'Professor Henrik Drever, a long-time colleague of Charlotte's. Excellent motive; equally excellent alibi.'

'Drever ... Drever,' mused Beryl. 'Nope, never heard of him.'

'Really? Nothing in the will?'

'Not a sausage. Which fits. Charlie and I have met up and written pretty faithfully over the years, and I think I could claim to recognise all the beneficiaries, if only by reputation. I'm guessing this Drever is some sort of slug or pondlife?'

'I confess I don't really know him either,' said Leyla. 'He's in university management.'

'Say no more. But I'm afraid I can't help you with him. Next!'

'OK, number two. Another professor, the art critic Shani Rajapalayam.'

'Oh, Shani?! No no no. Surely not. Not in a million years!' Beryl looked aghast. There was a moment's pause. 'On the other hand, maybe. Yes, actually I can absolutely see it.'

Leyla raised the more interrogative of her two eyebrows.

'Well you see, she's just that *sort*. Nice, oh yes, there's no one nicer. But hard to get a real grip on, you know? I've met her a few times, and she was never less than lovely to me, but I couldn't claim to have the first idea what makes her tick.' Another pause. 'Except art, obviously. The passion's clear enough. Maybe that's all it is, no mystery, just a total obsession with the painty stuff. If she's put all her real feeling into pictures, then maybe she's got nothing to spare for ordinary things like people. Though now I come to think of it, she and Charlie ...'

'Yes?' Leyla perched forward on the edge of her rocker, before realising her mistake, and scooting back just before the momentum pitched her out altogether.

'Well, Charlie's never been one to hold back when she has an opinion to offer – as you may have noticed? Yes, I can see you have. Well, that being the case, and her having known Shani for some forty-odd years, give or take – in fact I think Shani lodged with her at one stage – she was one of her protégées, that's what it comes down to ... well, given all that, it seems odd to me that she has featured so rarely in Charlie's letters and rants over the years. If Shani really *is* in the frame ...?'

'Oh yes,' said Leyla. 'She's definitely somewhere in the mix.'

'Well, then. For someone of such importance in Charlie's life and death – and given the rumours about her domestic goings-on – I'd have expected to know a lot more of the inside scoop than I do. All I know of Shani comes from her, and her public profile – not from Charlie.'

'I see.' Leyla tried to adjust herself to this unexpected negative inference. It seemed important. 'Can you think of any reason why your cousin might have been so ... discreet?'

'Yes, I can,' said Beryl. She sounded less than happy about it. 'The usual one.'

'Ah.'

For fanden, thought Torben, but these eco lightbulbs were useless. He had finished prepping his costume for the march. Cooked, eaten, washed up. Gone for a walk. Now he couldn't concentrate on a thing – it didn't help that the book he was currently reading was an eight-hundred-page single sentence by Jon Fosse – but the light was not *quite* good enough to do any work on the floorboards. Plus he was now on such good terms with his neighbours, and it seemed a bit late to start making that much noise. So what, exactly, was he meant to do with himself, for the long hours that remained before he could possibly go to bed?

He tried watching one of the remaining clips of Charlotte, to see if it could provide any last-minute inspiration. A gaunt male novelist who had been big in the eighties was grumbling on a BBC4 arts programme.

'All this *narrative non-fiction* about intellectual young women who've got something wrong with them,' he was saying. 'Like an illness – or rather a complex – or maybe a boyfriend who doesn't appreciate them properly, *yawn*. I mean, it's practically a cabal, a conspiracy – the publishers, the writers, the readers, they're *all the same people*, the exact same type of people, most of them women – and what do they reward, over and over again? Self-absorption, that's what – forever collectively fawning over a handful of them who get nominated to slap their names on the same introspective claptrap, with never a look-in for the rest of us. It's, it's vicarious onanism, that's what it is. They elect the most photogenic or diverse of these young women to perform a circle-jerk of—'

'Vicarious self-pleasuring,' Charlotte interrupted, 'I rather like that. The only problem, sweetie, is that what you've just defined there is "all literature". Only when you were at it with the other boys, back in the glory days, it didn't need a has-been on a panel discussion to point out who the wankers were.'

At this point, the host intervened. Torben gave up. Even the put-down had failed to hold his attention. If only he'd gone to football, he'd be tired enough to turn in early. But at this rate, he'd be up all night, and no good for anything in the morning.

There was nothing for it. He sighed. Removed his outer layers of clothing. And, in the dim-lit loneliness of a London townhouse, a Danish art historian began to do a series of silent star-jumps.

Inevitably, they had started on the sherry.

'Number three then,' said Leyla. 'Simon Grey, MP.'

'That two-faced git?' said Beryl. 'I'm glad he's on the list. Can't we just say it's him?'

'I fear the police may require more in the way of actual evidence,' said Leyla. 'Why the antipathy, may I ask?'

'Well, for one thing,' said Beryl, 'if you've dug into him, you'll know his recent record in government. The unacceptable face of big oil, with its fat arse firmly wedged into Westminster.'

Leyla raised her glass in acknowledgement.

'You've no idea how much it hurt Charlie,' Beryl went on. 'You know, she actually *liked* him? Apparently he knew a lot about van Dyck, kept a good wine cellar, and cut his political teeth campaigning for entry to the Common Market. All things to put her firmly in his favour. She had him down as another Ken Clarke, someone you knew where you were with. His about-turn on the fossil fuel thing really hit her hard. But frankly, I'd have had her down to murder him, rather than the other way round. What's his motive?'

'Preventing a leak,' said Leyla. 'Which makes it sound like he's either incontinent or a ship's carpenter, sorry – the short version is that he slipped up. He'd been accepting bribes from a big oil company in return for fixing licences in their favour. This happens a lot, of course, and people mostly get away with it – but that's because they don't usually email clear evidence of their wrongdoing to the person who's just accused them. I believe he was drunk at the time. Anyway, he knew Charlotte had the goods on him, and tried to silence her. We can't be certain to what lengths he went. But,' she concluded, 'he was on the scene of the crime earlier that afternoon. I can play you his testimony if you like.'

'I'd rather not hear his voice in my house, thank you very much,' said Beryl. 'But surely you've got him bang to rights? All you need is that email, and you'd have enough circumstantial evidence to get the police to look into it. Provable motive, clear wrongdoing, on the scene …'

'I fear,' said Leyla, 'you've been reading too many detective novels. But the real problem is, I suspect we can't lay our hands on the email *without* the police. Sort of a Catch-22. I don't suppose you have anything to add to the picture?'

'Well, he wasn't in the will, for obvious reasons ...' said Beryl, pouring them both another glass. Leyla reminded herself that each one was only tiny. They barely amounted to anything. Although she rather wished she'd taken note of how full the bottle was when they started.

It turned out that all Beryl had to add was more invective, some of it conspicuously borrowed from Charlotte's own indictment of the man she had once considered a friend. But Leyla had not supposed there would be any especial insights on this score. Time to move on.

'Number four: Jonathan Azawakh,' she said, the hackles rising on her neck as if they might, even now, be overheard.

For a moment, Beryl said nothing. Then she leant forward. Leyla prepared herself for revelations.

'Jonathan who?' said Beryl.

At three hundred and twenty star jumps, Torben stopped. Caught his breath. Took stock.

Nope, it hadn't helped. He was feeling as stir-crazy as ever.

For all Leyla's questions, Beryl really seemed never to have heard of the civil servant. At least, not by name – she was aware that a faceless 'Man from the Ministry' had recruited Charlotte, or so Beryl had surmised, at some point after her first trip to Russia. But the subject had never been discussed, for obvious reasons. 'She said it was all boring, routine stuff,' said Beryl. 'Of course, what she really wanted was to protect me. Plausible deniability and all that. I can tell you I was all ears at the time, I've read every John le Carré, but not a peep did I get out of her.'

All of which, thought Leyla, made the whole thing sound more serious than ever. But there was no mileage in going any further down this route, not when her interviewee had no knowledge of the suspect. Besides, she sensed it would nearly be time for the evening meal, and she wanted to get on to her own irrational obsession.

'Number five, then,' she said. 'Kath—'

An oven timer sounded from somewhere behind them.

'Oh, sorry, dear,' said Beryl, rising. 'That'll be the lasagne.'

Oh, well, in that case. Leyla was willing to wait a little longer for justice where lasagne was concerned.

Where, thought Torben, was the nearest Mexican restaurant? No, Google, *not* Taco Bell – something family-run and genuine ... This one was Californian, this one Tex-Mex ... He cast his net further afield. OK, a handful of them. And a Friday night – they'd be far busier than he could wish, but at least they'd all be open for a few hours. Time to start putting in some legwork on the biggest loose end in this case. Call it a warm-up for tomorrow's march.

Mushrooms, lentils, spinach – Leyla would have to reappraise Beryl; she had not had her down as a vegetarian-alternative sort of cook. 'What does Roger eat?' she asked.

'Road-kill, mostly. It balances out the meat-free kibble.'

Leyla wished she hadn't asked. The phrase 'meat-free kibble' was already having a retrospective impact upon her enjoyment of that lasagne. Instead, she finally introduced Katherine Trigg into the conversation.

'Kitty Trigg!' Beryl seemed taken aback. 'But she couldn't hurt a fly.'

Leyla began to outline their reasoning – the evidence of historic bad blood, her connection via the phone call to the day of the murder, her association with the other suspects – when something struck her. '"Couldn't"?' she said.

'I see you really *are* a lawyer,' Beryl said. 'Yes, I meant exactly that. There's always been a mean streak in that one – I knew her quite well when we were young, her people have lived around here for generations, still do in fact, though Kitty herself moved to London forever ago – but she lacks guts. I'm sure if she could simply press a button to do someone in, she wouldn't hesitate – the author of the unauthorised biography of John Mortimer comes to mind for starters, apparently she hates that man – but I can't see her as a flesh-and-blood killer. That's not me being ableist, either – I know what you young people are like – but her mobility issues are besides the point. She never was one for getting her hands dirty; one of those rather obsessive people, sort of only half *here* if you know what I mean … the type where reality is almost a sideshow to their actual interest, whether that's a long-held grievance or an all-consuming hobby. Of course in Kitty's case, it's both. So I can see how another person's right to life might not feature that highly among her priorities, which is probably the first sign of your classic killer, but still, the more I think of Kitty Trigg, the more I come back to this … I won't say squeamishness. It's more that she was always so … otherworldly. To push another person down the stairs – no; no, I can't see it. Why, in her lacrosse days—'

'Lacrosse!' Leyla burst in. Where was it …? 'Beryl, you've just reminded me, I found this picture. When Torben showed it to Trigg, she frosted over completely. I wondered if you could help me understand why?'

Beryl took the proffered printout. Traced it lovingly with a finger.

'Ah, yes,' she murmured. 'This takes me back. I would have been, oh, twelve? Thirteen? A first-former, anyway, when this was taken. Charlie was my hero back then – she still is, really' – and Leyla found herself automatically looking away from the swimming eyes, the lump-throated voice – 'but even I'll admit that this was not her finest hour.'

Perhaps it was just the falling temperature, with the setting sun. But the hairs on Leyla's neck were stiffening. This was, presumably, the incident that had not made the first draft of Charlotte Lazerton's memoirs. 'Go on,' she said.

'This was the summer of '62,' said Beryl, as if from a long way off. 'Not quite a Bryan Adams line, I'm afraid, but every bit as golden. And don't go thinking it was all swinging revolution and the Rolling Stones, there wasn't a peep of all that at Brook Hall School. Oh, by the time *I* reached the sixth form, some of the girls were smoking pot and listening to "far out" records, but I don't think they had the first idea what it was all about. And while Charlie and Kitty were still around, it felt like another age entirely – not exactly innocent, we're talking about teenage girls, after all ... no, I think the word I'm really after is *boring*. Dull as ditch water. It was never exactly a smart sort of school. There were only really two things that got the blood pumping at Brook Hall in those days – jolly hockey sticks, and boys. And this photograph is about both.'

Leyla waited. Beryl had the air of someone settling into a story.

'As you can see, Charlie – she looks good, doesn't she, even in all that get-up? – Charlie has her arm round Kitty. They're both seventeen, Charlie practically runs the place despite being endlessly in trouble, and we little squits in the first form worshipped the lot of them. Best of friends, these two – and perhaps more, if you believe what Laura Barrymore was putting about, about what she'd seen going on behind the pavilion. That's probably how Kitty made the team, come to think of it – Charlie covering for Kitty's flaws in practice sessions, speaking up for her, that sort of thing. And it was certainly a good lacrosse team – that's the schools county cup they've got there.

'The only blot on this summer's horizon is the person not in shot: Rick Stapleton, the gardener's boy. The one who pushed the roller, did the weeding, all through the summer. I think he was eighteen, nineteen? A "big boy", we first-years called him, and absolutely gorgeous into the bargain. Well, you can imagine most of the rest – what could be more natural, even in the strictest school, than that sixth-formers might run into gardeners out on the lower fields. And of course, boys being in such short supply, both Charlie and Kitty made a play for this one. Now, at that age, love, or what you take to be love, becomes the most important thing in the world …'

'And young Rick Stapleton opted for Charlotte?' Leyla hazarded.

'Well, *no*, actually,' said Beryl. 'Funnily enough his first choice was Kitty – she had the charm that went with the nickname, of course, but actually I always thought he just found her less intimidating. And she fell for him – but *really* fell for him. Went around talking of marriage, took it all very seriously. Most of it was in her head of course – but never underestimate the power of what goes on in the head of a boarding-school girl when it's all she's got. According to gossip, they had a few – well, we used to call them "trysts", probably all very tame by today's standards. Kitty, when pressed, said she was saving herself for after the wedding. Until one lacrosse practice – it can't have been more than a week or so after this picture was taken, come to think of it – Charlie went in for a tackle on Kitty that went wrong. At the time, most of us blamed Kitty for not committing to the contact, you know, go in hard and you won't get hurt? But there's no denying that

Charlie *did* go in hard, and Kitty *did* get hurt. In fact, she spent the rest of that summer laid up in the san.'

'San?'

'Sanatorium,' Beryl explained. 'The hospital bit, you know. It was a bad break – in fact I gather that leg's never been quite right since. Always relapsing. There've been spells when she's walked well enough, at least I've seen her walking round the village a couple of times over the years. But she never played lacrosse again, never rode, never swam. Hardly surprising, really; she spent her final year with a leg brace and crutches; we all thought what a pity it was, to blight the best days of her life so completely. Oh I know people do the most amazing things now, it's a real inspiration, but for Kitty, there was none of that. No medical expertise, and more to the point, no good examples. "Crippled," people said. What a word.' Beryl grimaced. 'But the more immediate consequence was, of course, that with Kitty off the scene, Charlie swept in and made off with Rick Stapleton. It fairly broke Kitty's heart when she found out. And in those days, girls' hearts really did break. Perhaps they still do, for all I know.'

Leyla, by now on her third glass of sherry, could well imagine it. The smell of fresh-cut grass. The long summer afternoons, that heavy, otherworldly quality to the air. Stolen moments. Illicit thrills. And a girl in agony, first upon the field in that hot intensity of violence, of blinding pain, and then stewing for weeks in a fusty invalid's bed, cut off from the world, conscious every moment of what was going on without her. The consequences of which would affect the rest of her life …

'Might I ask,' Leyla said at last, 'why your cousin acted the way she did? I would have thought, after the accident, that perhaps her sense of guilt—?'

Beryl spread her hands. 'I'm sure she began with the best

intentions. Probably played the go-between for Kitty and Stapleton while Kitty was laid up, and just got to know him a bit too well. Remember, Brook Hall was a *very* dull sort of place. My best guess is – Charlie got bored, and decided to make something happen. As I say, not her finest hour.'

No wonder, thought Leyla, as they washed up, hugged, headed for bed, that the anecdote had not made the first cut of the memoir. *Warts and all*, wasn't that what Charlotte had told Jonathan Azawakh? But even then, there are the warts you bear proudly upon your face for the world to see, and there are the ones that lie concealed in darker, more intimate places. The sort no one exposes voluntarily. This, presumably, was the life-long rift that, in Trigg's testimony, the two of them had lately sought to heal. But what if that reaching out, on Trigg's part, had been a mere pretext? A means of re-establishing contact, in order to take a very cold revenge? What if the timing of the whole thing, so close to Charlotte's death that a phone call between them had coincided with the very moment of the murder, had been no coincidence at all?

But there was the same stumbling block as ever: the phone call. And while Beryl had just given her the most convincing personal motive for murder she had yet heard, she had also flatly refused to believe Trigg capable of doing the deed in person. So how to reconcile those contradictions? Leyla felt sure there was somewhere these two things, far from standing in opposition to each other, came into fatal connection. But *where*? And why could she not escape the feeling that the key had been not in Trigg's, but in Shani's interview?

Leyla was still circling this question, like dirty water around a drain, when she fell asleep.

23

PICCADILLY

If Beryl's cottage was a dream, a mirage of paradise, then breakfast time was doubly so. Rodger was tearing over the slopes, disturbing ducks and sundry waterfowl. There was a haze rising from the stream in the sluggish summer sun. Tea and fresh juice out on the veranda, everything a little dewy, a little mournful, as if all this were already a memory, something recalled. A crock of local milk, fresh strawberries, accompanied somewhat at random by those mix-packs of children's cereals that Leyla remembered from long ago – it turned out that Coco Pops were as much fun as ever; no wonder that hipster cereal café had done so well.

'Must you go?' asked Beryl.

'I was just wondering the same thing,' said Leyla.

'Why not stay for the weekend? I'd love the company. Maybe we'd turn up something more that might get us further – I've got letters and postcards we could go through, there might be something—?'

Leyla shook her head. 'Really, I'd love to. But it's Torben's big day … It'll be a damp squib, of course, I'm sure of it, in which case he'll need bucking up. And then there's always the outside chance his mad plan actually ends up smoking out the culprit, in which case I'd hate not to be in at the finish.' She paused. 'Also, if I stayed, I'd need a new ticket, and I'm not sure I could justify that to my bank balance.'

'Then *both* come down next time. And soon! We could motor about, see the sights …'

Leyla suppressed a shudder. 'Actually, maybe I'll hire a car myself. But that's terribly kind of you; we'd love to. Well, I would, and Tor will soon cotton on.' She was aware of how much she sounded like his girlfriend, but it couldn't be helped. 'I've an idea he'd quite enjoy this Kingston Lacy place I've heard of nearby; is it worth it?'

'Kingston Lacy? Good lord yes! All a bit much for me, I think it was even called poncy by Georgian standards, but that's part of the fun. And the gardens alone …' Beryl broke off; she seemed to be wrestling the urge to laugh. Leyla tried out one of her speaking glances.

'Oh, nothing,' said Beryl, a little wistfully. 'I was just thinking – it would be perfectly safe, I don't think they have the peacocks anymore.'

'Why would peacocks be unsafe?'

'Well, quite. No, it was the silliest thing' – and she dabbed at her eyes – 'a phobia of Charlie's. We teased her about it for years, until she made plain the subject was *not* amusing. In my case, by flushing my head down a loo …'

'This was a childhood incident?' Leyla hazarded. Though she quite enjoyed the image of a distinguished professor shoving her elderly cousin down the lavatory.

'Mm,' said Beryl. 'The thing itself happened before my time, when she was just a babe in arms – well, a babe in a buggy. She was taken round the grounds at Kingston Lacy, and she must have had crumbs all down her, because this peacock got a little too friendly, and apparently she screamed, and out came its tail – I suppose it isn't funny really, those birds can be enormous, and the sudden shock to an infant at close quarters – anyway, she's had a terror of them ever since. It became this family legend, and followed her to school, so of course it was always a good joke for a certain low sort of girl – me, for instance – to flash a peacock feather at her, or imitate its cry, and see her jump out of her skin. At least, that is, until she caught whoever it might be and exacted bloody vengeance ... Leyla, love, are you ill? Oh, please tell me it wasn't the Coco Pops, they must be years out of date ...'

Lort, thought Torben, glancing at his watch where it lay, as ever, at his bedside. Even when that bedside was, as now, an upturned cardboard box. Nearly ten o'clock. Well, it had been quite the late night in the end, with precious little to show for it except a couple of tenuous leads from some kitchen staff in Camden to pass on to Gary Bassett, who might possibly be able to put a constable on it. But he had two hours, less, to be in position at the Bomber Command Memorial. Already, he could feel the heat rising from the street below; it was set to be a scorching day, and he regretted his choice of outfit. Mask and cloak were all well and good for skulduggery in a dank cellar, but not so much for a slog through a baking central London. Still, too late to change now. This was it. Time to count his pigeons.

She would not, Leyla told herself, as the X8 careered back south through the green of merrie England, tell Torben straight away. Her case was complete: motive, opportunity, method, all accounted for and psychologically satisfying. But there were still loose ends to tie up, email replies to await – if she could just be sure in crossing off a couple of the others, *then* she would feel justified in crashing his grand experiment with what she already felt sure was the awful solution to this cold and cruel murder.

Passing through Red Lion Square on his way to Holborn underground, Torben came up short. It was set to be a gruelling afternoon. Just time to stop at the garden's Chilean café and fortify himself with a light brunch before entering the fray. Really, when you thought about it, it was the prudent thing to do.

Safely installed on a London-bound train that was, miraculously, only a quarter of an hour delayed, Leyla checked her phone for only, oh, the twenty-ninth time that journey. One new email.

Subject: Re: Quick auditing enquiry
From: Maria Artois
Sent: Sat, 16 June, 11:17
To: Leyla Moradi

Cher Leyla
Thank you for your email. Yes, I can confirm Professor Drever was present for all the times you have mentioned. Every session. In fact, he made himself rather too much the life and soul of the party! I assure you 100% that not a conversation went by without a contribution from my respected colleague, if you know what I mean ...
Yours
Maria

At last! Leyla dashed off a hasty message to Torben. *The pigeon shoot has begun, and Drever is down I repeat DOWN*. Then, just in case her meaning was not entirely obvious, she sent another message: *See email I am forwarding: Drever's alibi confirmed watertight. It wasn't him.*

One down; four to go. Or rather, three, since Leyla was pretty sure who would be left standing at the end. And she was only expecting news of one of those three any time soon. How long had it been – thirty seconds? She checked her phone again. Why hadn't anyone messaged her in the last thirty seconds?!

Emerging from the depths at Hyde Park Corner, Torben automatically checked his phone. He had rather expected some sort of update from Leyla by now, if only of the snarky *having a lovely time, wish you were here, enjoy your wasted day* variety. But nothing. He had no phone reception of any kind, in fact. Looking up and around, he took in the obvious explanation. Of course the networks were out, they must be utterly frazzled. Forget London: the entire western world seemed to have assembled at this end of Piccadilly.

It was as if a music festival was, for one year only, being held in the centre of the city. Torben could scarcely move for milling people, tricked out in everything from the tourist's shorts and t-shirt, to the cargo trousers and dreads of the classic ecowarrior, to the national costumes of any number of countries and, in one especially disorienting squeeze past, a group attired in formal evening wear. Half the faces pressed round his were painted; the scents of cannabis and rollups mingled with a thousand perfumes and a hundred thousand varieties of human sweat. Boom boxes playing everything from reggae to acid house warred with a drum ensemble ... a lone trumpeter ... was that a mariachi band?! Any worries Torben had had about standing out in his disguise vanished; the only trouble now would be finding the right people.

He ducked beneath a banner reading 'Wot a COP-out', borne by someone in a police costume replete with helmet who was, perhaps, in danger of over-mixing their puns. Shimmied his way around a group of teenagers clad, despite it being a Saturday, in that undying undress version of school uniform where you used your tie as a bandana: nice to see that some things never changed. Two infants, joyously shouting slogans that they could not possibly understand, stood beside a more sullen group of face-painted children who had clearly been press-ganged by parents unable to find a babysitter. Torben laughed, and accepted a leaflet held up by one particularly mutinous-looking toddler. Why had he never done this before? It was glorious!

Pushing on past groups of friends, largely in their sixties, greeting each other and sharing sandwiches and flasks, he caught his first glimpse of his destination: the white neoclassical memorial and, in front of it, something extraordinary. The float his students had helped to make hove into view. The picture had not done it justice – it really was a vast scale replica of the *Titanic*, prow jutting sharp against the sky, speared by an iceberg of almost literally blinding whiteness. Torben had to shield his eyes as he approached. Talk about an inconvenient truth. So far as he could tell through his squint, all that whiteness was text, painted on a duller background ...

'It is made up of broken promises,' said a voice in his ear. He turned. '*Bonjour*, Catesby,' murmured Elodie.

Torben executed a deep courtier's bow. She giggled, and went on. 'Every agreement, every treaty – from Kyoto and Paris to all the little ones – every commitment that has been delayed, or evaded, or ignored. Well, as many as we could fit, I should perhaps say.'

'It's very neatly written,' he said, wishing he sounded less like a patronising schoolteacher.

'Stencilled,' she said. 'I think the font we used is called something like Bassington Old Face.'

'Baskerville,' he amended.

'Ah, *d'accord* ...'

Looking more closely, Torben could make out some of the words, as well as a legend towards the stern of the model ship itself – RMS *Hubris*.

Well, they were young and angry, you could forgive them for being a bit too on-the-nose.

'I *love* it—' he began, when his words were drowned – speaking of on-the-nose – in a turbulent sea of discords, as if a collective of tomcats had decided to devote themselves to free jazz.

'You found some performers then!' he shouted, once the tuning-up had receded to a mere background cacophony.

'Two flutes, a tuba and a string quartet,' Elodie beamed. 'We'll make it work somehow.'

It occurred to Torben, rather belatedly, that everyone seemed to be having the time of their lives. Perhaps, as the march progressed and the chanting got going, there would be more channelling of righteous fury. But this gathering phase was more carnival than po-faced rally. It might just be the weather, of course, another face-meltingly hot summer's day, with a hint of something in the air he couldn't quite place. Still, if you cared enough to show up, make a spectacle, get a basic message across, then why not enjoy the experience itself? He should really participate in a little more direct action if it was always like this, surrounded by smiling faces and merry babble.

Well, except for that little knot of people over there ...

'*Ouais*,' said Elodie. 'You warned us a party-pooper or two might be hanging around. Only I was not expecting—'

'All five of them,' said Torben.

Azawakh, Drever, Grey, Rajapalayam, Trigg. They had *all* turned up.

Somewhere around Basingstoke, Leyla's phone finally flashed up a WhatsApp message from Frances. *You owe me big time hun. See attached.* Three agonising minutes later – how could train Wi-Fi take so long to download a simple text document? – Leyla was reviewing an account of Shani's movements in late April. The meeting at Lucia Segugio's was there on the Monday, looking entirely innocent in its mundanity. And Tuesday 24th ... was block-booked with back-to-back team meetings in their shared offices. Frances' contact had added the note 'Can confirm she was there throughout Tue pm. Disagreement re Damien Hirst nearly got me sacked. Want me to rake up anything else? I am so up for that.'

Leyla just about refrained from punching the air. She was, after all, in Hampshire. *See below*, she dashed off to Torben. *SR's alibi cast-iron*.

Funny that he hadn't replied to the earlier message.

All five of them, each a might-be murderer, come in answer to his message. Circling the bait. They looked wary as hell. Not all in black, this time, but they might as well have been; the group seemed to suck in all the light and sound from around them, a vanishing point of suspicion and unease. Simon Grey was the most conspicuous, by virtue of the fact he was wearing a wide-brimmed hat and dark glasses. Little wonder: his big-oil paymasters would be less than thrilled to see him marching in defence of the planet. Jonathan Azawakh's smart-casual get-up, by contrast, was well calculated to deflect interest; of the five, he seemed the most at ease. Which wasn't saying much.

Torben had expected Shani Rajapalayam, of all of them, to be the most at home in this environment, where every third protestor was probably a subscriber to her newspaper. But she seemed tense as a stalked deer. Next to her, Henrik Drever stood impassive, incongruous in suit and tie, not even his usual open-necked shirt. It was the same tie, Torben realised, that he had been sporting at the Savoy; the old school tie of Lundsbergs. Once again, its perfectly arranged ends and exquisite knot were belied by its wearer's demeanour – although unlike on that earlier occasion, Drever could not have looked more out of place in his formal attire. He even had a macintosh draped over one arm. Either he knew something Torben didn't, or he was taking the Swedish reputation for prudence to new extremes. Heaven forfend he should allow his shirt and tie to get wet, what *would* the other marchers say? Oh but of course – the AWA presidency, the election – it was being announced today! Torben had received an email; the ceremony was scheduled to begin at three p.m. That Drever should nonetheless have shown up here with the defining moment of his career only a few hours off suggested either that he was utterly terrified of what might otherwise come out – or that, despite all appearances, he was capable of caring about something and someone other than himself. There was always a chance he was here to find out who had killed Charlotte, rather than to hide it. Torben considered. The AWA was mere streets away from Parliament Square, a great Edwardian wedding-cake of a building dominating Storey's Gate in

Westminster. Clearly, Drever was banking on a seamless transition. Maybe it was just curiosity that had summoned him?

Of all this awkward squad, it was Katherine Trigg who must have made the greatest effort to be here; she was leaning on her stick, her face shaded beneath the parasol she bore aloft with her other hand. Torben had to resist the impulse to offer to carry it for her. He doubted whether she would last the march – but then he remembered: the float had seats. So much the better. Their ensemble presence had made things much more complicated – no easy case of the sole culprit turning up in self-incrimination. Either his most left-field theory was correct, and the five of them were somehow all implicated, or they had been drawn by the odour of blood in the water, the mystery of that anonymous message.

Torben considered. What if he himself had received such a communication? And he knew at once that nothing in the world would have kept him away. *For helvede*. Well, he would just have to trust that the impassable throng, and the curiosity that had brought them all here, would hold them together long enough for something to happen. For one of them to let something slip. He adjusted his mask. Time to take up his position as eavesdropper. Beside them, the impromptu orchestra was striking up a scratch instrumental arrangement of REM's 'It's the End of the World as We Know It'. Maybe he should have brought a violin.

So, that was Leyla's due diligence accomplished: two down, and nothing more she could hope for on Grey or Azawakh right now. For as many as four, maybe even five minutes, she re-reviewed the case she had made out, wrestling with her internal devil's advocate. No, it was perfect. She thought about calling Torben at once, but the carriage was crowded, and for all she knew he was with the murderer right now. A shame to break the news by text, but at least the written medium allowed her to convey the revelation with clarity and detachment. She started to type.

Trigg! Trigg Trigg Trigg. IT WAS KATHERINE TRIGG!!!!

24

WHITEHALL

Understandably, it took a long time to get a hundred thousand or so people on the march. But march they eventually did. Torben fell in step behind his five shufflers, just far enough behind to avoid treading on heels without going out of earshot. He had planned for the proximity, wearing his handball trainers beneath his cloak rather than any of the shoes he'd been in at the interviews, some of which were rather distinctive, and spraying himself with a cheap aftershave bought for the purpose – but it became immediately apparent he need not have bothered. He had supposed whoever turned up would be looking out all around them, their senses alert for the unknown emailer. But the group's attention seemed to be turned entirely inward, away from the hubbub. And their conversation so far had been … well, the only word for it was *normal*. Strained, yes, obviously. But none of them had acknowledged the hippo in the room. It was as if they made a regular habit of getting together for protest marches.

Oh. But of course. Of *course* they weren't looking for an anonymous outsider who had sent that email. They all thought it was one of the five of them. And they were stalling, waiting to see who would make the first move.

'I can recommend the afternoon tea at the Palm Court,' Drever was saying, gesturing to their left. 'The décor is of course a little loud, but their Darjeeling is particularly fine.'

Shani was studying – or at least pretending to study – the finer details of the float. 'You know, amid all the fuss the mainstream makes about aesthetics, I think we've lost sight of how *representational* the art of this generation has become,' she said to Jonathan Azawakh. 'Yes it's all installations and assemblages of found objects, and it still needs a lot of textual mediation, but almost nothing's abstracted anymore. It always shouts exactly what it is.'

'It certainly leaves little scope for interpretation,' Azawakh replied, doing a passable imitation of an interested connoisseur. 'You could almost call it a form of taking back control – the new generation insisting on the legibility of their own voice, bypassing the cynical old critics. No offence intended, of course.'

'Only a little taken, Johnny dear ...'

Torben was glad to see that Elodie and her companions were leaving well alone; he had given strict instructions not to pester the celebrated art critic, nor to comment on the unlikely presence of a government minister in their midst – not that many people outside the Westminster bubble were likely to recognise Simon Grey, shorn of all the usual indicators.

'Eaton Square Senior School,' the politician was now pointing out to Katherine Trigg. 'I wonder my own alma mater doesn't sue for name infringement.'

Trigg seemed to be following her own line of thought. 'That was 112 Piccadilly we just passed,' she said. 'And then another hotel ... a pity, it doesn't look like 110A really exists. Peter Wimsey's flat, you know,' she elaborated, in answer to Grey's look of polite enquiry. 'A fine writer, Sayers, I've always thought – though when it comes to portraying the quirks and foibles of London's justice system, she's not a patch on the master ...'

And she was off on her favourite hobby-horse. It was, perhaps, a mark of Grey's nervous state that he continued to listen to her disquisition on John Mortimer. Torben reminded himself of the wording of his email. *Do not leave the procession until it reaches Parliament Square*, he had written. Clearly, they really were just biding their time, waiting for the rogue element among them to make their presence known. At least one of them must be in genuine fear of exposure. Waiting to find out if someone they had thought a friend had somehow got the goods on them. Had stumbled on their act of murder. With up to four of them hoping to learn what the unspecified other knew about – what? Their complicity, their guilt by unwitting association, the fallout of one of their close acquaintances turning out to have had a hand in Charlotte's death? Azawakh had his cover-up to think of, Rajapalayam her theft, Grey his misdirected email, Drever the obvious and enormous personal advantage he had gained, enough to taint him by proximity to the act if anything turned out to have been underhand, even if he hadn't been directly involved.

Really, the fact they were managing to keep up even this desultory conversation, this veneer of sociability, was greatly to their credit under such straitened circumstances. But then, they were professionals. Superficial friendliness was their bread and butter.

Green Park on their right, a verdant reminder of what the crowd was fighting for. Fast-food outlets and corporations to their left – the first real sign of rancour was the ripple of boos that broke out as successive waves of marchers passed an HSBC. A bottleneck as they reached the Ritz and a crossroads; the intersecting streets had not been closed to traffic, and a churn of honking taxis and private cars attracted more opprobrium from the waiting protestors. Someone with a megaphone was improvising a call-and-response song with a willing audience.

Jerrrr-emy Clarkson! (Jerrrr-emy Clarkson!)
Jerrrr-emy Clarkson! (Jerrrr-emy Clarkson!)
Jerrrr-emy Clarkson is a horse's arse!
He looks like a horse's arse,
He smells like a horse's arse,
He is a horse's arse!

'Disgraceful,' muttered Grey.

'Oh, I don't know,' said Shani Rajapalayam, who had gained some composure as the march went on. 'Granted it's not quite Woody Guthrie, but it expresses a certain, elemental truth. And it feels very much in the spirit of Char— I mean, who're they doing next? Ah, it's our orange friend across the water. *Donnnn-ald Tru-ump!*' she sang. 'Gosh that was strangely satisfying.'

After passing the Wolseley, where Torben had dined with Katherine Trigg, the procession headed right down St James's. So far, no one had betrayed themselves or broken cover. Grey was looking thoroughly fed up, but that was only to be expected. Drever had shed his wooden manner and was now positively twitchy, constantly fidgeting with his hands and sweating freely, though that might just be a combination of his suit and the weather. Sometime in the past half hour, the heat had built from idyllic to oppressive, and a wind was picking up; the sort of wind that brought no relief but whipped up the hot grit of London and threw it in your face. Torben didn't fancy the look of the sky much either. Surely those gathering clouds should have provided some respite from the mounting temperature; they seemed instead to be smothering those marching below in still greater heat. It was as if the protest was some form of inverse rain dance, the subject of the march summoned in evidence: *You don't believe in this climate crisis? Well, joining us live from the upper atmosphere, please welcome ...* And whether it was the heat, or the ever-jostling bodies backing up from Trafalgar Square up ahead, or the looming presence of St James's Palace and all it stood for, the crowd was responding. No more horses' arses now. Just a steady, growing chant that called for justice, for action.

As they left Woking, a thought occurred to Leyla. Torben's radio silence – might it not portend something more than preoccupation? Dear God, if anything had happened ... She tried calling him. Straight to voicemail, and she knew that was no good.

Maybe she had been too cavalier. Perhaps a sober statement of the facts ... If Trigg had somehow done something to him then she, Leyla, was powerless, but if he was still near her, then this might help convince him of the danger, put him properly on his guard? After all, what else could she possibly do?

Katherine Trigg murdered Charlotte, she typed, watching out for every false impulse of autocorrect as she went. *Motive: revenge. At school, in sixth form, C injured K during lacrosse. Broke her leg – with permanent consequences. Also, whilst K was convalescing, C stole her boyfriend and first true love, he's the RS in that note to self from her memoirs. Remember what it's like being 17 – and what that must have meant to K when added to the loss of mobility. Hence enormous grudge. Either K finally felt it was time to exact vengeance – before C's election as AWA President, so a certain poetic justice in forestalling that crowning achievement. Or C's attempt to reconcile with K re-awoke K's animus. With fatal consequences.*

Leyla considered deleting the final sentence as too melodramatic. But she was a sucker for a sign-off. She sent that message and began its sequel.

Opportunity: perfect. K visited C's in the run-up to the murder and scoped out the layout of her house. Crucial detail: the landline phone at the top of the stairs. This setup gave K all the tools she needed to stage a remote killing. Stay with me here. Method comes in two parts.

Leyla wished Torben had been with her, listening to Beryl; had felt the same sense of revelation as the key detail, unlooked for, had come into her possession. The cornerstone of the whole thing. Well, all she could do was tell him. Surely she had earned his trust by now.

C had a secret phobia from early childhood. Shani talked to you about it but none of us, Shani included, saw it for what it was. C was mortally afraid of peacocks. She'd basically been attacked in her pram visiting a country house. Beryl knew, and so did all C's school friends. Including K. C would jump with terror at the sight OR SOUND of a peacock. And that was K's murder weapon.

Feeling more confident, Leyla committed her discovery to the ether and pressed on to the clincher.

We know K phoned C immediately before C died. Yes, that was K, as verified by the police, calling from her own home. But she didn't speak. She played the recorded sound of a peacock down the phone line. C reeled in fright, toppled forwards, and fell to her death. No one entered or left the house, no one was present. And the phone call – the means of murder – also gave K an alibi. Her murder method became an instant defence if anyone came to suspect. The perfect crime. So unless a recording of that conversation exists, which I don't think is possible, you need to extract a confession somehow. But that is how she did it. Over to you.

Leyla was unhappy with the tone of this final message. It in no way conveyed the creeping feeling she had when she contemplated Trigg's crime, the sudden scooping out of her viscera, the prickling sweat of vicarious dread at a crime so calculated, so cold. Something born of ancient knowledge, stored against this cruellest, most implacable of revenges. It had about it the savour of obsession. Of remorselessness. Of the slow-grinding machinery and inexorable force that others, more fortunate, ascribed to justice, or to God, but which she, Leyla, now knew was the mark by which one recognised only one thing in this world: the certainty of death.

Pall Mall seemed to stretch for ever. So many white stuccoed buildings, so many columns and pediments, a monotony of bone, chalk, ivory, funereal white, sepulchral in their pallor. Storey after storey rising above on either side, a mausoleum, entombing the marchers. And the air. There seemed to be either much less, or much more of it – whichever it was, it was suffocating, stultifying. The communal sense of rage and frustration was being pushed down by the atmosphere, by the architecture – not suppressed, but condensed, the pressure rising even as the volume dipped and the pace slowed. Every investment bank they passed, every private members' club, drew more hisses and mutters. A less well-intentioned protest would have been hurling bricks by now. The momentary relief of much more sky as they finally crossed the wide expanse of Waterloo Place was immediately battened back down as they re-entered the road's final, narrow stretch, and the bottleneck up ahead backing up from Trafalgar Square began to tell.

Slowly, painfully slowly, they inched round the cordons of the square, to pour like grains of sand in a timer, down the grim grey artery of Whitehall. Out of nowhere and for no apparent reason, the scratch band on the float struck up Handel's Sarabande, the stately theme from the film *Barry Lyndon*. The tuba's bassline went through and through Torben's body. From somewhere, far off and very high, there came a low answering rumble. Something was stirring.

Torben's plan had patently failed. No one had bitten, no one had bolted, and before long they would all be peeling off – confused, bored, embarrassed, but free. For some time now Katherine Trigg had been sitting on the side of the float, legs dangling, and first Shani, now Simon, had taken it in turns to sit beside her, keeping up a low conversation. Jammed close at Torben's side now in the tightening press, Shani and Jonathan were silent, morose.

Unlike Henrik Drever. Earlier, he had seemed withdrawn, twitchy, his hay fever or whatever out in full force. Now he was gabbling away to a couple of the young protestors, now abandoning them for another interlocutor, now re-reading the text on the float, now craning his neck to see over the crowd. Maybe he was claustrophobic? Or just bored to distraction. And the mood was catching; everyone seemed increasingly desperate to get out of this farce.

Torben strained his ears, hoping against hope that the conversation on the float might at last touch on the one subject that had brought them all together. But no. Grey – to give him credit, he was being indefatigably polite – was once again venturing onto dangerous territory. John Mortimer, the subject of Trigg's obsession, had been a famous barrister in his day. But Grey seemed less than impressed with the hero worship. By concentrating very hard, Torben could just catch snatches of the MP's sonorous voice over the noise of the band, the crowd. 'All those libel cases though, when he was a QC, those high-profile defences, his reputation as a hot-shot barrister ... *Last Exit to Brooklyn*, *Gay News*, the Sex Pistols ... very minimal personal role ... experienced legal team ... European Court of Human Rights—'

'Nonsense!' Trigg fairly exploded at the suggestion. For half a bar, even the band was silenced. 'It was all down to Mortimer, I tell you! That was how they did it – he was ruthless, a machine. Yes, others were involved, but I tell you they just wound Mortimer up, pointed him in the right direction, and let him rip!'

She sounded faintly unhinged in support of her hero. 'Look, I've had enough of this,' said Grey, struggling to his feet. Even his schmoozer's patience apparently had a breaking point. 'She's mad, positively mad. Deluded—'

But anything further he might have had to say on the subject of Trigg's mania was lost in the echo of an almighty clap of thunder, almost right overhead. *'For helvede,'* Torben breathed, then caught himself – but no one could possibly have heard him. For now everything, but *everything* gave way before a total transformation of the world around them. The rain had begun.

And what rain. Bursting upon them with unimaginable fury, it was a deluge, a devastation – a reckoning. Torben jerked down the hood of his cloak, grateful at last for its meagre protection. All around him, the better-prepared were producing, as if from nowhere, cagoules, macs, ponchos. A bristling thicket of umbrellas was unfurling, imperilling the eyes of other marchers, fellow feeling abandoned to the base need to fend off the merciless rain.

He saw the musicians diving for cover, shielding their instruments with their bodies. Saw two middle-aged men struggling for possession of a short umbrella. Saw a testudo formed from placards, held horizontally by young protesters above a knot of children. Beneath his feet, dirty water was already streaking, a gathering torrent. And his world was shrinking, blurring, running at the edges.

'Screw this, I'm off.' That was Simon Grey's voice, somewhere beside him – Simon Grey, one hand clutching the brim of his silly hat like a man drowning; pushing past bodies, heading away. Torben spun about, looking for the others, conscious of the dead weight of his cloak now leeching to his back, his thighs.

Glimpses only. Of Azawakh raising high a cane-handled umbrella, giving Shani his arm, somehow finding a way to part the crowd. Shani pulling her arm free once clear of the press. Azawakh heading east, making for the Embankment, Shani doubling back northwest, perhaps towards the ICA. Of Drever pulling the folds of his raincoat about him, old school tie whipping in the wind like a streamer, a banner, its single wide blade of cloth somehow heraldic. Striding south, cutting west, aiming no doubt for the AWA on Storey's Gate. Of Trigg, abandoned on the float, unable perhaps to make her getaway, or else trusting to the meagre cover of the huge sculpture, itself now threatening to sag under all that water. Trigg, so small, making no move to shelter herself, and now slipping a little sideways in her seat. Trigg, silent, tiny, a thing to be carried off by so much rain, that ran through her hair, her clothes, through the red welling that now bloomed and mingled with the rain, an uncanny pink fountain that drenched her blouse as her body listed gently, ever so gently, onto its side, where it moved no more.

25

STOREY'S GATE

Then Elodie was there, and one of the violinists, bending over the body. Elodie's face, a mess of streaky paint, turned up to his. 'She is – she is dead.' Her voice, so uncomprehending.

'Don't touch her more than necessary,' Torben said. 'Try and find a doctor – there must be a doctor in this crowd – and police …' Already he was turning away from the body, the awful knife-struck wound in her chest, scanning the anonymous crowd.

'*Mais qu'est-ce tu—?*' but he could not attend to Elodie's plea, the tremble in it that threatened to undo him. He had to decide.

Grey had struck back north, away from the rally, away from the seat of government, from his office, from the places he was known.

Azawakh was eastbound, he had thought for the underground, perhaps the river and the bridge. Up Whitehall Place, past Scotland Yard.

Rajapalayam had splintered off, towards another great art institution, north and west.

Drever had gone full west, striking out through Whitehall itself, making for Horse Guards, the park, the back way to the Academy.

One of them had done this. And this time, there had been blood. Contact. There would be evidence.

Now, he told himself. Make your choice *now*.

And in that moment, he knew. '*Tilgiv mig*,' he said to Elodie. He wasn't sure she'd heard. Then he turned west, and went after Drever.

The rain had scattered the protestors. Behind him came sirens; looking back instinctively he caught a glimpse of police, mounted on motorbikes, corralling the crowd now streaming around Scotland Yard, herding them like cattle – feinting in formation, regrouping, going again. Angry yells of indignation contended with the roaring of throttles.

Somewhere further on, what remained of the crowd was chanting; it sounded like they were counting numbers. *Won*, he thought he heard them cry. *True. Free.*

Too many bodies. Biting down on his natural urges, Torben shouldered his way through the mass of ponchos and umbrellas now converging on the gates of Whitehall, surrounding the sentries, making for cover. Still the distant crowd was chanting. *Fore. Fire. Sticks.* He blinked rain from his eyes, almost knocked over a passing tourist, arrowed himself through an impossible gap and felt himself swallowed up by the open maw of Horse Guards itself.

Sever. Hate. Nein. Tear!

Reeling, Torben emerged into the vastness of the parade ground. Its sandy surface stretching away, churned to a quagmire by the scattering marchers. He broke into a run, heading for the far left corner – the only way to catch up with Drever would be to take chances, assume his destination. *For helvede*, where had the bastard got to? Torben vaulted the bollards, skittered between a couple of families, a gaggle of children, squinted down the curve of road. Was that him, that swaddled form, stalking away past the massive plane trees? No. Maybe?

Caught between impatience and caution, Torben kept himself to a brisk walk, trying to close the gap without attracting too much attention. Thank God there were still enough masks, placards and costumes amid the raingear to prevent him standing out. Yes – yes, it was Drever, tall and grey in a tight-belted mackintosh.

Torben fell in behind him, matching his pace. The park to their right, the avenue, the willows, the lake, its surface an endless plash of ripples as the driving rain struck and struck the stiller water. To their left, the monumental slabs of the Foreign Office. They were in the heart of it, here, this tiny patch of city, not just of government but of so much soft power – soft, but power for all that – the Academy, the ICA, the palaces, offices, clubs … Here he was on Drever's terrain, the natural territory of all his erstwhile subjects. But there was one authority he could bring in on his side. Fishing between the folds of his cloak, Torben sought the phone in his pocket, immediately speckled with raindrops as he fumbled it out, unlocked it, found the number. Reception restored as he broke free from the stranglehold of so many thousands in one tiny space, he was half-conscious of missed calls and messages popping up, Leyla, Leyla, Leyla. But it was Ruth's number he needed.

'*Hej*,' he said, cutting across her greeting. 'Ruth, you know how it's your last weekend as a serving police officer? Well – how do you fancy getting yourself fired?'

Torben made another call, this time to Gary Bassett. Now was the time for the policeman to prove his worth. And he just about clocked the substance of Leyla's many messages. *Trigg Trigg Trigg*. Well. So much for that. But he never took his eyes entirely off his quarry, across Birdcage Walk, on to Storey's Gate, past serried rows of hire bikes and red-brick arches and into the bowels of the Academy of Western Art itself. It always felt like a miniaturisation, stepping through the polished wooden doors, set so low into so tall, so grand a building that they might as well have been cat flaps in a giant's house.

'Excuse me, sir ...' Out of nowhere, a doorman had materialised, the politest of questions on his face. Oh *lort*, he was still wearing the mask and cloak!

'Sorry,' he whispered, hastily bundling them off to reveal the sober clothes beneath, regretting the trainers – surely the trainers were OK? Once again he dug into his pocket. 'Sorry – I'm a Fellow really,' he hissed, presenting his plastic ID card.

The doorman smiled. 'Oh, that's quite all right, sir,' he murmured. 'We're used to performance art here of course, but seeing as it's the election ...'

'Oh,' said Torben, 'that reminds me. In a little while, some police might show up. And they really *will* be police. I'm sure they'll be discreet.' He was sure of nothing of the kind. But before the doorman could respond, he was off up the great sweep of the central marble staircase, slipping into the mainstream of his fellow Fellows, all of them steaming in a mist of evaporating rainwater, heading upstairs for announcements, speeches and two glasses each of free champagne.

It was a hell of a space, the main auditorium. Torben filed quietly into the upper gallery, the plummet to the lower floor bound by gleaming brass rails, a sharp rake of seating stretching up to ornate *oeil-de-boeuf* windows set beneath an arching dome. Rain still hammering against those rounds of glass, but distant now, another world. Below, in the vast pit, the floor was cleared for circulating aficionados, critics, historians, makers, and all the other busily swimming piranhas who made up the AWA membership – himself, of course, included;

Torben was well aware by now that he was no better than he ought to be. A large digital screen was suspended above the stage, towards which some of those below were already directing covert glances between vol-au-vents. The main event was only minutes away, and the presidential candidates were clustering to one side, his quarry among them. At this distance, from this height, Torben could not read Drever's expression. But his body language was remarkable for a firm favourite: hands opening and closing, smoothing down his tie. One pace forward. One pace back.

Even up here there were waiters offering drinks to the more shy and retiring of the Academy's members. Torben accepted a glass without really realising. Five seconds later it was empty, and he was aware of a slight dizziness. A microphone squalled into life, and a *doyenne* of the art world began a fustian monologue. It was happening. It was happening now.

Images on the floating screen. The beaming faces of the remaining candidates flashed up: a maverick sculptor who'd been controversial in the eighties; Drever at his very slickest; a professor who'd done solid work at Glasgow; the ex-director of a well-known NGO; the outgoing head of a textile museum. Each was greeted with a brief spiel from the host, a smattering of applause. Some minor commotion at the back of the hall, a few heads turning. People moving closer to the stage, people shifting further away.

'Another glass, sir?' at Torben's elbow. Automatically, he took it.

Something sententious about progress, consensus, a storied tradition of innovation. Coughs, an elephantine sneeze, some awkward laughter from the floor. And at last – 'Without further ado, it falls to me, on behalf of the Committee' ... how much polish, Torben wondered idly, did it take to keep those Gothic doorframes gleaming? ... 'to announce, with the greatest pleasure' ... the stage itself was shiny

as an ice rink, you could practically see their reflections in the veneer
… 'that the first ever President of the Academy of Western Art is Professor Hen—'

Drever stepped forward in anticipation, towards the podium, the second microphone. And two more people stepped forward, out of the crowd on each side of the dais.

And didn't Ruth do it well? No hint of stage fright, not a stutter, as the mic just caught her words, broadcasting them to the assembled art world.

'—rik Drever, I am arresting you on a charge of murdering Katherine Trigg.' Then, more quietly, already leading him away from the microphone. 'You do not have to say anything …'

For a moment, the great hall of the Academy of Western Art was silent. Spellbound.

But only for a moment.

26

ALDWYCH CRESCENT

'And of course,' said Torben, 'half of them thought it was a piece of performance art, the other half thought it was a spill-over from the protestors outside – an eco-intervention for his views on sponsorship – which resulted overall in about a fifty-fifty split of boos and cheers …'

'Until,' said Ruth, 'they started twigging I was genuine …'

'At which point,' said Torben, 'it all kicked off.'

The three of them – Ruth, Torben, Leyla – were squeezed into a corner table at the Delaunay, a somewhat less formal sibling to the Wolseley, just off the Strand. It was late, the three of them tumbling in among the post-theatre crowd, delighted to find a kitchen still open, the last table still free. They were drinking house Martinis, which included akvavit, sherry and absinthe among the ingredients, and no one was entirely sure what mood they should be in. It was a bit like celebrating the end of exams you suspected you might have failed. Torben had finally given in and allowed himself to order a real sausage – 'Call it reverse carbon offsetting for going on the march' – and their little table, lit by low lamps, was clustered with the wreckage of central European cuisine.

Leyla exhaled. 'I can't believe I missed it. Delays outside Clapham Junction ... You were in mortal peril, Tor, I was stuck on this eternal train, and I had no idea which of our two positions I'd rather be in ...'

'And Ruth,' said Torben, 'was putting in the performance of her career. Shame you're not sticking around long enough to get a medal or whatever it is.'

Drever had, unwisely, attempted to run for it, and been brought down by a combination of a sturdy police constable and the surprisingly sprightly Glaswegian professor. The Fellows of the Academy of Western Art had gone mad for it. Canapés had perhaps been thrown, and champagne spilt in anger. As Torben had made his way out he had distinctly overheard one venerable historian comment to a much-garlanded restorer, 'If they don't arrest someone else at the re-run, it'll be a hell of a letdown. Haven't had this much fun since we de-bagged Brian Sewell in '94.'

The almost-president's rash bid for freedom had left few in doubt as to his guilt, and Bassett's team had soon produced the murder weapon: Torben had told them to search every bin, drain and gutter between Admiralty House and the Churchill War Rooms. Half an hour later, a surprisingly professional-looking knife had been recovered, with Trigg's blood all over its blade, and Drever's DNA all over its handle.

'A Mora knife,' Torben had observed, almost proudly. 'He may have gone native for English culture, but he was still a Swede where it mattered most.'

Confronted with the evidence, Drever had ceased his indignant bluster and gone quiet, making only a polite request for a lawyer. Before the hour was out, this representative had opened negotiations around what mitigation they might expect for entering a plea of guilty.

Leyla had listened to the full story with a remarkable lack of interruptions. On the other hand, she had gone through three cocktails, for which Torben had optimistically offered to pay. She had saved him paying for Simon Grey's lunch, after all. Oddly, she had accepted the offer with a quiet 'thank you'. She couldn't possibly be ... shamefaced? Leyla? Surely not.

'What you still haven't told us,' she observed at last, 'presumably out of a weakness for the dramatic, is how you knew to go after Drever in the first place. Four suspects, each headed in a different direction. Lucky guess?'

Torben smiled; sipped his Martini. He had spotted a bottle of Tokaji at the bottom of the wine list, and was sorely tempted. He shifted the menu towards him and found it would set him back a hundred pounds. Temptation receded.

'It was his tie,' he said at last. 'When they all left. The thin end was tucked inside his shirt. Now, he may have been wet, and bored, and desperate to be elsewhere. But the Henrik Drever I knew would never commit such a sartorial infelicity unless it was a matter of life and death.'

It was the sort of line he'd always wanted to deliver. Like a real detective. Yet it was not as satisfying as he'd hoped.

'And it struck me,' he went on, 'that a stabbing, at close quarters – well, there'd be bound to be *some* blood. As he leant over her – or more likely as he straightened back up – the trailing end must have brushed against the wound. Or else he used the tie to wipe his hand clean. Of course, he couldn't take it *off*, we'd all seen him wearing it, and he needed it for the ceremony. So he had no choice but to tuck it in.'

They both looked suitably impressed with this. Well, time to disillusion them.

'The only problem is,' he admitted, 'I haven't got the faintest idea *why* he killed her.'

Leyla almost spoke, but didn't.

'What?' he said.

'Oh,' she said, not meeting his gaze. 'I was only wondering ... if it could have been an act of ... revenge?' She addressed the final word to the bottom of her glass, barely audible over the clinks and chatter of the restaurant.

'Ah,' said Torben. 'You mean he found out about "Trigg's Peacock".'

'I still think it sounds more like a chess opening,' said Ruth.

They had been a little bit mean about this earlier. Hence his paying for the cocktails. In Torben's view, 'Trigg's Peacock' sounded like either an avian subspecies or a mathematical theorem. Ruth had held out for either a chess move or a provocative piece of twentieth-century philosophy.

'Well, yes,' said Leyla, her face now glowing even more than the rest of them. 'Is that so hard to credit? Katherine Trigg murders Charlotte in ice-cold blood after decades of festering hatred. She lets something slip to Henrik Drever, during the march. Who in turn—'

'Jeopardises his career and financial prospects an hour before its absolute zenith by taking justice into his own hands, for the sake of a rival whose death profited him enormously, by means of a deadly knife he just happened to have about his person in case he felt an urgent need to whittle a spoon?' said Ruth.

They both stared at her. '*For helvede*, Ruth,' said Torben. 'That was devastating! I think the fame has gone to your head.'

Already, more than one diner had turned to look at Ruth less than surreptitiously, check their phone, and whisper. Footage of the arrest was threatening to go viral, and even the BBC were using the upload from someone's phone to accompany their news story. Ruth's face, alongside Drever's, was suddenly everywhere. Maybe going into local government was not such a bad thought after all; a starring role in a high-profile murder case would do wonders for her own electoral prospects.

'Fine,' said Leyla. 'It was just a suggestion. And until you can prove how Drever killed Charlotte whilst hobnobbing in Brussels, and why he was possessed by an overwhelming urge to do in an innocent old lady, "Trigg's Peacock" is still the most convincing theory we have in play.'

'Coke users can do some pretty wild things,' Ruth offered. 'What – oh, come off it! Don't tell me neither of you had realised that?! Why you dear little lambs …'

Oh. And he had thought it was hay fever. A weak bladder. And it had been staring him in the face for – for how long?

'*For fanden,*' he said. 'One up to you, Ruth. But that's a catalyst at most, not a motive. Now that I know, it obviously fits – yes, he must have been craving a dose at the start of the march, and then fixed himself some at an opportune moment – perhaps when that first rumble of thunder grabbed all our attentions – because he was certainly under the influence of *something* by the time we reached Whitehall. I can see why that might have affected his judgement, precipitated his action – but it didn't give him his reason. I must have missed something …'

He *had* missed something, he knew it. Perhaps gazing into the distance would help. No, the only result was that Ruth was laying a hand on his arm.

'Tor,' she said, 'are you OK?'

He started. 'Of course! You mean—'

'It wasn't your fault that Katherine Trigg died,' she said.

'Ruth,' he said, '*mange tak*, but I know. Please don't think I blame myself because a paranoid murderer struck again.' This was not, of course, true, but he didn't think he could bear the full weight of Ruth's sympathy, not yet. 'Yes, in retrospect, the whole scheme does start to look a little dangerous. But it was their choice to turn up, each of them. And I am *not* responsible for Drever bringing a knife to a climate fight.'

'Hear hear,' said Leyla, raising her almost-empty glass.

'It is not my conscience that troubles me,' he said, only now becoming aware of quite how much he had drunk that day, 'but the dictates of justice not yet done. He killed them both, I *know* he did. And I know *why* he killed Charlotte, and *how* he killed Katherine. Now I just need to fill in the blanks.'

And he did know. Know that Drever had killed them both. Because he had stood on the other side of the two-way mirror with Gary Bassett and Ruth and two other officers as the subject of Charlotte was raised in the interview room. Drever had been gaunt and hollow-eyed, and his fancy tie had long-since disappeared within the sealed bag of a forensics specialist. But Drever had laughed at the question. Laughed! And, patting aside the concerns of his lawyer, he had looked the mirrored glass full on as he replied. 'Supposing we entertain the frankly ludicrous hypothesis that I *did* kill Charlotte Lazerton. I would be very grateful if you could inform me how and when I did so. Because I' – and here his laughter had become a hyena's cackle – 'I myself have not the faintest idea!'

And in that moment, Torben had seen with perfect clarity what Drever was too cocky to deny: he *had* murdered Charlotte Lazerton. But he had also said that he did not know how.

And Torben believed him.

27

THE ROYAL ACADEMY

Torben had not forgotten Elodie. To make it up to the traumatised young woman, he took her to the Helene Schjerfbeck exhibition that had just opened at the Royal Academy. Strange, to see Piccadilly without its marchers, just the usual run of traffic, tourists, passers-by. Elodie, too, with no trace of reflected death on her features. Looking at that fresh face, practically radiating hope and resolution, it was hard to believe there were such things as avarice and murder – the very things, he reminded himself, that she and her friends had been marching against. There was no need to idealise the young, they had principles enough, and the spirit to fight for them.

Still. 'I'm sorry you had to see that,' he said, as they ascended another vast staircase – this one rather more austere than the spangled sweep of the AWA, all whitewash and dressed stone. And, he thought, sorry that she had not only had to see but to *deal* with it all; to find the police, amid the crush, to watch the body, to answer questions. To grow up, so fast, in all that rain.

'But no, it was very interesting in the end,' Elodie said. And she was smiling as she said it, possibly a little too bravely. 'Almost beautiful, really. I have never seen death before. So it can help my process, maybe; my aesthetic? Oh, and it was shocking too of course, quite terrible. But then, she was a *very* old woman.'

Katherine Trigg had been seventy-three. Torben repressed a shudder at the callousness of the young. What was that he had been thinking, about idealism?

The exhibition was split across two rooms. By the time they entered the first, he'd already decided to buy the catalogue – always a mistake not to, you could never get it cheaper online – and the design qualities of the whole exhibition were making him go all gooey inside already. That main image on the poster, where Schjerfbeck looked a bit like Tilda Swinton. The exquisite plaster-pink of the background colour scheme. The font, the delicious serif font of the body text, elegant but tough, juxtaposed with the hard-hitting slabs of the sans serif titles. He ran his mind over fonts he had known; these were definitely up there with the best.

The first room was light, decorous, and seemed to be playing host to about three painters in one. Schjerfbeck was probably Finland's greatest artist, unless you had a *really* soft spot for Tove Jansson, and her dates – 1862 to 1946 – meant she had straddled almost every major movement in modern art history. Beside him, Elodie practically tutted at the earliest works, idyllic representations of rural life, coastal landscapes, small blonde children. Sort of realist, sort of nationalist. Their one defining feature was a certain quality of light, which redeemed them all. He tried to express this to Elodie, who was having none of it.

The second room, he could see, was smaller, darker. Part of him wanted to hold back.

'*Allez*,' said Elodie. '*Viens*. Oh, but these are something else!'

A stretch of self-portraits ran right round the walls. Year after year, executed as she aged. First a little passive, even pasty, that sense of unflinching scrutiny leavened with compassion. Then a flattening, a reduction of complexity to essence, spots of colour in high cheeks, a growing cold, a gauntness. And then – but he could scarcely bring himself to look.

It was almost harder to take, in a way, than confronting the corpse of Katherine Trigg. That had been a body, a crime, a thing perpetrated in an instant, upon an innocent. A horrific act, but one he could respond to. This – this was too much. Schjerfbeck's late self-portraits were nothing less than an exercise in annihilation. How an artist could do this to herself – how *any* human being could see so far into their own mortality, their own dying, and record it. Picture by picture she stripped away what was good and living. Hair, then skin, reduced to harsh lines, to flat lime white. In this one, she was half person, half carnival mask. In this, an orc; in this, a spectre. The very last images, ghoulish, were little more than half-remembered nightmare, a fading dissolution of a memory of a ghost glimpsed through a window. This was living, and ageing, and dying, in full knowledge of that final fact. He had seen nothing more true, and nothing more terrifying. They were images that would haunt him for ever more.

From somewhere, impossibly, the scent of fresh flowers. Elodie leant herself against him, and he saw her own eyes were moist.

'Her old face,' was all she said.

Torben, his mind on death, started. 'Say that again,' he said.

'I only said – "her old face".'

'"Her old face",' he repeated. Something there. What was it?

Old face.

A font, the one she had used on the protest float. Baskerville Old Face.

Baskerville …

For helvede.

He had forgotten the dog.

He turned to Elodie. *'Cherchez le chien!'*

'Quoi?!' She regarded him as a child might a madman.

'Never mind. Look, I have to go – I think I've worked it out!'

And he ran, actually ran, out of the Royal Academy. As if all the hounds of hell were at his heels.

28

REGENT'S CANAL

If only Meera had given him her number. Still …. It was a long shot, but worth a try. He called Cameron Plott.

'Oh, hi, Torben – a *phone call*, that's so retro – look, I'm kinda busy right now—'

'Cameron, is Meera with you?'

'How the *fuck* did you—'

'Never mind, just put her on.'

Meera's voice on the line. 'Look, Torben, this really isn't a good ti—'

'You can go back to the sex in a minute. And speaking of which, I just need to know – that "sex dungeon" you said Mortimer found, the first day you took him for a walk—?'

'Actually we made a bit of a cock-up on that one,' Meera said. 'Turned out it wasn't kinky business after all, just some weird kind of dog-training room. The Human Trafficking guys took the piss pretty hard about that when they told us; they had to look into it when we called it in, and all they found were a load of dog hairs and saliva over everything. But—'

'*Tak*, Meera, that's just what I wanted,' Torben said. Two minutes later, having ensured that he, Meera, and – for the next stage of the plan – Leyla all had each other's numbers, he rang off. Rude, he supposed, to crash Meera's lazy afternoon. But maybe the subject of the sex dungeon would inspire her and Cameron to try out something more adventurous in the bedroom; they'd thank him for it one day.

Gary Bassett picked up on the third ring. 'Jesus, you call every day, who are you – my wife?'

'Don't get your hopes up,' said Torben. 'Listen, did you follow up those names I gave you, from the burrito place in Camden?'

'Torben, that was less than two days ago, and in case you've forgotten we've had the small matter of a mass protest, a stabbing and a murder confession to deal with since then.' A pause. 'But yes, as it happens, I've got an address for you. I'll text it over now.'

He sounded so proud of himself. And why not. If Gary Bassett didn't come out of this business with at least some kind of medal, there really was no justice in the world.

Surfacing at Camden Town, Torben rechecked the address on his phone, then headed north. His quarry was apparently living in the last ungentrified pocket of the canal – a corner of the northern bank that was still forever old London, all graffiti, scummy water, and a rundown sixties pre-fab, its grey-grim walls streaked with water stains. It struck him uncomfortably, somewhere in the region of his conscience, that this was the closest thing to normal London life he had encountered in the whole investigation. The lock on the communal door was helpfully broken; the stairwell stank of piss and broken dreams. Correction: piss and marijuana. Broken dreams were more—

And there she was, emerging up a basement staircase, a young woman – a girl, frankly – answering exactly to the description he had got from the late-shift waiter: slight build, waif-like, brown hair tied back, skinny jeans worn high on the waist, yet in truth resembling nothing more than a startled deer, poised to bolt.

'Ximena,' he said, 'please – you're the only person that can help me.'

Afterwards, he was never entirely sure what had held her there. God knew she owed him and his world less than nothing. Perhaps it was the appeal for her aid, surely a rare enough occurrence to merit curiosity if nothing more. And the £200 in cash he had produced moments later clearly hadn't hurt, though she had become doubly suspicious and he had felt like the lowest kind of worm. Whatever it was, she let him into the basement room she was sub-subletting from a council tenant, and gave him five minutes. He gave her both Leyla's and Gary's contact details. 'You may not believe it, but these people can and will help you. Go to them.'

A bare lightbulb, dangling from a rose-less aperture. A sofa spilling half its polyester stuffing. A splintered coffee table adorned with a startlingly beautiful arrangement of wild flowers in a chipped mug.

'Whatever you want,' she said at last, 'it's clearly something big. And I'm not going to like it.'

He took a deep breath, feeling absurdly long-legged, outsized, perched on the edge of the subsiding sofa. 'Charlotte Lazerton,' he said, and placed the battered business card from Charlotte's desk upon the table. 'You walked her dog.'

'*No chingues,*' she muttered to herself. 'They said no one …' and she looked up at him, defiant. 'I did nothing illegal,' she said. 'They told me it was only for money, something harmless. Never did I know that she would die.' A pause. 'I liked her very much. I …'

She looked at her hands, turning over in her lap. '*¡qué pendejo!*' she breathed. 'I was, I was an *imbécil* to think they would not hurt her.'

'When you walked Mortimer,' Torben said slowly, 'you took him to a house nearby, didn't you?' And he named the address of the abandoned 'dungeon'.

'How do you—? *Sí*. They paid me and said "come back in an hour". I never saw inside.' Her eyes flashed. 'They did not hurt the dog. He is a good dog, he was never unhappy.'

Torben nodded. 'Ximena,' he said, as gently as he knew how. 'All I want … is a name. Or an address. Nothing written down, no police, at least not today. Just a word, now. You can whisper if you like.'

Her hands were trembling. 'If they find out,' she said, 'then they will kill me.'

'They will not find out. And they will kill no one, not anymore.'

Silence. For a very long time.

Then she scooted up next to him on the sofa. 'OK,' she said. 'I whisper it.'

So now he had a decision to make. He needed to act fast, because he knew she would run and she would talk, or someone would see: no way would an operation like this let someone like Ximena just disappear on them. He didn't think he'd been seen going in. But then, he had to admit to himself, he didn't have the first idea how to tell if someone was tailing you.

Which meant his own movements were predetermined: Northern

Line, then Jubilee, and pray there were no Sunday engineering works. The address Ximena had whispered ran through and through his head, blazed from the app on the screen in his pocket. He was heading straight there, to see and do whatever he could before they realised someone had split on them.

But as to the police. Ruth was out, she had played her part, and he could never ask her to work on a Sunday. Aside from her beliefs, she'd be stuck in the middle of some community thing by now. Gary, Meera, now *they* could be reached. They would mobilise like a shot for what he had to offer.

And that was his problem. Because he needed them to pick up Ximena. Wherever she bolted now, she was in danger. He had no means to hold her. The only hope – the only thing his conscience could stomach – was for sympathetic officers who would not charge her to pick her up and offer her protection. But if he asked them this, and also forwarded them the address, what were the Met going to do? Split their already overstretched resources, prioritise the safety of an illegal alien hiding somewhere in north London over the scoop of the year in a known location?

Were they hell.

So the decision was made for him. Get them after Ximena, and go on alone. Only after they informed him she was secured would he give them what they really wanted. And he laid this out in a text, to ensure they acted as efficiently as possible.

A perfect solution both logically and morally. Flawless, in fact.

What could possibly go wrong?

29

ISLE OF DOGS

By the time he arrived, it was entirely dark. A dozen-minute dash from Canary Wharf underground station, over a dock, beneath the rails. It felt like New York, or at least what New York looked like in films, until he rounded the final corner, past the playpark and the council housing. In the space of a hundred metres, he'd gone from shiny new money, thirty storeys high and boxing out the sky, to any old where, bricks and pebbledash, and now – now this dead end, in a too-high wall of hoardings.

He checked the address. Westferry Printworks, the name borrowed from a long-gone factory, its fabric blasted, ripped, wrecking-balled down to leave this swathe of no man's land between housing estate and deep-watered dock. It was the right name on the hoardings, the one Ximena had whispered. Grimm & Maier Holdings. Laggardly redevelopers of a five-hectare compound, behind the walls of which who knew what was happening – from the feel of the place, it could be practically anything except for building works.

One of the posters showed an artist's impression of their plans for the site. It looked lovely. It also featured a lot of people, unlike Torben's actual surroundings. Sunday night, and no one around.

Darkness, from what he could tell, beyond the walls. Not even security lighting. So much the better.

He began to skirt the compound. The south wall ran along the waterline, just a thin strip of brick concourse and iron railings, between himself and the deep dark water. A few trees, the start of a notional boulevard – a few more had been left standing inside too, their trunks and thicker branches just about rising higher than the wall. His way in.

Just don't slip, he told himself. Because falling in the water is the lucky outcome.

For fanden, this had been easier when he was nine. And that had generally taken place in daylight, and he had been able to make a noise. *Hup!* And he was over, down, landing with gratifying lightness on the balls of his feet. Hunkering down in an instinctive crouch, he took stock. Waste ground stretched before him, broken concrete, rubble, sand and scrub. Forlorn, a couple more trees stood sentinel over the emptiness. Beyond, a low glow from a squat building, a Portakabin, roof corrugated, slatted blinds at the mean windows shedding a miser's pittance of light. Next to this building, a cluster of sheds, large iron cages, sliding doors ... kennels. At least a dozen out-sized kennels.

Exactly what, he wondered, was he hoping to achieve? He had a phone; he supposed his plan must be to document whatever he could, whatever might be incriminating, before whatever Ximena did next let them know that they'd been rumbled.

He was using words like 'them' and 'they'. He had absolutely no idea what they meant.

Crossing the wasteland was a slow and faintly ridiculous

manoeuvre. Yes, there was light from the Portakabin, someone was inside, but no way was anyone keeping watch. Who apart from bored teenagers would ever try and get in here? And even they would be likelier to content themselves with tagging the outside face of the walls, where others could see. There was nothing here for anyone who did not know exactly what they were looking for.

For all that, he squatted, crawled, used every scrap of available cover – a pile of bricks, a heap of sand, a rusting wheelbarrow, what looked incongruously like a ball of tumbleweed straight out of a Western …

At last, his clothes and hands filthy – which might at least help him blend in to the background – Torben had crossed the gaping expanse. Rising to his feet, he glued himself to an unlit corner of the building, and waited for his breathing to slow, to quieten.

London at night was a strange beast. Never exactly what you could call dark, not true dark, but this sick sort of darkening, the nagging glow of light pollution like the prickling heat of a fever victim's brow. Distant noise serving only to highlight the unlikely quiet close at hand. Still far too warm. And a smell. A rising smell of dog.

OK, what now? His pumping blood was no longer the loudest thing in his ears, and Torben could just make out a murmur of voices, drifting from a cracked-open window round the corner. Even villains must need ventilation on hot summer nights.

What was underfoot? It was disconcertingly gravelly here, perhaps for reasons of drainage … Leyla's voice in his head, heavenly Leyla, *the drainage is immaterial* … when this was all over, assuming he made it out alive, he would have to do much more than buy her some cocktails. He began to edge closer, his back to the wall. Would taking off his shoes help? Probably not, he'd only step on something and yell …

Light within; dark without. He felt emboldened to glance through the glass of the window from a narrow angle, trusting to optics to keep him hidden. A squalid little room. Stick furniture. A desk, an open ledger – handwritten accounts! Presumably to render them untraceable and easily disposed of. An old metal filing cabinet, a man hunching over one of the drawers, a screech from its runners and a bag withdrawn, dainty in the man's large hand, weighty with white powder. Well, that made sense. Just as even bad guys needed fresh air, they presumably also needed to diversify in the current economic climate. Multiple income streams. And, in this case, cocaine was itself the gateway drug to a rather greater thrill …

Apparently the sachet in question was for personal use only, though. Both the occupants of the office were now fussing about the table, cutting, shovelling, snorting.

'We celebrating a new client?' one said.

'Yup. A—'

'No, lemme guess. In-law.'

'Correct.'

'The husband?'

'Yeah, but also—'

'Oh, *gay* husband?'

'Yeah.'

'Takes all sorts. OK, gimme a compass direction.'

'South-west.'

'Not Chelsea, too obvious.'

'Cold.'

'Wimbledon?'

'Think more west.'

'Richmond!'

'Bingo. Right on the river and everything.'

'OK, and it's his husband's … mum?'

'Yeah, but statistics got you that one.'

'Well, statistics would also say Alsatian, but I'm guessing … Newfoundland?'

'Nope.'

'Great Dane?'

'Miles off.'

'Er … Schnauzer? Boxer? Fuck me, not a Saint Bernard?'

'You'll never get it.'

'Why not? Oo, that Tibetan one?'

'Alsatian.'

'Oh, you sneaky bastard! It's never—'

'Look here, it's in the book.'

And he swivelled the ledger so the light fell full across it. On the far side of the table, both bent their heads closer. It was a perfect tableau – the coke, the lit faces, the open page that might, at high resolution, be legible … Torben reached for his phone, framed the shot, zoomed in, snapped it.

At this point, he realised he had forgotten two things.

He had not disabled the flash. Nor was it set to silent, and that funny artificial shutter sound that they persisted in adding to digital phones rang like a bell in that bright and awful second.

A face loomed in the window. A guttural bout of swearing. And, just before everything went entirely to hell, five more words that rewrote Torben's world.

'Frank – let the dogs out.'

30

ABOUT FIVE METRES HIGH

Leyla was having one of her less predictable Sundays. It had begun with a hangover, routinely enough, which had rather set the tone for the morning. Bloody Torben, pushing cocktails on her full of evil Scandi spirits. Then, still abed, an unhealthy dose of doom-scrolling through hot takes on Ruth's perfectly choreographed arrest, and a wander through the more esoteric online theories about Drever and who the mysterious Katherine Trigg had been. Leyla had noted that, with grim inevitability, the media was going to town on the murder and giving the march, let alone its purpose, only the scantiest of mentions. Finally up, and almost half alive, she had tempered wickedness with virtue, running the kilometre or so to the Shoreditch branch of Dishoom for a bacon naan roll and a Virgin Mary. The run back had been rather slower.

A listless enough afternoon followed, albeit brightened by a long phone call with Beryl, who took the news of Katherine Trigg's death with just the right blend of sadness, ghoulishness and rampant speculation. She had let Leyla talk through her peacock-and-revenge theory and was very kind about it, but even on so short an acquaintance, Leyla could tell when she was being humoured.

She was *not* calling Torben. Not when he was, reading between the lines of a single, brief message, taking Elodie sodding Griffon on a trip to a museum like some benevolent godfather to make himself feel better about having drowned the girl's innocence in a welter of blood and rain.

Things got more interesting later on. She had exercised, cleaned, ironed, prepped a supper. Put off eating it, cursed the endless sunshine of the midsummer days ... finally curled up with a slim French novel, and had just got to an especially existential bit, when a message came through on her phone. *Hello. My name is Ximena. I think I need a lawyer. Is it possible to meet?*

Before an hour was out, she was serving Ximena a light selection of *mezza* and starting to fill out forms, ring round the right people, generally lay the foundations of the legal fortress that would keep this brave young woman in the country, off the street, and out of danger.

Then had come the call from Meera Rampur. 'Leyla, I'm texting you an address, can you get there asap? I don't think you're gonna want to miss this. And we could do with someone who might know what the hell he's likely to try and do.'

It took two minutes to reassure Ximena that she would be safe alone in the apartment. Thirty seconds to look up the address. And four minutes flat to run as she had rarely run before, right the way down East Road to Old Street station.

She could tell it was the right place because of the police cars, backed up down the road. Someone was making moves with a roll of tape as if they were about to cordon off the site. A little way off, two figures, arms behind their backs, were being cajoled into the back of a van. Lights everywhere. From somewhere out of that light, an 'Excuse me, ma'am—'. But then, there was Meera, her face a perfect picture. 'It's all right, she's with me. Leyla, you absolutely *have* to see.'

Past a special-looking van parked askew with, rather wonderfully, the words 'Dog Section' stencilled on the side. Past an artist's impression of idealised modern living. Through a splintered pair of metal gates, looking for all the world as if they had been battered down with a ram. Which, she supposed, they had.

'Stay behind me,' said Meera, and only now did Leyla clock the padding on her chest and arms. 'And keep this side of the wranglers at all times. They're about to go in and secure them all, but they promised to wait a minute – I think one of them's filming …'

More lights, and a row of what might have been ice-hockey players – or, she supposed with a pang of sadness, lacrosse goalkeepers – all of them chuckling at something Leyla could not yet see. And an unholy din … as well there might be, she realised, as she finally saw past a padded shoulder, and took in the scene.

Fifteen, maybe twenty dogs were circling a tree. None was smaller than Rodger, Beryl's otterhound. Some would have put Mortimer himself to shame. She was no expert, but there were woolly ones, stubbly ones, black and tan and white and grey, all of them sleek and gleaming with health and muscle and power. Every one of them was baying, slavering, yowling away, as they paced and rolled and scrabbled around the trunk of a solitary, scraggly tree. In the upper branches of which, teetering precariously, an unlikely shape, blacker against the blackness of the sky—

'*Hej*, Leyla,' said the tree. 'You know, it's at times like this that you come to appreciate deep and essential truths about yourself.'

'Such as?' she said.

'I have finally realised, there are no two ways about it. On balance, I am definitely a cat person.'

31

A STATIONÆRY CUPBOARD

'What I had forgotten,' said Torben, 'is the propensity of the Metropolitan Police to ride roughshod over basic civil liberties. All the time they were meant to be looking for Ximena Podenco – who, to her undying credit, went straight to Leyla – they were tracking my movements via my phone, as Bassett told me afterwards. He'd tampered with it during Drever's interrogation, as soon as he found out how I'd gone after him on my own. Definitely irregular, if not downright illegal. So as soon as I stopped moving across London, they mobilised. Meaning that, while I was creeping like a particularly shy sort of crab across a patch of scrubland on the Isle of Dogs, they were closing in. No respect for the agreement I thought we'd made, no concern for the welfare of a vulnerable young woman—'

'Or as you could also put it,' interposed Wilson, 'they bent a rule to cut a corner, knowing you were likely to do something else stupid, and took the sort of swift, decisive action that allowed them to catch two dangerous crooks in the act and rescue a fatheaded Scandinavian from having his face chewed off by a pack of slavering hounds.'

'Well, there is that,' Torben conceded. 'And the criminals soon squealed and grassed up their controller, who squealed in turn—'

'And everyone was plea-bargaining everywhere right up to the top, yeah,' said Wilson. 'But don't jump ahead, OK? We'll go again from my responsible citizen's defence of police priorities.'

They were back in the recording studio of the Hayford Theatre – or, as the sign on the door now officially proclaimed, the 'stationæry cupboard'.

'Thanks to you,' Wilson had told him. 'A diplomatic borrowing from the Danish alphabet to appease both sides of the pedantic divide.'

The final episodes of *Crimeward Ho II: Ho Let The Dogs Out?* would not be uploaded to the servers until after the court proceedings were wrapped up, but Wilson wanted everything ready to release the moment the embargo was lifted. 'In fact,' he said, more to himself than to Torben, 'I think we'll cut here to Meera Rampur for her description of the first arrests, then get in that guy from the Dog Support Unit – he's prepared to go on the record if we plug their recruitment programme ...'

Most people, it seemed, were prepared to go on the record. They could not, as yet, discuss Simon Grey in the forensic detail Wilson was hoping for, since he still retained his parliamentary privilege, which protected him even though he was now sitting as an independent MP, pending an enquiry. This was because the police had applied for access to Charlotte Lazerton's email account as part of their separate investigation and 'accidentally' stumbled upon a rather interesting piece of correspondence concerning a multinational oil firm, some drilling licences, and a six-figure sweetener.

Meanwhile, Torben had insisted on anonymity for Shani Rajapalayam – 'What's the point?' Wilson had argued, 'Everyone knows who it is' – ever since receiving a handwritten letter in the wake of all the revelations.

Dear Torben,

I believe I owe you an explanation. Your neighbour and my friend, Lucia Segugio – yes, I think I'll still call her my friend – has told me of your conversation, and you are quite correct in what you have surmised. On what transpired (though I did not know this for some time afterwards) to be the day before the murder of my beloved and benighted mentor, colleague, and sometime lover Charlotte Lazerton, I abstracted from her house a small portrait in oils by Lucian Freud. I did this by means of a hatch and fire corridor that corresponded between the top storeys of the two houses. I believe that Charlotte remained unaware of my removal of the portrait, and my action had no bearing upon her untimely death the following day, which I regret more than I can ever begin to say.

Obviously I would appreciate it if you kept this information to yourself, and, reluctant as I am to commit such a cliché to pen and paper, please burn this letter after reading it. Or shred and recycle, since you have evinced some sympathy to the environmentalist movement.

I think you may perhaps look more kindly upon my actions in the light of my motivation. The portrait in question is of myself. It was painted in 1978, when I was still in my teens; a first-year undergraduate student at the Ruskin. I had been introduced to the artist by Charlotte, who had just begun to take an interest in me – at this point, only as a protégée, a pupil, a girl of intellectual promise. Freud, unsatisfied with some detail of the execution, gave me the portrait upon completion, making me promise never to sell or exhibit what he considered to be a sub-standard work. For my part, I found the whole experience at once the most wonderful and the most terrifying thing that had ever happened to me.

Some years later, my career and independence from Charlotte's influence now safely established, we became lovers. We were neither exclusive nor constant, reconnecting as and when it suited, often in concert with a third party – Rome in 1988 will remain forever etched upon my memory; I wonder what became of that boy Matteo – but I digress. Over time, our relations soured. I was, perhaps, further gone in my affections for Charlotte than either of us realised at the time, and certainly more so than she was for me. But she was, despite herself, a sentimental creature, and fond of me, and requested the gift of the Freud portrait as a memento of our years together. For auld lang syne. I was happy to oblige, having no especial love for the picture which, I had come to agree along with its maker, was a flawed and indeed problematic rendering. Moreover, it had begun to embarrass me, and I kept it locked away. Charlotte knew this, and accepted with the gift Freud's original stricture: that it remain entirely private.

In recent decades, Charlotte and I have had our ups and downs. Certain inequalities in our past liaisons began to rankle with me and I frequently took her to task for what I saw as a somewhat cavalier, unreconstructed attitude to various matters. I was both aggrieved and deeply shocked when, at a party early this year, I found that she had reneged upon or forgotten her promise and exhibited my portrait in her house – which, whilst technically a private space, was a de facto gallery for a certain section of our mutual acquaintance. You have probably gathered that the painting was a nude, and a graphic one at that.

Of course I immediately confronted Charlotte, who

promised to take the picture down, but she flatly refused to return it to me, and I could not help suspecting that she wished to keep it as a gentle form of leverage. Not blackmail as such, nothing so sordid, just a reminder that she still held something of our shared past over me. The fact of this began to weigh upon me, leading me finally to act in the manner I have already described. I had to wait, of course, until Lucia had returned from abroad, to give me a means of access. Otherwise I would have retrieved the painting much sooner. It was doubtless a rash act and, possession being nine tenths of the law, probably an illegal one. But my conscience is clear as to the spirit of the thing and, while I could never countenance the destruction of an artwork, I intend to keep it from view in future. I will not be leaving it to Lucia in my own will. But then I very much doubt, living as she does, that I will predecease her. She is now, of course, your neighbour; do keep an eye on her and convince her to moderate some of her indulgences if you can.

I began by craving a favour and end by imposing further upon you – not a very creditable letter. It had better end here. Thank you, in advance, for doing the right thing. So few of us know how to do that. I'm sure we'll see each other now and then; please, don't allude to this. Increasingly, I find myself inclined to a belief that professional relationships should remain professional.

Yours ever,

S.

The more charitable view, Torben had thought, was that Charlotte had kept the painting of Shani, not as collateral, but because she liked it. And because she still remembered their relationship fondly. But then, he would want to think the best of her, and even were it true, it was a luxurious position to be in. He remembered Charlotte's own pen-and-ink sketch of Rome, 1988, and blushed. Shani had known what she was doing in writing that letter. Her secret would be safe with him.

Speaking of secrets. He, Ruth, Leyla and Gary Bassett had all received invitations to Katherine Trigg's funeral, sent from her London address. These had been written by a man called Craig Wendolyn who, on enquiry, turned out to be Trigg's lover of some thirty years' standing, keeping this running alongside a happy family home on the other side of London and a job selling Bentleys. The funeral would take place in town, rather than down in Blandford, due to the 'decades of happy memories' he and Trigg had apparently shared. These included many years of wheelchair tennis at a club in Dulwich, where the wake would be held.

Leyla took the news with better grace than might have been expected, given her evident embarrassment at getting so hung up on one incident in the youth of a much more complex woman. 'I blame Beryl's sherry,' was her only attempt at self-defence. 'After three glasses of that, trust me, you'd believe anything.' And, to Leyla's credit, she seemed almost as happy as the rest of them. And it was Leyla, now addicted to googling even the remotest acquaintance, who found out that Craig Wendolyn was also the life secretary of the John Mortimer Appreciation Society.

As to Jonathan Azawakh's involvement, Torben had been given no choice: this stayed off the record. So Azawakh had informed him on an early-morning walk along the Thames.

'Really,' the civil servant had said, 'you two gave us far too much credit. A flag came up on the system when the police filed the death of Charlotte, and ever since our private altercation about her memoirs last year, I had been keeping an eye out for any unusual activity from that quarter. We went in first thing the next morning; I don't think we were seen—'

'You were,' said Torben. 'But my source must remain anonymous.' He thought Marko Posavac would appreciate being referred to as an anonymous source.

'You see!' said Azawakh. 'We're just not as good as you think. We never suspected foul play until you came round, poking your noses in. Even then I thought you were just playing silly games, disturbing the peace without good reason; it's why I warned you off. So thank you. While in general we would prefer to have avoided the scandal of a double murder by a high-ranking university administrator, I happen to have been very fond of both victims. I'm glad you gave them justice.'

'And Simon Grey's corruption case?'

Azawakh waved that away. 'Oh, we can't move for wrongdoing in Westminster as it is, what's one more felonious politician among so many? We won't interfere with his case, I promise you. But as I was saying, we acted in all innocence when we went in to Little James Street; my department's really very single-minded. We just got in there, went through the records – what a mess *that* was – took the compromising pages of the memoir, and got out. Of course, we cleaned up after ourselves.'

'Rather too well,' said Torben. 'Even the police noticed that much. And you failed to spot yourself in her papers, too – you were under MM, not JA.'

'MM?' said Azawakh. Then, 'Oh – Man from the Ministry!' And he laughed. 'That takes me back. She really was out of another age. You know we nicknamed her "Sir Anti-Blunt" in the service? But though she loathed the man for his views on art, she wouldn't let anyone say a word against him for his politics. "Hang him for his prose if you like, but let's not be so vulgar as to bring up the other thing", or words to that effect. Silly old Charlotte.'

'Might I ask,' said Torben, 'since you've made it plain that I can never speak or write a word of this, what it was in her memoirs that you were so desperate to keep quiet?'

'Code-breaking,' said Azawakh at once. 'Plain and simple. She could publish and be damned about all the actual Soviet secrets she extricated – that's just historic colour, declassified stuff. But we also brought her in to crack a bunch of codes that were based – the Kremlin was going through a patriotic phase – on a comprehensive knowledge of canonical Russian artists and their masterworks. You know how fond she always was of word games, all those terrible puns. I believe she was once crossword-setter for the *New Statesman* for about a month, and they received more angry letters about her clues than for their stance on nuclear disarmament.

'Until very recently I wouldn't have minded if she'd talked about her code-breaking on primetime television. But the funny thing is, Russia's started using the same codes again – these fads come and go – and it's awfully nice knowing what they're up to just at present. I'm sure you understand.'

Torben inclined his head. 'That I *can* square with my conscience,' he said. They walked on. 'Oh,' and he came up short. 'Your downstairs neighbour, the one who inherited from her aunt …?'

'Arrested,' said Azawakh. 'My, you *do* know your stuff, don't you? Ever considered a career in my line of work?'

'Wouldn't I have to be a British citizen?'

'That could be arranged.'

'Arrange it,' said Torben, 'for Ximena Podenco. You owe us that much at least.'

Azawakh smiled. 'I think Charlotte would have approved. Consider it done. Oh – and I look forward to hearing all about it … suitably redacted of course … on *Crimeward Ho*.'

'Actually, Tor,' said Wilson, 'I've managed to get myself a bit lost. How about you just monologue for a bit, I'll chuck in some interjections, and then I'll tidy it up in the edit? Give it the full Poirot, from the top.'

'If you insist,' said Torben, trying – and patently failing – not to sound delighted to be asked. 'It begins, as you know, with the death of Dame Charlotte Lazerton. From the outset, I was convinced it was murder. She was too young, too with-it, to be the sort of person who just falls down the stairs. It quickly became apparent that a number of people stood to gain a little too conveniently by her death, and five suspects stood out from the first. The greatest problem by this point was that the crime scene itself was cold. Even if two forensic investigations – sorry, what did we agree with Azawakh that we should say, a botched forensic investigation that removed all DNA evidence? – even if the botched forensic investigation hadn't accidentally wiped the place clear, by the time I gained access the house had been cleaned and its contents removed. There were, however, certain material indications, some of which misled us, some of which aided us, and some of which I only remembered much later on.'

He paused for breath. Wilson gave him a big thumbs up. 'A used tea service for two turned out to be a total red herring. Simon Grey has proved to be far too petty a criminal to rise to the level of murder at first-hand. We were seriously set back by considering him as a suspect, and drugged tea as a potential method.' He looked at Wilson.

'Yep, that's all good, apparently we can assert his criminality, his legal team aren't contesting the charge.'

'*Strålende!* Next, there was the location of the crime itself: a narrow set of stairs, at the top of which was an old, wired, landline telephone. This proved to be crucial, and we did factor it in, but we got our details wrong. I'm sure Leyla is a good enough sport to fill you in on Trigg's Peacock as a theory—'

And Leyla herself opened the cupboard door. 'Not late, am I?'

Wilson grinned. 'Exquisite timing. Tor's just settling into his Great Detective act; feel free to chip in.'

'Budge up then,' she said, scooting in alongside Torben. 'I heard you mentioning Trigg's Peacock – a logical, coherent explanation of a perfect crime. Albeit one with, I now concede, no actual basis in fact.'

'What we ultimately established,' resumed Torben, 'was that Katherine Trigg was an unwitting earwitness to the act of murder, because that murder was precipitated – quite literally – by her phone call, which Charlotte answered. It was this phone call, or rather the answering of it, that was the means of murder—'

'So in a way, I was entirely right,' said Leyla.

'—but in such a manner that Katherine Trigg's role was entirely random and incidental. At this point, I had nothing more to go on. With doping set to one side, the most credible solution was that someone actually pushed Charlotte down the stairs. Katherine Trigg was incapable of this, due both to her physical condition and the demonstrable fact that she was in her own home, at the other end of the phone line. Simon Grey had left the house an hour earlier, furious at his failure to recover a compromising email, and played no further part.

'Incidentally, we have just found that email printout after an exhaustive search of Charlotte Lazerton's papers, concealed within a – all right, within *my* PhD thesis on Caspar David Friedrich, pasted to the back of an image of Friedrich's painting *The Sea of Ice*, which depicts a shattered iceberg and a shipwreck. Our conclusion is that Charlotte's choice of hiding place was meant to be satirical. And also that, just because one has found the thing one is looking for, that's no reason to stop looking.' Leyla stuck her tongue out at him.

'Three suspects remained,' he pressed on, 'but the one with by far the best motive for wishing Charlotte dead just so happened to be in Brussels at the time, as corroborated by a wholly independent and respectable witness.'

'Notice,' said Leyla, 'that he makes free use of the passive tense when it's something *I* contributed.'

'Nonetheless,' said Torben, '*I* remained convinced that Henrik Drever was psychologically by far the most likely killer, and therefore I left this possibility or even probability open. And so we had reached an impasse.'

'Both of us,' said Leyla, 'favoured a solution in which the murder had been committed by someone not actually in the house with Charlotte.'

'Which led Leyla to concoct a charmingly esoteric theory based upon Charlotte's pavophobia—'

'Pavophobia?' said Wilson, leaping in before Leyla could object.

'Fear of peafowl. Look it up; it's a proper thing,' she said.

'Note to self,' said Wilson, 'need short segment on pavophobia. OK, carry on, Torben.'

'This apparent dead end,' said Torben, 'led *me* to conduct a rather rash experiment. Attempting to flush out the perpetrator, I in fact brought all five suspects together under highly stressful conditions for a brief but intense period of time. These conditions were liable to induce paranoia and anxiety in any guilty party, which is what I wanted. However, this paranoia manifested itself in a second murder, that of Katherine Trigg. This was a crime of opportunity committed under extreme weather conditions that entirely concealed the act itself: anyone in proximity to Trigg, who was sitting exposed on the side of a carnival float, would have been able to carry it out amid the confusion and the downpour, provided they had a weapon to hand. It was, however, a crime entirely unlike the first: spur-of-the-moment, visceral, and extremely risky. Only someone as disturbed as Henrik Drever would have acted as they did.'

'And we got all this the other day,' Wilson added. 'You clocked it was Drever because of the tie thing, and he was super-hyped because of the coke and the presidential election.'

'Exactly,' said Torben. 'Drever's appearance and manner indicated his guilt, which was subsequently proven by the DNA evidence on him, the victim, and the murder weapon. What I entirely failed to grasp, however, was his motive. Why kill the wholly harmless Katherine Trigg?'

'Obviously I'll cut there,' said Wilson. 'Rhetorical question always equals ad break in my book. But you'd better be about to answer your own question, or this cupboard is about to become a whole lot less stationary.'

'*Klap lige hesten*,' said Torben, 'I'm getting there. So. The knife that Drever had brought along, while ill-advised, was clearly intended for use, if required, on whoever had sent that anonymous email: the person who claimed to have information about the murder of Charlotte Lazerton. Why else would he be armed?'

'Another rational explanation,' said Leyla, 'was that he wanted to avenge Charlotte's death: learning it was murder, but with little hope of recourse to the law, he was out for justice himself. As we were. Only with extra stabbing.'

'Which held together logically,' said Torben, 'but did not fit his psychology at all. Drever is no vigilante and had no love for Charlotte – there's only one person he'd kill for, and that's Henrik Drever. So the only thing that made any sense at all was that *he* had murdered Charlotte, suspected someone was on to him, and that something Trigg had said or done during the march *had convinced him that she was the source of the compromising information*. His career was on the line, his election hours away. The rain gave him the perfect chance: if he could silence Trigg and get out of there, he would have eliminated the only source of danger. He would ditch the knife; clean the tie that bore the incriminating bloodstain. Easy to do it, in those mad minutes of chaos. The anonymity of the crowd.'

'Tor,' said Wilson, 'stop milking it, or I swear—'

'OK, OK. So. The only possible motive for Trigg's murder was to cover up *Charlotte's* murder. Meaning whoever killed Katherine, also killed Charlotte. And we know Drever killed Trigg, therefore he also killed Charlotte. *And* – as I realised quite embarrassingly late in the day – the corollary of this equation was that whatever Trigg had said or done that made Drever think she was on to him, would in turn provide the clue to the first murder. If it was something worth killing her for, it had to be central to the mystery of how he had killed Charlotte despite being in Brussels.'

'Huh,' said Wilson. 'When you put it like that, it does sound kinda obvious.'

'Which is the problem,' said Torben, 'with walking through my process like this. It makes me look so much more basic.' *For helvede*. Had he actually just said *my process*? Out of the corner of his eye, he saw Leyla grinning, and hurried on before Wilson noticed. 'I didn't realise what it was she had said until the next day, when a chance remark from Elodie Griffon made me think of *The Hound of the Baskervilles* – and I remembered: Charlotte had not been alone in the house at the time of her murder. She had been with her dog.'

'Her dog, Mortimer,' added Leyla.

He glared at her. That was meant to have been *his* line. 'Now, Katherine Trigg's pet obsession was the barrister and writer *John* Mortimer, creator of *Rumpole of the Bailey*. And at this point it came back to me that, just minutes before her death, she had been arguing with Simon Grey, who then abandoned her, loudly proclaiming that she was mad, leaving free the space beside her on the float. She was insisting that, in his days as a barrister, it was Mortimer's individual genius that had won his landmark cases, not the wider judicial process. And the final thing she had said to drive him away had been something like this … "It was all down to Mortimer, I tell you! That was how they did it – he was a ruthless machine. They just wound Mortimer up, pointed him in the right direction, and let him rip!"

'We all heard her say it. And she referred to him only by surname. In the absence of any other explanation, I could only infer that Drever, manic as he was, had mistaken this as a reference to Mortimer the dog. For how else could it possibly relate to Charlotte's murder, and therefore bring about Trigg's own death?'

'Which meant,' said Wilson, 'that Trigg's words – all that about winding him up and letting him rip – held the secret to how Drever killed Lazerton? By the way, would it be too crass if I got a voice-actor in to re-record those lines of Trigg's?'

'Yes,' said Leyla.

'It's your show,' said Torben. 'And you're quite right. Drever thought he was hearing a recapitulation of his own method of murder, along with half of Whitehall. Luckily, Grey sounded entirely incredulous. But others might be less disbelieving. And so he killed her.'

'Great,' said Wilson. 'I mean, boo. But that's an episode end right there. You OK to go on?'

'He's just getting started,' said Leyla.

'Quite,' said Torben. 'From here, it all fell into place. All I had to do was put Mortimer at the centre of my thinking. Suddenly, Ximena Podenco – his dog walker, remember? – became the number one person of interest. But only *person* of interest; Mortimer himself was the real focus. For some months, Ximena had been taking him for regular walks, without Charlotte. Why her? Charlotte had told me herself, shortly before her death: because Ximena's employers were very cheap, and insisted upon cash. As their card put it, "Five-star service at one-star prices. Large breeds a speciality." Remember that. Note also that they had zero web presence, and chose to employ vulnerable young illegal immigrants like Ximena.'

'Which isn't uncommon for the London grey economy,' said Leyla. 'But, since beefy grass-fed types capable of reining in gigantic hounds would be the more logical employee profile, it does suggest a company motivated by a need for discretion and total power over their staff.'

'Now,' said Torben, 'Charlotte had been recommended their services by an acquaintance. What if this had been Drever? Working from the basis that Drever, the dog and the murder were all connected, this seemed a promising hypothesis. The inference was that the dog-walking was part of the plot. Already I was blundering around the notion of Mortimer as a murder weapon – a ruthless machine, pointed in the right direction and let rip.

'Next: Meera Rampur informed me that on his very first day's walk as a police dog, Mortimer made straight for what she at first took to be an unlicensed sex dungeon, but was later shown by specialists to be an unorthodox kind of dog-training facility. Clearly, this was where Ximena had been taking Mortimer on his walks – a fact she later confirmed when questioned.'

'Ximena's a great interviewee,' said Wilson. 'We've just done background so far for her showcase, but she's a natural. I'm thinking maybe, when her papers come through, of introducing her to some people. That girl has talent.'

Torben beamed. 'So: Mortimer was being trained up as a murder weapon, by Ximena's employers, on behalf of Drever.'

'You're making it sound like Drever had set this whole thing up,' objected Wilson. 'Let me feed you a line … You mean, Drever was behind the whole operation?'

'Oh no,' said Torben, 'he was merely a client. Because I was starting to remember other things, you see, now that I was taking the dog-centred approach. Gary Bassett had told me as much at our first meeting: an old man in a Knightsbridge townhouse, an old woman in a Mayfair flat, a pensioner in Bloomsbury. All dead in the last few months. And what did they have in common, besides being on their own, vulnerable, and possessed of high-value real estate? A Leonberger, a St Bernard and a Newfoundland, all on the scene at the time of death. All of them large breeds. And Jona—'

Leyla coughed.

'—I mean, and from another source, I heard of an old maiden aunt in a seven-figure property in Pimlico, who died all alone, except for a pair of Tibetan Mastiffs.'

'Let me get this straight,' said Wilson. 'You mean, there's been a spate of similar deaths recently?'

'Not deaths,' clarified Leyla. 'Murders. All of them.'

'Organised crime,' said Torben.

'London,' said Leyla. 'City of opportunities. If there's demand, then there's supply. Frankly, I'm just annoyed Torben got there before I did; I'm meant to be the cynical one. There's a hell of a lot of money in London, and where there's money, there's crime.'

'Most of that money circulates quite efficiently, whether it's legitimate or not,' said Torben, who wasn't keen on having his reasoning stolen. 'But there are two current phenomena that, taken together, have created a unique form of demand. The value of property has risen astronomically, especially prime residential property in central and western postcodes.'

'Hence the inability of anyone without either a vast amount of cash, or a supremely jammy legacy, to get on the housing ladder,' said Leyla. 'Even the likes of us, Wilson, who aren't exactly without unfair advantages, have to pour all our earnings into the open mouths of landlords.'

'There are, however,' said Torben, 'an awful lot of older homeowners who bought their properties decades ago, before prices skyrocketed. But this is where the second phenomenon comes in: people are living longer. And those who can afford to look after themselves remain healthy for far longer. Meaning there are quite a lot of impatient people out there in their forties, fifties, even sixties, who consider themselves entitled to inheritances that just aren't coming. All that property, all that capital, tied up in the possession of a generation sitting tight and refusing to die.'

'And of course,' said Leyla, 'a percentage of those impatient people are also deeply unscrupulous. Career professionals, mostly – bankers, managers—'

'Lawyers,' said Torben.

'Quite,' said Leyla. 'And they're prepared to … shall we say, expend some of their liquid capital in order to … hasten things along a bit. Shell out a little in order to reap a much greater reward.'

'Bump off their elders,' said Torben. 'Which gives us a ready market for old-age assassinations. Now, there's also been a recent trend, especially among widows, for keeping large dogs as pets. Replacements for lost partners, in a way: company, a source of exercise, and a great big reassuring impression of security.'

'Big dogs are about as high maintenance as husbands,' said Leyla, 'but more useful in self-defence. Unlike most men, they're biddable, loyal and physically impressive. However, those very qualities that recommend them as guardians also make them a source of danger.'

'Sleeper agents,' said Torben. 'They just need activating. All it takes is one entrepreneur ready to exploit the market. It worked like this: a client looking to rub out a wealthy relative – the target was usually an in-law, a step-parent, an aunt – would recommend this particular firm of dog walker, the beauty of the thing being that large dogs take a lot more walking than the average elderly homeowner can provide. Those long walks would involve a trip to one of a number of discreet locations – the police have tracked down eleven of them so far, I think – where the dog would be trained in secret.'

'Not harmed, or mistreated,' said Leyla, 'which might give the game away. Just trained to respond to a particular trigger, at which they would leap up and overpower the target – with the result of knocking them down the stairs, smashing their head on a marble worktop, precipitating a heart attack, et cetera et cetera. Hard on the victims – and almost as hard on the poor dogs, tricked into acts of violence undertaken in good faith, in the belief that they were doing nothing more than performing as they had been trained. I'd imagine some of the dogs got put down too: two innocent lives for the price of one.'

'An imprecise method of murder,' said Torben. 'I'm guessing you got your money back if it only resulted in mild concussion or a hip replacement. But it was that element of chance that made it so brilliant. The attacks took place while the victim was alone, and could only possibly appear from the outside to be accidental. Better yet, neither the perpetrator nor the agency they employed would have any way of knowing precisely *when* the victim would trigger the attack, giving the guilty parties no need to construct alibis that might appear artificial; they could go about their daily lives in the perfect knowledge that an entirely random, hairy bomb was ticking away without any further input on their part.'

'Gary Bassett also told us,' said Leyla, 'that the criminals were trialling a new "express" service of doppelganger dogs, switching a trained killer in for the real pet during the walk. That's why we found Torben up a tree when the police raided the compound, surrounded by all these substitute canines. Wilson, *please* tell me you're going to devote proper airtime to Torben up the tree.'

'It's the series highlight,' he promised.

'Anyone trying that would really have to be in a hurry though,' said Torben, 'or else the target would have to be pretty far gone. There can't be many owners who'd be taken in by a dog switch for any length of time. That's part of the horror of it: the usual method was so carefully calculated to exploit the genuine bond between pet and victim.'

'And Charlotte Lazerton,' said Wilson, 'was one such victim?'

'Exactly,' said Torben. 'The day before her death, she even told me that someone had abstracted one of her slippers: this was Drever, months earlier, when he had first commissioned the assassination. That gave the dog handlers in that basement flat an object imprinted with Charlotte's scent, to help teach Mortimer what to do. Ximena, knowing only that something underhand was going on but in no position to make a fuss, would drop off Mortimer every week. And every week, the training went in a little deeper. No one could say when Mortimer would respond to the trigger. It just so happened to be when Drever was in Brussels; he could as easily have been at his home a few streets away. What mattered was that he was getting on with his own affairs, with a total appearance of innocence.'

'Ah, you mentioned a trigger?' said Wilson.

'Ach, *for helvede*, sorry – but that's obvious: it was Charlotte answering the phone,' said Torben. 'Everyone who knew her, including Drever, knew she had this affected, old-world way of answering her landline – "London seven-four-two-six-triple-four-oh", she would trill. *For fanden*, she *also* told me that she could hear her phone being tapped. That was the agency, monitoring her habits, getting a consistent recording of the triggering sentence. They would play the recording back to Mortimer, in combination with the slipper, and encourage him to knock down the handler when he heard the line. Given that the well-padded handler would bounce back up and reward Mortimer with a treat every time, he would understand it to be play; desired behaviour. Less desirable, of course, when your phone – as Drever knew well – was right at the top of a very steep staircase.'

'Jesus,' said Wilson. 'So eventually, the lesson went in fully, and the next time Mortimer was nearby when she answered the phone—'

'Bam,' said Leyla.

'Bastards,' said Torben.

'Poor Mortimer,' said Wilson.

'Quite,' said Torben. 'Imagine it from his perspective – joyfully jumping up to embrace his mistress, confident of reward. Next minute – everything wrong, and no way of escape from this thing that he had done.'

'All of which was accomplished in time,' said Leyla, 'to clear the way for Drever's election as AWA president.'

'What a guy,' said Wilson.

'A fair example of the sort that wins elections these days,' said Torben. 'I wonder where it went so wrong for him. Maybe he never stood a chance from his schooling on – so driven, so moulded, so empty. I really think he and Charlotte were friends, once, when he was still a scholar who cared for his subject. But, over the years, the less time he spent teaching, researching, the more time getting on, estranged from his old colleagues, getting used to taking decisions based purely on budgeting, made from a great height and distance …'

'The more time,' said Leyla, 'he spent using a highly addictive substance as a support mechanism, rather than anything so bothersome as other human beings …'

'So that in the end,' said Torben, 'he saw in his way, not an old friend, but an expendable inconvenience. Just some old woman who happened to be blocking his path to—'

'Status, wealth, opportunity,' supplied Leyla. 'And no one any the wiser—'

'Except, of course, for the firm he'd hired,' said Wilson. 'I'm guessing he was introduced to them through his coke dealer?'

'*Rigtig*,' said Torben. 'Luckily for him, he lived in the right neighbourhood. Because his dealer was also the one used – and, in a very real sense, owned – by the brains of the entire operation. A man named—'

'Stop,' said Wilson. 'That's all I want from you two. I'm recording an entire, separate special on the many criminal enterprises of the bored and brilliant playboy capitalist Zak Cremello.'

32

A VERY NICE TABLE

Torben was cooking. He was also on a diet. This latter decision, whilst patently necessary and even welcome after the excesses of recent weeks, was slightly spoiling the former act. However, he was working from a very decent recipe for a lentil and mushroom lasagne, courtesy of his new acquaintance and some-time correspondent, Beryl Cabell-Fowell. And, prompted by the urgings of a digestive system stretched to breaking point, he was substituting half-fat crème fraîche for double cream.

Beryl had sent the recipe inside a table – an unlikely form of packaging, but not unwelcome, since the table in question was a rustic yet exquisite dropleaf example of vernacular Gustavian carpentry, circa 1780: a gift of thanks, for solving the murder of her beloved cousin. A weekend in the country was also on the cards, complete with excursion to Kingston Lacy.

As he cooked, he was listening to a podcast. *Not* a true crime pod, but one from a year or two back, featuring guest interviews from older women about life in the public realm over the age of seventy. He was trying to get tips on interviewing, for the book he now desperately needed to start work on – the real version of the tribute to

Charlotte that he was contractually obliged to produce for Carmen Sabueso. Still. Only a month lost. As academic writing went, he was still way ahead of schedule.

The previous episode of this podcast had been mostly Judi Dench talking about her favourite trees. This one, of course, featured Charlotte herself. 'I wonder whether,' she was saying to the interviewer, 'as you age, you share this increasing sense I have – of having a piece of string coming out of the centre of my head, drawn taut, and going up somewhere I can't see. I can practically *feel* it, this string, just here between my temples, and every now and then I catch it being yanked ... and I hate it, you know, absolutely *hate* this feeling that I'm having my movements directed. All the people up there on the other end, just bloody well tugging away. I never noticed them when I was young, I was too busy dancing to the tune.'

Torben checked the simmering ragù, added a couple of drops of liquid smoke, another sprig of rosemary.

'And you don't feel,' said the interviewer, 'that there's a way to just take a pair of scissors and, I don't know – cut the string?'

'Oh,' said Charlotte, and she sounded very tired, 'it's much too late for that, I'm afraid. I can still fight for causes, but there's nothing much to be done for me personally. That's the problem with looking the fact of age square in the face. It's the sort of thing we think about, people like us, dear, on evenings alone, sitting in a pleasant chair, beside a low light. There are thoughts that wander into the room, brush against our legs, nuzzle up to us, insinuating. They have about them the savour of mortality, and at times like that you sense their presence. And then, in the quiet of your lovely, dim-lit room, you know a moment's fear – real, physical fear of dying – until you master yourself, and put the thought away tidily in some small, shut-away place, so that you can go on a little longer, and pretend to forget that the fear was ever there ...'

Torben removed the lid from a pot of simmering mushroom stock, and added several pasta sheets to steep for a few minutes.

'And then,' Charlotte continued, 'there are those other epiphanies, quite as bad in their way, when you suddenly remember that, not so long ago, you knew a happiness, an energy within yourself, that is now quite departed, and it isn't coming back. And you think – it only took a couple of turns, a silent shifting of stones, for that beating joy to just slip from your life, *unnoticed*, you didn't notice it go – and now here you are, accustoming yourself with quite terrifying swiftness to something altogether *lesser*. And perhaps, you think, one more great effort, one act of will, could reawaken that joy, and quicken the streams of your life again. But then, once again, the scale of it is all too much for the moment, and you put that thing too in some small, still place. And you go on. Diminishing by degrees of infinitesimal smallness. Settling, ever settling ...'

Torben thought again of the Schjerfbeck self-portraits. And suddenly, there was no need to add more salt to the pan, nor more water.

Half an hour later, Leyla arrived. 'Nice table,' she said. 'Have you thought about adding a couple of chairs?'

'Chairs, she says!' said Torben. 'Well, lah-di-dah, you don't ask for much, do you? Here I am, inviting you over for dinner, and all you can think to say is that you'd like to be able to *sit down*?'

'I also,' said Leyla, plonking it upon the tabletop with an abandon that made Torben wince for the woodwork, 'brought a bottle of Chiroubles.'

'Hurrah!'

*

'I like the music,' she said, a little while later, between mouthfuls raised perilously from table to head height.

'I thought you'd never mention it,' he said. 'Rued Langgaard's *Rosengårdsspil*, played by the Nightingale String Quartet.' He had chosen the record with extreme care.

'That twiddly bit that keeps coming back,' she said.

'Good, isn't it?'

'Mm.'

They ate on.

'You know,' he said at last, when they had eaten, and cleared, and taken themselves upstairs to perch, a little perilously, upon the two-seater sofa, 'there are two morals I think we should draw from the case of Henrik Drever.'

'So few? You astonish me. I'd have thought you'd want to propound at least a round dozen.'

'The first,' he pressed on before he could think better of it, 'is a question of method.' The music was still playing. That twiddly bit came back again. 'We went wrong, Leyla, because neither of us was privy to all the key information first-hand. *You* never saw Drever's face, the callousness in him, nor the essential harmlessness of Katherine Trigg. *I* never saw Grey's weakness and venality, the sort of greed that rarely rises to decisive action. If I'd had you with me when I took Meera to the pub, or talked to Gary Bassett, or heard Katherine's outburst on the march, you might have spotted the things I passed over, the clues to what was really going on.'

'So the moral is, let Leyla come to the expensive dinners?' she said.

Again, those violins. That thing they did.

'The moral is, I should share everything with you. *Every* meal. Every moment going. This house, this sof—'

'Oh, Torben,' she said, and went for him.

Luckily, in the interests of preserving historical artefacts, they soon fell off the sofa.

Later again, the music long since finished. The bed, to their great relief, had proven itself equal to the challenge.

'Torben,' said Leyla.

'Mm?'

'You mentioned a second moral?'

'Oh, *ja*.' He sat up. There was an ominous creak that he didn't exactly like. But it didn't touch him. Nothing could get to him here. He was so very, very happy.

'Well?' she said. 'What was it?'

'One I should have realised right at the start,' he said, and looked her full in the face. 'A lesson for the ages. Never trust a Swede.'

ACKNOWLEDGEMENTS

The problem is, people quite liked the acknowledgements for *Helle & Death*, and I just don't think I can top them. They still apply – the same people have been unfailingly brilliant, from Miranda and Charlotte calling the shots, to Joanna pulling the strings, to Samantha Johnson coming up with another sumptuous cover. Hayley Shepherd remains the copy-editor that dreams are made of. Or should that be 'of which dreams are made' – Hayley? Back at Profile, and along with Robert and Emily, I should also credit Sarah Kennedy on the copy-edit, and the great Angie Curzi and Rachel Quin for knockout marketing on both books. Family and friends as ever amazing, Emma's still the best and hey, we have a baby now, but he did bugger all to help. Special credit to new early readers Jakob Reckhenrich and Emily MacGregor, specialists in barristering, writing in general, and the arcane arts of owning a dog in London. In essence, those who were amazing, still are, which is so much more than I deserve.

Now, I have new debts to pay! First up, the rest of the Nest of Vipers, a quite outstanding slither of authors among whom it would be invidious to particularise, but you should buy all their books if you haven't already.

Next: London itself, a city I have only briefly called home but with which I seem to have a longstanding literary fascination. *Helle's Hound* is something of a panegyric to *my* London – everyone's is different – the one I knew as a young academic. Those wise to its every-changing panoply of shops and restaurants will clock that I have stepped out of historical time, in having Torben pig out at places that never co-existed. I also brought forward the Schjerfbeck exhibition at the RA by just over a year. To those unhappy with the liberties I have taken in this regard I say: have you seen what I did with the *actual plot?!* For which I must also apologise to the ghost (if anyone's got one, it's him) of Arthur Conan Doyle. If anyone can spot all the allusions to a certain shaggy dog story, I'll buy them a vegan *pølse*.

If there is a grain of emotional truth amid the referential silliness, it inheres in all that Torben owes his mentor, Charlotte Lazerton. As I write this, life is echoing art in the darkest way possible, and I find myself co-editing a journal that was to have featured an article by the toweringly brilliant Bruce R. Smith, whose sudden and shocking death has left academia much the poorer. I knew him only a little, but a kinder, cleverer, and better man would be hard to find.

Finally, then, to those who really did do for me what Charlotte did for Torben. I have been taught and championed by so many deeply good people – Kathryn Gleadle, Colin Jones, Kirsten Gibson … This book is dedicated to the three I owe the most. Mark Philp: supervisor, inspiration, friend, to whom I stand forever in awe. Roger Parker: my first 'boss', whose research ambitions first brought me to London, who taught me about musicology and loyalty. And John Street, who gave me a job when, unemployed at the start of the pandemic, I was on the way out of academia; who gave me a bed in his basement; and who gave me an eternal respect for a certain kind of quiet wisdom. He mingles scholarly enquiry and sincere friendship as few can. From which you will gather that none of them are *quite* like Charlotte Lazerton, and I suspect none of them has ever slept with two Soviet security guards simultaneously. Though if any of them have, my money's on Roger.

To all of the above: thank you.

ABOUT THE AUTHOR

Oskar Jensen is an author and academic. He researches songs at Newcastle University and has written scholarly tomes on Napoleon, ballad-singing and, most recently, the London streets in *Vagabonds: Life on the Streets of Nineteenth-century London*. He is a BBC New Generation Thinker, appearing frequently on Radio 3 and 4, as well as showing up in the *New Statesman*, on *Who Do You Think You Are?*, and as historical advisor for 2018's *Vanity Fair* and the forthcoming biopic of Mary Wollstonecraft, *If Love Should Die*. *Helle and Death*, Oskar's debut adult novel and the first to feature Danish sleuth Torben Helle, was published in 2024. Oskar will be returning to these characters for the third instalment in the Torben Helle series, which will be published by Viper in 2027. Find him on X @OskarCoxJensen.